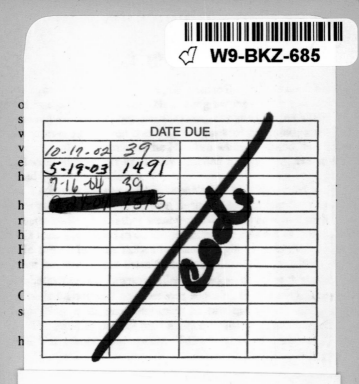

DATE DUE		
10-17-02	39	
5-19-03	1491	
7-16-04	39	
9-21-04	7575	

WILDERNESS

FRONTIER STRIKE

David Thompson

LEISURE BOOKS **NEW YORK CITY**

To Judy, Joshua, and Shane

A LEISURE BOOK®

June 1996

Published by

Dorchester Publishing Co., Inc.
276 Fifth Avenue
New York, NY 10001

Printed in the United States of America.

WILDERNESS
FRONTIER STRIKE

Chapter One

The three horsemen rode down out of the foothills into the dark valley.

Ages ago it had been known as the Green River Valley. Over the centuries it had been home to Indians, frontiersmen, farmers, and ranchers. After the great cataclysm, it reverted to its natural state until the arrival of the one who would become known as the Dark Lord. Now it was known as the Valley of Shadow.

The new name was fitting in more ways than one.

On this particular day, roiling dark clouds swept savagely over the bleak landscape, casting

David Thompson

the twisted trees and brown grass into twilight shadow. The thudding hooves of the riders' mounts sounded dull and hollow, as if muffled somehow by the heavy air itself. An otherwise oppressive silence gripped the somber terrain.

In all that vastness, nothing else moved.

The three men reined up on a low knoll to survey the sweep of valley before them.

"I don't like this, pard," said one of the riders. "I don't like it at all." He was a wiry, lean man, his whipcord frame clad in buckskins. Blond hair crowned a ruggedly handsome face. A sweeping mustache drooped below alert blue eyes.

The man he addressed could only be described as a virtual giant. Close to seven feet in height, he was endowed with bulging muscles that seemed to ripple even in repose. Faded brown pants and a black leather vest molded his powerful form. His wavy hair was dark, his eyes a penetrating gray. He stared somberly at the object in the distance, and responded, "Who does, Hickok? But it's up to us. We can't let him get away."

The third man nodded grimly. Shorter and stockier than his companions, he had black hair and brown eyes and features that mirrored his Indian ancestry. "It ends today, Blade. One way or the other, the slaughter ends."

Hickok glanced at him. "You got that right, you mangy Injun."

Surprisingly, the short man was not insulted by the remark. Instead, he smirked and replied, "At last we agree on something, oh wise, white ding-a-ling. Will wonders never cease."

8

Their levity was forced. Their humor was that of men so closely bonded that they could insult one another and not take offense. Anyone who knew them well knew that they were the best of friends.

Blade lowered a brawny hand to the hilt of one of the twin Bowies that adorned his hips. "Who ever thought it would come to this?" he said, more to himself than to them. "Just when everything was going so well. Just when the Freedom Federation had reunited the country, he had to appear."

Hickok snorted. "Nothin' in life is set in stone, pard. About the time we get to thinkin' that everything is going our way, life hauls off and wallops us on the noggin to show us the error of our ways. Ain't that how it is, Geronimo?"

The stocky man glanced at the blond. "My ears must be deceiving me. You can't be right twice in one day. It would be a new record."

Blade clucked to his horse and rode down into the Valley of Shadow. The Commando Arms Carbine slung over his back rubbed against him with every loping stride. He wished that they had brought binoculars so he could study the immense structure at the center of the valley. It was their destination. It might also serve as their tomb.

The Dark Tower was home to the Dark Lord. Within its towering walls, evil had spawned and spread across the land like a plague of locusts, devouring all in its path until the final battle between the vicious hordes of the Dark Lord and the combined might of the Freedom Federation. The Federation had won, but at a staggering cost. His darkling army destroyed, the Dark Lord had fled to his sanctuary.

Now it was up to the three Warriors to put an end to him, once and for all.

Geronimo was slightly in front of the others. On purpose. His eagle eyes were keener than theirs. If danger arose, he wanted to be in a position to spot it well ahead of time. And he had no doubt that they would encounter opposition sooner or later. No one before had ever entered the Valley of Shadow and lived to tell the tale.

Hickok whistled softly as he rode. Of the three, he was the most relaxed. It was not an act on his part. It stemmed from his supreme confidence in his ability to beat any enemy, no matter how many or how strong. He never fretted about dying. His philosophy could be summed up by one of his favorite sayings: "If it's meant to be, it's meant to be."

The Dark Tower grew closer. Rising into the clouds like a gigantic black needle, it cast an eerie dark green glow. For over a mile around it, the vegetation had long since withered and died. Beyond that distance, to the edge of the valley, the grass had turned brown, the trees had become stunted. It was as if the Tower had sucked the life from the surrounding countryside and drawn the energy into itself.

Hickok took the ominous monolith in typical stride. "What was this jasper tryin' to do? Make a new Tower of Babel?"

Geronimo had a retort on the tip of his tongue, but he never uttered it. His eyes narrowed and he abruptly drew rein. "Trouble coming," he announced.

Blade halted and unslung the Commando. At first he did not see what his friend saw. They were too far off. Then stick figures materialized in the distance, figures that resolved into ranks of plodding creatures that had once been human beings.

"Zombies," Hickok spat in disgust.

Geronimo was unslinging his FNC Auto Rifle. He patted the shirt pockets of his fatigues to insure spare magazines were handy. "There are thirty of them in three rows of ten."

"Really?" Hickok rose in the saddle. "I knew I should have ate more carrots when I was a sprout."

Blade worked the bolt of the Commando. "Only thirty?" he said. "Can it be that easy?"

"We're not to the Tower yet," Geronimo pointed out.

Hickok dismounted. A Marlin .45–70 hung across his back, but he made no move to unlimber it. Instead, he rested his hands on the ivory-handled butts of a matched set of Colt Python revolvers strapped around his waist. "We'd best do this on foot. You know how skittish horses are around zombies. It's that awful smell."

The suggestion made sense to Blade. Climbing down, he let the reins dangle and strode forward flanked by his friends. "If something should happen to me, I'm counting on the two of you to see this through. The Dark Lord must die."

"Don't you ever get tired of lookin' at the bright side all the time?" Hickok scoffed. "We're not about to let you buy the farm. Your missus would have a hissy fit."

The three men stopped and spread out. Blade

felt his skin crawl as the ranks of awkwardly shuffling horrors approached. Soon he could see their pale faces and sunken eyes, their spindly limbs and matted hair. Since the wind was blowing from west to east, he also caught a whiff of the pungent odor the zombies always gave off. It was the foul reek of a month-old corpse.

"Some of them have guns," Geronimo warned.

"So?" Hickok said. "These yahoos couldn't hit the broad side of a mountain with a tank."

As if to prove the gunfighter wrong, one of the ungainly scarecrows raised a Winchester and fired, and the slug smacked into the ground at Hickok's feet.

Blade elevated the Commando and let loose with a burst on full auto. The .45-caliber rounds punched into the chest of the zombie that had fired, jolting the scarecrow backward. Where a normal man would have collapsed on the spot, the zombie straightened and tried to raise the Winchester again. A second burst chopped him down.

"Go for the head, remember?" Hickok said, and did just that, his hands twin blurs as he drew both Pythons and triggered them in ambidextrous precision. He had to angle the pistols because of the range, yet each and every shot scored. Not once did he take deliberate aim.

Geronimo chimed in with the FNC. The Auto Rifle chewed up four zombies in a span of seconds, the .223-caliber hailstorm crumpling their deceptively frail forms into disjointed heaps.

The remainder of the unearthly company were fanning out at a brisk if clumsy gait. Most carried knives and swords and axes and had to get in close to be effective.

Blade's revulsion caused him to make a mistake. He emptied his magazine much too fast instead of spacing his shots. A metallic click prompted him to eject the spent magazine. Or to try, at any rate. For when he tugged, it refused to budge. He tugged once more, all too aware that reeking figures were converging on him from several directions at once.

Hickok saw the giant's plight. Heedless of his own safety, he swiveled and rushed over, dropping any pale specters that posed a threat to the man he would never admit he cared for as a brother. Planting himself in front of Blade, he shot a lurching zombie in the left eye, another in the right. That was when his Pythons went empty.

"Damn!"

A zombie wielding a sword raised it to strike the gunman. The blow never landed. A glittering knife parried it, backed by the steely sinews of the man who waded into the ranks of walking monstrosities with his two Bowies flashing.

Blade was in his element.

While the Warriors were trained in a variety of fighting arts, each of them had a weapon he or she favored above all others. With Hickok, it was his Pythons. With Geronimo, the tomahawk he always carried. With Blade, it was his prized Bowies.

Weaving a gleaming tapestry of shining steel, the giant countered the sword a second time, pivoted, and decapitated the zombie with a backhand stroke. He did not wait to see the body fall.

David Thompson

Already two more were on top of him, one swinging a large axe. He ducked, drove his left Bowie to the hilt into the abomination's abdomen, and followed through with a thrust into the base of the jaw that stiffened his attacker like a board. Wrenching both blades free, he stepped back.

The third zombie showed a bit more intelligence—if that were possible. It circled, waggling a butcher knife, seeking an opening.

Blade feinted. The loathsome horror took the bait and went for his chest. Sidestepping, Blade slit its throat with a forward slash, then completed the job with a reverse thrust.

More zombies lumbered toward him, the second and third rows of the undead platoon concentrating on him as if they somehow sensed that he was the leader of the three Warriors and therefore the prime target. Even he could not withstand so many at one time. He retreated a few steps, then crouched at bay, but refused to run.

From the right came Hickok, his Pythons reloaded. In cracking cadence the gunfighter downed foe after foe.

From the left darted Geronimo, the FNC burping in staccato rhythm, felling zombies right and left.

Side by side now, the three friends held their ground. The zombies, while awkward in motion, could move surprisingly fast when they wanted to. At close quarters battling them was little different than battling normal men.

The FNC emptied and Geronimo cast it behind him, resorting to his tomahawk to face his next enemy, a tall scarecrow who tried to impale him

14

on an iron-tipped spear. Whipping to one side so the spear missed, Geronimo took a single bound and brought the tomahawk down on the crown of the zombie's head with all the power in his muscular shoulders. The keen edge sheared through straggly hair and pale flesh into solid bone, stopping the zombie in its tracks.

Blade lost count of the number he slew. Bodies littered the ground in front of him when he drew back a Bowie to slash and realized there were no more left. Only then did the stench assail him, churning his stomach. He covered his nose and mouth with one hand and walked to where he had set down the Commando.

"They almost had us," Geronimo remarked, wiping gore from his tomahawk on the tattered pants of a stricken zombie.

"These wimps?" Hickok laughed. "I could have licked these coyotes with one arm tied behind my back."

Blade was bending to pick up his SMG when he happened to gaze to the east. Off across the valley were three plumes of dust. "Just wonderful," he said. "There go our horses."

Hickok slid a shiny cartridge from his gunbelt and inserted it into a chamber in one of his Pythons. "I reckon we walk, then."

It was not all that far. The Tower reared above them, more sheer than a mountain, starkly alien in design and construction.

"They say that Thanatos built it in nine months," Geronimo marveled. "Do you think it's true?"

Rumor had it that the Dark Lord's true name was Thanatos, that he had once been a top scientist in the Civilized Zone, a genius who came to believe that he could run the world better than anyone else. It was also rumored that he had delved into arcane knowledge, that he had uncovered secrets lost to humankind since the dawn of time.

Blade had heard all the stories. The only one he'd had reason to believe true was Thanatos's name. Now, in the shadow of the looming edifice, he wondered if maybe, just maybe, the other tales contained germs of truth as well. How else had Thanatos accomplished so much in so little time?

The Tower was but one of the Dark Lord's feats. He had gathered an army of zombies to be his cannon fodder. Renegade humans and mutants had flocked to his banner, serving as commanders of his scarecrow legions. From out of nowhere the army of the night had struck, launching a three-pronged attack against the Freedom Federation.

Luck, more than anything else, had given the allies the victory. The zombie army was no more. The few mutants who survived had scattered to the four winds. All that remained was to finish off Thanatos himself.

"I think we're expected," Hickok declared.

At the base of the monolith loomed a door twenty feet high and equally as wide. It had been left halfway open, permitting more of the green glow to spill out. A strange, low rumbling emanated from its bowels, along with the occasional clank and rasp of heavy machinery.

"Spooky place," Hickok said, his brows knit-

16

ting. "Say, what was it the old-timers used to call out?"

"When?" Geronimo asked, not quite sure what the gunfighter was getting at.

"When they dressed up in silly outfits and went out beggin' for food?" Hickok snapped his fingers. "I remember now." Walking up to the door, he pounded on it and called out, "Trick or treat!"

Geronimo glanced at Blade, who rolled his eyes. Together they moved warily into the Tower, pausing on the threshold to openly gawk.

The interior was as black as the exterior surface, only shinier. It pulsed with the shimmering green radiance. Except where doorways were evident, the walls were seamless, as smooth as polished glass. The rumbling was louder and definitely came from under the ground.

Hickok noted three flights of stairs and at least six doors. "Which way do we go?"

Blade was asking himself the same thing. There were bound to be guards. More zombies, perhaps. Or creatures much worse. "Your guess is as good as mine," he said, cautiously advancing with the Commando tucked to his side.

Geronimo's scalp prickled as he, too, stalked into the madman's lair. He had what he could only describe as a terribly bad feeling deep within the core of his being, a premonition that they should get out of there while they still could. "Wouldn't it be smarter to wait for the rest of the Warriors to join us?" he asked.

"They're busy mopping up," Blade absently answered. "It will be days before Rikki-Tikki-Tavi and Yama and the rest can get here."

Hickok stared straight up and was shocked to

discover that he could see countless stories above them. "It's now or never," he concurred. "The sooner we get this over with, the sooner we can get on with our lives."

At the bottom of a spiral flight of stairs, they drew up short. "Which way?" Geronimo repeated. He looked up and glimpsed something flit across an open space high, high above. Something big with fur and wings. He would have gotten a better look, but he was distracted by a gust of cold air from an inky doorway near the stairs. The air brought with it a foul stench worse than the odor of the zombies. It also carried to his ears the leathery scrape of feet. At least, he *thought* they were feet. "We'll never be able to find Thanatos in here."

"I still have some Civilized Zone money on me," Hickok revealed. "Let's flip a coin." Suddenly loud humming broke out to their left. Automatically, they swung toward the source, a solid black wall that towered up into the remote heights.

Hickok pulled his six-shooters with uncanny speed, cocking them as he cleared leather. The humming was like the buzzing of bees. It rose and fell in volume, the peaks increasing in intensity. For some reason it provoked a fluttering in his gut, just as the rasping of fingernails over a chalkboard would cause some people to quake.

The sound rose to a fever pitch, then inexplicably died. For all of five seconds there was total silence.

"I guess it was nothing to worry about," the gunman said.

On cue, part of the black wall slid aside, revealing that it was in fact a door, and that behind the door was an elevator a lot like those the Warriors had seen in the Civilized Zone and elsewhere. Only this elevator was three times as big as it should be. As for the grotesque nightmare that waddled out of it, no one on the planet had ever beheld its like.

The beast was as big as a gorilla and hairy like one, but there the resemblance ended. Scaly skin covered a reptilian head. Talons like those of eagles clicked together in bloodthirsty anticipation. Eyes sizzling like red-hot emeralds, the creature uttered a roar that would have done justice to the wild lions that roamed the continent.

It charged.

Blade was nearest the elevator. Instinctively, he squeezed the trigger. The Commando hammered, and he had the satisfaction of witnessing holes blossom on the monster's chest. The thing was hit ten or twelve times, more than enough to slay any mutant on the continent. But this one only slowed for a few heartbeats, swatting the air as if seeking to bat the swarm of lead aside. Cocking its head as a lizard might before pouncing, the living devil came on faster than before.

Blade held the trigger down. He was still firing furiously when the mutant reached him and lashed out. Its thick arm caught him across the torso. He went sailing, head over heels into the stairs. His ribs were jarred almost to the breaking point, and the breath whooshed from his lungs. He saw the floor rush up to meet him.

Geronimo was next to bear the brunt of the creature's rampage. The FNC bucked, its rounds drilling into the beast's forehead. That should have been enough to end the clash then and there. Yet the mutant never slowed. Geronimo tried to evade a swing that clipped him on the shoulder and sent him flying.

Hickok was last in line. His mouth quirked as he extended both Pythons. "Is this any way to greet guests?" he quipped, and shot the creature's eyes out.

The monster roared, clawing at the holes where its pupils had been. In a mad rage, it blundered to one side, then weaved wildly. The roar swelled as it filled the doorway. A moment later the thing was gone, tromping on out into the twilight.

The gunfighter twirled his Colts into their holsters and turned. His fellow Warriors were slowly rising, bruised but unbowed. "How many times must I tell you galoots? It's not how many shots you get off, it's where you put 'em that counts."

Blade walked past, to the elevator. The door had not closed. A control panel revealed that it would go as high as the one hundred and fiftieth floor and descend as low as Subbasement Fourteen, whatever that was. He entered.

"Either of you coming?"

Hickok hesitated. "Are you sure you know what you're doing, pard? It could be a trap."

"Or a blunder on Thanatos's part," Blade said. "He might take it for granted that his pet will dispose of us."

Geronimo strode into the car. "Let's show him how wrong he is."

"All for one," Hickok said, joining them. He tried to keep a poker face, but it was difficult not to betray his intense dislike of enclosed spaces. No sooner did he step in than the door closed of its own accord. Without warning, the elevator shot upward so rapidly that he was nearly dumped on the floor.

Blade positioned himself in front of the door so he would have first crack at Thanatos. From what he had heard, the mastermind was as big, if not bigger than he was, and a formidable hand-to-hand fighter. With any luck he could take Thanatos down quickly, sparing the others from possible harm.

A vibrant hum filled the shaft, swelling to a peak and tapering, over and over again. The lights on the control panel flashed one by one, each lit no longer than the blink of an eye.

"What floor do we pick?" Hickok asked.

"We'll start at the top and work our way down," Blade said.

"Good idea," Geronimo interjected. "The size of this Tower, it shouldn't take us more than four or five years."

Tense seconds ticked by.

Blade did not expect to hit pay dirt on the upper floor. So he was taken off guard when the elevator coasted to a smooth stop and the door flung open to reveal a spacious, gloomy room dominated by a huge square metal cage with no top. The cage was ringed by banks of sophisticated electronic consoles and computer banks.

None of the equipment was of any interest when Blade set eyes on a tall, hooded form that stood beside the steel contraption. He caught a glimpse of a thatch of red hair, of eyes that blazed like suns. "Thanatos!" he cried.

21

The figure snarled and leaped into the cage. In a twinkling, it disappeared.

"There must be a trap door!" Blade shouted, springing to overtake their quarry. Straight into the cage he ran.

The universe exploded.

Chapter Two

The year was 1840.

Trapper Nathaniel King and his young son, Zach, were hunting. They had been in the saddle since first light and now the sun was directly overhead. Nate's keen eyes were glued to meandering elk tracks they had been following for the better part of the morning. "Soon," he whispered to the boy.

Young Zach squirmed with excitement. The family was low on jerked meat, and an elk would provide enough to last them through the summer into the fall. Besides that, he looked forward to roasting the heart and liver as soon as the bull was slain. In his opinion, no meat was quite as tasty as elk heart. Unless maybe it was painter.

Nate raised his bearded face to survey the mountain slope above. They were high in the Rockies, west of the remote valley where his cabin lay. A bald eagle soared above a snow-capped peak. Ravens glided on uplifting currents. In the forest around them, birds sang, squirrels chattered, and chipmunks scampered. It was a veritable paradise.

It was his home.

Nate seldom thought about New York City anymore, of the crowded streets and sooty buildings, of the frenzied pace of life, of the power-hungry politicians who felt they knew better than anyone else how the common man should live. He had given all that up, had turned his broad back on a promising career as an accountant, to take up the life of a free trapper.

There was no denying that life in the wilderness had its drawbacks. Hostile Indians had to be dealt with. Grizzlies and panthers and wolverines were constant menaces. A man had to always be on the lookout for rattlesnakes and black widows and such. But even so, even with the daily dangers, Nate would not trade the wilderness for all the so-called culture New York had to offer.

Out here there was freedom, Nate mused. True freedom, not the sham where politicians kept telling people how free they were while all the time imposing more and more laws and more and more strict controls on those gullible enough to believe them.

True freedom. The words peeled in Nate's

mind like the chimes of the Liberty Bell. No man or woman could fully appreciate what their Maker had intended for mortal life to be until they had drunk from the cup of genuine liberty, until they had savored pure, unfettered existence.

It was a revelation to be able to do as one wanted, when one wanted, with no self-appointed busybodies looking over one's shoulder to criticize or nag or bully.

Nate straightened in the saddle and drank deep of the crisp mountain air. It invigorated him clear down to his toes. "Lord, I love this life," he said softly to himself.

Well he should.

He had a beautiful Shoshone wife, a son who would make any father proud, a daughter who was sunshine and strawberries and merry laughter all rolled into one energetic bundle, and a comfortable cabin situated near a lake in a valley where game was abundant and they could add fish or fowl to their table whenever they wanted. Plus, while money was no longer the priority in his life it had once been, he had a couple of thousand dollars safely cached.

In short, Nate rated himself one of the luckiest men alive. No storm clouds loomed on his personal horizon. His family was healthy. Their needs were being met. And at the moment he was on friendly terms with all the local tribes, even the Utes, who had been striving to drive him off for years.

No doubt about it, Nate King reflected. He was living a charmed life.

What could go wrong?

No sooner did the thought cross Nate's mind than an odd event occurred. A clap of thunder rocked the mountains, a thunderclap that echoed and reechoed off the majestic peaks, a thunderclap so loud that it caused Nate's black stallion to shy and nicker.

Drawing rein, Nate looked up, puzzled. The sky was perfectly clear, not a single cloud marring its azure expanse. Where then had the thunderclap come from?

"What was that, Pa?" Zach asked. Remembering the time they had visited St. Louis and witnessed an Independence Day celebration, he added, "A cannon blast, maybe?"

Nate grinned. "I doubt very much that someone has gone to all the trouble of lugging a cannon up into these mountains. Last I heard, no one is waging war on the chipmunks."

"Oh, Pa," Zach said, laughing.

Nate lifted the reins to go on, then froze. His son's gasp confirmed the bewildering testimony of his own eyes. Where moments ago the sky had been a deep blue, it had suddenly acquired a dark green cast, a strange, glittering effect, the likes of which he had never beheld before.

"Goodness gracious, Pa!" Zach exclaimed. "Am I seeing things?"

Nate merely shook his head while trying to make sense of the dazzling heavenly display. Once, a few winters ago, he had seen something similar. But that had been at night, and the lights that had streamed and darted and flashed and rushed about had been of a reddish hue, not green. The Northern Lights, the mountain men called them.

Again a thunderclap shattered the tranquility of the Rockies. This one was louder than the first. As it fell on their ears, the green light crackled and sparked, seemingly about to set the sky on fire.

"Pa?" Zach said nervously. The spectacle terrified him, and he was trying hard not to show it.

"It will pass, son," Nate said, wishing he felt as confident as he sounded. Truth was, he had no idea what they were seeing, or whether it might be harmful in some way. Would the sky rain green drops? Would green lightning start blistering the ground around them?

Craning his neck, Nate noted that the peculiar effect was a local phenomenon. The sky was only green in the immediate area. Farther north, south, east, and west, it was a normal shade of blue.

"What do we do, Pa?"

Nate looked around. To their right the slope dipped into a verdant valley. He jabbed his heels into the stallion's flanks and headed for it, saying, "We'll get under cover, just in case."

The trapper fingered the heavy Hawken that rested across his thighs. In addition to the rifle, he was armed with a pair of smoothbore single-shot .55-caliber flintlock pistols, wedged under his wide brown leather belt on either side of the buckle. Above his right hip nestled a butcher knife in a beaded sheath his wife had made. On his left hip was a Shoshone tomahawk. His clothes were typical fringed buckskins, adorned with beads where Winona had decorated the sleeves and front. His moccasins were thick-soled and warm. A beaver hat crowned his black mane of hair.

A third thunderclap rent the crisp air as they wound down into thick pines bordering a wide meadow. Nate dismounted, tied the reins to a low limb, and hunkered to wait for the green light to fade away.

"Wait until I tell Ma!" Zach said as he alighted. "She won't believe it."

Who would? Nate asked himself. It was so bizarre, it bordered on the supernatural. Tales the Shoshones had told him cropped up unbidden. Tales of mighty beings endowed with unearthly powers, stories he had always chalked up to superstition and legend. The display above was enough to give him doubts.

"Maybe Apo is angry," Zach ventured.

Nate did not answer. Apo was the Shoshone version of what other tribes referred to as the Great Spirit. Since the boy spent every summer traveling with his mother's people, he knew all about their beliefs. Among them, Zach was known as Stalking Coyote, little Evelyn as Blue Flower, and Nate himself as—

The loudest blast of thunder yet shook the ground under their feet. Both horses whinnied and tried to pull loose. Nate leaped, catching hold of the stallion's bridle. His son did the same with the sorrel. Around them the air glittered, as if from the glow of a million fireflies. An acrid scent filled their nostrils. A sound, much like frying bacon, grew louder and louder.

Zach gazed across the meadow and felt his hair stand on end. *"Pa!"* he screamed, aghast, pointing. His impulse was to bolt, but he was too petrified to move.

Nate looked.

On the other side of the meadow an ungodly apparition had appeared out of thin air. It was the figure of a tall man, a virtual giant, ablaze with coruscating green light. He stumbled a dozen feet, his arms flailing, writhing green flames covering him from head to toe. His momentum spent, he slapped at the flames to no avail. His knees began to buckle and he turned his face to the heavens. From his lips burst a strangled cry. "*Jeeeennnnnnnyyyyyy!*" With that, he pitched forward and was still.

"Lord Almighty!" Zach exclaimed, and had to remind himself to breathe again. "Was that a ghost, Pa?"

Nate was numb with shock. In all his life he had never observed anything like the bewildering horror. Being taller than his son, he could see over the top of the grass and knew that the giant form lay where it had fallen. A ghost, surely, would have vanished into the nether realm that spawned it.

"Pa?" Zach prompted.

"No, I don't think it's a spirit," Nate conceded in an awed whisper. Part of him yearned to vault onto the stallion and get out of there while they still could. Yet another part of him, the same intense curiosity that had lured him to the frontier, the same sense of wonder and excitement that made every day in the mountains a joy to live, spurred him to move stealthily to the edge of the trees.

Hefting his Hawken, Nate said, "Stay here,

son. I'm going to take a closer look."

Zach's mouth went dry at the prospect of being left alone. The sky was still green, the air still crackled. "If it's all the same to you, Pa," he said, "I'd like to tag along."

Nate was about to refuse, but changed his mind when another thunderclap shook the pines. "All right," he said. "Cover my back." Leveling the Hawken, he crept into the high grass, parting it with his barrel. A new odor tingled his nose. It was like sulphur, but different. How, exactly, he couldn't be sure. Suffice it to say that it made him feely slightly queasy. He almost turned around.

Then the figure ahead groaned. Whoever or whatever it was, it was in pain. It must need help, and Nate King had never refused aid to those in need. Ever.

The trapper gingerly stepped near enough to inspect the prone form. No green flames were evident. To all intents and purposes, it was a man, a big man, a big man to be sure, but a flesh-and-blood man wearing a black vest unlike any Nate had ever encountered and pants of a fashion unknown to him. Of special interest were two large knives strapped around the man's waist.

Nate King pondered. Among his peers, the fraternity of mountain men who made their living raising beaver plews, he was widely regarded as one of the strongest and toughest. His size had a lot to do with it, since the Good Lord had blessed him with a physique most men envied. Yet he was puny in comparison to the figure before him. The man had to be a full foot taller and six inches wider at the shoulders. And where Nate had always prided himself on his powerful sinews, the man in the grass had muscles on top of his muscles.

"Is he like us, Pa?" Zach wanted to know. "Or is he a demon of some kind?"

Every night without fail, Nate read to his family from the Bible. The boy knew about Satan and demons and the like, and the devilry they practiced on humankind. Once, Zach had asked him if demons still walked the earth, and Nate had answered that he honestly did not know. Could it be? Nate wondered.

"Should we shoot him?" Zach said.

The query gave Nate pause. On the one hand, the idea had appeal. If the giant were hostile, finishing him off was the right thing to do. On the other hand, Nate had never slain anyone who could not fight back. Enemy or no, dispatching a helpless man went against his nature. "Only if he tries to hurt us," he said.

"Is he going to live, you reckon?"

To find out, Nate squatted and placed his hand on the giant's wrist. There was a pulse, weak but steady. "I think so," he said. That brought up the issue of what to do next. Should they just leave him there? Or should they take him back to the cabin and let Winona tend him?

Just then, to their rear, the sound of frying bacon erupted. Nate whirled, dreading that he had erred by bringing his son into the open, afraid that another flaming giant was about to materialize out of the ether.

It was far worse.

Near the trees a lean shape did appear. Like the man in the vest, it blazed with dancing green flames. But where the giant was apparently human, the thing taking shape before the startled eyes of the mountain man and his son was definitely not. "A demon!" Zach cried.

Nate's brain seemed to shut down, to go blank with astonishment. His breath caught in his throat.

The thing was six and a half feet tall. It was clothed in what Nate could only describe as chain mail, but black, not silver as medieval knights had worn. The mail was scaly, which proved fitting since the thing itself had scales covering every square inch of exposed skin. The head resembled an alligator's, but the features were much more expressive and hinted at a mix of reptilian and human characteristics. It had four fingers but no thumbs, and fingers tipped with black claws. There were also claws on its feet, which were vaguely human in shape but only had three toes and a heel twice as long as it should be.

A demon! Nate's mind echoed as the creature lurched a few feet, then recovered its balance. It tossed its head as if to clear it and slowly looked around, the green flames gradually dying without inflicting any harm. Eyes like molten rubies fixed on the trapper and the boy.

Zach, scared witless, scooted backward, bumping into his father. Without thinking, he whipped up his Hawken and thumbed back the hammer.

The thing tilted its head. Nate would have sworn that it leered at them in blatant contempt. Then it hissed just like a viper, flicking a foot-long red tongue out, a tongue, appropriately enough, that was forked. "What *are* you?" he heard himself say.

The creature opened its maw, disclosing rows of tapered teeth. It took a step, its claws spread wide. Only then did Nate discover that it had a tail half the length of its body, a tail that bore a vicious black spike at the end.

"This just can't be!" the mountain man blurted.

Zach glanced at his father. He sensed that the vile beast was about to attack them, yet his pa stood there gaping. The thing took another step and his nerve broke. He fired without aiming, the recoil smacking the stock against his shoulder.

The shot jolted Nate out of his befuddled state. He saw the creature knocked onto its back, saw it half rise with a hand pressed to a furrow on its temple, a furrow moist with *green* blood. Snarling, it coiled as if to spring. Suddenly a noise Nate had never heard before made it glance at an object on its wrist. The noise was repeated several times, an odd series of chirps that were not quite chirps.

Another second, and the creature spun and departed at incredible speed, faster than the fleetest antelope, faster than any living thing of which Nate knew. It flowed over the ground, a blur among the trees, its tail extended just as some lizards would do when running.

Within moments it was gone.

Nate did not know whether the shot or the chirping was responsible for the thing's departure. He was just glad it had left. "You did right, shooting it," he complimented his son.

Zach was quaking. He sought to stop, but his limbs went on trembling regardless. Fear such as he had never known, potent fear that practically paralyzed him, brought bile to his mouth and weakness to his knees. He had never been so afraid, not the first time he tangled with a bear, not the first time he went up against a painter, never.

A groan reminded Nate of the giant. "Go fetch the horses, son," he directed. "We're heading home before that thing comes back."

"Is it safe, Pa?" Zach said. "What if he's not friendly? Think of Ma and Sissy."

"Would you rather they were alone with that creature on the loose?" Nate countered.

The idea increased Zach's fright. Swiftly reloading, he dashed off to comply.

Nate, meanwhile, knelt and rolled the giant over. To be on the safe side, he plucked both knives from their leather sheaths. What knives they were, too! The blades were longer than his by over three inches. The hilts were bigger as well and polished to a sheen. Oddly, though, both knives were lighter than his Green River blade. How that could be, he had no idea.

The quality of the steel in the blades was another surprise. Nate knew enough about blacksmithing to appreciate the superior tempered metal used in the construction of the giant's weapons. The blades were thinner than his yet much more sturdy. It was inexplicable.

Rising to see what was keeping Zach, Nate spotted something lying in the grass near where the giant had initially appeared. He investigated.

It was a gun, yet a gun unlike any known to the trapping fraternity. It had a barrel and a trigger and a stock, but there any similarity ended.

There were more metal parts, for one thing. Instead of a wooden forearm under the barrel, this gun had an outlandish wooden grip. The sights were much more elaborate than the peep variety on a Hawken. Yet another unusual feature was a bolt in a recessed groove above the trigger. It served no useful function that he could see.

The fantastic gun had to belong to the giant. Nate slung it over his shoulder and retraced his steps. Zach was hurrying their mounts over.

"We'll drape him over your horse and you can ride double with me," Nate proposed.

"Fine by me, Pa," Zach said. "I don't want to get close to him. He's hoodoo, if you ask me."

Nate handed his rifle to his son, hunkered, and got the giant into a sitting posture. From there it was a simple task to hoist the man onto his shoulders, then transfer the unconscious burden to the sorrel and tie the giant down. Neither of the horses betrayed any alarm. That told Nate the man was indeed human. Had there been anything out of the ordinary about him, the horses would have acted up.

Stepping into the stirrups, Nate lowered his arm so his offspring could scramble up behind him. He wheeled the stallion and led the sorrel eastward at a steady lope.

Zach kept looking back to assure himself the giant was still there. Although he was not yet fourteen years old, he had seen many a sight to behold. But few could hold a candle to the blazing giant, and absolutely none had prepared him for the creature that showed up afterward.

Nate checked on the man from time to time. Once the giant stirred, calling out the same name as before. In moments he had passed out again. Other than a few groans, he uttered no other outcries.

Early afternoon found the trapper and the boy on a ridge that overlooked their valley. Smoke spiraled from the stone chimney of the cabin. Ducks, geese, and brants swam idly on the lake. South of it a small herd of deer boldly grazed in the open. A red hawk banked over a thicket, seeking prey.

"It looks peaceful enough," Zach said.

Nate knew what the boy was thinking. He shared the same worry. That creature they had seen earlier could easily have reached the valley before them. If it were to run into Winona and Evelyn, he had no illusions about the outcome. Clucking to the stallion, he trotted down a game trail. On gaining the valley floor, he broke into a gallop.

The ground around the cabin had been cleared of brush as a precaution against surprise attack. When Nate passed the last of the firs, he was overjoyed to spy his wife and daughter on their way to the lake, Winona carrying a bucket. They stopped and little Evelyn waved.

Zach could hardly wait to tell his mother and sister the news. As soon as the stallion started to slow down, he jumped off and sprinted down the path.

Nate let the boy go. Winona had to be told, and he could use her advice on how to deal with the stranger. In a crisis she was always levelheaded, a trait he could not claim to share.

Reining up in front of the cabin, Nate slid from the saddle and stepped to the sorrel. The first order of business was to tote the giant indoors. Leaning his Hawken against the wall, he proceeded to untie the stranger. One of the knots proved to be stubborn. Drawing his butcher knife, he cut it rather than waste time fiddling around.

Nate carefully lowered the bigger man to the ground, feet first. He was bending, and the giant sagged on his back when the man's eyes snapped wide open. Mirrored in them was pain, confusion, and anger.

Before Nate could say a word, the giant's right hand swept up and clamped onto his throat.

Chapter Three

Geronimo came awake with a start. He bolted upright. His hand swooped to his side and he began to yank out his Tomahawk. Belatedly, his surroundings sank in. He paused, confused, then rose unsteadily and turned in a three-hundred-sixty-degree circle to verify that his senses were not playing tricks on him. "How can this be?" he said aloud.

The Warrior stood in the middle of a vast plain. For as far as the eye could see there was nothing but rolling prairie and rippling grass. He shook his head in disbelief, closed his eyes, and opened them again. The plain was still there.

Geronimo saw the FNC at his feet. Retrieving it, he checked the magazine, which was full. He was glad he had not lost it, just as he was glad that his .357 Arminius revolver still hung snugly in its shoulder holster under his left arm.

There was no sign of the Dark Tower, no trace of the withered countryside in which it stood.

The last Geronimo remembered, he had followed Blade across the room where they found Thanatos. He recalled seeing the Dark Lord disappear. Only a pace behind Blade when they came to the strange cage, he had slowed, concerned that it was a trap. But when Blade had bulled fearlessly into it, he had done the same. Vaguely, he remembered seeing his friend vanish. "Blinking out" would be a better description. One instant Blade had been there, the next he had been gone.

Geronimo had assumed Blade was right about a trap door, and he had lunged to grab the head Warrior before Blade fell through. His fingers had grasped empty air. Then there had been a sensation of falling. He had clawed for support that was not there. Radiant green light had enveloped him, and the moment it did, he had grown unaccountably dizzy, dizzier than he had ever been, so dizzy he had feared he would be sick.

After that, everything was a dim jumble of impossible images. Geronimo seemed to recall being caught up in a swirling green vortex. He had spun and spun, or his mind had. The end result had been the same. His vertigo had grown worse, to the point where he had not known which way was up or which way was down, to the point where he had been unable to form a coherent thought if his life depended on it.

The last sensation had been of slipping into a void. He had taken it for granted that he was dying, that he would never wake up again on this side of the vale.

Here he was, though.

It beggared a question. Where, exactly, was *here?* The prairie resembled Dakota Territory, a region under the control of survivors of the holocaust who called themselves the Cavalry.

Geronimo squinted at the sun to get a sense of direction. He blinked, more from surprise than from the glare. The sun appeared to be bigger and brighter than he ever remembered seeing it. That was impossible, of course. The sun was a star, and stars did not simply up and grow whenever they felt like it.

More mystified than ever, Geronimo mulled over which direction to go. The angle of the sun and his own shadow indicated that it was the middle of the morning. If he truly was in Dakota Territory, the Rocky Mountains were west of him, the Valley of Shadow even farther west.

Shouldering the FNC, Geronimo turned his back to the sun and started hiking. He did not have a watch, but in his estimation he had been on the go for over an hour when he was brought to a stop by a loud, guttural grunt, just such a noise as a mutant or, worse, a *mutate* might make.

It came from directly ahead.

Bending low, Geronimo stalked forward until he heard a distinct crunch. More ensued, along

with loud cracking and snapping and grunts ga-
lore. On cat's feet he came to a broad area where
the grass had been trampled flat. Silently moving
the last stems aside, he discovered the grunter.

In the middle of the flattened tract stood an
enormous bear. Yellowish-brown with white-
tipped hairs, it was five feet wide at the shoulders
and over eight feet tall. A large hump over the
front shoulders added to the impression of massive bulk. It was preoccupied, eating the remains
of an animal Geronimo could not identify. As he
looked on, the brute tore a bone from the ravaged
carcass. Its iron jaws closed, shattering the bone
as if it were a twig.

Geronimo recognized a grizzly bear when he
saw one. What made this specimen of special interest was its robust health. Most of the bears he
had run into previously had been deformed in
one respect or another. Either they were geneti-
cally warped mutants or they were chemically
deformed *mutates*.

Thankfully, the wind was blowing from the
bear to him, so Geronimo needed not worry that
the beast would detect his scent. He backed off
a few feet and worked his way around to the left,
circling the trampled area, giving the bruin a
wide berth. The shoulder-high grass hid him
completely.

Geronimo had taken a dozen steps when the
breeze, which had been fanning his face, suddenly fanned the back of his head instead. He
tensed, hoping against hope that the bear was so
busy eating it would not pay much attention to
a random scent. He should have known better.

Grizzlies had a reputation for being some of

the most aggressive animals alive. They were belligerent, short-tempered, and fierce. They would eat anything they could catch, and they went after everything that blundered into close range.

Geronimo heard a piercing growl. He could not see the bear, but he could hear the pad-pad-pad of its heavy paws as it came toward the grass. He ducked to foil the breeze, but the harm had already been done.

Five feet away a ponderous head and immense shoulders rose above the top of the grass. The grizzly's black nostrils flared. It sniffed several times. Mighty jaws quivering, it swung its head from side to side, evidently to pinpoint the Warrior's scent.

All was not lost. Geronimo was confident the bear would lose interest if it failed to locate him, and go back to feeding. If he stayed low, he should be able to slip off unnoticed.

The grizzly picked that moment to tilt its head and look right at him.

Instantly, Geronimo shoved erect and bolted. Grizzlies could overhaul horses over short distances so he had little chance of outrunning it. But he could put distance between them, could buy himself the precious seconds it would take to core a vital organ with a well-placed shot.

He ran flat out. The stems lashed him, stinging his hands and face. They snared the FNC. He had to keep a firm grip on the Auto Rifle in order not to lose it. Twisting, he glanced over his shoulder.

The grizzly was after him. Like a great, fur-covered ship, it plowed through the sea of stems without missing a beat, flattening those in its path as effortlessly as if they were not there. Its head and the hump were visible, its eyes locked on his back.

There was never a tree around when a man needed one. Grizzlies were poor climbers. Eluding his pursuer would be simple if Geronimo could clamber onto a high limb and wait until the bear lost interest or its belly goaded it into going after other quarry.

Geronimo glanced back again. He had a ten-yard lead, hardly enough. The bear was taking its sweet time, either because it was already full or because it saw no need to exert itself to overtake him. Either case had bought him extra moments. He poured on the speed.

A knoll offered the Warrior a spot to make his stand. He veered to the right, losing a few feet, but it was worth the sacrifice if he could get above the bear.

It sounded as if a steam engine were after him, the way the beast wheezed and panted. Geronimo resisted an urge to snap off a few shots on the off chance that they would discourage it. A wounded grizzly was much more savage, and it would not rest until it had hunted down the cause of its pain.

Geronimo reached the knoll. Flying to the top, he spun and dropped onto one knee, the FNC glinting in the sunlight as he trained it on the onrushing behemoth's skull. He tapped off a short burst.

The monstrous bear tucked into a forward roll that brought it to rest at the bottom of the knoll. Scarlet rivulets trickled from holes near its left ear. The great carnivore still breathed, but it did not move.

Pleasantly surprised at how easy it had been, Geronimo took deliberate aim.

The beast was far from finished. Venting a roar that could be heard for a mile, the grizzly pushed up on all fours, yawned wide its slavering mouth, and charged up the slope.

Geronimo flicked the selector lever to full automatic, then held down the trigger. Lead thudded into the grizzly's face, its head, its neck. It staggered but would not drop, its four-inch claws digging furrows in the earth as it sought extra purchase. Like a ball shot out of a cannon, it hurtled higher. Those rapier teeth were only seven feet away, then six, then five, then four.

The FNC went empty. Geronimo leaped to the right, a futile act at best since the bear would be on him before he went a yard. Something slammed into his side, catapulting him halfway down the knoll. His shoulders bore the force of the impact. He lost hold of the Auto Rifle. Rolling to a stop, he unlimbered his revolver and rotated to confront his bestial adversary.

The grizzly lay atop the knoll, its front paws extended. Holes riddled its head and neck. Its head was cocked, as if casting an accusing eye at the Warrior. Other than a trembling in its rear leg, it was still.

Geronimo slowly rose. Keeping the .357 Magnum on the bear, he climbed to the top, picking up the FNC along the way. He could not quite accept the mighty engine of destruction was dead, but it was.

Sighing in relief, Geronimo holstered the Arminius, ejected the spent magazine, and pulled another from a pocket. He realized that he only had two spares left. That was bad news. He had hundreds of miles to cover, and he was bound to stumble on more wild beasts and genetic horrors. From then on he must use the ammunition judiciously, never wasting a round.

Turning, Geronimo shielded his eyes with a hand and surveyed the prairie to the west. There was no end to it. To the southwest were several large animals, but they were too far away for him even to hazard a guess as to what they were.

He was about to resume his trek when more large animals appeared to the northwest. There were seven or eight, strung out in single file, bearing to the west. In the haze of midday they shimmered like ghosts. He squinted and their shapes solidified. They were horses and riders.

Members of the Cavalry, Geronimo decided. Perhaps they had heard the autofire and were looking for the person responsible. All he had to do was bang a few shots into the air and they would come on the run. Since the Cavalry and the Family had long been staunch allies, they would help him rejoin his friends. He could hardly wait to greet them.

Drawing the revolver, Gernonimo cocked the hammer and elevated the gun over his head. A noise behind him, as of someone or something exhaling, brought him around in the blink of an eye. For a second he thought that he had been mistaken, that the grizzly was alive after all and about to pounce. But it had only been the spasmodic release of air left in the beast's lungs. He poked it with the FNC to be sure.

Geronimo grinned over his bad case of nerves and faced northwest. The grin faded into a frown of disappointment. The horses and riders were gone. He scoured the plain diligently with no result.

Rather than waste a bullet when the Cavalrymen might be out of earshot, he slid the revolver under his left arm. He lingered a few minutes in case they should reappear. No such luck. Reluctantly, he headed westward, tramping through the high grass with more care than he had exercised before. He did not want to repeat the incident with the grizzly.

The sun passed its zenith, arcing lower. Geronimo grew thirsty. His stomach growled. He regretted not cutting off enough grizzly meat to last him a day or two. There was no telling when he would stumble on game.

About the middle of the afternoon, a line of cottonwoods and a few willows broke the monotony of the grassland. Where there were trees, there had to be water. And where there was water, there had to be wildlife.

Geronimo jogged to the vegetation. He did not throw caution to the wind. There had been no trace of mutants yet, but they were out there, blighting the landscape with their festering presence, ravenously feasting on every living creature they found. Abominations all, they were far worse than grizzlies.

The welcome gurgle of flowing water brought Geronimo's grin back. The belt of trees and undergrowth was thirty to forty yards wide. He penetrated less than halfway and came upon the stream, a blue ribbon five feet wide and about that many inches deep. Eagerly, he threw himself down and was going to drink when common sense gave him pause.

Was it tainted? Geronimo wondered. As a result of the cataclysm, many waterways were polluted with radioactive toxins and man-made biological poisons. A single sip could induce swift death.

This stream looked safe. The grass that grew at its edge was green and lush. The soil was a rich brown, not bleached or orange or some other ungodly color.

Fish were the clincher. Geronimo glimpsed something small flitting about in a shallow pool to his left. Peering closer, he wanted to laugh for joy. A small school of minnows were proof positive that the water was not contaminated. He lowered his face into it and drank; seldom had water tasted so delicious.

Geronimo knew better than to drink too much. His thirst quenched, he rolled onto his back and rested. He could not get over how green everything was. The trees, the grass, the wildflowers, even the weeds, they all enjoyed a vigor rare in his day and age. He had found a rare pocket completely untouched by the global holocaust that had brought every government in the world to its knees and transformed the pristine planet into a nightmare.

The gay chirp of birds and the gurgling of the stream combined to lull the Warrior into a state of drowsiness. His eyelids drooped, and he was on the verge of drifting off when a twig snapped loudly.

Geronimo rolled to his knees, the FNC locked and loaded. Ten feet away was the creature that had broken the twig. It was hard to say which one of them was more astounded, Geronimo or the splendid ten-point buck that stood riveted for a few moments and then bounded off into the brush, flashing its tail as was the custom of its kind.

The Warrior was so amazed, he forgot to shoot. The buck had been in sterling health, just like the grizzly and the fish and the birds. No sores or bald spots had marred its hide. No pus had oozed from its nose or eyes.

"It's a Garden of Eden," Geronimo said softly, making a mental note to bring his friends and their families back there one day so they all could enjoy the treat. Rising, he waded in the stream and moved through the cottonwoods to the plain.

Geronimo was loath to leave his little paradise. But five or six hours of daylight remained and it would be foolish to waste them. Casting a fond glance at the stream, he ventured into the open. The sight of the buck had rekindled his appetite. The next one he saw would not be so fortunate.

Time passed. The cottonwoods and willows dwindled until they were lost to view.

Geronimo was the only living creature in the whole vast ocean of waving grass. He had lapsed and was not paying much attention to the terrain. Pushing through a thick cluster, he halted at the brink of a large depression the likes of which he had never set eyes on.

The grass had been worn clear down to the roots. Dust covered the bottom of the saucer-shaped basin, which he guessed to be ten feet wide and over a foot deep. It reeked, bringing to mind what it was like to be downwind from a urinating stallion.

"Odd," Geronimo kept up his new habit of talking to himself. He skirted the depression, went another twenty feet, and came on another. On a hunch, he walked to an earthen spine not much higher than he was. Even so, from its crest he saw that there were dozens of similar basins, scattered for hundreds of yards in all directions.

Stumped for an explanation, Geronimo forged on. A few buzzards circled over him briefly, then lost interest and went elsewhere. Twice he spooked rabbits. Once he spotted a brown snake winding off into the grass. Unlike Hickok, who was partial to rattlesnake meat, Geronimo had never been fond of eating reptiles. He let the snake go.

Minutes later the Warrior looked down to avoid a rut, and when he looked up, a four-legged animal went sailing past him so swiftly that if had he blinked, he would have missed it. Halting in midstride, he looked to see what it had been. As he did, another zipped past in incredible leaps that covered twenty feet at a bound. He had a dazzling image of a deer-like, long-legged, reddish-tan animal with relatively short, thick horns, each with two prongs at the end.

Pronghorns. Geronimo had never seen any up so close. They were rare to begin with, and normally they kept a wary distance from humans. Since they had eyesight an eagle would envy and could attain speeds of over seventy miles an hour, they were as elusive as will-o'-the-wisps.

Another flashed by. Then another. Swiveling,

he realized that he was in the middle of a stampeding herd, that dozens and dozens were streaking from north to south in reckless abandon. None posed a threat to him. Exhibiting uncanny reflexes, those that came anywhere near him swerved quickly aside.

Geronimo's stomach grumbled, letting him know that he had gone most of the day without eating. He brought up the FNC but he did not employ it. Trying to hit one of the four-legged bullets would be more a matter of luck than skill, and he did not have ammo to waste.

What had spooked them? Geronimo pondered. Clear to the northern horizon was nothing but grass and more grass. He suspected a predator, or maybe even a prairie fire, although no smoke blackened the sky.

It was a thrill to stand there with antelope hurtling by on all sides. They made no sound except for the drum of their small hooves and an occasional bleat by a young one. The Warrior laughed, his first since the war against the Dark Lord had begun.

The thought revived memories Geronimo did not care to dredge up. He vividly recalled the sneak attack the Dark Lord had launched on the Family. The stench of blood seemed as fresh as it had been that night. The screams of the wounded and the wails of the dying still rang in his ears. Had it not been for the Warriors, the Home would have fallen.

A Warrior by the name of Rikki-Tikki-Tavi was generally regarded as the hero of the Night of the Zombies, as the Family Chronicler called it.

Rikki had been alone on the west wall when

the undead horde launched its assault. Single-handedly, armed only with his cherished katana, he had resisted a floodtide of merciless legions, dashing from point to point to push scaling ladders from the ramparts or to behead zombies that managed to gain a foothold. Later it was estimated that he had slain forty-seven of the enemy before more Warriors arrived to stem the flow.

Geronimo had done his share that terrible night. He had been assigned to the south wall, and with the help of Samson, Achilles, and Sherry, he had fought off hundreds of the enemy.

Their automatic weapons had decimated the zombie ranks, stopping all but a handful from reaching the top. The few that had were crushed by Samson. *Literally* crushed. Geronimo would never forget the sight of the burly strongman perched on the parapet with zombies clinging to his shoulders, zombies clinging to his legs, zombies dangling from his arms, all trying to topple Samson as he pulverized them with his mallet fists or reduced them to splintered wreckage with iron kicks.

The Founder would have been proud.

Giving his head a toss, Geronimo shut that dreadful night out. Too many had died, among them friends he had known since childhood, people he had cared for dearly. The Dark Lord had a lot to answer for, and Geronimo was going to see to it that the butcher paid.

First, he had to reach the Valley of Shadow.

The antelope had stopped going by. The Warrior took up where he had left off, holding to a brisk pace. Sixty feet from where he started, he halted again. Was it his imagination or was the ground under his feet quaking? A faint rumbling arose. He turned to isolate the source.

It came from the north, the same direction the pronghorns had come from. Whatever was responsible, a thick dust cloud now choked the horizon, a cloud that grew bigger and denser as the rumbling grew louder and louder. A dark line materialized at the bottom of the cloud, a line as wide as the cloud itself.

A full sixty seconds elapsed before Geronimo discerned what the dark line was. Thousands upon thousands of shaggy animals were strung out over a mile-wide front, so many that they darkened the heavens with their dust and induced an earthquake with the hammering of their heavy hooves.

Geronimo could not quite credit his eyes. It was impossible, and yet it was happening. Those creatures barreling toward him were buffalo, more of them than anyone had ever guessed existed. They bore down on him in a thunderous phalanx of bristling horns and bobbing humps. He could not possibly outrun them, and he had nowhere to take cover.

Chapter Four

The words echoed in Hickok's skull like shouts in a cave. At first he could not make any sense of them. Gradually, as he struggled up through a clinging fog of partial awareness, he comprehended more and more although he was not yet fully awake.

"... not wolf meat, I reckon. See how the coon's eyelids are a-flutterin'?"

"Is he hurt, hoss? See any wounds? Any bruises?"

Vaguely, Hickok was aware of rough hands turning his head from side to side and raising his shoulders.

"Not a scratch on him, Kittson. Don't it beat all? If I didn't know better, I'd swear this fella just laid down to take a nap."

A third party interjected a comment. "Out here in the middle of nowhere, Clyman?"

"Strange-lookin' varmint," said the man named Kittson. "You'd think he was a sprout, what with that hairless chin and all. And look at them fancy guns. I've never seen the like. Pass one over."

Someone touched Hickok's right Colt. It sent a bolt of indignation rippling through him. No one laid a hand on his pistols. Ever! The Pythons had been his since before he became a Warrior. More times than he cared to count, they had saved his hide. They were his, and his alone, until the day he died. He'd be damned if anyone was going to take them.

Outrage brought Hickok out of the mental fog that had befuddled his mind. He opened his eyes to find a stocky form bent over his chest. He saw a matted tangle of beard, saw weather-beaten features. "Back off, *hombre!*" he warned, shoving hard.

The man was flung backward. Two others, startled, took a step back.

With the speed of an uncoiling sidewinder, Hickok was on his feet, his hands poised above the grips of his precious Pythons, his blue eyes ablaze with the cold fury that had been the last sight most of his enemies ever saw. "Hands off the hardware, you coyotes, unless you're partial to lead poisonin'!"

The three men shared bewildered looks. They were dressed alike, in grungy buckskins and moccasins. To a man, they carried rifles and had a brace of pistols wedged under their belts. Slanted across their chests were leather bags and other items.

"Hold on there, hoss," said a man whose voice identified him as Kittson. "We didn't mean no harm." He offered his right hand. "It's good for these old eyes to see a young beaver like yourself. It must mean we're closer to the gateway than we figured. Give me your paw."

Wary of a trick, Hickok hesitated. "The gateway?" he repeated.

"Sure," Kittson said amiably. "St. Louis. Leastwise, that's what them newspaper writers have taken to callin' it. 'The Gateway to the Fur Trade.' Everybody knows that."

The other two men were regarding Hickok with a mixture of curiosity and amusement. Convinced there was no threat, Hickok shook Kittson's hand. The power in Kittson's bronzed, calloused fingers was unexpected, but Hickok matched it, tit for tat.

"Have you got any 'bacca in your possibles?" asked the man named Clyman.

"Hell, Cly," said the third man, chuckling, "this coon ain't even got a possibles bag. Ain't you got eyes?" He swiveled. "For that matter, he ain't got no horse, neither." His brow furrowed. "Say, Mister, how in the hell did you get out here, anyway?"

"Maybe he flapped his arms and flew, Ogden," joked Clyman.

Hickok had not given much thought to where he was until that moment. He was astonished to discover that they stood in the middle of a vast grassy plain. A dozen feet behind the unkempt trio stood several horses and ten heavily laden pack animals. "Where in tarnation am I?" he blurted.

Kittson arched a bushy eyebrow. "You don't know, hoss?"

The Warrior shook his head, the simple act provoking an intense wave of dizziness that nearly caused his legs to fold. Tottering, he put a hand to his head. His tongue felt thick and coated with hair, as if he'd downed a jug of rotgut all by his lonesome. "The last I recollect, my pards and me were in the Valley of Shadow."

Kittson did a double take. "The valley of the shadow?"

Hickok, striving to collect his thoughts, nodded. "You've heard of it?" That was a good sign. He couldn't be far from Blade and Geronimo. The sooner they were reunited, the sooner he would learn what had happened. The last he remembered, he had been following them onto a metal contraption. He'd spotted a pair of mutants jumping onto it from the other side, and he thought that he had shouted a warning. Then a keg of gunpowder had gone off inside his noggin.

"Who hasn't, Mister?" Clyman was saying. "It's in the Good Book, ain't it?"

The Good Book? Hickok was about to ask the man to explain when the worst bout of dizziness yet made his stomach flop around like a frog with its leg caught in a snake's mouth. He was worried that he would pass out again.

"Say, are you all right, young feller?" Kittson inquired. "You're as white as a sheet."

"I've felt better," Hickok allowed. Embarrassed

by his weakness, he stuck to the subject at hand. "You still haven't told me exactly where I am."

Ogden, who was the youngest of the three and had a big wart on the tip of his bulbous nose, snickered impishly. "Exactly, huh? Well, let me see." He scratched his thick brown beard and made a show of being deep in thought. "You're on the planet Earth, in North America, smack dab in the Great American Desert, about two days' ride from the muddy Mississippi and civilization." He glanced askance at the sun. "Give or take a day or two, mind. It's awful hard to be exact without decent landmarks."

Hickok stared at the grass rustling nearby. "The Great American Desert?" he said. "What are you tryin' to pull, jasper? I don't see no sand or camels hereabouts."

"Camels?" Ogden said, and laughed uproariously. "That's a good one, Mister. I'll have to remember it. The boys do like to poke fun at Major Long every chance they get."

"Who?"

Kittson answered. "Major Stephen Long, the idiot the government sent in a few years back. He was the one who branded the plains as the Great American Desert. Claimed it wasn't fit for man nor beast."

Clyman, whose left shoulder drooped lower than the right, tittered. "I reckon Long forgot to tell that to the bufflers and the Injuns. But the American government believed him. Which ain't all that surprising. Politicians are so good at spreadin' tall tales that they just naturally believe every one they hear."

Too much was being thrown at Hickok too

fast. What was this Great American Desert they were talking about? And why was it that he had never heard of Major Stephen Long? Or had he? The name jogged a faint bell. Then there was this business of the government. Everyone knew that the U.S. had ceased to exist at the time of the holocaust. "Are you telling me that the American government is still around?"

Kittson pushed the blue cap he wore back on his head. "What kind of tomfool question is that? Who do you think runs St. Louis nowadays? The French and Spanish had their turns, but all they did was squabble. So now the Americans have come along. Knowing them, they'll probably spoil everything with all their laws and regulations and rules and such."

Hickok's confusion mounted. The last he'd heard, St. Louis had been under the control of a bunch of bikers who called themselves the Leather Knights. He'd never been there himself, but Blade and Rikki-Tikki-Tavi had, and they'd told him all about their escapades. Was it possible the Leather Knights had changed their name in honor of America, the land of the free and the home of the brave? He couldn't see them doing it, yet it was the only possible explanation.

Another thought occurred to him, even more troubling. If his new acquaintances were right, he was close to St. Louis. But the city was hundreds of miles from the Rockies. How had he gotten there from the Valley of Shadow? Did that wierd metal contraption have something to do with it?

"I've got to find my pards," Hickok stated his first order of business aloud.

"You're welcome to tag along with us to St. Louis," Kittson said. "Maybe your friends are there."

The idea had merit, Hickok decided. Since the Resistance was in the Freedom Federation's debt, he could contact the government and ask them to help locate Blade and Geronimo. In no time at all they'd be on their way to the Valley of Shadow to settle accounts with the Dark Lord.

"What do you say, hoss?" Clyman asked while opening the leather bag draped across his chest. He removed a dark square object, jammed a corner into his mouth, and bit off a piece. Beaming happily, he chomped greedily, his left cheek bulging.

"What are you eating?" Hickok asked, his own belly as empty as could be.

"Eatin'?" Clyman said, and laughed. "Lordy, if you ain't a caution. Don't tell me you ain't never set eyes on chewin' 'bacca before?"

Ogden hooted. "I'll tell you, Mister. You sure do tickle a man's funny bone." He extended his right hand. "Never did catch your handle, fancy guns."

Hickok told them. The comment caused him to look closely at their weapons. Then he looked closely at them. Suddenly he realized that something was not quite right. Their weapons were unlike any he had ever seen except in books in the Family library. Their buckskins, while like his, were thicker and coarser. To their credit, they had a rugged, untamed air about them that he found refreshing, and there was no denying that they were genuinely friendly.

"Where did you get those antiques?" the gunfighter inquired, nodding at the rifle Kittson held.

The man acted puzzled. He was the oldest of the bunch, his hair gray at the temples, his beard flecked with gray streaks. "What are you talkin' about, friend? I bought this here long gun five years ago from Jake Hawken himself. That don't hardly make it no antique."

Now it was Hickok's turn to be puzzled. He reasoned that the gunsmiths in St. Louis lacked the skill to make six-shooters, pistols and automatics, and were manufacturing old-time flintlock and percussion guns instead. But it amazed him that the gunsmith who made Kittson's had the same name as one of the famous brothers who had made exceptional rifles in another day and age.

If there was one subject Hickok was an expert on, it was the history and development of six-shooters and rifles. As the Family's premier gunman, he knew more about weapons from the frontier period than any other Warrior. Yama was a walking encyclopedia when it came to automatics in general, Ares had specialized in SMG's, but neither could hold a candle to him where early firearms were concerned.

Kittson tapped one of the flintlocks at his waist. "As for these, I traded for the pair at rendezvous two years ago, so they're even newer."

Ogden nodded at the Warrior's gunbelt. "What about those shiny guns of yours, hoss? We ain't never seen the like. Mind showin' 'em to us?"

Hickok was glad to oblige. But at that moment the horses acted up. Every last one looked to the north and half of them uttered nervous nickers.

"Injuns must be out there," Ogden said, raising his rifle.

"This close to St. Louis?" Kittson said. "What do you use for brains, boys? It had to be a painter or a griz."

Clyman moved his stooped shoulder up and down. "If it's a silver-tip, I get first shot. I owe them for what that one on Ham's Fork did to me."

Ogden found the remark humorous. "Hellfire, Cly. You got only yourself to blame for the chunk that she-bear took out of you. Even greenhorns know better than to traipse off into the brush without a rifle handy."

"I was only heedin' Nature's call," Clyman defended himself. "I never figured a griz would be so close to camp."

Kittson was hurrying to his horse. "Mount up, you box-headed jokers, before whatever it is takes a notion into its head to taste horse meat. Or human."

Hickok's own head was clearing. He scanned the prairie but saw no trace of the thing out there. "Maybe it's a mutant," he speculated.

Kittson glanced at him. "A mu-who?"

"A mutant," Hickok clarified. "You know. Something part bear and part something else. Or maybe a bear with two heads and eight legs. I saw a wolf once that had two—" He stopped. Ogden was cackling to beat the band, and the older men were showing more teeth than a school of piranha. "Something the matter?"

"A bear with two heads and eight legs!" Ogden guffawed. "Where do you come up with these? They're priceless."

Clyman winked at his companions. "Don't be pokin' fun at our new friend. He's tellin' the truth. Why, once up in the Missouri River country, I saw a dragonfly with four heads and four tails."

"What was it doing?" Kittson asked, trying his best to keep a straight face.

"Makin' love to itself."

The three men howled, leading Hickok to conclude that they were all a mite touched in the head. He'd seen it before. Decades of radiation poisoning had reduced whole populations to raving lunatics.

Clyman bent. "You can ride double with me, friend. That way if we run into any of them two-headed varmints, you can keep them off my back."

More laugher peeled out. It abruptly died when some of the pack horses started to shy and pull at the rope that linked them into a string. Kittson, who had hold of the end of the rope, immediately prodded his dun into motion. Ogden fell back, taking up position about the middle of the line, his long rifle centered on the dense grass.

Clyman's roan pranced a few yards when Hickok climbed on, then calmed. The man with the drooping shoulder was as serious as could be now, his dark eyes roving from east to west. "Well, whatever's out there had better keep to itself. After all the hard work and sweat we put into raisin' our plews, I ain't about to let anything run our animals off."

"Plews?" Hickok said.

Clyman twisted. "What country are you from, pilgrim, that you don't know what a plew is?" He bobbed a chin at the bulky packs. "Beaver hides, Mister. We have a full year's worth that we're fixin' to sell in St. Louis. Came all this way 'cause we can get a better price than if we sell them to company reps at the rendezvous."

Hickok had no idea that there were so many beaver left in the world. "Just like in the old days," he said softly.

"Not hardly," Clyman said. "We had to travel clear to the Snake River to find enough beaver to make the trappin' worth our while. Most of them in the central Rockies have been kilt off." He saddened. "Damn shame, too. Ain't a more fittin' profession in the world for those that cotton to freedom and excitement than raisin' plews for a living."

Hickok wondered why the people of St. Louis were in the market for so many beaver hides. The city had been largely untouched by the final World War. There were skyscrapers and highways and running cars. But no plants to make clothes, he reckoned. The citizens must be in desperate need of new duds to wear and were sending trappers into the mountains to get furs.

The rear pack animal let out with an ear-piercing neigh, more a shriek than a whinny. Ogden reined his mount around and galloped to the end of the string, where the animal was stamping back and forth and tossing its head and mane. He examined it, swallowed hard, and called out, "Something took a swipe at its hind end."

"Impossible!" Kittson responded. "We would have seen."

"I'm tellin' you there are six claw marks in its rump, plain as day," Ogden insisted. "As high as

63

my chest, maybe higher."

Hickok was as perplexed as his acquaintances. It would take a large predator to make slash marks that high up, yet none of them had caught sight of it. How could that be?

"Has to be a painter," Clyman said. "No griz could be that sneaky."

"What's a painter?" Hickok asked.

The stooped frontiersman looked around. "You really are a danged foreigner, aren't you? Painters are panthers. The Frenchies like to call them cougars, or some such. Other folks have taken to callin' them mountain lions. Same thing. Big cats with bad tempers."

"Maybe it's a mutant cougar."

Clyman jabbed a finger at the gunfighter. "Don't start with that nonsense again. This is hardly the right time. We have to keep our eyes skinned or that infernal critter will cost us a horse we can't rightly spare."

No one spoke for the longest while. Hickok had begun to think that the culprit had drifted elsewhere when a raspy whisper from deep in the grass proved him wrong. It was a whisper that resonated with suppressed ferocity, that hinted at immense vitality and inhuman vocal chords.

"Waaarrrrriiiooorrrrr! It's you I want! Let the others go on without you!"

Kittson and Clyman drew rein. "What in the name of all that's holy!" the older man declared. Straightening, he hollered, "Who the devil's out there? Show yourself, Mister! There's a painter on the prowl and it's liable to cut you to ribbons if you keep on playin' games."

From the deep grass boomed guttural laughter, laughter that could only be described as demonic, laughter that sent a chill of recognition down Hickok's spine. "You gents had better ride on to St. Louis without me," he said, beginning to slide off. "That thing out there is only interested in me."

"Hold on," Kittson said. "What thing? All I've heard is some jackass tryin' to spook us. If he shows his head, I'm of a mind to blow it plumb off. No grown man should be so childish."

"Man?" crackled a taunting challenge. "You insult me, human dog. Here. See for yourself. Do I look like a man to you, fool?"

Forty yards out a brown knob rose above the grass and kept on rising. The knob was the top of a head, the head identical to that of a Brahma bull, only this one was attached to shoulders as wide as a wagon which were part of a body as muscular and hairy as that of a Neanderthal.

A *minotaur*, Hickok observed. One of the Dark Lord's favored lieutenants. Every zombie company had a minotaur commander. They were impossibly strong, impossibly tough, absorbing punishment that would pulverize a regiment. Now that he thought about it, a minotaur had been one of the creatures he had seen jump into the metal cage right before the world turned topsy-turvy.

The three frontiersmen were flabbergasted, acting as if they had never seen a mutant before. Kittson actually slapped himself. "I'm seein' things!" he said, appalled. "I have to be!"

"If you are, that makes two of us," Clyman whispered in undisguised horror.

At the rear of the string, Ogden called out, "Is

that a talkin' buffalo? Or just someone's idea of a poor joke?"

The minotaur tossed its curved horns. "Joke, am I?" It dropped onto all fours and charged, the tips of its horns the only part of it visible above the tall grass, which snapped like stalks of grain before a scythe as the juggernaut hurtled toward them.

"Skedaddle while you can!" Hickok bellowed, springing from the horse and spinning to face the genetic aberration. For once he did not resort to the Pythons. Slipping a hand under the sling that banded his chest, he pulled the heavy Marlin over his shoulder and into his hands. The lever ratcheted flawlessly, feeding a .45–70 cartridge into the chamber.

Geronimo had once teased Hickok about not favoring a Winchester, widely hailed as the rifle that won the Old West. But Hickok had known what he was doing. In a era when massive mutations were everywhere, when sheer stopping power counted for more than muzzle velocity and penetration, the .45–70 was ideal. It packed more of a wallop than a .30–30 or .30–06. A single shot was often sufficient to drop an adversary, where it might take three or four with a smaller caliber. So the gunman had stuck with the .45–70, teasing or no.

Now, as the grass thirty yards out bent toward him and loud snorts signified the minotaur had hit full stride, Hickok flipped the rear sight up and aligned it with the front sight. He was so intent on being ready for his enemy that he did not realize Kittson and Clyman had dismounted until they assumed places on either side of him and cocked their antique long guns.

"Didn't you hear me?" Hickok demanded more gruffly than he intended. "Light a shuck or that thing will pound you to a pulp."

"What kind of men would we be if we turned tail and ran?" Kittson said. "My sainted ma would roll over in her grave if she thought she had raised a coward."

Hickok wanted to argue, to plead, to beg them to get out of there before it was too late. But it already was. With stunning rapidity, the minotaur was on them.

Chapter Five

Nate King had never run into anyone so immensely strong, not in three decades of living among some of the hardiest—not to mention, rowdiest—roughnecks in all the world.

The life of a mountain man did not breed weaklings. From dawn until dusk during trapping season, a free trapper tramped all over creation, toting heavy traps and stakes, wading in and out of ice-cold streams and ponds, lugging forty-pound beaver carcasses back to camp, and so on. It would harden any soul. Muscles were turned into bands of steel. Weak constitutions were forged into iron ones.

Nate had always taken pride in the change that came over him after he gave up the sedate life of a New York accountant for the active life of a free trapper. He had grown broader at the shoulders, wider across the chest. His stomach, once so flabby that when he smacked it, it quivered, resembled a bed of rocks. Legs that once tired if he walked more than a mile could now take him up and down mountains all day. He was healthier than he had ever been, more powerful than he had ever dreamed he could be.

It was not enough. Nate swatted at the bulging arm that held him, but he might as well have struck it with a feather. He attempted to tear the giant's hands from his throat, but could not. In desperation he brought up his other arm, intending to use both to batter his attacker senseless. In the heat of the moment, he forgot that he still held his butcher knife.

Blade took a lurching step. He was confused, unsure of where he was or what had happened after he chased the Dark Lord onto the metal grid. The first sight he had seen when he came to was a big man in buckskins standing in front of him, clutching a long knife. Bitter experience had taught him that strangers were more often hostile than friendly, so he took it for granted that the big man intended to do him harm and acted accordingly.

When the man in buckskins raised the knife, Blade's head cleared in a rush of adrenaline. He grabbed the stranger's wrist to hold the knife at bay. Locked together, they strained, Blade slowly gouging his fingers into the man's thick neck.

Nate King could feel himself growing red in

the face, could feel the breath being gradually choked from him. He was far from beaten, though. He was not the type to give up without a struggle, especially when his family was close at hand and would be the next targets of the giant's wrath. He tensed, about to hook an ankle behind the giant and trip him, when an unforeseen element effected the outcome of the clash.

Now that Blade could think straight, he realized that the man in buckskins was not really trying to stab him, that the big man was more intent on simply breaking free. He relaxed his hold a trifle to see if the man would take the hint and stop resisting. Suddenly, to his right, rasped the metallic click of a gun hammer being pulled back.

Zach King had been racing down the trail to the lake when he had seen his mother stiffen in alarm. Looking back, he had been horrified to behold the giant and his father locked together in combat. Fearing for his father's safety, he sped toward the cabin, halting at arm's length and pointing his Hawken. "Let go of my pa, Mister, or so help me, I'll shoot!"

"Stay back, son!" Nate cried, afraid the giant would turn on him.

Blade was so startled by the youngster's appearance that for a second he just stood there.

"Didn't you hear me?" Zach demanded. "I won't tell you again!"

The Warrior looked at the father. All he saw in the man's eyes was worry for the boy. There wasn't a trace of bloodlust. Slowly lowering his arms and straightening, he responded, "I'm sorry, son. I thought your father was about to attack me."

Zach did not lower his rifle. The giant appeared to be sincere, but he was taking no chances. "Attack you? Why would he do that after all the trouble we went to lugging you home?" It annoyed him that the giant was not more grateful. "We could have left you out in the woods for that scaly critter to eat, but we figured you needed mending after being on fire and all."

"On fire?"

Nate spoke up. "You were covered with green flames when we first saw you." To confirm his peaceful intentions, he slid his butcher knife into its beaded sheath. "I thought you had been burned alive, yet your skin and clothes were untouched. How that could be, I don't know."

Blade tried to piece together the fragments of those final moments in the Tower as he chased Thanatos. Where had the Dark Lord gone? How had he gotten from the Dark Tower to wherever he was? The patter of footsteps heralded the arrival of a woman and a child. An Indian woman, no less. That was a surprise, since few tribes had survived the holocaust and its aftermath. The Flatheads in Montana were exceptions to the rule, but this woman did not appear to be a Flathead.

Winona King stood beside her man, her right hand on the hilt of her knife. "What is going on, husband?" she asked in her impeccable English, never taking her eyes off the giant. He intimidated her, although she did not let it show. A Shoshone did not show fear to an enemy, and she did not yet know whether the man her husband had brought back was friend or foe.

Nate explained briefly. He wanted to get their visitor inside and ply him with questions. Despite their misunderstanding, his gut instinct was that the giant could be trusted.

Blade listened with half an ear. He smiled at the little girl, who grinned impishly from behind her mother's buckskin dress, then shifted to take in his surroundings. The breathtaking sweep of mountains, lake and valley were dazzling. The forest was virgin, the lake crystal clear. Nowhere was the taint of contamination in evidence. "Where am I?" he breathed in awe.

Nate caught the comment. "You don't know, stranger?"

"The last I knew, I was near the Green River," Blade disclosed. The contrast between the blistered landscape there and the Garden of Eden in which the cabin was located was staggering.

The Green River valley was familiar to every mountain man. Several times the rendezvous had been held there. "You're hundreds of miles from the Green, friend, high in the central Rockies," Nate said. He pointed at a peak to the south. "That there is Long's Peak. Maybe you've heard of it?"

Blade had. He recalled seeing it in the distance during his last visit to Denver, the capital of the Civilized Zone. That meant he was west of the city and not all that far. "I have to get to Denver right away and see President Toland."

"Where?" Nate asked. He had never heard of a place by that name.

Zach chuckled. His folks made it a point to keep abreast of current developments in the

States. At the annual rendezvous they mingled with travelers from all over, getting the latest news. Even he knew that the President of the United States was John Tyler, not Toland.

Blade misunderstood. He assumed they were amused by his audacity in proposing to meet their president. Little did they know that Toland and he had known one another for years. It was imperative that he get word to all the leaders of the various Freedom Federation factions. They had to be warned that Thanatos was still alive and on the loose.

Idly, as was his habit, Blade dropped his hands to the hilts of his Bowies to rest them there. Only this time his fingers closed on empty air. He slapped the leather sheaths in dismay. If he had lost them, they would be impossible to replace. They had been made before the cataclysm by a master knife maker using state of the art techniques that could not be duplicated. The steel had been the best money could buy, tempered until it was diamond hard and razor sharp.

Nate saw and hesitated. Returning the knives might put his family at risk. Yet it also might inspire the giant's trust. He weighed the benefit against the liability, then stepped to his stallion. "Looking for these?" he said, opening a parfleche and removing the pair. His left hand stayed on the butt of one of his pistols.

Blade accepted the big knives gratefully. He'd owned them so long, wearing them day after day, year after year, that they were as much a part of him as his arms and legs. "Thanks for looking after them," he said.

"There's also this," Nate said, unhooking the

sling to the strange gun from his saddle.

Blade hefted the Bowies, gave both deft flips, and caught them again by the hilts. After sliding the pair into their sheaths, he took the Commando.

Young Zach could not take his eyes off those glittering knives. They were the finest he had ever seen, bigger than his pa's. "What kind of knives are those, Mister?" he inquired. "Where can I get myself a pair?"

"They're known as Bowies," Blade revealed. "Named after a man called Jim Bowie who—"

"Died at the Alamo along with Davy Crockett and William Travis," Zach excitedly finished for him. "I know all about it. Folks say they're some of the greatest heroes who ever lived, right up there with George Washington and that lion fella from Greece."

"Leonidas," Blade said.

"That's the one." Zach loved to hear about battles and such. Every summer when he stayed with his mother's people, one of his favorite pastime was to sit near the warriors at night around the campfire and listen to them recount their coup. One day he was going to be a respected warrior, just like his father and uncles. "I wish I could have been there. I would have taught that Santa Anna a thing or two."

Blade smiled knowingly. All boys shared daydreams about glory in combat. It was as natural as breathing. Yet there had been a time, long before the cataclysm, when those who ruled society had frowned on it. All toy weapons had been banned. Children had not been allowed to read books that contained violence or to indulge in any form of entertainment that had a shred of violent content. It was thought that by denying children contact with violence, they would grow up to be peace-loving citizens who could do no wrong.

As was often the case back in those days, those who tried to impose their will on society at large had been terribly wrong. They completely overlooked that violence was an inherent part of nature, that in the wilderness there was only one law, the survival of the fittest. Granted, most people back then had lived in the cities, but the cities were little better than concrete jungles where violence was just as rampant.

In light of that, trying to shield children from violence had been an exercise in utter stupidity. But that was how things had been way back then, when those who thought they knew it all imposed their ignorance on those who should have known better.

Now, staring into the boy's excited face, Blade remarked, "The Alamo was a bit before your time. But the Freedom Federation could use you when you get older."

Nate had been momentarily distracted by Evelyn, who came over and tugged at his pants. He looked up, saying, "What was that you mentioned?"

As for young Zach, he laughed lightly and said, "I'd hardly say the Alamo was before my time, Mister. It was only six years ago."

"Six?" Blade said, and waited for the youngster to chortle at his little jest. But neither the boy nor his father did so. "What year do you think this is, anyway?" he asked, half-jokingly.

"Don't you know?" Zach said. "1840."

The Warrior glanced at the father, waiting for the punch line. There had to be one. No sane person could stand there and claim the Alamo had taken place just a few years ago. It was ancient history, as ancient as the rifles and pistols the family was armed with. As ancient as the type of saddles they used, and the traps that hung from pegs on the wall, and the kind of knife the father possessed.

A peculiar feeling came over Blade, a feeling that caused his skin to prick as if from a heat rash and his stomach to ball into a knot. "You can't be serious?" he said, his voice sounding strained even to him.

"Of course we are," Zach said innocently. "Why? What's the matter?"

Nate King saw an unusual glint in the giant's eyes, as if the man were extremely troubled. He could not fathom the cause. "What year do you think it is, friend?"

Blade barely heard. Once again he gazed out over the valley at the ring of snow-capped peaks. He stared at the azure sky, bluer than he ever remembered seeing it. He noted the lushness of the vegetation, the health and vitality of every living thing within sight. The awful truth crept unwanted into his mind and he shook his head. "It's not possible," he said.

Winona was as puzzled by the giant's behavior as her husband appeared to be. She wondered if the stranger was one of those whites whose brains were always in a whirl. Touched in the head, her man called them. They were like rabid wolves, and would turn on a person without warning or provocation. She grew aware that the giant had turned toward her. She stiffened.

"What tribe do you belong to?" Blade asked.

"I am Shoshone," Winona said proudly. He had to be new to the mountains not to be able to tell from the style of her hair and her dress.

"And there are other Shoshones alive?"

"Of course," Winona answered. "That is a silly question."

"Humor me. Exactly how many are there? And where do they live?"

Winona did as he requested. "Over five thousand of my people live in the region drained by the main forks of the Bear and Green Rivers. Our country extends as far west as the Snake River."

Blade racked his memory of early American history, his unease growing. Pointing eastward, he asked, "Is there a city called Denver on the other side of that range?"

Zach found it uproarious. "A city out on the prairie? Where did you ever get such a harebrained notion, Mister? The nearest big city is St. Louis, clear back on the Mississippi."

The queasy feeling that had come over Blade grew worse. "Humor me again," he said. "Tell me that this valley is located in the Civilized Zone, and that you know who President Toland is."

"I never heard of any Zone," Nate said. "As for the President, his name is Tyler. Before him, it was William J. Harrison, but he only lasted a month in office and died of pneumonia. Harrison took the place of Martin Van Buren—"

"That's enough," Blade said, raising a hand. "I get the picture." Or did he? Because if what the man was telling him was true, the impossible had been made possible, the unreal had become real, and he did not quite know how he should deal with it.

Winona's resentment of the giant was fading. It was plain that he posed no threat to her loved ones. He was clearly upset, growing more so by the moment. She tried to put him more at ease by saying, "I do not believe we have been properly introduced." She told him her name, and made introductions all around.

The Warrior went through the motions, but his heart was not in it. Over and over in his mind the same words screamed: *It can't be! It can't be!*

"Blade?" Winona said quizzically. "Is that your first or your last name?"

"My only one," Blade said absently. "I had another before my Naming, but—" He broke off and moved past them, heading down the trail toward the lake, keenly anxious to be alone. "Please excuse me. I'll be back in a while."

Nate let the giant go, grabbing Zach when the boy started to go after him. "I think the man wants to be by himself, son."

"What's wrong with him, Pa?"

"I don't rightly know."

Zach was confused. "Is it me, Pa, or is he a peculiar cuss? Why in the world did he get all bothered when we told him what year it is?"

"You can ask him when he returns," Winona broke in. "Meanwhile, I need wood for the fireplace, and the horses need to be put in the corral."

"Ah, Ma," Zach groused.

"Get to it, son," Nate said sternly. He saw the giant look back at them as if to convince himself that they were still there. "Keep your eyes skinned for grizzlies," he called out. He had done his best to keep the valley free of the savage brutes, but every now and then one slipped down to the lake from the high country.

Nodding to be polite, not hearing a word, Blade went on. He was dazed to his core, unable to comprehend how every natural law he ever knew had been ripped asunder. It couldn't be 1840. It *couldn't* be. For if it was, he had been thrust back in time hundreds of years. And time travel did not exist. H. G. Wells to the contrary, no one had ever been able to work out the mechanics, to create a nuts-and-bolts device capable of breaching time with the same ease a ship plied water or a bird cleaved the air. It just wasn't done.

The Kings had to be up to something, Blade reflected. They were playing an elaborate ruse on him. They had even gone so far as to get their hands on antique weapons, ancient clothes, and long lost artifacts. Yet that idea in itself was preposterous. What possible motive could they have?

Frustrated by the mental dead end, Blade swatted at a tree limb, accidentally breaking it off. He flung it down and stalked to the water's edge before his frustration gave way to a budding kernel of despair. His emotions swirled. One moment he was convinced that he had to be in his own day and age no matter what the King family claimed. The next he felt a gnawing doubt.

Blade had seen what the Dark Lord was capable of. He had fought the zombies and the minotaurs and the snake-men. He had seen the Dark

Tower with his own eyes, had witnessed the technological marvels Thanatos had mastered.

Science, not sorcery, was the secret of Thanatos's power. The darker shades of science, the depths of genetic depravity manipulated by warped genius. Science wielded like a sword to satisfy the Dark Lord's lust for domination. Science at the pinnacle, where the impossible was made probable. In short, science perverted to do whatever Thanatos wanted it to.

Was it conceivable, then, that the Dark Lord had achieved the inconceivable? Was it within the realm of reality that Thanatos had mastered the unreal? Had he done what no one had ever been able to do before? Had he perfected a form of time travel?

Blade remembered the strange cagelike affair in the top chamber. He remembered how it glowed and vibrated right before Thanatos blinked out of existence. At the time he had jumped to the conclusion that Thanatos had escaped through a trap door. Now he was not so sure.

Perhaps, just perhaps, the cage-like affair had been the time-travel device. Perhaps, just perhaps, it had been the Dark Lord's ace in the hole, as Hickok might say, to be used as a last resort if the Dark Lord were brought to bay.

Blade gave a harsh laugh and stared at his reflection in the lake. Listen to him! A grown man standing there seriously accepting the likelihood of time travel. It was too ridiculous for words.

The Warrior got a grip on his surging emotions and ran a hand through his hair. There had to be a simpler explanation. Maybe the device had been a teleport, and he had been cast deep in the mountains where the holocaust had not effected the ecological chain.

But that still did not account for the Kings.

Blade saw a fish swim languidly past, a fish as big as his forearm. He bent for a better look and it promptly darted off into deeper water. Further out geese and ducks swam, unperturbed by his presence. Across the lake a buck was taking a drink.

The deer had the right idea.

Setting the Commando down, Blade sank onto his right knee and leaned forward. He took a sip, the cool water soothing his dry throat. Splashing some on his face and neck was invigorating.

The Warrior wiped his hand on his pants, twisted, and went to rise. A throaty growl froze him in place. Glancing at the top of an embankment that bordered the shoreline, he saw the largest mountain lion it had ever been his privilege to encounter. It was as long as he was tall, every square inch packed with rippling sinews. And as he set eyes on it, the enormous cat sprang.

Chapter Six

Life is in and of itself tenacious.

Whether a single person or an entire race, people will exert their utmost to preserve their lives against overwhelming odds. Only cowards curl up and die without a struggle, and if the truth were known, their souls had withered of neglect long before the fateful day.

A brave person never gives up. A person who possesses true courage will fight for life as long as breath remains. That has been proven time and again throughout the course of human history by ordinary men and women who were unbelievably valiant in the face of crushing adversity.

And so it was with the Warrior who had taken the name of Geronimo. He was stranded in the middle of the prairie with no cover at hand and a horde of stampeding buffalo thundering down on him, yet he did not give up and collapse in abject fear. He did the only thing he could do. He ran, even though he had nowhere to run to.

Geronimo headed west, vainly seeking to outflank the immense herd. There was no way he could do it, and he knew there was no way he could do it, yet he did it anyway. Legs pumping, eyes riveted to the densely packed mass of shaggy hides and curved horns, he flew on through the grass without any regard for what lay in front of him.

Without warning the ground seemed to give way. Geronimo tumbled into a roll that brought him up on his knees in the middle of another one of those odd depressions he had stumbled on earlier. This one was the same size, but it did not reek quite as bad. The grass around the edge had started to regrow, indicating the bowl had been there longer.

The west rim of the depression had partially collapsed. Geronimo ran to it and was about to scramble out when the loose dirt sparked an inspiration. Kneeling, he clawed at the side of the bowl, digging a hole large enough for him to crawl into.

The whole time, the ground rumbled, the grass above trembled. The herd was so close that Geronimo could hear the buffalo snorting and grunting. He dug faster, ignoring the pain when a fingernail ripped on a rock.

The hole was not as big as Geronimo would

have liked it to be when the hammering hooves spurred him into tucking himself into the pocket he had excavated and pulling the dirt up over him. He scooped frantically, every second counting. In moments he had sealed himself in an earthen cocoon.

It wasn't much protection, but it would have to do.

Geronimo was on his left side, his knees tucked to his chest. He lowered his chin, covered his head with his arms, and waited. He did not wait long.

The hammering became continuous thunder. Above him and on both sides, the earth shook, the vibrations so strong they nearly rattled his teeth.

Then the earth Geronimo had painstakingly piled over him began to break apart. A hole appeared, large enough for Geronimo to see an unending stream of dark hooves flash past. Buffalo after buffalo leaped from the rim of the bowl to the bottom, sped on across, and pounded up the opposite side.

The Warrior's position was precarious. At any moment the whole side of the depression might collapse, exposing him to the river of driving flesh. He would be trampled in seconds, reduced to so much pulp and splintered bone.

Geronimo tried not to think of that. He breathed shallowly, blinking dirt from his eyes now and again. The reek he had noticed before was stronger, so strong it was almost overpowering. It came from the buffalo. That jarred his recollection.

He knew what the depressions were. Buffalo

wallows, basins made by the bison rolling and rubbing repeatedly over certain spots to relieve the constant itching caused by insects in their thick coats. Bulls urinated in the dirt and then caked themselves with mud to ward off more pests. Once a wallow was created, the bison would use it again and again, whenever a herd passed by.

It was ironic that one might—just might—save his life.

Just then the top of the hole commenced to crumble. A chunk of earth the size of his fist smacked his cheek. Another stung his ear.

The side of the wallow had taken more punishment than it could withstand.

Buffalo continued to pour past. With every one that did, a little more dirt rained down than before. He had to cover his mouth and nose in order to breathe. The biggest clod yet hit his shoulder. He knew the hole was on the verge of collapse and he braced for the inevitable.

Minutes later it came.

With a muted swish, the ground above the Warrior buckled, covering him from head to toe. His face was smothered by dirt before he could take a breath. He pushed at it, but more rained down, getting into his eyes and blinding him just when he needed most to see. He was pinned. He was trapped. His lungs needed air, yet if he broke free, he would very likely go down under the sledgehammer hooves of the buffalo.

What choice did he have? Geronimo exploded into action, shoving against the earth with all his limbs at once. Some of the dirt gave way, but not enough. He shoved again, and again, growing desperate as his lungs strained for release. Punching at the hard sheath of soil, he opened a small hole that grew noticeably larger when he applied both knees against the barrier and heaved.

Suddenly the ground above him shifted and split, cascading on either side. Geronimo found himself partially in the clear, exposed and vulnerable. He sucked in dusty air, threw his arms over his head, and tensed for the worst.

Nothing happened.

It took several moments for it to dawn on Geronimo that the hammering had ceased, that the ground around him was still once again. Warily, he raised his head high enough to see the entire wallow and part of the plain above. No buffalo were in sight.

Geronimo sat up, brushing dirt from his shoulders, coughing from the dust. To the south the great tidal wave of bison washed on over the plain, a few calves and older animals straggling at the rear. He had survived!

"Wait until Hickok hears this one," he said aloud.

A snort warned the Warrior that he might have been premature. He twisted, expecting to see a buffalo. Instead, a horse stood twenty feet away, a fine roan with its ears pricked in his direction. Astride it sat a man.

Fleeting elation coursed through Geronimo. A member of the Cavalry had found him. He would go see Boone, their leader, and request help in finding Blade and Hickok. It was a stroke of luck long overdue. Then he looked more closely at the man and his elation evaporated.

It was an Indian, a warrior in fringed buck-skins, armed with a bow, quiver, and knife. His black hair was braided on both sides. At the back of his head jutted a lone eagle feather. His expression was one of utter astonishment. Although he had an arrow notched on his sinew bow string, he made no attempt to use it. He was that stunned.

Geronimo did not know what to make of the man. So far as he knew, few tribes had lived through the terrifying days of the holocaust. Only the Flatheads in Montana had been miraculously spared. But the man gawking at him did not appear to be a Flathead. His features were different, his buckskins, too.

Since the warrior did not act hostile, Geronimo did not resort to his revolver. "Hello there," he said genially while slowly rising. The effect was not what he anticipated.

Yelping, the warrior wheeled the roan and galloped to the north, quirting the horse with the bow.

"Wait!" Geronimo called. "I won't hurt you!" But it did no good. The man fled as if the demons of Hades were on his tail.

The Warrior would have run after him, but the FNC was still buried under the dirt and he was not about to leave it there. Squatting, he dug until he found the Auto Rifle and pulled it out. By brushing and blowing, he cleaned the weapon off. But he worried that dirt had gotten into the FNC and might foul it when he needed it most.

Geronimo elected to field strip the rifle on the spot. Moving onto the trampled grass that now bordered the wallow, he sat and ensured the chamber was clear. He carefully broke the FNC down, used the sleeve of his fatigue shirt to wipe the parts, and had it reassembled in half the time it would have taken most men.

Training was the key factor. Every Warrior was required to become expert with the weapons he or she favored. Long hours were spent disassembling guns and putting them back together to the point where the Warriors could do it blindfolded.

Patting the barrel, Geronimo rose and turned to the north. The ground looked as if it had been chewed up by a gigantic machine with colossal spikes. In many spots the grass had been reduced to bits and pieces, the earth gouged and grooved.

About a hundred feet away lay a buffalo on its side. Geronimo assumed that it had tripped and been trampled in the stampede. Then he saw another beyond it and still another even farther away. Surely not all of them had suffered the same fate?

The Warrior walked to the nearest. He was surprised to hear it breathing and to see its eye swivel toward him as he approached. Its legs did not appear to be broken, nor was there any damage to its hide. Leveling the Auto Rifle in case the brute lumbered upright and charged, he saw something sticking from its ribs. Venturing closer revealed it to be an arrow. Part of the shaft had broken off, no doubt when the bull went down.

Geronimo thought of the warrior with the bow. The catalyst for the herd's flight became clear. Those buffalo had been fleeing for their lives. But it was unlikely a single warrior had spooked so many.

A sweep of the prairie turned up no others. Geronimo slung the FNC, drew his revolver, placed the muzzle behind the buffalo's ear, and fired. The beast grunted and lurched upward, rising no more than a few inches. Exhaling loudly, it slumped, its horn digging into the ground.

Geronimo traded the revolver for his tomahawk and helped himself to a choice piece of the haunch. There was so much meat, surely the warrior would not begrudge him enough for one meal. He also cut off a section of hide to wrap the meat in until later.

His trophy under his arm, Geronimo resumed his westward trek. In due course he was in high grass once more. He pushed on until the sun framed the western horizon, hoping, without success, to come on another stream.

A low knoll to the southwest was the only break in the plain. Hiking to it, he flattened grass on the east side where he would be sheltered from the stiff wind, then busied himself gathering dry grass. He left the meat and hide lying at the base of the knoll.

His arms burdened with fuel for his fire, Geronimo headed back. He was a stone's throw from the knoll when a feral growl brought him to a halt. Dropping the grass, he hurried on.

Several coyotes had caught scent of the bloody meat. They were pacing a few yards from the bundle, held at bay by the man scent on the hide. One was growing bolder than the rest and kept taking quick steps toward the bundle, then back again.

Their growling and whining drowned out Geronimo's footsteps until he was virtually on top of them. The Warrior booted one in the rump. Yipping, it rolled end over end, bolting into the grass when it regained its feet. The second one was just as timid. But the third, the brazen male, stood its ground long enough to snarl in halfhearted defiance; then it, too, made itself scarce.

Geronimo climbed to the top of the knoll to make sure they left. The three crafty predators regrouped a hundred yards off in a clear area and sat, their tongues lolling.

Taking the bundle with him, Geronimo reclaimed the grass. Half he spread out in a rectangle to serve as his bedding. After clearing a spot a yard in diameter and digging down an inch to reduce the risk of igniting the prairie, he tore some of the other dry grass into equal lengths and arranged them like the spokes of a wheel on top of the bare patch.

In his left front shirt pocket was a pack of matches. The Family had long since used up its hoarded supply, but thankfully the Free State of California had plenty to spare and was willing to trade.

The first match did the job. Geronimo deliberately kept the fire low, adding grass as warranted. Unwrapping the hide, he cut the meat into strips, took one, impaled it on the tip of his knife, and held it over the flames.

The tantalizing aroma was enough to make the Warrior's mouth water. He watched the meat sizzle and brown, scarcely able to control himself. It was still half rare when he tore into the strip with gusto, chewing ravenously. Even unsalted, with no garnishment or sauce, it was just about the most delicious meat he had ever enjoyed.

Three strips were wolfed in no time. Geronimo cooked a fourth but did not hurry eating this one. Leaning back against the knoll, he savored every morsel while watching the sky darken and stars blossom. It was probably his imagination, but the night sky seemed different somehow. Studying the stars, he concluded that there were more of them than he was accustomed to, which was ridiculous.

Then the moon rose.

Geronimo was munching on his final mouthful of tangy buffalo when the crown reared above the earth. Ablaze with celestial glory, the Earth's satellite hove majestically into view. Never in his life had he seen the moon so huge or bright. It was spectacular. In awed fascination he admired its breathtaking beauty.

In a short while bedlam broke out. Initially, a few coyotes yipped. More joined in, until the yipping was a constant chorus. Soon throaty howls were added to the mix, howls that grew in number as the night waxed. Wolves were abroad. From the sound of things, Geronimo guessed there were scores in his vicinity and hundreds more within earshot, far more than he had ever heard at any one time.

As if that were not enough, the screech of big cats and the throaty roar of big bears added to the din. Grizzlies and other things were in search of prey. Geronimo rested the FNC across his lap as a precaution.

The sounds swelled into a raucous cacophony. It seemed like every carnivore within a hundred miles had gathered in the area. Geronimo was wrapping the leftover meat in the hide when a pair of red eyes flared in the darkness. More followed suit, until a ring of fiery orbs hemmed him in.

Wolves, Geronimo suspected. The pack kept its distance, content to sit and stare. Even so, he sat on the bundle to stifle the odor, and he never took his finger off the Auto Rifle's trigger.

The Warrior had intended to get to sleep early. The presence of the bestial multitude prevented him. He was loathe to drift off when at any moment one of the predators might make bold to dash up and take a bite out of him. He let the fire burn lower to conserve fuel but not so low that the wolves could creep closer undetected. He figured that after a while they would become bored and wander elsewhere. To his consternation, they didn't.

It must have been near midnight when a ferocious roar silenced the primeval refrain as abruptly as if a switch had been thrown. The ring of red eyes promptly faded. That was good news in itself, but Geronimo had a much greater worry.

The roar had come from the other side of the knoll.

Flattening, Geronimo peered at the rim. A gargantuan shape took form, a bulging hump the telltale sign. It was another grizzly and it had caught his scent. He aimed at where the head should be, but he did not fire. At that distance the bear would be on him before he got off a second round.

Sniffing broke out. The bear banked its oversized head from side to side. Teeth gleamed in the pale glow of the crackling flames. It took a long stride down the slope, but hesitated.

Geronimo took a calculated risk. He dared not let the bear get close enough to use those wicked claws. So, dropping to his knees, he uttered a war whoop. For a span of seconds his life hung in the balance. Then the grizzly rotated on its hind legs and trotted into the gloom.

The Warrior did not relax until long after the monster was gone.

It surprised Geronimo that no mutants or mutates put in an appearance. Campfires usually drew them like magnets drew metal. Many had learned that where there was a fire, there was a two-legged meal just waiting to be consumed.

Shortly after the bear departed, the night quieted. Geronimo settled back and folded his arms across his chest to catch some sleep. He was almost asleep when the terror-stricken bleats of an animal being slain snapped him awake. Ferocious snarling and crunching and the thrashing of grass testified to the tenacity of the creature's struggle. A final bleat strangled off into a lapping noise.

Geronimo had been to the Dakota Territory a year ago. He had slept out on the prairie with Hickok, Blade, and Spartacus. Yet it had been nothing like this. They had not run into a single grizzly. They had seen only two wolves and those from a long way off. Coyotes had been nonexistent.

How then had the animal population increased so dramatically in so short a span?

The Warrior could not shake the nagging feeling that something was amiss, that all was not as it should be. The paradise he had discovered earlier—the horde of buffalo, the mysterious Indian, the abundance of game where there had been so few—all added up to a question mark of major proportions.

He was mulling the prospects when dreamland claimed him. And dream he did, of an evil figure in a dark cloak stalking him from out of the night, foiling him when he attempted to escape, cutting him off again and again, laughing sadistically all the while. The laughter rose to a frenzied peak, stark fear welling in his breast, fear such as he had never felt, fear that shattered the nightmare's hold and brought him awake with a start.

Geronimo sat up. He was caked with sweat. His mouth was as dry as sand. Dawn was still an hour off. Stretching to relieve a kink in his lower back, he realized that he had sat on the bundle all night. It was squashed flat, the meat so much mush. Still, it was food and he was famished. Collecting more grass, he soon had a fire going and treated himself to breakfast. A solitary wolf padded by, stared at him awhile as if hoping for a handout, then sulked off.

As the eastern sky became painted with vivid streaks of pink and gold, Geronimo licked his fingers clean, put out the fire, and walked up the knoll. The wind had died. The plain was still for once, not a blade of grass stirring. None of the wild things were sounding off. It was a rare peaceful moment.

Geronimo gave inward thanks to the Great Spirit for another day of life as he moved on. Of all the Family members, he was the only one who routinely referred to the Creator in that fashion. His Blackfoot heritage had a lot to do with it.

As the only Warrior with the blood of the red man in his veins, he felt obligated to carry on the practices of his forebears. It was safe to say that no one in the Family had read more about Native American history, as it came to be called, than he had.

The Blackfeet had believed that the sun was the great power in all things. Their Father, the Sun, they called it, and did their annual Sun Dance in its honor.

Other tribes had believed in the Great Medicine, or Great Mystery, as the supreme power. Others used a title that translated into Great Spirit. Geronimo adopted the latter when in his teens.

The Warrior had often wondered what would have happened to the red race had there been no Third World War. The records taught that at the time of the cataclysm, America was torn by turmoil. White had turned against black and red, black against red and white, red man against everyone else.

None of the Elders seemed to know why hatred had been so widespread. Some blamed the government, saying that government policies were designed to spawn mistrust, that politicians wanted the people divided to make it easier to control them.

One Elder believed that there had been something in the water or the food or the air that had bred mass hatred, much as lead utensils had bred widespread insanity among the ancient Romans.

Geronimo's train of thought was derailed by the nicker of a horse. The warrior from yesterday had returned, and he had brought friends. Seventy feet out on either side rode six Indians strung in single file. Most had bows, a few carried lances. One held a flintlock rifle, of all things.

Geronimo did not want trouble with them. "Hello again!" he hailed the warrior he knew. "I am a friend, not an enemy. Get down and we can talk."

The man who had been addressed did not accept the offer. He said something to a burly warrior behind him, then elevated his bow, kneed his horse, and bore down at a gallop.

"No!" Geronimo cried. "There is no need for us to fight!"

The warrior on the roan must have felt otherwise. He trained the tip of his arrow at Geronimo's chest.

Chapter Seven

Passing out was an embarrassment.

He had planned with the utmost care. His calculations had been honed to the nth degree. His device had been tested and retested on lower life forms. Once he even sent a minotaur through, to an island known as Crete in the dawn of recorded history. At no time had there been any clue that being rendered unconscious was part of the transit state. He had wanted to be fully sentient the whole time, to experience undiminished that which no mortal man had ever experienced in all the long history of the human race.

Thanatos stood and brushed off his cloak of

many pockets, patting each to insure the contents were intact. Without his bag of scientific tricks, as it were, accomplishing what he intended to do would take years longer than he had planned on. That would not do.

Wooden walls hemmed Thanatos in. He smiled. The old maps had been correct. He had materialized in an alley in the heart of the city. But he had not taken into account the nauseating odor that rose from mounds of garbage on one hand and yellow puddles on the other. His nose wrinkling in disgust, he strode to the end of the alley to survey the new world in which he found himself. *His* new world.

A small figure dashed out of thin air, colliding with Thanatos's tree trunk of a leg. It bounced off and landed on its backside, uttering a tiny peel of surprise laced with fear.

"I beg your pardon, sir. I didn't watch where I was going."

Thanatos glanced down. A disheveled waif in a dress and shawl little better than rags bowed her head as if afraid to meet his gaze. "Look at me, girl," he commanded.

The waif did so. She had a pear-shaped face streaked with grime and dark hair that cascaded in oily curls. "As you wish, sir."

"You have manners, child. I like that." Thanatos swept his hood back, freeing his red mane to tumble about his broad shoulders. His lake-blue eyes glued to hers. If she noticed that his pupils were vertical slits and not rounded as they should be, she did not betray it. "What is your name, child?"

"Felicity, sir."

Thanatos lowered his hand. She let him lift her to her feet and did not pull away when he entwined a thick finger in one of her curls. "Tell me, Felicity. What city is this?"

"Why, it's St. Louis, sir. Everyone knows that."

A low rumble issued from Thanatos's chest, much like distant thunder before a storm. It was an unconscious habit of his, done when he was displeased or angry. "Never compare me to the common herd, child. I am as different from them as night from day. Were you to collect the intellects of every other mortal on this wretched sphere and place them on a scale, they would weigh less than mine."

The child giggled. "How could you do such a thing, sir? Cut open their heads?" She had two upper front teeth missing. The gap lent her added charm. "That would be a sight to behold, wouldn't it?"

Thanatos cracked a rare smile. He liked this girl, even if she was much too thin. "Yes, it would," he agreed. "Now, tell me something else. What year might this be?"

Felicity did not laugh or even arch a brow. With the frankness of youth, she accepted the extraordinary question as being perfectly normal. "It is 1840, sir. May fifth, to be exact."

The news pleased Thanatos greatly. He was right where he wanted to be, when he wanted to be there. In an era when electricity had not yet been invented, when the light bulb was unknown. Steam power was all the rage, but even it had not been harnessed to its full potential. In such a benighted world, in an age where ignorance was not just due to mental neglect but was actually a common state of being, knowledge was truly power. Which made him the most powerful man on the planet.

"I really should be on my way, sir," Felicity said. "My mother sent me on an errand, and if I don't get back quick enough to suit her, she'll take a switch to me."

"Will she indeed?" Thanatos said. He looked up.

They were in a narrow street choked with passers-by and people standing in front of doors and leaning out windows. If cleanliness was next to godliness, then those Thanatos saw were as far from heaven as it was possible to be and still not be in hell. They were a motley assortment, many wearing buckskins, the majority with holes or rips in their attire. Here and there city dandies strutted about like peacocks, their immaculate store-bought apparrel in marked contrast to the shoddy clothes of their poorer brethren.

"What is this errand you are on?" Thanatos inquired.

The girl looked both ways as if to make sure no one was spying on them. Then she slipped a dainty hand down the front of her thin dress and produced a thick silver coin. "I'm to buy our supper, sir, and take it back to our apartment." She fondled the coin as if it were the wealth of Minos. "This is the first real money we've had in days. If I lose it or let it be stolen, my mother will have a fit."

Thanatos was hungry himself. Time sliding, it seemed, heightened one's appetite. "Tell you what, child," he said, taking her free hand. "How about if I go along to insure that no one takes your money? I'll even escort you back to your apartment, if you have no objections."

Felicity balked. "I don't know, sir. My mother says not to dally with strangers."

"And a wise mother she is, too." Thanatos poured on the charm. "But we've been talking for several minutes and no harm has come to you. That should prove my friendly intentions. If not, perhaps this will." He slid a hand into an inner pocket on his cloak and palmed a leather pouch. With a flourish, he brought it out, unfastened the draw string, and upended the contents into his palm. The girl's eyes grew as wide as saucers at the pile of coins, each as shiny and new as if they had recently been minted. And in truth, they had.

"Goodness gracious, sir! You must be rich!"

Thanatos did not tell her about the precious gems and small gold bars he carried. "That I am," he conceded. "So why not let me treat your mother and you to a meal, and you can keep your own coin." As subtle incentive, he went on, "Your mother need never know. You could spend it on whatever you wanted."

The girl's eyes widened again, duty and avarice battling for supremacy. Avarice won. "I suppose that would be all right." The coin went down her dress faster than it had appeared. "It's not like I would be stealing or anything. And it has been ages since she let me have money of my own."

"That's hardly fair of her." Thanatos offered his arm and the waif reached up to take his elbow. They made an incongruous picture, he with his flowing red hair, luxurious cloak, and polished black leather boots, she with her oily locks, tattered dress, and scuffed shoes. "Guide me, my dear," he said.

St. Louis was a dump. At least, that was Thanatos's considered opinion after ten minutes of winding along cramped streets where uncouth people had dumped chamber pots and rotten food with no regard for the consequences. Even minotaurs had more brains than that. Half the time he held a white handkerchief to his nose to spare him from the stench.

The child led Thanatos toward the waterfront, to a district of seedy taverns and grimy grogshops. Out on the Mississippi, mighty steamboats plied the water. He halted on spying them, dazzled by their size and grace. Studying the past, it turned out, had not adequately prepared him for the reality.

"Is something wrong, sir?"

"No, child," Thanatos told her. "I've just never seen steamboats before."

"Really? A grown man like you?" Felicity giggled some more, paying no mind to the low rumble that came from his chest. "You must be new here, then. Not a day goes by that there aren't a dozen or so in port. Mother took me on a ride on the *Jefferson* once with one of her uncles. It was great fun."

"I bet it was." Thanatos had not included a steamboat in his original plans, but he now saw where one would expedite matters quite nicely. He filed the tidbit for future consideration.

Going on, the child entered the shabbiest tavern Thanatos had seen yet. The interior reeked of spilled ale and wine, of sweat and tobacco and worse. Ruffians lounged at tables or stood at a dirty bar. Some were trappers, some rivermen. Some were gamblers, some merely drunks.

All eyes fixed on Thanatos and the girl. She showed no fear, but walked right up to the counter where a portly man in a stained apron greeted her with a cockeyed smile.

"Hello, little Felicity. Haven't seen you in a spell. What can I do for you today?"

"Mother sent me," the girl said. "I'm to fetch a pot of beans and some cornbread." She turned to Thanatos. "I almost forgot. What about you, sir? Would you like a pot of beans, too?"

"I prefer meat."

The man behind the counter gestured toward the back. "I can have the cook whip you up a plate of venison. There might even be some buffalo left over from last night. How about a thick, well done steak, charred around the edges?"

The image was enough to turn Thanatos's stomach. "The one pot of beans will suffice."

"Certainly, sir." The portly man glanced at Felicity. "Um, I hate to bring this up, but which one of you will be paying for this? Her mother, you see, still owes me for two meals I let them have on credit, and—"

Thanatos silenced the upstart by doing as he had done with the child. He knew it was a mistake the instant the coins tumbled out. Sharp intakes of breath and the scraping of chairs showed that it had not gone unnoticed. The owner looked as if he were about to gag.

"Yes, sir! Whatever you want, you just say the word. Maybe some imported wine? Or the finest Scotch this side of the Atlantic Ocean?"

"I have no interest in anything else." Thanatos

slipped the pouch into his cloak. Out of the corner of his eye, he saw a beefy character in homespun rags whisper to three others, and the four promptly rose from their table and left. They were so transparent, it was pathetic.

The owner cleared his throat. "So, are you one of Abigail's uncles?" He winked on the sly so the girl would not notice. "It seems as if a new one comes to visit every week or so."

"I am not," Thanatos said stiffly. He had no patience for fools, less for those who did not know enough to mind their own business. He was tempted to say as much, but the man might be of some use after all. Resting an arm on the bar, he waited until the portly specimen returned from the kitchen, then remarked, "A prosperous individual in your fortuitous position must be privileged to an abundance of information concerning the uncharted realms beyond the waterway."

"Huh?"

Thanatos was peeved by his lapse. When dealing with those who had intelligence quotients in the single digits, it was advisable to use language a simpleton could comprehend. "You must hear a lot about the country west of here."

"Oh. Yep. Sure do. I get an earful from every trapper and mountain man who comes in."

"Is it as wide open and untamed as the books claim?"

Lifting a used glass from the counter, the owner paused. "Books? What are you talking about? I didn't know anyone had written about the frontier, unless you mean the account of Lewis and Clark's journey."

Thanatos had made another minor blunder. The volumes he referred to had yet to be penned. They were in his private library, just a few of the many thousands he had collected. "I hear that some of the Indian tribes are not kindly disposed toward whites."

The portly man chortled. "That's one way of putting it, Mister. Outright hostile would be better. Anyone who crosses the plains takes his life in his hands." Warming to the topic, he lowered his voice so as not to be overheard by his customers. "Between you and me, only an idiot would risk his hair for a bunch of beaver skins. Sure, I know that some of those boys earn upwards of two thousand dollars a year, but no amount can bring a dead man back to life. Savvy?"

Thanatos gestured at the dregs of humanity that filled the room. "What about these men? Think any of them would go to the mountains if they were offered enough?"

The owner snickered. "Hell, Mister. Some of them would kill their own mothers for the price of a drink. If you had money to spare, you could hire yourself a small army."

"Interesting."

"But even that wouldn't save you from the Indians. There are thousands of Blackfeet and Bloods and Piegans. Not to mention the Sioux and the Arikaras and half a dozen other tribes I could name. They all hate us with a passion."

Thanatos could sympathize. He despised inferiors as much as the Indians despised the whites. "That is the only way to hate," he mentioned, eliciting a curious stare.

For the next quarter of an hour Thanatos plied

the talkative bartender with questions about the wilderness that stretched from the muddy Mississippi to the Pacific Ocean, confirming details he had previously memorized and learning new information of value. He was so pleased that he gave the owner a tip when he paid for the meal.

It was growing dark when Thanatos and Felicity stepped into the street. The girl insisted on carrying the pot and the corn pone. Frequently she would sniff at both and smack her lips. Watching her, Thanatos felt his own mouth water. "You act as if you are starved to death, child."

"I am. We haven't ate a bite since yesterday morning."

"Why so long?"

Felicity pouted. "It's awful hard for my mother to come by money."

"What does she do for a living?"

"She spends a lot of time entertaining my uncles. Last night an uncle from Chicago stayed with us. He's the one who gave us my coin."

Street lights were few and far between. For the most part they walked in murky shadow, surrounded by flitting shadows, just two more spectral shapes adrift in the land of the mentally dead. Thanatos, who stood head and shoulders above them all, was filled with contempt for the puny insects who would soon call him lord and master.

Stealthy footsteps reminded him of the four dolts from the tavern. He did not let on that he knew, even when two passed them and ducked around a corner ahead. A brief diversion was just what he needed to whet his appetite.

Felicity took the corner first and nearly tripped

over her own feet to keep from bumping into the pair who awaited them. One was the beefy character, the other a broomstick with a scarred cheek.

"Howdy there, friend," said beefy jowls.

Thanatos placed a hand on the child's shoulder to reassure her. "I am not, never have been, and never will be your friend, you miserable excuse for animate matter."

"What did you call me?" the man blustered.

"I do not repeat myself for the benefit of morons," Thanatos said in disdain. He inched his hand into a concealed pocket, then thought better of the idea. Why waste valuable items he might need later when he was more than capable of handling the quartet with his bare hands?

The leader of the foursome puffed out his hairy chest. "You're one of those uppity rich bastards, aren't you? Well, me and the boys will take you down a peg or two if you don't cough up that pouch with all the money."

Thanatos moved the girl back against the wall so she would not be harmed when the simple-minded robbers made their move. He did not want anything to happen to her after all the trouble he had gone to on her behalf. Turning toward the spokesman, he threw salt on the gaping wound of their profound stupidity by taunting, "Get this farce over with, will you? I do not have all night. I'm hungry."

Beefy jowls swooped an arm behind him. When it reappeared, he held a dagger. "Suit yourself, rich snot. We'll carve you into pieces and leave you for the rats."

The broomstick and one of those on Thanatos's left also pulled blades. The fourth man favored a short wooden club. They fanned out to keep Thanatos from running off. Little did they realize that he had no intention of depriving himself of the intense pleasure he would derive from disposing of them.

"Last chance," the leader said.

Thanatos planted himself in front of the child. "Is it your intention to talk me to death?" he baited the lout. "Or are you more of a man than you appear to be?"

Beefy Jowls flushed with outrage. "Them's fighting words! Get him, boys! Teach him what for!"

Broomstick was the quickest, as Thanatos expected. The skinny ones usually were fast on their feet, and this one streaked in like lightning, spearing his long knife in low, going for the groin. Thanatos easily sidestepped, seized the man's right arm, broke it over his knee, and cast Broomstick aside.

The next ruffian only slowed a trifle. He feinted left and went right. Thanatos was ready. Wrapping his huge hand around the would-be thief's wrist, he twisted. There was a grating crack. The man screeched, clutching at his arm. Thanatos put him out of his misery with a kick to the temple.

That left Beefy Jowls and the tough with the club. The latter closed first, swinging savagely, seeking to drive Thanatos against the wall where he would have no room to maneuver. Thanatos humored him. He let two blows land on his jaw and was rewarded by blatant shock when the man saw that neither blow had any effect.

"Weakling," Thanatos hissed, grabbing Club by the throat and lifting the man off the ground with one hand. With the other, he gripped the top of Club's head and gave it a brutal wrench. The crack of the spine was much louder than the crack of the wrist had been.

In a span of seconds one man was dead, another unconscious, and one flopping about on the ground with a broken arm. Beefy Jowls looked at them and began to back away, showing his true colors.

"No you don't," Thanatos said, taking a single bound. The leader cried out and slashed at Thanatos's neck, a feeble attempt at best. Thanatos blocked it, took hold of the man's right wrist with both hands, pivoted, and drove the dagger into Beefy Jowl's privates. Poetic justice, Thanatos reasoned.

The leader screamed and back-pedaled, gushing blood. He looked down at himself in rising horror while sinking to his knees. "No, no, no, no, no, no, no, no, no, no!" he blubbered.

"Yes," Thanatos said, looming over him. Gripping the man's lower jaw, he pried Beefy Jowl's mouth open, hooked his fingers under the man's upper teeth to prevent him from biting, bunched his shoulder muscles, then snapped one arm up and one arm straight down. This crack was the loudest of all.

The girl had not moved. She was petrified, and she flinched when Thanatos gently grasped her arm. "Do not be alarmed, child. They can not hurt you now." He motioned. "Lead on. I'm sure your mother is eager to eat."

Another six irregular blocks brought them to a

shabby building. As usual, the interior smelled offensive. The child brought him to a door at the end of a dark hall. At his knock, a woman twice as portly as Beefy Jowls flung it open.

"About damn time you got here, brat! Where in the world have you—" She saw Thanatos and stopped. "My word! Who are you, and what the devil are you doing with my baby?"

Thanatos adopted his most courtly air. "I am a lonely traveler, madam, who saw fit to escort your charming offspring safely home." He patted his cloak so that his coins jingled. "Perhaps you will see fit to let me in so that we might become better acquainted?"

Like daughter, like mother. Abigail flung the door wider and beckoned. "Mercy me! Where are my manners? It's as plain as the nose on my face that you're a regular gentleman. Do come in and tell me how you happened to meet my little girl."

"As you wish. But you really should enjoy your beans before they get cold."

The apartment was as decrepit as Thanatos had known it would be. Abigail placed the pot on a rickety table and rummaged in a peeling cabinet for bowls. She gave a cracked one to her daughter and offered the other to him.

"No, thank you," Thanatos said suavely. "Don't mind me. Dig in. I'm not particularly fond of beans." He took a chair by the door. "I'll be eating soon, anyway."

Mother and daughter were so famished that they ate the entire pot and polished off the corn pone without uttering two words. Abigail consumed the lioness's share. Thanatos found himself admiring the plump contours of her ribs and stomach. She had to weigh three hundred pounds if she weighed an ounce. It was a bonus he had not foreseen.

"Well, now," Abigail said, pushing her bowl back. "Let's get acquainted, like you wanted."

Practically drooling, Thanatos rose and slowly walked over to stand between them. Leaning down, he patted both their wrists. "Your gracious hospitality means more to me than either of you can appreciate. I have come a long way, and I am quite ravenous."

Abigail batted her thick eyelashes at him. "What would you like, dearie? I'll send Felicity out to fetch it."

"That's not necessary. I intend to eat in."

"Pardon?"

Thanatos smiled, really smiled, his upper and lower lips parting three times as far as ordinary human lips ever could. His teeth were fully revealed. So was his true nature. At the last instant the mother comprehended and opened her own mouth to scream for help, but to Thanatos it was as if she moved in slow motion.

He struck.

Chapter Eight

Venting a tigerish roar, the minotaur burst from the tall grass and reared to its full eight-foot height. Its bull head swung from side to side, regarding the three humans with cold malice. Its horns glinted in the sunlight. Its muscles were banded into bulging cords.

The sight so shocked the two trappers that neither Kittson nor Clyman got off a shot.

Not so Hickok. Without hesitation he squeezed the trigger. The .45–70 boomed and bucked, the slug slamming into the minotaur's forehead, smashing it backward. The monstrosity tottered but did not go down. Hickok worked the lever and fired again, again going for the head. He aimed for the eye, but just as he fired the genetic deviate shifted and the bullet caught it above the eye instead. Bellowing more in baffled wrath than in agony, it raised a ham-sized fist.

The Warrior banged off two shots in swift succession. They would have dropped a hippo, but the minotaur had been bred to absorb more punishment than most living things could endure. It was jolted onto one knee, thick green mucous oozing from the wound. Bellowing, it started to rise.

That was when Kittson and Clyman recovered their wits and fired simultaneously, their long guns spewing smoke as well as lead. Kittson's shot tore into the minotaur's throat, Clyman's into the chest about where a human heart would be. The twin .60-caliber blasts at so short a range slammed the minotaur onto its back.

"Run!" Hickok said, giving the two men a push.

Neither listened. Fingers flying, they commenced reloading their rifles.

The genetic abomination snorted and lurched onto its hands and knees. Its inhuman gaze, blazing raw hatred, locked on the Warrior. *"Another time, another place!"*

Hickok was reaching into a pocket for a cartridge for the .45–70. The Marlin was one of the most powerful rifles ever made but it had a drawback; the bullets were so big, the magazine could only hold four rounds.

The minotaur spun and plowed off into the grass. It ran unsteadily, weaving as if drunk, uttering growls and snarls and snorts, the minotaur equivalent of cursing. It was gone before any of them could fire again. The last they saw of the beast was grass waving in the distance.

Hickok swiftly replaced the four spent rounds. Where there was one minotaur, there might be more. Or others of the Dark Lord's playthings, vile creations not fit to exist. He felt eyes on him and turned to find his two new friends staring at him as if he were from another planet.

"What in the name of holy was that critter?" Kittson asked in astonishment.

Clyman jabbed a bony finger at the gunfighter. "It could talk! And it knew you!"

To Hickok it was unbelievable that the trappers did not know what a minotaur was. Everyone in the country had heard about the fearsome Dark Lord and his unholy legion of undead and mutations. The only explanation he could think of was that the trappers had left for the mountains to trap before Thanatos first appeared and by some miracle had not run into any of his vicious minions before this.

Ogden came trotting up. He was as bewildered as his friends, and he had a question he wanted answered, too. But his had nothing to do with the mutant. "You fired four shots at once! I saw you! What kind of gun is that you've got there, anyhow?"

"A Marlin," Hickok said, figuring that would suffice. There were still plenty of pre-holocaust rifles around, and most folks knew about Winchesters and Marlins and the like.

"Never heard of it," the young trapper declared. "Where can I get me one? Why, with a gun like that, I could hold off the entire Blackfoot Confederacy."

Hickok did not see why the man was so excited. A rifle that only held four rounds was hardly exceptional. Some held nine or better. One he knew of could hold thirteen. "Look, friend," he said, "now is hardly the time to stand around jawin' about hardware. That varmint might come back, and the next time we might not be so lucky."

Kittson, in the act of pouring black powder down the muzzle of his rifle, lifted the powder horn. "It might? Then we can't waste another second. The next time it could run off the pack animals."

The threat of losing their precious hides spurred the trappers into quickly reloading and mounting. Hickok once again swung up behind Clyman. Without delay, they headed to the east.

The afternoon passed slowly, the clomp of hooves, the creak of leather, and the occasional nicker of a horse the only sounds. The mountain men, for once, were not talkative. They took turns riding at the rear of the string. Toward sunset, when it was Clyman's turn, he glanced over a shoulder at the gunman.

"I don't mind tellin' you, hoss, that I think there's a lot more to you than meets the eye. And I ain't so sure it's healthy for us to have you around."

Hickok had been thinking the same thing. The minotaur apparently had it in for him, which put anyone he was with in danger. "You have a point," he conceded. "Maybe you jaspers should drop me off and go on without me. I can get by alone."

Clyman took offense. "Now hold your horses, dang it. I didn't say anything about leavin' you by your lonesome. That wouldn't be the decent thing to do." He clucked to his mount. "All I'm sayin' is that it would be nice if you would come clean and let us know all there is to know about you and that spawn from the pit we tangled with."

"Fair enough," the gunfighter said. "When we make camp, ask me anything you want."

They took him up on it, and this time they did not poke fun when he mentioned mutants. In fact, they did not utter a peep until Hickok had concluded a short account of the rise and fall of the Dark Lord. He leaned against a saddle, taking a sip of his piping hot black coffee. "That's it in a nutshell, gents. While you were off in the mountains playin' Daniel Boone, the world as we know it almost came to an end."

The three trappers were a somber lot. They shifted uneasily, Kittson the first to speak.

"Now don't get me wrong, Hickok. I ain't calling you a liar. But some parts of your story are mighty confusing."

"Such as?"

"Such as that city you mentioned, Denver. How come we've never heard of it? Or the Freedom Federation? Or the Civilized Zone? And why, when we've spent most of our adult lives up in the Rockies, haven't we ever seen hide nor hair of one of those mutants before?"

"Mighty peculiar," Clyman agreed. "Yet we all saw that critter earlier with our own eyes."

"I'd like to know what a zombie is," Ogden threw in. "And why the United States Army didn't put a stop to this Dark Lord you mentioned before he got too big for his britches. Hell, old Colonel Leavenworth would have marched on out at the head of the Sixth Infantry like he did against the Arikara once, and that would have been that."

Again Hickok was bothered by the mention of the United States. The Leather Knights in St. Louis had a lot of gall renaming themselves after one of the greatest nations that had ever existed.

Even more perplexing was how the trappers had never heard of the Freedom Federation. The factions that made it up were widespread, its fame much more so. He found it hard to accept that there was a single soul on the North American continent who was not familiar with the Federation's accomplishments. Hell, even the Lords of Kismet knew about the Federation, and *they* ruled most of Asia.

Kittson was talking. "We'll get the answers we need soon enough. Tomorrow we'll reach St. Louis."

Ogden cracked a grin. "I can't wait to sell our peltries and get some real spending money." Poking his fingers into his possibles bag, he sorted through his effects and held out a small, battered coin. "This is all I've got to my name. Can you believe it?"

Hickok, on an impulse, said, "Mind if I take a gander at your wealth?"

"Be my guest, hoss." Ogden flipped the coin in a high arc.

The Warrior caught it. The first odd thing he noticed was that it bore UNITED STATES OF AMERICA on one side in big, bold letters, along with the words HALF CENT. Turning it over, he saw the image of a woman with long curly hair, along with the date. "Where did you dig up this relic? It's from 1828."

"I got it in change when we were buying supplies, just before we lit out for the high country," Ogden said. "And I wouldn't call a coin twelve years old a relic."

"How old?"

"You can see the date for yourself. Since this is 1840, that makes it twelve years. I may not be much of a hand at reading and writing, but I always could cipher with the best of 'em."

1840? The man just said *1840?* Hickok looked at the coin again, then at them, at their bullet pouches, and their powder horns, and their Hawkens. He thought of their reaction to the minotaur, of how they had never heard tell of the Freedom Federation or the Civilized Zone or the Free State of California. He thought of everything that had happened since he revived, and he came to the only logical conclusion.

"Damn."

Ogden was pouring himself a cup. "What's wrong, friend? You look as if you just swallowed a passel of worms."

Hickok handed the coin back and stood. "I need to be by myself a spell." Taking the Marlin, he moved from the circle of firelight, over by the horses.

The way he saw it, there were three possibilities. Either he was unconscious and dreaming the whole thing, which was absurd, or the three trappers were insane, which was improbable, or he had to accept that the Dark Lord had somehow sent him back in time hundreds of years.

Hickok recalled the metal contraption and how Thanatos had vanished in the blink of an eye. He recalled the sky-high Tower, the legions of men and women transformed into zombies, the creatures Thanatos had created from test tubes.

Above all else, Thanatos had been a scientific genius. A perverted genius, but still a genius. And a genius undeniably capable of performing seeming miracles. Such as time travel.

"It's 1840," Hickok said softly. He did not feel shock or astonishment. He did not want to curl into a ball or burst into tears. More than anything, he was mad, furious that unless he could find a means of reversing whatever Thanatos had done, he was stuck in the past for the rest of his life. He would never see his wife or children again. Never hold Sherry in his arms at night and cuddle under the blankets. Never taste her delicious lips on his.

"That lousy Thanatos," Hickok grumbled. He'd have loved to get his hands on the fiend. Or, better yet, have Thanatos on the business end of his Pythons. But that was a pipe dream.

Or was it?

Hickok pondered while pacing in a small circle. If he had been shot back in time, then that must mean that his friends and the madman had gone back, too. Thanatos had been first onto the grid and promptly winked out. Seconds later Blade had done the same. Then Geronimo. He had been the last.

A remembrance jarred him. No, that was not

quite true. A minotaur and a snake-man had burst onto the grid and were closing in when he had tumbled into what he thought was a bottomless pit. They must have been sent back as well.

Hickok perked up. He knew next to nothing about time travel, but it seemed logical that if the minotaur and he had wound up in roughly the same area at roughly the same time, then his friends and Thanatos must be there, also. The Dark Lord undoubtedly knew how to return them to their own time period. So, if he wanted to see Sherry again, all he had to do was track down Thanatos, shove a pistol up his nose, and tell him to reverse the process, or else.

Piece of cake, Hickok mused. Whistling, he sauntered back to his spot near the fire and sank down to polish off the rest of his coffee. The three trappers closely observed his every move.

"About that stuff I told you awhile go," the Warrior said. "It appears I didn't quite get the story right."

Ogden chuckled and slapped Clyman's shoulder. "I knew it! Didn't I tell you that he fed us another of his tall tales?" He hefted his tin cup in a mock salute at the gunman. "I've got to hand it to you, Mister. When it comes to whoppers, you beat 'em all. Even Jim Bridger can't hold a candle to you."

"I didn't make it up," Hickok set him straight. "I just got a few of my facts mixed up."

"Which ones?" Clyman inquired.

"The Freedom Federation and those other outfits I told you about don't exist yet. The Dark Lord figured out how to make a device that could send him back in time. It was just my luck to step onto it when he made his getaway." Hickok motioned at the prairie. "And here I am, in the past."

The Warrior waited, certain the three mountain men would badger him with a slew of questions. To his chagrin, they exploded in hearty mirth, Clyman laughing so hard that he had tears rolling from his eyes.

"I do declare!" the maimed trapper said between guffaws. "You had us goin' there for a while! We actually fell for your story!"

Ogden was rolling on the ground, his arms across his stomach. "Oh, Lordy! Claiming to be from the future! Don't that beat all!"

Hickok supposed that he shouldn't blame them. From their point of view, either he was plumb loco or the biggest liar in all creation. But in their merriment they were overlooking the proof of his claims. "Was that minotaur something I made up, too?"

That shut them up. Kittson sobered fastest and thoughtfully tugged at his bushy beard. "I'll be honest with you, friend. I don't know what to believe anymore. That thing seemed real enough. But if you're going to sit there with a straight face and claim that it came from the future, well . . ." He did not finish his statement.

Ogden nodded. "Me, I'm inclined to think you're talking straight tongue, Hickok. But it's so far-fetched, I can't help but think that you're poking fun at our expense."

Hickok let the subject drop. It occurred to him that maybe he should keep the time travel a secret once they got to St. Louis. Folks were bound to regard him as missing a few marbles. The only reason the trappers halfway believed him was thanks to the Dark Lord's gruesome monstrosity.

The Warrior stayed up long after the mountain men had fallen asleep—on the off chance that the brute would try to sneak up on them when they were off guard. But the night was uneventful.

The next morning, Kittson, Clyman, and Ogden behaved like children preparing to go on a picnic. They were so excited at the prospect of returning to civilization, they could barely contain themselves.

"The first thing I'm going to do after we shed the hides is to pay Mabel's place a visit," Ogden boasted. "I'm going to rent me a room, pay for the three prettiest fillies in the joint, and treat myself to a week of frolic under the sheets."

Kittson snickered. "The first thing you should do is take a bath. It's been over a year since your last one and you've gotten a mite whiffy."

They bantered back and forth as they tied on the packs, saddled their horses, and forked leather. Hickok had to ride double with Clyman again, and the trapper talked his ear off most of the morning.

The waterfront, it turned out, was Clyman's favorite haunt when he was not off in the wilds. The trapper went on and on about a grogshop called Finn's that had "the best ale, the hottest food, and the willingest wenches this side of the Atlantic."

Hickok somehow got it into his head that St. Louis was no more than a quaint rustic village with a dock or two. Toward the middle of the afternoon he learned how wrong he had been when they came to a rutted dirt road that wound through a stand of maples and oaks. As they emerged from the trees, there was their destination, spread out for mile upon mile before them.

St. Louis was a flourishing city. As the Warrior subsequently learned, it boasted sixteen thousand inhabitants. Steamboats and other craft plied the Mississippi daily. The waterfront district bustled with activity twenty-four hours of the day. Above the beehive were stately neighborhoods where large frame homes and limestone residences testified to the wealth of those who owned them.

Little did Hickok realize that St. Louis had not one, not two, but three newspapers, plus a rarity west of Chicago—a bookstore. There were also theaters where popular plays were put on every night.

"Yes, sir," Clyman enthused. "St. Louis is the closest thing to heaven on earth you're apt to find. It's wide open, friend. Whatever a man wants, he can likely find if he has the money to pay for it. Scoundrels are right at home here, because they know they can get away with practically anything, even murder."

Hickok found that last tidbit tantalizing. Thanatos would be right at home in a den of iniquity like St. Louis. It made him suspect the Dark Lord had picked that time and place on purpose. But to what end?

"The same holds true for the well-to-do," Clyman was saying. "Only they don't call it murder. They call it dueling." He pointed off shore at a small island. "See that there? It's where the rich and powerful go to settle their differences.

Bloody Island, it's called. Hardly a week goes by that it doesn't live up to its name."

The nearer they drew to the St. Louis, the more traffic they encountered. People on horseback, people in wagons, people in carriages, people afoot.

Hickok slung the Marlin over his back so as not to draw attention to it or himself. He intended to keep a low profile. His time would be spent nosing around in search of his pards and their enemy. If the others were anywhere in the city, he was bound to hear about it sooner or later. Especially Blade and Thanatos. Both were seven feet tall. They'd stand out anywhere.

The road wound toward the levee, branching off here and there. Hickok marveled at a steamboat churning upriver. It had twin black stacks the size of large trees and paddlewheels as big as log cabins.

Clyman saw it, too. "That's Harry Jessup's boat, the *Paragon*. He's headin' for the mouth of the Missouri, so he must be going inland. His vessel is small enough to make it clear to Fort Union."

"The army has forts along the frontier?"

The mountain man spat tobacco, then answered. "Trading forts, hoss, not military posts. Owned by the likes of the American Fur Company and others. Trappers can stop over whenever they like, and pick up supplies. Friendly Injuns bring in hides for blankets and trinkets or whatever."

Presently, they turned onto the busiest avenue yet. Hickok marveled at the bustling throngs. He saw women and girls in bonnets and long dresses, boys in woolen shirts and britches, men dressed in a variety of ways, depending on the work they did. Horses were everywhere. Dogs ran freely. Even pigs and fowl were allowed to roam at will.

A pink sow and her brood spooked Kittson's horse by darting in front of it, sparking a string of swear words the likes of which Hickok had never heard before.

Clyman was scanning the street. "If folks keep streamin' in here from the East like they're doin', it won't be long before St. Louis is as big as New York City."

They were passing a tavern, The Bull and Crown. Hickok glanced at the entrance just as a giant figure filled the doorway. The man wore a dark cloak. A hood shadowed his features. But Hickok did not need to see the man's face to know who it was. He had glimpsed that cloak once before. Only one person wore a garment like it.

As the giant stooped to step under the lintel, Hickok leaped from the back of Clyman's horse. *"Thanatos!"*

The figure swung toward the Warrior. A grin curled his thin lips.

Hickok forgot where he was, forgot his plan to keep a low profile. His hands on his Colts, he barreled through the crowd, shouldering bystanders aside right and left.

The giant backed into the tavern, lingering in the doorway just long enough to taunt the gunfighter with a mocking wave.

"Get back here, you mangy polecat!" Hickok shouted. A dog got in his way, and he kicked it in the butt to hurry it along. Men were cursing him, women were yelling, children cowering, but he didn't care. Fate had put him at the right spot at the right time. He was not going to let Thanatos slip through his fingers.

Suddenly a man in a beige jacket and cap barred his way. Extending an arm, he said, "Slow up there, Mister. You can't be pushing folks around the way you're doing."

"Move!" Hickok thundered, and pushed the busybody aside. He dashed to The Bull and Crown. The door hung open. The interior was as black as pitch after the brilliant midday sun. He took a step, seeking to orient himself, alert for movement. The scrape of a foot behind him registered a hair too late to do him any good. He started to pivot just as the roof caved in on top of his skull and he pitched into limbo.

Chapter Nine

Blade had time to grab the hilt of his right Bowie before the huge mountain lion rammed into him. They both went down, tumbling into the lake, the cat hissing and spitting and clawing at his chest and legs. He swung a backhand that clipped it on the head. The cougar retreated, but only to the water's edge. There it crouched and screeched like a banshee.

Blade was up to his waist in water stained a rusty hue by the blood he was losing. None of the cuts were life threatening, but one was deep enough to demand immediate attention. He started toward shore, drawing his other Bowie.

The mountain lion did not seem to like the water. It backed up again, only a few feet. Rear legs coiling, it eyed him carefully, and when he was almost out, it leaped a second time.

Blade met it with the Bowies, cutting crosswise, the keen blades catching it across the chest. Now it was the cougar's turn to bleed. The cat skipped to one side, instantly reversed direction, and came in low and hard.

Claws tore at Blade's leg, at his thigh. Water sprayed him in the face as he drove a Bowie at the mountain lion's neck. It blinded him, causing him to miss. He blinked rapidly, but before he could clear his vision the cougar was on him, leaping onto his right shoulder, its claws tearing into his flesh, its teeth seeking his throat. He got a forearm up, almost crying out in torment when those teeth bit clear down to the bone. At the same instant he lanced his right Bowie up and in.

There was the familiar sensation of steel slicing into a body, the muffled *thunk* of the hilt hitting home. The cat arched its spine and screamed like a woman being murdered. It lost its grip and fell, its tail thrashing madly. Blade jerked the Bowie out as it dropped. A fountain of blood gushed forth, soaking his pants.

Mortally stricken, the mountain lion refused to give up or to flee. Marshaling its reservoir of feral stamina, the big cat lunged at the Warrior's midsection. Disemboweling was a favorite tactic of its savage breed.

Blade was not caught flat-footed. His right Bowie impaled the cougar in the neck, his left sank into its chest. For a few seconds he had a clawed whirlwind on his hands as the mountain lion went berserk, spending the last of its strength in a frenzied attempt to grapple with him again—to take him down with it. He held the predator at bay, his arms bulging from the exertion, those lethal claws missing his face by the length of the beast's whiskers.

At length the mountain lion weakened. It made a few feeble attempts to cut him, then went slack, its sides heaving. It growled when Blade placed a boot on its shoulder for leverage, growled louder when Blade pulled the dripping Bowies out.

The Warrior backed away in case the cougar rallied. It hissed at him, flecking its mouth with scarlet spittle. Eyes that could memorize prey locked on his in blatant hatred. Its dying wish was as plain as its expression.

Blade sank to his knees at the water's edge. He was covered with blood, a mix of his and the beast's. His left wrist throbbed where the creature had bitten him. A dozen cuts and gashes seared him with misery. Setting the Bowies down, he bent to wash his arms.

A hint of movement behind the Warrior alerted him to his mistake. It had been rash to turn his back on the mountain lion before it expired. Twisting, he saw it on its feet, crouched for one more spring. It jumped as he lunged for one of his knives, knowing full well that he could not possibly grab it before the cougar reached him.

The shot that rang out echoed off across the lake and reverberated among the distant peaks. A cloud of gunsmoke marked where the shooter stood twenty yards away.

The cat was hammered to the ground, this time never to rise again, the spark of life gone before it stopped rolling.

Nate King slowly lowered the Hawken. His family had heard the cat's cries clear up at the cabin. Telling them to stay put, he had raced down the trail. With all that had happened since he encountered the giant, he had almost forgotten about the newcomer to the valley. A number of times in recent weeks he had found fresh spoor left by a large painter. Although he had tried to backtrack it to its lair and twice hid out near the lake at dawn, it had eluded him.

Usually mountain lions were abroad at night. It had not occurred to Nate that his visitor would be in any danger. What were the odds that the cat would pick that very moment to come down for a drink?

Nate had burst on the scene just as the giant thrust both big knives into the feline. Like his guest, he had figured that the painter was a goner. When the giant turned to the lake and the cat started to rise, he had whipped the Hawken to his shoulder. At that distance, there had been no risk of him missing.

Now, cradling the rifle, Nate crossed the rocky shore. "How bad is it, friend?" he asked, nodding at the bloody arm.

Blade was lowering it into the cold water. "I'll live," he said, and looked at the mountain man. "Thanks to you. This makes twice I'm in your debt."

Nate shrugged. "You'd do the same for me, I reckon." To confirm the panther was dead, he nudged it with a moccasin. "Looks like we're in for a treat tonight. My son will be tickled pink. Painter is his favorite."

"You eat mountain lion?" Blade asked, swirling his arm so the blood would wash off that much sooner.

"I know what you're thinking," Nate responded. "When I lived in New York, the thought of chewing on one of these critters would have made me sick. The first time I took a bite, I was afraid I'd make a fool of myself and gag. But you know what? Painter meat is the tastiest you'll find anywhere. Most mountaineers like it better than venison and buffalo."

Blade did not doubt it. People would eat just about anything. Case in point, the Technics in Chicago. Overpopulation had driven them to eating whatever they could get their hands on. The dish they liked the most consisted of roasted worms covered with mushroom sauce.

Nate recalled that the giant had wanted to be alone. "I'll come back in a while to tote the carcass to the cabin. You can stay down here as long as you like, but I wouldn't stay too long, if I were you. Those cuts need tending."

The attack had done what little else could have. It had jarred Blade out of his shock. He reflected that if he truly had been catapulted back in time, then he had to deal with the fact and take steps to remedy it. "No need to rush off," he said.

"Something on your mind?"

Blade straightened. The trapper was right about his wounds. Without proper treatment they might fester and become infected. But first he had a few words to say. "I want to apologize again for the way I've acted. Something happened, something I don't know how to explain, something that rattled me so badly, I wasn't myself."

"Think nothing of it." Nate had seen men before who were half out of their minds with worry or who lost their heads in the heat of battle. It wasn't right to hold them accountable for their actions when they had no control over what they were doing.

Blade held out his hand. "I'd like to start over, as friends. Deal?"

Impressed by the giant's sincerity, Nate shook his hand.

Up by the cabin, Winona King clutched her rifle and wished her man would return. She had not liked being left behind, but she had done as he wanted. It was only a panther, after all, and her man had slain many.

Winona could not quite make up her mind about the giant. She had been wary of him at first, just as she would be rightfully wary of a war party of Blackfeet or a roving grizzly. His size had a lot to do with it. He was the biggest man she had ever met, even bigger than her cousin, Touch The Clouds, who was the largest Shoshone alive.

But there had been gentleness in the giant's eyes when he looked at her and her children. Gentleness, and something else. A haunted aspect, such as a person might have if they had lost a loved one, or a calamity of equal magnitude had befallen them. She did not know why he should be so upset.

Nor did Winona know what to make of her

son's tale. As Nate rushed off, Zach had told her about finding the giant in flames. Green flames, no less. And of seeing a creature that was half human and half snake.

It was bewildering.

Suddenly a pair of tall figures appeared on the trail. Winona moved forward, relieved that her man was unharmed. He carried a panther across his broad shoulders. The giant was caked with blood. She saw his many cuts and volunteered, "Come inside. I have herbs that will help you mend."

A cooking fire had made the cabin warm and cozy. Blade did not realize how tired he was until he stepped over the threshold and felt the relaxing warmth seep into every pore in his body. He slumped into a chair by a table and placed the Commando on it. The little girl was fascinated by him. He grinned at Evelyn, and she scooted behind her mother, then peeked out to grin back.

Zach drew his butcher knife and stepped to the doorway. "I'll carve up the painter, Ma." He chuckled and winked at Blade. "She was fixing to make rabbit stew for supper, but now we'll have us a real treat!"

On a peg near the fireplace hung a parfleche. Winona carried it to the table. Inside were her herbs—roots and leaves and even a few whole dried plants. There was plantain, as her husband called it, used for wounds like those the giant had suffered. There were sagebrush leaves, chewed to relieve indigestion. There was *pannonzia*, or yarrow. A tea made from the roots was excellent for treating gas pain. She also had juniper sprigs, or *sammabe*. The tea made from them treated stiff joints and muscles. Plus many more.

Nate sat across from their guest. Since he had neglected to reload the Hawken after shooting the panther, he commenced to do so now, extracting the ramrod and placing it across his lap.

Blade had been thinking all the way to the cabin, and he had come to a few conclusions. "Did you happen to see anyone else near where you found me? Other than the mutant, I mean."

Nate paused. "What's a mutant?"

"The scaly critter, as your son called it."

"We saw no one else." Nate took a ball and wad from his ammo pouch. "What was that creature, Blade? Where did it come from? I don't mean to pry, but I can't help it. What if that thing shadowed us? It might attack Winona or the children."

Blade pursed his lips. The mountain man had a point. But there was an even greater danger than the Dark Lord's underling. That was Thanatos himself. Unleashed in the current day and age, there was no limit to the havoc Thanatos could wreak. No one could stand against him. He would be free to do as he saw fit, maybe even to take up where he had left off. It would be child's play for Thanatos to conquer the country. From there, the whole world was the Dark Lord's for the taking.

"The thing you saw can be killed by a bullet or a knife. It's not invincible," Blade said.

"But what *is* it?"

Blade did not respond right away. How much should he reveal? he wondered. How much was it *safe* to reveal? Was it smart to spread knowledge about the future? Could it somehow effect the chain of events that made the future what it was?

An idea that was even more troubling added to the Warrior's trepidation. Namely, would his presence in the past affect the future he knew? Was it possible for him to somehow change what would be by something he did now?

Blade flashed back mentally to an evening years ago when he had been at his mentor's, Plato. They had been talking about the holocaust and how different things would have been if it had never happened.

"Now and then I like to contemplate what I call the great 'What Ifs,'" Plato had said. "What if Rome had never fallen? What if the American colonies had never rebelled? What if Hitler had never been born? Or Michelangelo? Or Mozart?" The Family's leader had sighed wistfully. "What if genetic engineering had been used to benefit humankind instead of to increase our capacity to make war? What if the global elite that once controlled human affairs had humanity's best interests at heart, instead of only wanting to grow more powerful and to increase their wealth?"

Blade had swirled the wine in his glass. "What has been, has been. What is, is. What will be, will be. All the thinking in the world won't change it."

"True," the wisest man in the Family's long history had said. "Still, one can't help but dream. The human race had every opportunity to turn our planet into paradise. Instead, we nearly destroyed it and ourselves in the bargain."

"Sometimes the only way we learn is the hard way."

To Nate it was apparent that his guest was

deep in thought. He poured the appropriate amount of black powder into the barrel of his rifle, then tamped the ball and wad down. "You haven't answered my question," he remarked.

Blade did not know what to say, so he hedged. "Only because I don't want you to think I'm crazier than you probably already do." He smiled at Evelyn, who had stepped to the table and was peeking at him over the top. "All I can say is that it has to be killed. It and any others like it that might have made it through."

"There are more like that thing?" Nate said, appalled at the notion.

"There might be," Blade admitted. "Is there any way we can find out if anyone else has seen unusual creatures roaming these mountains?"

It was Winona who replied. "That is easy. The Indians who live in the surrounding territory would know."

"Can we go talk to them?"

Nate was sliding the ramrod back into its housing under the barrel. "We can if you have a few months to spare."

"That long?" Blade said, thinking of all the harm Thanatos could do in that amount of time.

"It would take at least two weeks to reach the nearest Ute village. We're on friendly terms with them, so it won't be a problem." Nate rose to lean the Hawken against a wall. "About a week's ride to the north live the Crows. It's risky going into their country, though. If they're in a friendly mood, they'll smoke a pipe with us. If not, they'll be after our scalps."

"Then there are my people, the Shoshones," Winona took up the narrative. "They live northwest of us. We would need two weeks or so to get to the village of my uncle, Spotted Bull. He would be happy to help us hunt these creatures down." She paused. "If they have not been sent by Coyote, that is."

"Who?"

Winona explained while taking tin cups and plates from a cupboard. "My people believe Coyote is their father. He made us from clay when he was a man. Now Coyote lives in the spirit world. When we die, we go to his land."

"How can these creatures have any connection to him if he's a spirit?" Blade asked.

"Coyote is a trickster, giant one. No one can say what he will do next." Winona walked to a counter and picked up a coffee pot. "He has always been willful. He married a girl who killed and ate anyone who stopped at her lodge, and together they gave birth to the ancestors of my people."

Blade did not see how that applied to the mutant. To her, he said, "Coyote did not send the creature I am after. It was created by someone known as the Dark Lord. He is as evil a man as ever lived."

"I have an idea," Nate chimed in. "We could go to Bent's Fort. It's only a few days south of here. Indians from all the tribes visit all the time to trade. If anyone has seen or heard of critters like the one we saw, someone is bound to know about it."

Winona liked the idea. They had not been to a post in ages, and she needed material for a dress and other foofarow. "We will take plews to trade," she said. "And the wolf hides from last winter."

"All of us are going?" Blade said. It would be dangerous enough with just the trapper and him. Taking a woman and children along was just asking for grief. He would rather they stayed.

"Of course," Winona said. "We are a family. We do everything together." She patted her daughter. "Would you have me leave Blue Flower and my son behind?"

Blade held his tongue. If the mountain man and his wife were willing to put their offspring at risk, it was out of his hands. He had no right to butt in. "How soon can we leave?"

"Is the morning soon enough?" Nate asked.

"Perfect," Blade said. The sooner they got underway, the sooner he could foil whatever plans the Dark Lord had.

Bel Aram had paused to consult the triangulator on his wrist when a small herd of four-legged creatures caught wind of him, rose from the high grass in which they had been concealed, and fled in long leaps. He was after them in the blink of an eye. No, faster, for Bel Aram could cover ten feet in the time it took mutant or human to bat an eyelash.

He liked how the grass rustled with his passing. He liked the feel of it on his exposed scales and wished he were not burdened by the body armor Thanatos made him wear.

The animals sensed that he was closing on them and increased their speed. Bel Aram did the same. They were great sport, these creatures. They were swifter than any animals he had ever chased. In the end, it did not save them. Or, rather, the one that Bel Aram overtook.

At the last moment the straggler turned on him and tried to slash him with pronged horns. Bel Aram evaded the blow, seized the animal by the neck, and bit its throat. The spurt of warm blood tasted delicious. He lapped at the geyser until it ran dry, then satiated his gnawing appetite, wolfing his food—as was his custom.

Soon Bel Aram was underway again. The triangulator showed him that the one he sought was close, under a kilometer away. It was strange that the blip had not moved in a long, long while. Perhaps Ghanata was dead.

The dot of light brightened. A low series of beeps came from the device. Bel Aram slowed. Loud snoring guided him the final few yards. He parted stems in front of him, and there was the lieutenant.

Another snore beat at Bel Aram's tiny ears. Some among the puny humans believed that snake-men did not have ears, but they did.

Bel Aram strode to the snoring hulk and shook a shoulder. All it did was provoke the dullard into snoring louder. "Ghanata!" he hissed. "Wake up, you pathetic oaf! How can you sleep at a time like this?"

Ghanata's only reaction was to mumble in his sleep and roll onto his side, exposing gashes in his head and wounds in his neck and chest.

"Wake up, I say!" Bel Aram snapped, punching the lieutenant on the temple.

The minotaur came up off the ground in a fit of rage. He looked around him, blowing and huffing as his kind were wont to do, then saw Bel

Aram, and stiffened. "Captain!" he exclaimed thickly. "I did not know it was you."

Bel Aram was in no mood to tolerate the cretin's stupidity. "I catch you sleeping when you should be seeking our master?"

Ghanata touched a hand to his chest. "I hurt, Captain. Humans shot me."

"Too bad they did not do us a favor and finish you off, oaf," Bel Aram said. "Must you always be next to worthless?"

The minotaur pouted, another trait that Bel Aram found idiotic. "I was shot," he repeated stubbornly, then added sullenly, "I was doing my job. I was trying to kill a Warrior. The one they call Hickok."

Bel Aram found the news worthwhile. "So at least two of them made it through. The third one must be here as well."

"Do we go look for him?" Ghanata asked hopefully. "I will crush his bones and mangle him to a pulp for you to digest. It will be like old times, as it was in the field, before we were assigned to the Tower guard."

"Fool," Bel Aram said. "The Warriors can wait. First we must let Thanatos know that we came through. He is southeast of us, and not all that far."

Ghanata rubbed a furrow above his eye. "Will he be mad at us? I do not want him to punish me. The last time he almost broke me in half."

Bel Aram grinned. He rarely did, since grinning did not come naturally to his kind. Their facial muscles were not built for it. "You deserved to be punished. You slept on guard duty."

He started off, moving slowly. "Try to keep up, sluggard."

"I will try," Ghanata promised, "but it hurts to breathe, even to talk."

"You'll heal," Bel Aram noted. "Our master incorporated accelerated healing into our DNA matrix, did he not? Unless we are hit in the brain or the heart, we seldom die. Maybe being shot will teach you to be more careful."

The minotaur stomped faster, but he did not appear happy about being forced to do so. Bel Aram did not make an issue of it. The truth was that he did not know how their lord and master would take their being there. Hopefully, if it angered the Dark Lord, Thanatos would break the minotaur's neck and spare him.

Thanatos always had valued brains more than brawn.

Chapter Ten

Geronimo had no desire to kill a fellow Indian. As the only member of the Family with the blood of the red race in his veins, he had always taken pride in his lineage and done his best to uphold the warrior traditions of his ancestors, the Blackfeet.

To some, that made his choice of a name rather odd, but he'd had his reasons.

Every Family member was permitted to pick their own name at the age of sixteen. The ceremony was called the Naming. It had been initiated by the Elders many decades ago to instill in the young an appreciation of their roots. Understanding history, the Elders believed, was the key to social maturity.

In his studies of the various tribes and their leaders, few had appealed to Geronimo as much as his namesake. In order to honor the memory of the wily Apache of old who had defied the might of the United State government long after the rest of the Apaches had been herded onto reservations, he had taken Geronimo's name as his own.

It had been a shock and a revelation for Geronimo to learn that other Indians, the Flatheads, had survived the cataclysm. He had spent time among them and had grown to respect them highly.

Later, Geronimo had learned there were a few other widely scattered Indian survivors. His wife, Cynthia Morning Dove, was part Sioux.

There were rumors that a large number of Indians had taken refuge in northern Canada at the time of the holocaust, but so far no one had been able to confirm it.

Geronimo hoped so. It would be a tragedy if his kind had been wiped off the face of the earth by the death merchants who had started the conflagration.

Now, hemmed in by two groups of mounted warriors, with the man he had seen before bearing down on him, Geronimo had a decision to make and a split second in which to make it. Already the warrior had an arrow fixed on his chest. He brought the FNC to bear, but instead of triggering rounds into the man on the horse, he fired at the ground in front of the animal. The short burst kicked up dirt. Whether it was that or the blasting of the Auto Rifle was hard to say, but the horse slid to a stop, rearing just as the warrior let the shaft fly.

The arrow whizzed past Geronimo's ear. He raised the rifle higher to fire again if need be. To his surprise, the other warriors were taking flight. The man on the rearing horse tried desperately to stay on, but the plunging animal was more than he could handle. He hit the earth hard and the horse dashed off.

Geronimo ran over. The warrior had been stunned by the fall and was rising unsteadily. Geronimo tapped the muzzle on the man's nose, freezing him in place.

"I told you that I meant you no harm. Why won't you believe me?"

The warrior's hand was poised inches from the hilt of a knife on his right hip. He had recovered enough to glare.

Geronimo felt it prudent to relieve the man of the weapon. It consisted of a rather primitive iron blade with a hilt fashioned from an elk antler. He tossed it over by the warrior's bow.

"Who are you? What tribe are you from?"

In glum defiance, the warrior said nothing.

Geronimo glanced toward the fleeing band, which was galloping northward. He did not understand why they had run off when they had him so greatly outnumbered. He stepped back to give himself room in case the one he had caught got any ideas. One more time he tried to communicate.

"Do you speak English? Is that the problem here?"

The warrior barked a curt response in a language Geronimo had never heard. Geronimo shook his head to signify that he did not comprehend.

Straightening, the captive cocked his head and scrutinized Geronimo from top to bottom. He grunted; then his hands flowed in a series of gestures. When he was done, he looked expectantly at the Warrior.

Geronimo knew the gestures for what they were: sign language. A few of the older Flatheads sometimes used the one-time universal language of the plains and mountains tribes. The younger ones had no interest in learning it. To them, it was outdated and worthless.

Unfortunately, Geronimo knew few of the signs. A medicine man had taught him a half-dozen or so. But it had been so long ago that he only remembered one clearly. Cradling the FNC in the crook of his left arm, he held his right hand in front of his neck with the palm facing out and his index and second fingers pointed up. Then he raised his hand until the tips of his fingers were level with his head. It was the sign for friendship, and meant literally "brothers growing up together."

The warrior's dark eyes narrowed in suspicion. He responded with a flurry of motions.

Geronimo did not recognize a single sign. It frustrated him. When he shook his head, the man made a gesture that had nothing to do with sign language.

By this time the band had disappeared. Geronimo mulled what to do next. Letting the man go would show that he was not an enemy. But what was to stop the warrior from circling around and jumping him when he least expected it?

A whinny sounded to the south. Geronimo had forgotten about the warrior's skittish mount, which had gone fifty yards and stopped to graze. A horse would enable him to reach the Rockies that much sooner. He wagged the Auto Rifle so the man would precede him, and together they hiked toward the animal.

Geronimo had to keep one eye on his prisoner, one on the horse, and still scan the grass for mutants and mutates. Gunshots often drew them like honey drew bears. It was highly unusual that he had not seen one since he revived. He was long overdue.

The horse lifted its head but did not run off. Its gaze stayed on the man who owned it. When they were almost there, the animal turned and plodded toward the warrior. Geronimo immediately walked between them, holding out a hand to grip the bridle. The horse would not allow it. Pulling away, it started to skirt him.

Without warning the warrior shouted a single word. His mount responded superbly, breaking into a lope that brought it alongside him. In a lithe bound he gained its back and instantly slid off the other side, hanging by an elbow and a knee.

Geronimo brought up the FNC, but he held his fire. To drop the man he had to drop the horse and that he would not do. The crafty warrior sped northward, never once exposing himself until the horse was well out of range. Then he swung up, pumped a fist overhead, and yipped like a coyote.

"Well done," Geronimo conceded to himself,

smiling. He had been snookered nicely.

Slinging the FNC, Geronimo walked to the spot where the bow and knife lay. He was going to take them. But it was just possible that the warrior would come back, and the man might take it as a good-will gesture on Geronimo's part if he left them there.

More alert than ever, Geronimo continued his journey. The morning gave way to noon. By the middle of the afternoon, he was starved and thirsty enough to drink one of the Great Lakes.

It must have been four or so when dark spots appeared high in the sky. There were eight or nine banking in wide overlapping circles. Buzzards.

Geronimo was inclined to pass by whatever had attracted them. His growling stomach and the thought that it might be a fresh kill bent his steps toward it anyway. On hearing growls, he slowed. A bone crunched. An animal snarled. He eased onto his hands and knees to cover the final twenty yards.

A pack of wolves were feasting on an old bull elk. Seven, all told. The elk had not been dead very long. The pool of blood in which it lay had not yet congealed.

The Warrior watched a wolf rip a strip of pink flesh off and gulp it down. His own mouth watered. It would be a long time before the wolves gorged themselves and wandered away to sleep it off, and he did not care to wait that long. He rose and boldly walked into the open.

The wolves leaped to their feet, all of them bristling and growling. A male bigger than the rest advanced partway to challenge the intruder.

Geronimo did not stop or slow. To show fear invited a concerted rush. He made a beeline for the dominant male. Bluff it, and the rest would give ground.

The big male was not inclined to relinquish their prize. It crouched, the hair on the back of its neck rigid, lips pulled back to expose rapier-like fangs. The gleam in its eyes spoke volumes.

"Scat!" Geronimo hollered, waving. Sometimes the sound of a human voice was enough to scare wildlife off. "All I want is one little piece!"

The dominant male was not scared at all. Head low, it took a step toward him, its bushy tail as tense as its body.

Having already wasted ammo once that day, Geronimo was not about to do so again. He would shoot only when he had to, and he would shoot to kill. "I won't warn you again," he blustered. "Get out of here!"

Two of the smaller wolves darted into the grass. One other began to, but halted. Another moved to help the leader of the pack.

It was all or nothing. Geronimo rushed them, swinging the FNC, bellowing at the top of his lungs. For a moment it appeared the dominant male would not retreat. He had almost reached it when the wolf spun and ran a few yards. That was as far as it would go. The other wolves joined their leader. None attempted to interfere when Geronimo moved to the far side of the elk and squatted.

Teeth marks were everywhere. Geronimo found a portion of haunch the wolves had not touched and helped himself to a large steak. As he had done with the buffalo, he wrapped it in a section of hide.

The wolves were slinking closer when the Warrior rose. They stopped, giving him the lupine equivalent of the evil eye as he headed westward. "It's all yours now, my brothers," he said cheerfully. They responded with an indignant chorus of growls and snarls.

As the end of the second day neared, Geronimo took stock. He still had not caught sight of the mountains. He still had no idea what had happened to his friends. Or where, exactly, he was. All he had done so far was manage to survive, which, in hindsight, was a feat in itself.

The sun dipped lower.

No more than an hour of daylight remained when Geronimo spied trees to the southwest. He adjusted course and soon was near enough to see sparrows frolicking in the cottonwoods. Since the stand covered only four acres, the source of the water had to be a spring, not a stream. He threaded into the trees, stopping when he heard a sound that was out of place.

Someone was talking, softly.

Geronimo moved to a wide tree and quietly climbed to a stout branch. From his vantage point he saw the spring, a pool ten feet in diameter. Seated on the bank was a grungy man in filthy buckskins. A mane of straggly hair was crowned by a beaver hat, a bushy beard hung halfway down his chest. He had a long knife in one hand and was bent over his left leg. Geronimo could not quite see what he was doing.

The talk was muttering, which the man did in bursts. Half the time the words were indistinct.

"Damn that Baxter and damn the Company and damn the whores that gave birth to those red vermin!" was the latest outburst. "Damn those heathens for begrudgin' a man the right to make his livin' where and how he sees fit! It ain't fittin'!"

Geronimo saw a rifle near the unhappy character. It was another antique, similar to the one the warrior had carried. He slid behind the trunk and approached until he was close enough to reach out and touch the unsuspecting figure. "Make no sudden moves," he warned.

Which was exactly what the man did. Yelping, he twisted, fright animating his craggy features. The tip of the long knife had blood on it. His blood. He had slit his right legging open above the knee and a red rivulet trickled out.

"What in tarnation do you reckon you're doin', pilgrim, sneakin' up on Old Hugh like that?" the man demanded. He had a wild look about him, accented by the fact his right eye was vivid blue, his left a deep gray. "You scared me out of ten years' growth!"

Geronimo scoured the vegetation across the pool. "Are you alone?"

Old Hugh snorted. "I should say I am! Those savages done killed off every last coon except me. And I suspect they'll do that if they get their paws on me before I'm shed of their country." His blue eye jiggled up and down of its own accord, a nervous tic that was to repeat itself every twenty or thirty seconds.

Geronimo wondered if the man had clashed with the same Indians he had encountered. Lowering the FNC, he introduced himself, adding,

"Maybe you can help me. I'd like to know where on earth I am."

Old Hugh was glancing right and left. "Geronimo, you say? That sounds like an Injun handle to me. And you sure enough look like an Injun." He leaned toward the Warrior. "But those clothes you're wearin' ain't like any Injun clothes I ever saw. And what kind of gun is that you're holdin'? One of them new English models?"

Geronimo moved to the spring, keeping a safe distance between the older man and himself. "It was imported before the holocaust. I'm not sure which country it came from. Hickok would know. He's a friend of mine."

"You're spoutin' nonsense, son," Old Hugh said. "Talk straight tongue or don't talk at all. That's my motto." He bent over his leg again. "Time enough to palaver later. You'll have to excuse me. I have an arrowhead to dig out before my leg gets infected and I lose it."

"I can help," Geronimo offered.

"Not necessary," Old Hugh said. "I was diggin' arrows out of my hide when you were knee high to a grasshopper. I reckon I can get this one out without too much fuss." He inserted the tip of his knife into the slit he had made. "Only thing is, the darned barbs are buried in the bone. I just hope to heaven it's not tainted."

"In what way?"

Old Hugh glanced at him. "Where have you been livin', son? On the moon? Don't you know that Injuns like to dip their arrows in rattlesnake venom and polecat livers and such? That poison get into your system and you're a goner. Mark my words." He paused. "But that's Injuns for you.

They're no account any ways you lay your sights."

Geronimo could not help himself. He would not let the memory of his ancestors be tarnished without defending them. "I'm part Indian," he revealed.

"Just like I figured," Old Hugh said while nonchalantly working his knife back and forth in the wound. "But at least you ain't hostile. If you was, you would have rubbed me out when you had the drop on me."

"What are you doing out here in the middle of nowhere?" Geronimo inquired.

The older man tittered long and loud, then caught himself and covered his mouth with his free hand. "We had us a brainstorm, Baxter and the Kellum boys and me. We figured we could sneak on into the Lewis Range without them blasted Injuns bein' the wiser. Prime beaver country up that way still."

"You trap for a living?"

Old Hugh stopped prying and poking to toss his head in merriment. "No, you blamed greenhorn. I'm the President of the United States, out for a Sunday stroll." He snickered. "Of course I raise plews! Been doin' it for well nigh thirty years, since before beaver was all the rage."

Geronimo wanted to keep the man talking in order to learn more about the country he was in and its inhabitants. "Did you find any beaver in the Lewis Range?" he asked.

A dreamy look came over Old Hugh. "Did we ever! You should've seen all them critters swimmin' and gnawin' on trees and workin' on their lodges. Hundreds of them, there were! We laid our traps and set to work, but we hadn't taken but five when the Injuns found us."

"Did they kill your friends?"

"I expect so, but I ain't for certain sure. I know one of them parted Baxter's hair with a tomahawk. Then them Kellum boys ran off as fast as rabbits with a pack of hounds on their tail. Half the Injuns followed. The rest came after me."

Geronimo stared toward the plain. "Are they still after you?"

Old Hugh jabbed a gnarled finger at his leg. "How do you think I got this arrow hole in me, sonny? I sure as blazes didn't put it there myself." He squinted with his good eye as he lowered his head so close to the wound that blood smeared the end of his nose. "I just hope I got out all of the arrowhead."

"Want me to take a look?," the Warrior offered.

"That's mighty gracious of you, stranger. But I don't like anybody's fingers but my own diggin' around inside of me. Who knows where your finger has been?" Old Hugh found his comment hilarious.

"Mad Bull and his boys caught me nappin' around sunset yesterday," the trapper continued. "I was out in the open with nowhere to hide. When I heard their whoopin' and hollerin', I turned, and that's when one of them red devils put an arrow into me."

"You were lucky they didn't catch you."

"Hell, luck had nothin' to do with it. Fear saved my bacon. I was so scared, I lit a shuck as if my hind end was on fire." Old Hugh chuckled. "That must of been a sight to see! Me a' hobblin' and

jumpin' on my good leg and them varmints clo-
sin' in, thinkin' they had me."

Geronimo had to ask. "How did you get away?"

"The sun saved me. It went down about the
same time I figured it'd be smarter to make like
a snake than a jackrabbit. I crawled off through
the grass, sure those rascals would find me at any
second. But you know what?" Old Hugh cocked
his blue eye at the Warrior just as it jiggled again.
"They rode within six feet of where I was and
never seen me." He spoke quieter as if to confide
a secret. "I figure I turned invisible."

"You did what?"

Old Hugh inserted a thumb and a forefinger
into the hole and worked them back and forth
like they were a pair of tweezers or pliers. "Sure.
Ain't you ever seen Injuns do it, you an Injun and
all?" A grunt escaped him. "I knew a Crow medicine man who could turn invisible. He could
walk right up to you and you'd never see him
unless he wanted you to."

Geronimo quenched his thirst while listening.
In his estimation the trapper needed a physician.
The wound had nearly rendered the man deliri-
ous.

"I asked him how he did it, but that old Crow
never would say. From what I gathered, it had
something to do with his diet." Old Hugh muttered several words, then said, "Eat the right
things and you too could turn invisible, sonny. It
would come in handy when heathens were after
your hair."

"I have no doubt," Geronimo humored him.
The shock of being wounded and the strain of
the chase had rattled the older man's thinking.

"Hold on!" the trapper declared. "I do believe I've struck pay dirt." The wound made a sucking sound as he peeled his dripping fingers from it. Holding his hand out, he displayed a flattened arrowhead. "Lookee! Just like I told you! It hit the bone but didn't go through. Appears I'll keep my leg a while longer yet. Good thing, too. I've grown right fond of it over the years."

"I'll heat some water to dress it," Geronimo offered.

"Are you loco? And have those Injuns spot the smoke?" Old Hugh shook his mane. "I'm partial to livin' a few more winters, if it's all the same to you."

Suddenly Old Hugh stiffened, turning his nose into the wind as would a meat-eater that had caught a tantalizing scent. "Hellfire and brimstone! Those coyotes are comin'."

The man was extremely agitated. "Coyotes can't harm us," Geronimo said to soothe him.

"Not real coyotes, you idiot. Mad Bull and his boys are headin' our way."

"You can smell them?"

"The bear fat in their hair—sure. What's the matter? You got a cold or something?"

Before Geronimo could respond, the old trapper picked up his antique rifle and hastened around the spring to the northwest. He moved with remarkable agility for someone who had just pulled an arrowhead from his leg. Geronimo kept pace.

"I knew it was too good to be true, me gettin' away like I done," Old Hugh muttered. "Mad Bull ain't about to let me go peaceable-like. He's still mad over that time I stole a horse out from under his nose."

The wind had grown stronger, as it invariably did toward evening. Brilliant red and orange bands painted the western horizon. Half a mile out on the prairie was a knot of riders, too far off for Geronimo to distinguish features.

"Yep. It's Mad Bull," Old Hugh stated. "We're in for it if that rascal learns where we are."

"We can hide until they go by."

The trapper smirked. "Now why didn't I think of that, sonny?" Beckoning, he hurried back into the undergrowth.

Geronimo cast a last glance at the riders, then dogged the older man's heels. "What kind of Indians are we up against?" he offhandedly asked.

"Don't you know anything, greenhorn? Mad Bull and his bunch belong to the worst tribe in all creation." Old Hugh covered the wound with a hand to stem the crimson trickle. "They're Blackfeet."

Chapter Eleven

Hickok sat up and wished he hadn't. Terrific pounding hammered the top of his head. He felt woozy. Putting a hand to his temple, he waited for the awful sensation to subside.

Someone had dumped him on a cot. A barred door was in front of him, a barred window to his right. The room stank to high heaven. If not for stray shafts of sunlight filtering in the window, it would have been as dark as the pit.

Slowly standing, Hickok licked his dry lips. Whoever had walloped him on the noggin was going to regret the day they were born. He patted his right holster and was horrified to discover the

Python was gone. So was his other Colt. Boiling fury propelled him to the door. He tried the latch, but it was locked.

"Let me out of here!" the gunfighter demanded, shaking the bars for all he was worth.

From the end of a narrow hall wafted a gruff voice. "Simmer down back there, Mister. I'll be along shortly."

"Now!" Hickok roared, nearly beside himself. Some might call it childish, but those pistols meant more to him than anything. They were his stock in trade, the tools that enabled him to do his job as it should be done. Time and again they had saved his life and the lives of those who meant the most to him. All the gold in the world would not induce him to part with either. It was unthinkable that someone had taken them.

"Draw in your horns, Mister," came the reply. "I'll get there when I get there."

Hickok stepped back, planted himself, and kicked the door. It shook a little, but it was plainly far too thick to kick down. He didn't care. He kicked it again and again, each blow resounding in the narrow hall.

On about the tenth time, the door at the far end of the hallway flew open and in stormed a man in a uniform and a matching cap. It took a moment for Hickok to place him as the busybody he had shoved aside before rushing into The Bull and Crown. "I remember you, you thief!" he declared.

The man had a walrus mustache and bulbous nose. At his waist hung a large key ring containing many large keys. He folded his arms and regarded the Warrior with smug spite. "Now isn't that rich! A troublemaker like you accusing *me* of breaking the law! You just don't know when to quit, do you?"

"I want out of this place," Hickok demanded. "And I want my guns back, pronto."

"This place, simpleton, is the city jail," the man informed him. "I gather you didn't know that St. Louis is getting civilized. We have a police force now. Have had one for two years, in fact. There's only four of us constables, which is far too few for a city this size. But we do the best we can."

"You're a law officer?" Hickok said, genuinely surprised. He'd read about marshals and sheriffs and the like in books in the Family library, but he'd never expected to be arrested by one.

"Sinking in, is it?" the man said. "You're just lucky I happened to be on the scene when you raised a ruckus. If I hadn't followed you into the tavern, that big fella in the cloak would have stomped your head in."

Thanatos. Hickok gripped the bars. "He's the one I'm after. You've got to let me out. There's no tellin' what he'll do if he isn't stopped."

The lawman shook his head. "Anyone arrested for disturbing the peace has to spend at least twenty-four hours in the calaboose. You have six or seven hours to go yet."

"I've been out that long?" Hickok said. "What did you hit me with? A crowbar?"

"I wasn't the one who knocked you out. The gentleman in the cloak did when you tried to shoot him."

Hickok inwardly fumed. "That lyin' scum. I never got a chance to even pull a pistol." He paused. "Speakin' of which, where the blazes are they? If you let anyone take them, I'll—"

"Those peculiar pistols of yours are locked in my desk," the constable revealed. "Your rifle is in our gun rack." He paused. "Where did you get those guns, anyhow? I've never seen the like. How much powder do they take? And why do the pistols have those round parts in the middle? What are they for?"

Hickok was so glad that the Pythons were safe, he leaned his forehead against the bars and silently gave thanks. To the tin star, he said, "Forget about my guns, ding-a-ling. You should be more concerned about Thanatos. He's the murderin' butcher you let get away."

"Thanatos?" the lawman said. "Do you mean Lord Seth, the gentleman who hit you? To tell the truth, I was all set to arrest him, too, until he told me who he was. It isn't every day that European royalty pays us a visit."

"He's claimin' to be a ruler of some kind? That figures."

"Lord Anton Seth of Latvia. I never heard of it myself. But who can keep track of all them tiny countries they got over there? Why, some aren't no bigger than Rhode Island, where I was born, yet they have the gall to call themselves a whole country." The constable snickered. "That's those Europeans for you. They're forever putting on airs."

Hickok did not care one whit about Europe or anywhere else at the moment. Softening his tone, he said, "Look, would it do any good if I apologize for raisin' a ruckus and give you my word that I'll be a mite more careful in the future? I really need to get out of here."

"Forget it," the man said stiffly. "The law is the law. Twenty-four hours is the minimum. You'll get out of here when I say so, and not before."

The Warrior wanted to land a solid right on the lawman's jaw. "Didn't you hear a word I've been tellin' you? That jasper who's callin' himself Lord Seth is a killer. If he isn't stopped, he's liable to run your streets red with blood."

The man sighed. "Spare me your lies. Lord Seth told me that he's outfitting an expedition to go off into the prairie and hunt buffalo. He'll probably be gone by the time you get out."

Hickok stared at the constable's retreating back and suppressed an urge to curse a blue streak. To have been so close to Thanatos and then be foiled like this was too aggravating for words! He couldn't let the madman give him the slip. He just couldn't.

It was a ramshackle building on the waterfront, a storehouse for merchandise brought in by steamboat. Thanatos halted outside the entrance, his hood up, his cloak flapping in the wind. From within issued the murmur of men. Human ears could not have heard it, but then, his ears were more than human. One voice out of the ten brought a scowl to the Dark Lord's visage.

". . . don't care how rich this Lord Muck-a-Muck claims he can make us. There's something about him I don't like, something spooky. If you ask me, we're all better off fighting shy of him. He's nothing but trouble."

Thanatos stalked inside, deliberately slamming the door to silence the men, who were congregated in an open area flanked by stacks of crates. All eyes were on him as he strode past them and turned.

"Greetings, my friends," Thanatos began suavely. "It gladdens my heart that you have shown up. I promise you that your lives will never be the same. Soon you will all have more wealth and power than any of you ever dreamed of."

"Oh, I don't know, your lordship," said a scrawny cutthroat whose voice gave him away as the carping critic. "I can dream of more money than old Midas owned."

"And you are, sir?" Thanatos asked, maintaining the facade of civility.

"Folks call me Bucktooth Bob."

Thanatos could see why. The critic's upper front teeth bulged his lip out at a grotesque angle, as if they were trying to work their way out of his mouth. Half were discolored, one stained bright yellow. A twinge of revulsion rippled through the Dark Lord.

"I'm a footpad," the unsavory specimen bragged. "One of the best in the city. Ask anyone. I always pick marks with money. A bash on the head, and it's all over." He swung his scrawny right arm. "A blackjack is my secret. One blow is all it ever takes if you know where to strike."

"A man should always know his craft well," Thanatos said dryly. "But you have failed to explain why you question my judgement." He took a casual step closer and surveyed the ten thieves and killers. "It is only fair that I inform all of you up front that I do not like to have my authority questioned. When I give an order, it is to be obeyed. When I give my word, you can wager all you own that I will do as I say."

Bucktooth Bob hooked his thumbs in his belt, his mouth curling in a partial sneer. "I'm sure you mean well, Lord Seth. But men like us don't take anything for granted. As for the promises others make, it's all hot air as far as I'm concerned. The proof is in the pudding, if you don't mind my saying."

"Actions do speak louder than words," Thanatos said, restraining himself from snuffing the worthless worm only with the utmost effort.

Another man, a bear of a frontiersman whose face bore scarred claw marks, remarked, "Maybe it would help, your lordship, if you could tell us a bit more about this grand scheme of yours."

"Yeah," said a third. "All we know so far is that you want us to do your dirty work, and you claim we'll all get rich."

Thanatos did not take offense. In their feeble-minded way, they raised legitimate points. "It would be rash of me to tell you everything. For my plan to succeed, secrecy is required. But I will say this." He rose to his full height and swept the hood from his head. In the murky light cast by the lone lantern, there was scant likelihood any of them would get a good look at his eyes.

"I intend to set myself up as the ruler of all the land between the Mississippi River and the Pacific Ocean," Thanatos elaborated. "Within two years I will have an army at my command the likes of which mortal eyes have not beheld since the dawn of time."

A few of the ruffians glanced at one another. One chuckled. Bucktooth Bob slapped his thigh and tittered like a high-strung woman. "I do declare! Don't you beat all? Just when I was beginning to think you'd do to ride the river with, you up and spout nonsense like that."

"An army?" another commented. "Did we hear you right?"

"You did," Thanatos said, incensed by their presumption.

Bucktooth Bob asked what all of them were apparently thinking. "Where is this army of yours going to come from? Are you planning to send to Latvia for troops? Or are you going to pull your soldiers out of thin air?"

"Not exactly, gentlemen." Thanatos used the term loosely. "I intend to forge my army from the ranks of the greatest natural guerilla fighters this continent has ever seen."

"Huh?" someone said.

Thanatos took another step. "The Indians, gentlemen. Every last warrior from every last tribe is going to fight for us and die for us. We will carve out an empire larger than the United States. Then it will be simple to—"

Rowdy laughter drowned Thanatos out.

"How in the hell do you plan to get all the Injuns to do your bidding?" Bucktooth Bob asked between giggles.

The bearish frontiersman nudged the wharf rat. "Only a danged foreigner could come up with a dumb notion like that, Bob!"

The Dark Lord made a mental note to make all of them suffer the most agonizing ends imaginable when they had outlived their usefulness. "Where there is a will, gentlemen, there is a way.

And I have a means of rendering the Indians as docile as lambs."

"Now there's something I'd like to see!" Bucktooth Bob said.

Thanatos came to a decision. "Very well. Perhaps it would be best to give a demonstration of my power. An object lesson, as it were." He faced the bearish hulk in buckskins. "What is your name?"

"Timothy Sistrunk, your lordship. Most just call me Scar, on account of what a griz did to me a few years back." Scar touched the furrows on his face.

"Come here," Thanatos directed. Reaching under his cloak into a hidden pocket, he palmed a small vial which he held up for all to observe. In it floated a thick greenish fluid, much like mucous, only this mucous glowed a faint shade of green.

"What's that?" Scar asked.

Thanatos gently shook the vial so that the mucous ebbed from end to end. "The key to my domination of this globe. The answer to your questions." Holding the vial at arm's length, he grasped the cap. "When I open this, Scar, I want you to take a few deep breaths."

"Why?" the frontiersman said. "What's that stuff going to do to me?"

"It won't harm you, I assure you," Thanatos said. He began to twist the cap off.

Scar was not very pleased by the turn of events. He looked at the others and fidgeted. His left hand strayed to the butt of a flintlock tucked under his belt. "I don't like this," he said. "It's not like cod liver oil, is it? The smell of that stuff about makes me gag."

"It hardly has any odor at all," Thanatos said. The cap was loose, but he did not remove it. Extending his hand until it was under the frontiersman's nose, he said, "It will only take a whiff. I want all of you to pay close attention." He removed the cap.

The instant air made contact with the green mucous, the substance grew brighter. Tendrils of green vapor rose from the vial. As he had been told, Scar inhaled deeply a few times.

Thanatos was quick to cap the vial as soon as the man obeyed. He placed it in the secret pocket. "There. It is done."

Bucktooth Bob, who stood closest to Scar, scratched his ostrich neck. "What's done? What was that all about? He's just the same as he always was."

"Is he indeed?" Thanatos countered. "Scar, would you be so kind as to strangle Bob until he is blue in the face?"

Some of them thought it was a joke. Bucktooth Bob did not know what to think. He looked at the frontiersman, then at Thanatos, his hand drifting to a dagger on his hip. "What kind of stunt are you trying to pull, Mister? Scar and me go back a long ways."

"Not long enough," the Dark Lord said.

One of the cutthroats gasped. Scar was turning. Slowly, awkwardly, as if he were not quite in complete control of his limbs. His expression was as blank as the surface of a rock, his eyes glazed. His skin was a sickly pale hue where moments ago it had been a robust bronze.

"Scar?" Bucktooth Bob said.

Thanatos smiled. The man who had once been Timothy Sistrunk did not answer. He couldn't. One sniff of the chemical had been enough to wipe all memory from his brain, to deprive him of his limited intellect, to render him incapable of any cerebral functions except for those involved in the most elementary of motor functions. Timothy Sistrunk was now a zombie, one of the walking dead, the first of a new undead army Thanatos was going to create.

Bucktooth Bob backed up a step. "Scar?" he repeated. "What in tarnation is wrong with you? Speak to me."

None of the other men moved. Mesmerized by the tableau, they awaited the outcome.

The man who had been known as Scar took another lumbering pace. His powerful arms rose, his thick fingers forming into claws.

"*Scar!* Damn it! Stop!" Bucktooth Bob shouted. His dagger sparkled in the lantern light. He crouched, his elbow cocked to thrust. "I'm warning you!"

It was a waste of breath. The zombie advanced as it had been ordered to do, its hands reaching for the riverman's neck. When Bucktooth Bob went on retreating, it went faster.

Bob was so intent on the unearthly apparition that he backed into a stack of crates. Trapped, he cursed, cried, "You asked for it!" then plunged his dagger into the zombie's ribs just as his former friend closed in on him.

No one else spoke. No one else moved.

The zombie had Bucktooth Bob by the throat now and was slowly throttling the life from the scrawny malcontent. A second thrust of the dagger had no more effect than would the sting of a bee. Bucktooth Bob grew frantic. He punched Scar in the face and on the neck. He rammed a knee into Scar's crotch. He tried to gouge out Scar's eyes. It was all fruitless.

Thanatos never tired of seeing his glorious handiwork in action. He must have witnessed thousands slain by his mindless minions, yet each new death was as fascinating as the last. He grinned when Bucktooth Bob sagged to his knees. Bob's face was beet red. Gradually, as Scar's fingers dug in deeper, the color changed to royal purple, finally to eggshell blue. By then his eyes bulged, his lips were pasty, and his chest had stopped heaving.

The zombie let go and stepped back, its arms going slack, oblivious to the dagger hilt protruding from its side.

"Well done," Thanatos complimented it as any proud parent would their offspring. Since he now had the undivided attention of the men who had responded to his clandestine invitation, he said, "I trust the demonstration has sufficed? Imagine, if you will, thousands of Indians in the same state as Mr. Sistrunk. Think of what we could do with such an army."

One of the ruffians found his voice. "There'd be no stopping us, Lord Seth. We could take over this whole country if we wanted."

Another caught the fever. "Anything we wanted would be ours for the taking! Why, we truly would be as rich as could be!"

A third man had a reservation. "But what about poor Scar? Can you make him like he was?

It ain't hardly fittin' that he spends the rest of his days lookin' as if he just crawled out of his own coffin."

Thanatos had them, hook, line, and sinker. "Never fear. I shall attend to Mr. Sistrunk shortly. For now, you are free to leave. We will meet here again tomorrow at the same time. By then I will have acquired the provisions and mounts we need." He glanced at Bucktooth Bob, who appeared even scrawnier in death than he had in life, if that were possible. "We need a replacement for Bob. If any of you know someone reliable, tell me tomorrow."

Thanatos dismissed them. The ruffian who had worried about Scar lingered but did not muster the courage to object. After their footsteps faded in the distance, the Dark Lord turned to the zombie.

"I have a new command for you. It seems that an accursed Warrior followed me through the portal. He is a minor irritant, at best, but one I would rather not have to deal with—not when you can dispose of him so effectively." Thanatos rested a hand on the zombie's shoulder. "Go to the jail. Kill everyone there."

A lantern suspended from a hook in the hallway cast uneven light into Hickok's cell. He lay on his back on the cot, his head propped in his hands, impatiently waiting for the constable to release him. Six hours, the man had said. It had to have been at least eight. He was about to explode.

There had been plenty of time for Hickok to come up with a plan. Since he was essentially a stranger in a strange land, he needed the aid of someone who knew St. Louis a lot better then he did. He would track down Kittson, Clyman, and Ogden, and ask them to help find Thanatos.

Once the Dark Lord was disposed of, Hickok would not rest until he located his pards. The three of them should be able to come up with a way out of the fix they were in.

The thought jolted him. In his eagerness to rid the world of the vile Dark Lord, he had nearly forgotten that Thanatos was the only one who might be able to send them back to the time period they came from. Without Thanatos, they would never see the Home again, never share any more happy moments with their families.

"Damn," Hickok groused. He had to take the Dark Lord alive. How in the name of all that was holy could he accomplish that major miracle? Thanatos was as devious as the year was long. It was rumored he had senses like a cat's and possessed the strength of five men. Or was it ten? Either way, subduing him would be as easy as wrestling a ten-foot alligator. While buck naked.

Just then the faint creak of metal hinges told Hickok that the outer door to the office had been opened. He had heard the same sound several times throughout the afternoon. What he had not heard before was the outcry that followed or the sound of a brief scuffle.

Hickok rose and stepped to the cell door. He peered down the corridor. Keys rattled. The hall door opened. A man in buckskins came toward him carrying the key ring.

"About time," Hickok said. "I was beginnin' to think you yahoos were going to leave me in here until I rotted." He hitched at his gunbelts, anxious to have the Colts where they belonged. "Hurry it up, Mister. I'm as antsy as a bear after hibernation."

The jailer had his head bowed and walked stiffly, as would someone with a bum leg. He halted at the door and took forever inserting the right key. At last he tugged and the gunfighter was free to go.

Hickok took a step and froze. The jailer had looked up. His pale skin and vacant stare were dead giveaways, as was the bloody hilt jutting from his ribs. It was a zombie.

The walking abomination attacked.

Chapter Twelve

Nate King was troubled. He would have preferred to leave his wife and children at the cabin, but Winona had insisted on coming. It had been nine months since the family last visited Bent's Fort, and for the others, going there was a rare treat.

Another factor weighed heavily in Nate's decision. The mutant, as Blade called it, might show up while he was gone. His wife and son were competent fighters but they would be no match for the snake-man. Nate wasn't even sure *he* would be.

The thing had been abhorrent, a violation of

all that was natural. It had radiated sheer evil, much like the sun radiated light. Nate's instinctive impulse had been to kill it, to rend it into bits and pieces.

Now, winding down through the foothills that bordered their hidden valley to the east, the mountain man never let his attention lapse. Remembering how fast the creature had been, he avoided deep timber and shaded patches where it could pounce on them before they knew it was there.

The morning had been uneventful. With the sun almost directly overhead, Nate looked for a place to rest the horses. On a hammock linking two hills he reined up. A pristine stream bisected it and there was ample grass for forage.

Winona and Evelyn were riding double. It was a precaution. Evelyn had been taught to ride, but she was not yet skilled enough to navigate some of the more treacherous terrain they passed through. Winona swung her daughter down, then slid off their pinto and arched her back to relieve a kink.

Zach brought up the rear. He was so glad to be going to Bent's that he bubbled inside. Life at their cabin was as grand as could be, but it did have a drawback. Except for the rendezvous and the three months every summer spent with the Shoshones, they did not get to socialize all that much. True, their friend Shakespeare McNair often came to visit, and on rare occasions other mountain men stopped by, but by and large Zach missed the company of other people, especially others close to his age.

At the Fort were several girls who were. Like

him, they had white fathers and Indian mothers. The last time the family had visited, Zach had spent hours in their company and had even gone on a stroll along the Arkansas River with a particularly pretty maiden.

Another attraction was the black cook, Charlotte. She had taken a shine to Zach and never failed to fatten him up with pie and other treats.

Zach dismounted and led his horse to the stream. The giant was already there, staring out over the prairie to the east. "Are you all right, Mr. Blade?" Zach inquired. It seemed to him that the man always wore a sad face. He reminded Zach of a trapper who once lost his wife to a flash flood and ever after went around looking as if he were upset to be alive.

"I'm fine," Blade answered. It would be a waste of breath to try and explain. How could he express how it felt to be cast adrift in time? To be cut off from all that one knew and all those who mattered in one's life? It was profoundly disturbing, a sense of alienation combined with a very real fear that he would never find his way home again. There was no experience to compare it to.

The Warrior strolled to the rim of the hammock. Below in the pines a jay squawked. To the north a pair of ravens took flight, the rhythmic beating of their wings as loud as if they were right next to him. Lower down, in a meadow fringing the pines, deer grazed. Out on the prairie were large dark forms that he could not quite place.

Nate came over. There was still so much the giant had not told them, still so much that he wanted to know. Yet he could not bring himself to pry. It was an unwritten rule of the trapping fraternity that no man had the right to meddle in the affairs of another. Unless the giant brought the subject up, Nate had to keep quiet.

Blade glanced at the mountain man. "You live in paradise. I envy you."

That gave Nate the opening he needed. "What's it like where you come from?"

"A few places are like this, but in many others you would think the world had gone mad. Streams and lakes are as poisonous as acid. Drink from some of them and you would be eaten out alive from the inside. Whole sections of the country are blighted and contaminated. It might take a thousand years or more before nature restores a balance."

Nate tried to imagine such a nightmarish landscape and could not. "How did all this come to pass?"

"How else? Man's inhumanity to man has always been our cardinal sin. One war too many was to blame."

"But how could a war turn lakes to acid or destroy so much land? The worst a cannon can do is blow a hole in the ground."

Blade knew he had already revealed too much, but it helped to talk. "Where I come from, war is much different than it is here. There are weapons that could wipe out every last man, woman, and child on the planet."

The mountain man was tempted to accuse the giant of exaggerating. Lord knows, all mountain men loved to tell a tall tale as much as the next fellow. But this was just too much to swallow.

"I know you won't believe me," Blade said.

"But think back in history. Once, war was waged with swords and slingshots. Then came bows and arrows and spears. Now they use guns and cannons. The next step will be bigger guns, bigger cannons. After that will come bombs and poison gas. Chemical warfare weapons won't be far behind."

Nate's brow furrowed. The giant was talking strangely again. What was "chemical warfare?" Did men run around throwing chemicals at one another?

Blade sighed. "At times it seems as if there's no end to our capacity to destroy ourselves. Just when things are going smoothly, along comes another madman who can't leave well enough alone. Each is worse than the last."

"This man you're after, the one you told us about last night. Can he do all these terrible things?"

"There's no limit to what Thanatos can do. Of all the menaces I've ever gone up against, he's the worst."

The giant fell silent. To keep him talking, Nate commented, "I knew a mountain man once who went bad. His name was Bill Zeigler. He turned cannibal."

Blade saw little similarity between a petty man-eater and a fiend who wiped out thousands without batting an eye. He did not bother to point it out. The magnitude of the Dark Lord's evil was impossible to comprehend unless someone had seen it firsthand.

Over in the grass, Winona had taken some pemmican from her parfleche and given it to Evelyn. While her daughter munched, she helped herself to a small piece. One of the horses nickered and she glanced at them. They were fine, but well beyond them, on the hill to the south, a spark of sunlight flared.

"Husband!" Winona said, rising, her Hawken in hand. She sought a repeat of the flash, but there was none.

The tone his wife used brought Nate King on the run. "What is it?" he asked, looking in the same direction she was.

Winona told him. Zach and the giant also came over. The four of them studied the crest of the hill with no result.

"Want me to go take a look-see?" Zach volunteered.

"No, Stalking Coyote," Winona said, using her son's Shoshone name. "It is best that we stick together. If they are hostile, we will know it soon enough."

Nate scooped his daughter into his arms and made for their mounts. "We'll head out onto the plain, then turn south. It will be hard for anyone to sneak up on us out there."

In single file they descended the hammock to a winding gully that brought them out at the east end of the meadow Blade had seen from the rim. The deer were gone. They crossed to a line of pines. Once they were among the trees, the mountain man reined up.

"Maybe we should lay for them here. If they're careless, we can catch them in the open and have the advantage of cover," Nate proposed.

Winona quickly climbed down. She led three of their horses into cover. Zach brought the other mounts and the pack animal. "Stay with them so they will not run off," she instructed him. Gunfire would not spook her husband's stallion or her mare, but the other horses were not quite as dependable.

"Ahhh, Ma," Zach groused, unwilling to miss any of the excitement should those who were shadowing them prove to be hostile.

"Do as you're told," Winona said sternly. Sometimes it seemed that the older her son got, the more trouble he gave her. Carrying Blue Flower, she rejoined the men who had crouched behind tree trunks. She picked one near her man.

Blade wondered if they weren't overreacting. Winona might have glimpsed the reflection of sunlight off of something other than metal. Rock outcroppings with quartz in them were common at that elevation. Many other rocks had shiny surfaces that would act just like a mirror if the angle were right.

It was then that a branch snapped in the forest on the other side of the meadow. Blade's doubt vanished. He pulled back the bolt on the Commando. Seconds later riders materialized among the foliage. He lost count at fifteen and estimated there were closer to thirty. The foremost reached the opposite tree line and stopped.

They were Indians. Husky warriors, primarily, wearing buckskins for the most part. Their faces were painted. The shields some carried also bore symbols of various sorts. To a man, they had shaved their heads except for strips of hair down the middle. The style reminded Blade of a Mohawk, only in this instance the hair style was more like a spiked frill. He had to admit that it lent them a fierce aspect.

"Pawnees," Nate said with animosity. Of all the tribes, he liked the Pawnees the least. They were a treacherous bunch. While they professed friendship for all whites, they were not above killing trappers they found traveling through their territory if they thought they could get away with it with impunity. He had been their captive once, and he harbored a grudge.

"What are they doing so far west?" Winona said. The Pawnees lived in established villages on the eastern plains and rarely ventured to the foothills.

"Hunting for Arapahoes or Cheyennes would be my guess," Nate said. Those two tribes regarded the Pawnees as bitter enemies. Every spring and summer war parties from both sides would raid the other.

"What do you intend to do?" Blade asked softly.

Winona raised her Hawken and braced it against the bole to steady her aim. "We will kill as many of them as we can and hope it delays the rest long enough for us to escape."

Blade glanced at her. She had not impressed him as the bloodthirsty type, yet here she was preparing to slay others without giving them a chance to explain or defend themselves. "Maybe they don't intend to harm us. Shouldn't we talk to them and find out what they want before we start shooting?"

Nate shook his head. "You don't know the Pawnees like we do. Trust us. The only reason they're shadowing us is to wipe us out, take our scalps, and steal everything we own." He elevated his own rifle.

Blade watched the lead Pawnees venture into the meadow. He had never liked slaying men from ambush. There had to be a better way. "Let me try," he said, stepping into the open.

"No!" Nate said, but it was too late. In dismay he saw the giant walk from the pines and halt. The Pawnees did likewise, clustering together. They did not know what to make of the stranger and jabbered excitedly.

"Is his brain in a whirl?" Winona asked. "He will get himself killed."

Nate agreed. There were over thirty Pawnees. They would overwhelm the giant before he could get off two shots. "It's up to us to cover him as best we can," he said, fixing a bead on one of the warriors.

Now that Blade had committed himself, he realized that he did not know how to communicate with the band. The Pawnee tongue was Greek to him. He could only hope that some of them spoke a smidgen of English. "Hello!" he called out. "Why are you following us? What do you want?"

The response was exactly what Nate and Winona knew it would be. One of the Pawnees straightened, hefted a lance, and uttered a war whoop. It was the signal for the entire war party to break into a gallop, fanning out as they bore done on the giant.

Blade did not want to harm any of them. In a last gap effort, he motioned for them to stop, hollering, "No! Go back! You don't stand a prayer!"

Nate admired the giant's courage, but he suspected that his wife was right. Blade's mind must be addled for him to think that he could withstand a war party that size. By the time it took the giant to reload, the Pawnees would be on him.

The Warrior tucked the Commando against his side. He had tried, but it had done no good. The savage countenances of the Indians left no doubt as to their intentions. Finger on the trigger, he let them come a little closer to insure he would not bring down their mounts by mistake. Then he opened up, the .45-caliber SMG, converted to full auto by the Family Gunsmiths, spewing lead in a devastating arc. In his first sweep five of the Pawnees went down, their torsos ruptured by the hail of heavy slugs.

Blade triggered another short burst, conserving his ammo even though he had a ninety-round magazine in the Commando and five spares in his pockets. Two more warriors catapulted off their mounts. He swiveled to drop others, but the Pawnees were breaking to the right and left, fleeing in what could only be called stark terror. They looked back at him as if he were some sort of demon.

At first Blade did not get why. When he raised the Commando higher and several of the warriors literally cringed against their mounts, he understood. It was his weapon. No one in that day and age had ever set eyes on an SMG. Single-shot rifles and pistols were the rule. A weapon that could spit dozens of rounds in under a minute must seem supernatural to the astonished war party.

The Pawnees were not the only ones amazed. Nate and Winona shared astounded expressions. Neither had ever seen nor heard of any gun that could do as the giant's had just done.

His ears ringing, Nate rose and walked from the trees. Shiny metal objects littered the ground at the giant's feet. Picking one up, he sniffed the open end. The scent was like that of the black powder he used in his Hawken, yet also different.

The war party did not stop once it reached the woods. In panicked flight, the Pawnees kept on going and soon were lost from view high on a hill. They showed no sign of stopping.

Blade felt sorry for the men he had slain. He had tried to warn them that they did not stand a chance, but they wouldn't listen. Now seven bodies dotted the meadow. Several riderless horses were nearby.

The giant glanced at his companions and was startled by how they were staring at him. Or, rather, by how they were staring at the Commando.

"Where did you get a gun like that?" Winona bluntly asked. She had to have one. A gun that could fire more than one shot at a time would enable her to protect her loved ones from any threat that might arise.

Blade was at a loss to explain. In order not to appear rude, he said, "They are quite common where I come from, but they are not available here."

"Could I send for one?" Winona asked, recalling the time her man had her pick a shawl and a pair of scissors from a catalogue, as he called it. A friend going to St. Louis had taken the order. When he returned, he had brought the articles with him.

"I'm afraid not," Blade said. Ejecting the magazine, he checked how many rounds were left, then slapped it back in. The simple act had added to the amazement of the Kings, who stepped forward to observe closely.

Nate held out the shiny object he had retrieved. "What is this for?"

Blade took out the magazine again, removed an unspent round, and handed it to the mountain man. "Compare them," he said. "See the lead at one end? That's the bullet. The whole thing is called a cartridge. Think of it as a miniature cannon and you'll get an idea how it works."

The Warrior stopped. He had already disclosed too much. Revealing secrets from the future might have an adverse effect on the past. What if an unscrupulous person were to gain such knowledge?

Then again, it seemed to Blade that the future was the future and nothing could ever change it. If it could be altered, if his traveling back in time derailed the sequence of events that led to the future he knew, then the future he knew would never have existed in the first place. The fact that it did indicated his time traveling was actually part and parcel of the very past that constituted the foundation for events yet to be.

"Where *do* you come from?" Nate inquired.

Blade was spared having to answer by a loud groan. Together they cautiously approached the bodies. Five of the seven were dead. One warrior had three holes in his chest but was still breathing, each breath a ragged gasp that by rights should have been his final one. The last Pawnee had taken a slug in the shoulder and his collar bone was broken. He also had a deep gash in his neck and a crease in his skull.

"I will finish this one," Winona said, drawing her butcher knife.

Blade moved between her and the prostrate Pawnee. "He poses no threat to us now. You can't just kill him in cold blood."

"He would gleefully slay us if the situation were reversed," Winona noted. The giant's squeamish nature was ironic, given his size. She hoped his weakness would not get all of them into trouble if they were attacked again. "You must stop thinking as a white man thinks and think instead as a Shoshone. Otherwise a hostile warrior from another tribe will slit your throat and make off with your hair."

"That may be," Blade said, "but I refuse to shoot down someone who can't fight back."

Winona frowned. "Then you will not last long in the wilderness." White behavior never failed to mystify her. They could be so bold, so outright arrogant, while at the same time so blindly trusting, so foolishly gullible. It was a paradox she had never been able to unravel.

Suddenly the wounded Pawnee lunged erect, drawing a knife as he rose. Only Winona saw him. Her husband was bent over the other stricken warrior. The giant was facing her. She saw the Pawnee spear the knife at Blade's back. Automatically, she cried, "Look out!" while shoving him aside.

Blade was caught off guard. He glimpsed the Pawnee, felt the man brush against him. He realized a knife had been thrust at his back and missed. But it did not miss Winona. She had saved him at her own expense. The blade sheared into her side, doubling her over.

The Pawnee wrenched the knife out and cocked it to stab again.

Without thinking, Blade drew his right Bowie, his hand flashing out, the steel caressing the Pawnee's neck. The man gave a convulsive start, staggered, tried to turn on him, then keeled over. Blood spouted in a torrent.

Nate had heard his wife's cry. He turned just as she was stabbed. "Winona!" he shouted, bounding to her as she crumpled. He caught her and lowered her to the ground. She sagged against him, quivering, her teeth clenched. He did not need to ask how bad it was.

Burning pain filled Winona from her ribs to her hips. Her hand was sticky where it covered the wound. "That should not have happened," she said. "I was stupid."

Blade sank beside her. "I'm to blame. I shouldn't have turned my back on him."

Winona mustered a wan smile. "You're learning," she said. The pain was growing worse, not slackening. She tried to rise but dizziness and her husband prevented her.

"Stay still until I've examined you," Nate directed, gently laying her on her back. Prying apart the four-inch slit in her buckskin dress, he found that the blade had entered her just below her right ribs. If it had missed vital organs, she would live. Provided infection did not set in. "We'll head home as soon as I've bandaged you."

"No," Winona said. "We go on." When Nate opened his mouth to object, she silenced him by placing a finger on his lips. "What if I weaken and cannot ride? You would need to make a travois and haul me back up the foothills into the mountains. It would take you almost as long as it will to reach Bent's Fort. We are almost to the plain. There it is flat. If you must drag me, it will be easier."

Nate did not like it one bit. She was right, but he did not like it. The deciding factor was that the Bent brothers had a man on their staff who was the next best thing to a genuine sawbones. He'd be of great help if the worst came to pass. "As you wish," he reluctantly agreed. "Don't move while I fetch wood for a fire."

"I'll do it," Blade said, hastening off. Guilt racked him. If he had let Winona do as she wanted, the Pawnee would not have stabbed her. He shuddered to think that the kindness the Kings had shown him might cost them the life of their loved one.

Chapter Thirteen

Geronimo and Old Hugh had barely settled themselves on their bellies in a thicket when the war party arrived. Hooves clumped dully as the warriors filed into the cottonwoods in small groups. At their forefront was a man Geronimo recognized: the warrior who had tried to kill him.

"That's Mad Bull hisself," Old Hugh whispered. "If that varmint catches our scent, we're goners."

Geronimo studied the warriors. So these were Blackfeet. It was a mild shock to discover that the tribe had survived the cataclysm. Apparently they had reverted to the traditions of their ancestors. Now that he had time to think about it, their clothing, weapons, and the style in which they wore their hair was exactly like the artistic reproductions and photographs he had so often admired in ancient history texts in the Family library. It was uncanny.

The old trapper extended his rifle. "I've half a mind to make wolf meat of that buzzard just for the hell of it. He's done aggravated me more than any heathen alive."

"No!" Geronimo said, placing a hand on the barrel. "Do that and we'll have them all down on us. I thought you wanted to get out of this alive?"

"I do, I reckon," Old Hugh admitted. "But it galls me to pass up a perfect shot. I may never get another chance at the bastard."

The Blackfeet neared the spring. Mad Bull rode in the lead, a lance in his left hand. Evidently, he had not returned to the site of his clash with Geronimo for his bow.

The Warrior felt a peculiar longing, an urge to reveal himself, to somehow let the Blackfeet know that there was a bond between them, that their blood ran in his veins. His practical side discarded the idea as reckless. Mad Bull had already tried to kill him once. The man would not hesitate to try a second time.

Old Hugh continued to mutter, even with the war party so close. Only he muttered quieter than before, his words only audible to Geronimo.

"Blamed upstarts! If they were friendly like the Shoshones and the Flatheads, it'd be a heap easier for us mountanee men to earn a livin'."

"You said yourself that this is their country," Geronimo reminded him. "How can you blame them for protecting what is theirs?"

"Whose side are you on?" Old Hugh rejoined, then blinked. "Oh. Almost forgot. You're part Injun yourself." His eye jiggled. "Well, I won't hold it against you. I've known a few decent breeds in my time."

"How white of you."

Old Hugh scrunched up his nose. "You're not one of those breeds who thinks the white half of him ain't worth a soggy buffalo chip, are you?"

"I am proud of the heritage on both sides of my family," Geronimo informed him.

"Your heritage, eh?" the trapper said, and snickered so loud that Geronimo was certain the Blackfeet would hear him. But they didn't. "That's a highfalutin word to be throwin' around. But I've got news for you, sonny. Britches are britches. It don't matter if a man fancies himself royalty or if he's a common field hand, he still has to pull 'em down to take a shit. Know what I mean?"

Geronimo nodded. He did not care to be distracted any longer by the old man's chatter with the Blackfeet so close. All of them had dismounted. Some were drinking, some tending to their horses, and a few were gathering wood to build a fire. They were going to spend the night, then.

Old Hugh noticed the same thing. "Look at those devils, playin' right into our hands! About the middle of the night we'll slip out and help ourselves to a couple of their horses. If we do it right, we'll be long gone before they miss 'em."

The animals were tied to the west of the water,

only ten feet or so from the fire a stocky warrior was making. Two other Blackfeet dumped armloads of dry wood next to him. Another pair, armed with bows, were talking to Mad Bull. Presently, they turned and came around the spring, heading straight for the thicket.

"They're huntin' game for their supper," Old Hugh whispered, flattening. "If they spot us, the jig is up."

Geronimo followed the trapper's example and molded his body to the ground. The thicket was dense enough and big enough that it should conceal them nicely unless the hunters made a point of peering into it. Which was exactly what they did. Arrows notched to their sinew strings, one moved to the right, one to the left. They crouched to scour the depths for rabbits or grouse or whatever.

The sun had nearly set. Twilight was poised to claim the land, and the shadows had lengthened accordingly. Geronimo was in deep shade. Only his left arm and leg were exposed. Since his fatigues were green, he blended in so well that it was unlikely they would see him.

The Blackfoot on the right gave up and stood. He turned to move on and the other warrior started to straighten when the unforeseen occurred.

Old Hugh sneezed.

Immediately, the two Blackfeet hunkered and sought the source, calling out to their fellow braves. Mad Bull and every last member of the war party came on the run, quickly encircling the thicket.

Geronimo glanced at Old Hugh, who

shrugged. There was no escape now, short of battling their way out.

Mad Bull barked in the Blackfoot tongue, going on at some length while poking his lance into the thicket. It was over six feet long but too short to reach the Warrior or the trapper.

Old Hugh fluttered his lips. "I reckon we don't have any choice, sonny. They know we're here. He says if we don't come out with our arms in the air, they're going to set fire to the thicket and smoke us out."

"We can make a run for it," Geronimo said.

"Me with my gimp leg? Are you loco?" Old Hugh rose on his elbows and called out in a language that had to be Blackfoot. "I told the coyotes that we're comin' out," he said to Geronimo.

Geronimo balked. He had no wish to harm the Blackfeet if he could help it, but neither was he willing to give up without a fight. He was convinced that if he cut loose with the FNC he could drop fully half of them before they knew what hit them. The rest, though, might nail Old Hugh, or get lucky and put an arrow into him.

"Why are you dawdlin'?" the trapper asked. "I may not think much of Mad Bull, but I'd never dispute that he's a man of his word. Hustle along, sonny, or we'll be fried porcupines." He crawled to where he could rise into a crouch, his Hawken held over his head to demonstrate he would not resist.

It seemed to Geronimo that Old Hugh was giving up much too tamely. He'd have thought the old-timer had more gumption. Several Blackfeet had arrows trained on Hugh, so further resistance was out of the question. Much against his better judgement, Geronimo showed himself and soon stood beside the trapper at the edge of the their hiding place.

Mad Bull seemed startled to find the Warrior there. Wagging his lance, he motioned to show that Geronimo should discard the FNC. Not until Geronimo set it down did he visibly relax and reacquire his cocky air.

A younger warrior relieved Geronimo of his revolver and tomahawk. Others gathered around to fondle the Arminius, marveling at it as if they had never seen a revolver before. A heavy-set warrior helped himself to the tomahawk and gave it a few test swings.

Mad Bull stood in front of Old Hugh, sneering. He addressed the trapper, using a combination of Blackfoot and hand gestures. It was sign language, but Mad Bull's fingers flew so fast that Geronimo had a hard time making sense of what was said. He need not have tried. Old Hugh translated.

"You didn't tell me that you and this heathen were acquainted, sonny. Seems that he has a mad on over something you did to him. He wants me to tell you that before he's done you'll beg him to put you out of your misery."

"Tell him he talks big when he has the advantage," Geronimo said. "I challenge him to put down his lance and meet me on equal terms, man to man."

Old Hugh laughed. "One on one? Where do you think you are? England? The Queensbury rules hardly apply here, friend. Mad Bull can do with us as he sees fit."

"Tell him anyway," Geronimo insisted.

"It's your funeral." The trapper conveyed the message.

Mad Bull darkened, a storm cloud ready to burst. Stepping over to the Warrior, he regarded Geronimo with contempt. He spoke for a while, accenting his remarks with gestures.

"I won't bother to repeat it all," Old Hugh said. "Suffice it to say he just called you every dirty name he could think of. He also said it was a nice try, but he's not about to do you honor by meeting you in personal combat. You don't deserve it."

"Tell him he's a coward."

"I do and he'll wallop you."

"Tell him anyway."

The trapper shrugged. "Some folks just never learn." He did as the Warrior requested.

No sooner were the words out of Old Hugh's mouth than Mad Bull hauled off and hit Geronimo across the face. Oddly, the Blackfoot resorted to an open hand rather than a fist. The blow stung, but Geronimo stood firm and matched the Blackfoot's glare. "Tell him that my ten-year-old hits harder than he does."

"Do you want to die? Is that what this is about?"

"Also tell him that he is an insult to his people, that no true Blackfoot would refuse a personal challenge."

Old Hugh grinned. "It's been nice knowin' you, sonny. You're a mite strange, even for a breed, but you've got grit. Too bad you don't have the brains to go along with it."

The next blow was a punch, delivered to the pit of Geronimo's stomach. He doubled over but did not go down. Struggling for breath, he told the trapper, "Now tell him that if they are going to kill me, to get it over with. But say that I want one of the others to do the job. It would shame me to have a coward take my life."

The trapper hesitated. "You didn't by any chance escape from a madhouse not long ago, did you?"

"Say it just as I told you."

The insult was too much. Mad Bull hissed and started to elevate the lance. But he checked his swing when he realized that the other warriors were staring at him, and that the collective look in their eyes hinted at confirmation of the Warrior's accusation. Slowly, the lance lowered. Mad Bull was now the color of a strawberry, and his lips twitched as if he were on the verge of a fit.

Geronimo seized the moment. "Now say this, and say it quickly." He collected his thoughts. "I have long respected the Blackfeet. I have long believed they are people of honor, that their warriors are the bravest anywhere. Say that I challenge them to prove me right by agreeing to ritual combat between Mad Bull and me."

"They'll never go for it, sonny. Why should they when they hold all the cards?"

"*Do it.*"

The Blackfeet listened attentively. Mad Bull snorted, but the others were somber as they clustered and consulted. An argument broke out between several warriors and Mad Bull. The upshot was that Mad Bull whirled on Old Hugh and vehemently spat a reply.

"Well, I'll be!" the trapper exclaimed in awe. "I never would have thought they'd fall for it, but they have. Mad Bull has accepted your challenge. You'll fight him at dawn. If you win, we get to go free." He looked at Geronimo. "How did you know they'd go along? Most everyone else who has fallen into their clutches has been tortured, then rubbed out."

"I know how they think," Geronimo said, and let it go at that. He did not resist when he was hustled close to the fire and tied hand and foot. Old Hugh was plopped down next to him and given the same treatment. Once they were bound, the Blackfeet lost interest in them and gathered around the fire. The same pair who had gone off hunting did so again.

"We're still breathin'," Old Hugh said, mostly to himself. "Will wonders never cease!"

"How is your leg?" Geronimo asked. The bleeding had resumed, a thin if steady trickle.

"I'll live. I've been hurt worse, like the time a she-bear with cubs caught me nappin' up near the Tetons. That bitch took a chunk out of my side big enough to gag a horse. Remind me to take off my shirt sometime and show you."

"I'll take your word for it."

Old Hugh glanced at the Blackfeet, then leaned toward the Warrior to whisper, "You've done right fine so far. Be ready tomorrow when I make my move."

"What are you talking about?" Geronimo responded, afraid the trapper would jeopardize his scheme to free them both. "There's no need for you to do anything. I can beat Mad Bull."

"Goliath thought the same about David and look where it got him." Hugh shook his head. "Any man who straddles fences is bound to get gouged in the butt. Me, I like to keep my fate in my own hands."

Geronimo grew more worried. "All you have to do is play along and we'll both be let loose. There need not be any bloodshed."

"Anyone ever tell you that you're livin' in a dream world?" Old Hugh said. "These are Blackfeet we're dealin' with, the biggest pack of liars ever bred. So what if Mad Bull promised we'd go free? Do you really expect him to let it get around that he was beaten by a breed? He'd never live it down."

"The others will not let him break his word."

Old Hugh was tickled by the statement. "It's not as if he took a blood oath or anything. These are Injuns, friend. They don't hold to the same standards white folks do. They talk with two tongues and never bat an eye."

Geronimo held his peace. It would be pointless to debate the issue with someone so set in his ways. Leaning back on his elbows, he contemplated the state of affairs. One of the Blackfeet was examining his revolver. Mad Bull had the FNC in his lap and was fiddling with the bolt. "You'd think they had never handled firearms before," he commented.

"That reminds me," Hugh said. "I've been meanin' to ask. Where did you get those guns of yours? I've never seen their like in all my born days."

Geronimo shifted onto his side. "I've heard that rifles and pistols can be hard to come by out here."

"What's so hard about it? Just go to St. Louis, look up the Hawken brothers, and they'll make you a spankin' new rifle. Won't have to wait more than a week or two—less if they have some on hand." Hugh grinned. "Ain't progress grand? I never thought I've live to see 1840, but I'm glad I did."

The Warrior was not certain he had heard correctly. "What was that you just said?"

The trapper repeated himself, adding, "Why? What's the matter? What year did you think it was?"

"You just claimed it's 1840."

"And it is. I know it for a fact because I was in St. Louis a year ago and saw a calender on the wall of the shop where we bought our Newhouses."

"Eighteen forty?" Geronimo said, waiting for the old-timer to cackle at his little joke.

"You'd make a fine parrot, son. I hear tell that some of them birds will say whatever we do over and over. 'Course, '1840' ain't half as interestin' as 'Polly wants to get drunk and fall flat on her face.'"

Geronimo smiled at the older man's antics. Imagine. Trying to persuade him that it was hundreds of years in the past. Then he glanced at the Blackfeet. He thought of the virgin land, of the pure air. He remembered the metal grid in the Dark Tower. A shudder passed through him.

"You catchin' a cold, sonny?" Old Hugh asked. "All of a sudden you look as peaked as a corpse."

Geronimo did not answer. He barely uttered two words the rest of the night, even when Mad Bull came over to inspect his fatigues and plucked at the pockets but did not figure out how to unfasten them.

Old Hugh tired of trying to get him to talk. Midnight came and went. Most of the Blackfeet had dozed off, and Old Hugh was snoring like a drunken sailor. Geronimo lay staring at the stars, feeling lost and confused and not a little scared, at a loss to explain how Thanatos had accomplished the devil deed he had.

Immersed in introspection, the Warrior lost track of the passage of time. He should sleep, should rest for the conflict with Mad Bull, but he was too high strung, too overwrought by the incredible revelation that explained everything that had happened to him since he awoke after stepping into the metal cage.

"What of Cynthia?" Geronimo said to himself at about two in the morning. He closed his eyes and curled into a ball, wishing he could go to sleep and wake up in the morning to find that it was all a bizarre dream. It had to be, didn't it? Time travel was impossible.

Geronimo napped. He was sure he had only slept for a few minutes when a rough shake on the shoulder brought him back to the reality he would rather not deal with. A Blackfoot had awakened him.

It was dawn.

The war party was astir. Mad Bull sat crosslegged by himself at the far end of the spring. His eyes were closed, and he was singing quietly.

"It's his death song. Just in case, I reckon."

A night on the hard ground had not affected Old Hugh much. His hair was no more disheveled than it had been, his buckskins just as rumpled. Yawning, he scratched an armpit.

Geronimo felt sluggish. Lack of sleep and food

was the cause, along with the jolt to his system on learning the truth. That was not all. When he sat up, his arms and legs nearly buckled. His circulation had been constricted for so many hours that they were next to useless. He moved them as much as the rope allowed, but it did not get his blood flowing again.

Several Blackfeet, holding knives, surrounded the captives. Both were hoisted to their feet. Old Hugh was carted to a tree and shoved flat. He sat up, his back to the trunk.

Geronimo was carried to the center of the cleared space and unceremoniously dumped. A warrior cut the ropes, smirked at him, and stood back.

To restore his arms and legs to normal, Geronimo tried to rise. Crippling anguish racked him. His legs were so weak they would not support his weight, his arms so weak that he could not lift them. Tingling broke out in his wrists and spread rapidly up his arms to his shoulders. It was almost pleasant at first, but the pleasure soon faded. In its stead was exquisite pain.

The same sensation began at Geronimo's ankles and spread up his legs. He felt paralyzed. He would be helpless if attacked.

At that moment, Mad Bull came toward him. In each hand the Blackfoot held unusual weapons. They were clubs, thicker at the top than at the bottom. Imbedded in the tip of each and slanted at right angles was a wicked metal spike.

"Eyedaggs," Old Hugh informed him. "They can take out your eyes, puncture your lungs, or shear clear through to the brain pan. Watch your step, sonny. That crafty varmint wouldn't have picked them unless he was as good with them as a wolverine is with its claws."

Geronimo made a supreme effort to stand. It was in vain. The pain had not increased, but neither had it abated. He could barely lift his arms; his legs had a mind of their own.

"You'd better quit nappin', friend, or you're liable to sprout a new nostril."

Mad Bull halted a few yards away. He hefted the two clubs, picked the one he liked, and tossed the other down beside the Warrior. A string of sentences were addressed to Geronimo, who shook his head to signify that he did not understand.

"The scamp said that he's lookin' forward to rippin' your eyeballs out and feedin' them to the ants," Hugh explained. "He says that you're scum. He would not soil his hands on you if you had not challenged his honor as a warrior."

"How nice," Geronimo quipped, struggling to extend his hands as far as they would go.

"That's not all, sonny. He thinks that of the two of you, you're the coward. He wants to know to which tribe you owe the blood in your veins. He thinks it is must the Snakes or the Crows, since both are craven."

"It is neither," Geronimo said, rolling onto his stomach and pressing his hands against the earth. The pain increased, but he had to make his muscles respond or he was as good as dead. "I am part Blackfoot."

Old Hugh was so surprised that he neglected to translate. "You're what?"

"You heard me. Tell them."

The disclosure sparked an angry outburst from

Mad Bull and heated discussion among the others. Mad Bull took a step, shaking the eyedagg in a threatening manner.

"He says that you're a liar," Old Hugh reported. "He believes that you're mockin' him, and he takes it as an insult." The trapper thrust out both arms. "Look out!"

The warning was not needed. Geronimo saw the Blackfoot raise the eyedagg and spring.

Chapter Fourteen

The zombie filled the cell's doorway, preventing escape. White fingers hooked like talons, it shuffled toward the trapped gunfighter. Not the slightest trace of life shimmered in its blank eyes. Its face was a marble mask, the mask of undead death.

Hickok did not have his cherished Pythons or the Marlin, but that did not render him defenseless. Every Warrior was required to study hand-to-hand combat techniques under the tutelage of the most skilled martial artist in the Family, Rikki-Tikki-Tavi. Hickok had always been an adept pupil.

Suddenly launching himself at the lumbering specter, Hickok planted a kick on the knee that would have brought a normal human crashing to the floor. Whipping around, he delivered a backhand to the zombie's cheek. It was like hitting a wet sack of grain. The zombie kept coming, maneuvering to drive him into a corner where he would not be able to evade it.

"Try this on for size, hombre," Hickok said. He executed a spin kick, smashing the creature's jaw, but it did no more to deter the shambling horror than the other blows had done. The thing shuffled closer, its hooked fingers reaching for his throat.

The Warrior ducked and rammed a fist into the zombie's gut. The flesh yielded, absorbing the blow much as a sponge would do. He tried to back pedal before the creature could grapple with him, but the thing was on him too rapidly. An iron hand closed on his arm, another sought his windpipe.

Hickok flung himself backward. He collided with the wall, attempted to slide to the right, and found himself boxed in. Inadvertently, he had done just as the zombie wanted and trapped himself in the corner. The only way out was through the Dark Lord's abomination.

The creature's dirty fingernails clutched at Hickok's buckskin shirt below his neck. He swatted at the zombie's forearm but could not dislodge it. Suddenly his skin creeped with gooseflesh. The thing had a grip on his throat, its icy flesh pressing into his.

Hickok hated to be touched by zombies. They were cold and clammy. They gave off a faint, of-

203

fensive odor that brought to mind bubbling chemicals in a laboratory vat. Combined, it made their hideous features all the more unnerving.

He whipped to the left, holding the zombie by the arm. It slammed into the wall but did not slacken its hold. He drove his knuckles into its chin, into a cheek. The zombie was not fazed. In desperation he resorted to the oldest and dirtiest trick in the book. He pumped his knee into its groin. He might as well have struck a eunuch.

Inexorably, the zombie clung on. It solidified its grip, its fingernails biting deep. Its dull eyes were devoid of triumph or hate. It did not have the least degree of casual interest in what it was doing. The demented biological and psychological imperatives implanted by Thanatos compelled it to kill, kill, kill, without regard for itself or those it slew.

Hickok's breath was choked off. He pummeled the thing's arm, striving to snap it. When that failed, he spun away from the wall and let himself fall. Gravity and his momentum pulled the zombie down on top of him. Or it would have, had he not jammed his feet into the creature's gut and heaved.

With a loud thud, the zombie flew into the wall, tottered, and nearly fell.

The Warrior scrambled erect, hurtling out the doorway with the thing in pursuit. He raced along the narrow hallway to the next door. The office was undisturbed except for a few papers that had been knocked off the desk. On the floor by a chair lay the lawdog, his head bent at an unnatural angle.

Hickok glanced back. The scarred zombie was

still coming, moving as fast as any of its kind could, its gait all the more ungainly when it attempted to run. He slammed the door shut, threw a metal bolt. That should buy him a little time.

Dashing to a desk, Hickok yanked open the top drawer. It contained a sheath of papers, a quill pen, and odds and ends. No guns. He tried the next drawer and the next.

A resounding crash reverberated through the building. The zombie had smashed into the door. It did so again. The jamb bulged and cracked.

Hickok spied a rifle propped in the far corner. He darted over. It was another Hawken and he had no way of telling if it was loaded or not. The zombie was staring at him through the barred window high in the door. He thumbed back the hammer, aimed, and squeezed. A mocking click was the only sound.

The creature renewed its onslaught. This time the door itself cracked.

Casting the Hawken aside, Hickok scoured the office. There were no gun racks such as the Family had in their Armory. Across the room, though, stood an oak cabinet, much the worse for wear. Flying to it, he tried the handle. It was locked.

Hickok bounded to the dead lawman. As he knelt to search the man's pockets, the zombie battered the door once more. The door partially buckled, the top hinge breaking. The creature shoved, getting a shoulder between the door and the jamb. Its unholy gaze never left the Warrior.

Hickok found a plug of tobacco in a pants pocket, a folding knife in another. He tried the shirt, smiling when his fingers wrapped around the unmistakable contours of a small key. Jerking it out, he scooted to the cabinet.

The zombie was wedged fast but had not given up. Thrashing and kicking, it slowly forced the door wider. The next instant the other hinge gave way and the thing was through. Arms out, it stalked in for the kill.

Stay calm! Hickok told himself. If he didn't let the thing rattle him, he could do what had to be done. Inserting the key, he twisted. The lock was old and stubborn. It creaked but did not open. He tried again, the scrape of soles a reminder, as if any were really needed, that he had almost run out of time.

The Warrior jiggled the key. The stubborn lock obliged, and he pulled the door wide. Inside on the left hung a coat and a spare shirt. Leaning against the coat was his Marlin. On a small shelf rested a sight for sore eyes—both Colts.

Hickok grabbed them and turned, cocking the pistols as he pivoted. The zombie reached him just as he swung around. Icy fingers zeroed in on his neck.

The creature's mouth hung partly open, a typical trait of the undead breed. Hickok shoved the barrel of his right Python between the man's lips, angled it upward, averted his face, and squeezed the trigger. At the report, the zombie stiffened. Hair, flesh, and brain matter splattered the desk, the body of the constable, and the wall.

The zombie staggered. It feebly raised an arm, then melted to the floor as if made of wax.

Hickok did not waste another second. The shot was bound to draw attention. He twirled the Colts into their holsters, reclaimed the Marlin, and bolted for the door. It opened when he was a step away. Framed in it was another man in uniform, this one a burly customer who took one look at the bodies and leaped to the wrong conclusion.

The lawman jumped at Hickok, balled fists raining down. The Warrior took several punches to the face. Dodging an uppercut, he introduced the man's chin to the stock of his rifle. One swing sufficed. The lawman toppled like a felled tree.

Hickok ran from the jail and nearly collided with a passer-by. The street was crowded with the night life of St. Louis. A few of the nearest pedestrians looked at him, then at the building. Anxious to get out of there before they put two and two together, Hickok hurried off, adopting a nonchalant air to convince the suspicious that everything was all right. The ploy didn't work.

The gunfighter had gone seventy feet when a strident cry brought most people to a stop. He walked briskly on as the fevered yells increased, swelling toward him like the pounding of surf on a shore.

"There's a murderer on the loose!"

"Two men were just killed at the jail!"

"One was a deputy!"

"A blond guy in buckskins is to blame! He should be around here somewhere!"

That last outcry came as Hickok rounded a corner on a side street. The shout of a woman he had just passed echoed along it.

"Here! Over here! I just saw him! He just went down Hancock Street!"

The Warrior fled. It would be a study in futility to try to explain. The outraged citizens of St.

Louis were not about to buy his story that a member of the walking dead had slain their law officer and that he in turn had killed the creature to save himself. He had to elude them.

At the next corner, Hickok turned right. A check showed about a dozen men were after him, only two carrying rifles. He paced himself in order not to tire too soon. Three winding blocks he covered, always picking the darkest streets, but he could not shake the mad pack baying for someone to hold him long enough for them to catch up.

Then someone tried.

Hickok had turned onto a narrow artery that wound down toward the levee. A man in a stovepipe hat and an expensive jacket heard the mob and raised a cane.

"Stop, sir, or I will thrash you!"

"Be serious," Hickok said, slanting to one side. The man evidently was, because he moved to bar the way and swung.

"Take that, you scoundrel!"

A sweep of the Marlin blocked the cane. Hickok followed through by whacking the do-gooder over the skull with the barrel. The stovepipe hat folded like an accordion. So did the man who lay in the gutter groaning.

The delay had permitted several of the fleetest pursuers to close the distance substantially. Hickok was tempted to snap a few shots off to discourage them, but he dared not risk hitting one. They were innocent dupes, not pawns of the Dark Lord. They were only doing what he would have done had the situation been reversed.

It seemed that the lower Hickok went, the

more jammed the streets became. The waterfront district was the hub of the wild goings-on that the city was notorious for between dusk and dawn. Grog shops, taverns, and inns of ill repute were everywhere.

Hickok rounded yet another corner and had to spring against a wall to keep from being run down by a drunk driving a wagon. He hastened on past an inn and was passing a doorway when a slim arm snagged his and he was hauled into Stygian shadow.

"Hold on there, handsome! What's your rush? Wouldn't you like to cuddle some?"

The voice was sweet but the breath was not. It stank of alcohol and decay and who knew what else. Hickok pried at the slim fingers holding his arm. "I'm sorry, ma'am, but I'm married."

"So? What does that have to do with anything?"

The woman's face was a pale blob, her hair flaxen. She leaned forward, her mouth almost brushing his, her breath worse than ever, her ample bosom mashed against his arm.

"Give ole Sally a tumble, Mister. You won't regret it. I've done half the men in this city at one time or another."

Hickok did not see where that was a fact to boast about. "No," he insisted, moving toward the street. The drum of boots and shoes gave him pause. The wolf pack would spot him if he stepped from the shadows. Pushing the street walker into the recessed doorway as far as they could go, he gripped the Marlin, prepared to fight them off.

The prostitute took it as a sign that he had

changed his mind. Tittering drunkenly, she embraced him, her moist lips finding his neck. Her tongue lathered it as if she were intent on licking him clean. She nibbled at his earlobe.

In another moment the mob pounded past. There were twenty or thirty now, mostly men. A few glanced into the doorway. If they saw the gunfighter, they did not connect him with the one they were after.

"Oh!" the woman said, giving a start. "What the devil is that all about?"

"Your guess is as good as mine, ma'am," Hickok said.

From down the block came more cries.

"Which way did he go?"

"I think he went this way."

"No. He went that way."

"You're both wrong. I say he went toward the docks."

"Let's split up. If anyone sees him, fire two shots into the air and the rest of us will come running."

Hickok listened as their footsteps diminished in the distance. By then his neck and ear were sopping wet and the woman had started in on his face, sucking on his jaw as if it were hard candy. It sort of tickled. "That's enough, ma'am," he said. "I have to be going."

"What are you trying to pull? I thought you wanted to cuddle."

"I gave my word to my missus to be true to her when we were hitched, and a man should always keep his word," Hickok detailed. He'd rather extricate himself without the woman causing a fuss. "Surely you can respect that."

The woman placed her hands on her broad hips. "You know what I think? I think you wanted a kiss and a feel without having to pay. That's what I think."

Hickok backed toward the street. "Believe me, nothin' could be further from the truth. If I wasn't married, and if I had any money, I'd take you up on your generous offer." The last was an outright lie, but Hickok did not have time to waste. He thought it would appease her and he could go on his way in peace.

"*What?* You don't have any money?" Sally screeched. "Now I know you were trying to pull a fast one! I have half a mind to let Blackjack know. He don't like it when johns take advantage of his working girls."

Another stride and Hickok would be gone. "My name isn't John, and the last thing I would ever do is try to trick a fine lady such as yourself." He spun and darted from the doorway like a rabbit from a thicket. He didn't have hounds after him, just an irate streetwalker who started to follow, then turned and ran to a shabby building across the way.

Good riddance, Hickok thought. At the first corner he came to, he bore to the right. It would take him to the river, where a belt of trees and brush grew. He could hide out there until dawn. By then the hue and cry would have died down and he could resume his hunt for Thanatos.

None of those Hickok passed looked at him twice other than a few sultry women in tight dresses who gave him come-hither invitations he silently declined.

Out on the Mississippi, boat traffic was heavy.

Steamboats ablaze with lantern light plied the murky water. Some only carried cargo. Others were mobile gambling dens, crowded with residents out enjoying themselves. The tinkle of glasses and laughter pealed constantly.

Hickok wondered what had happened to Kittson, Clyman, and Ogden. He'd never had a chance to thank them properly for all they had done on his behalf.

Ahead was a park. Cutting across it would shave blocks off. Hickok was well into it before he realized that he was the only one there. The park was strangely empty, almost as if it were being shunned.

The Warrior slung the Marlin across his back so his hands would be free. He avoided hedges and areas where trees grew close together. In the center a statue had been erected. Pigeon droppings coated the shoulders. He circled it. That was when three vague shapes reared up out of a flower bed and arrayed themselves in front of him.

"Hold up there, mate," a man with a heavy accent said. "We want to have a word with you."

Hickok had stopped. "Stand aside," he directed. "I'm in no mood to be pestered by polecats."

A man whose shoulders were as broad as a bench found the comment humorous. "We've cornered us a tough one, boys," he taunted. "I reckon we'll have to whittle him down to size to learn him some respect."

The third man gestured. "It's like this, Mister. Your money or your life. Which will it be?"

"None of the above," Hickok quipped. "Go

away before you rile me. My daughter could whip the three of you morons with one arm tied behind her back."

"Is that so?" the biggest of the robbers said. He patted a pistol wedged under his belt. "I'd think twice before I smarted off like you're doin'. You're only makin' this hard on yourself. Give us your purse and you can go your merry way."

"Since when do men tote purses?" Hickok responded.

"Quit stalling, damn you," growled the man with the accent. "Give us your money right this second, governor, or else."

The Warrior sighed. "I've had runs of bad luck before, but nothing to top the past couple of days." He wagged his fingers at them. "Scat or make your play, you mangy low lifes."

They took him at his word. The three cutthroats grabbed for the big flintlocks at their waists. To say they were slow would be an understatement. They were pathetic. Molasses made human. It was not entirely their fault. The fast draw, as it would become known many decades later, had not yet been perfected. In that day and age, unlimbering a pistol and firing was not so much a matter of speed as accuracy. The trio thought they had the edge because they outnumbered their victim. How wrong they were.

Hickok drew, his right Colt leaping up and out before any of the three could pull their weapons. In the blink of an eye, they were covered. Had they froze, or had they let go of their pistols and backed off, that which followed could have been avoided.

"Don't, gents!" Hickok commanded. Either

they misunderstood or they were too cocky. None of them did as he said. Three flintlocks slid out from under three belts and were leveled in his direction.

The gunfighter resorted to a trick he rarely employed. He fanned the Colt, the calloused edge of his hand slapping the hammer once for each brigand. So swiftly did he fire that someone listening nearby would have sworn there had only been one shot. Each slug hit the point he aimed at.

The robbers were dead on their feet, shot through the heart. The tall one whined as his insides turned to mush. Of them all, he was the only one who tried to rise again. It was automatic, a motor response rather than a conscious effort. He got as far as his elbows when the spark of life left him.

Hickok puffed on the end of the barrel. It had been no contest. When he claimed his daughter could have beaten them, he meant it. She was a chip off the old block; one day she might become the greatest Warrior in the long history of the Family.

Verifying the three chowderheads were dead, Hickok began replacing the spent cartridges. Shouts spurred him into reloading on the run.

"Did you hear that?"

"It might be him!"

"Let's check!"

The Warrior selected a maple with a wide trunk to hide behind. At the other end of the park a knot of people appeared. They stayed close together, a man with a long rifle in the lead. It galled Hickok that they were still after him.

Didn't they have anything better to do?

"I don't see anyone."

"Then what was that shootin'?"

"Most likely some fool with too much redeye under his belt."

The vigilantes halted shy of the statue. Hickok entertained the hope that they would not spot the dead men and leave. Once again he was severely disappointed.

"Wait! Look yonder!"

"Are those bodies?"

"It's not a bunch of dogs takin' a nap."

In an agitated hubbub the group descended on the robbers. While they were occupied, Hickok slipped away, availing himself of what cover there was until he came to a street as black as the bottom of a well. Huge buildings, possibly warehouses, lined it. The Mississippi lapped at busy docks only a block away. A thick scent of water and smoke hung in the humid air.

Hickok congratulated himself on having given the vigilantes the slip. Soon he would be at the river and would follow it to the belt of vegetation he had noticed on his entry into the city earlier that day. Tomorrow he would find a hat and a coat to disguise himself so he could scour St. Louis for his recent acquaintances. By then, surely, the hunt would be over.

An alley offered a means of reaching the docks sooner. Sailors were unloading a steamboat that had recently arrived. Others were outfitting a barge.

The Warrior strolled to the end of a vacant pier to savor a rare peaceful moment. Judging by the size of the pilings, the river had to be deep, the current strong. He hunkered to watch a steamboat approach. Fascinated by the bygone vessel, he gazed on her churning paddle wheels and the smoke pouring from her high stacks. So enrapt was he that he did not hear anyone come up behind him, had no warning at all that he was in danger until someone snarled almost in his ear, "No one stiffs a whore of mine, jackass!"

Hickok shoved to his feet and tried to pivot. His head exploded in pain, in vivid fireworks. Vaguely, he felt something connect with his stomach, with his shoulder. His feet left the dock. Cold, clammy water closed over him, jarring him to his core, reviving him as nothing else could have. Staying underwater, he swam away from the pier to thwart anyone hankering to shoot him.

When his lungs were close to bursting, Hickok surfaced, pleased at how cleverly he had outfoxed his attacker. Then he saw the steamboat bearing down on him.

Chapter Fifteen

The King family and the Warrior were a day out from Bent's Fort when the infection set in.

Winona had been doing well. She had not lost too much blood. While weak and pale, she had every reason to think that she would be on her feet shortly after they arrived. Her husband had made her as comfortable as he could on a pine travois covered with blankets, and she was taking small amounts of food regularly to keep her strength up.

Little Evelyn rode with her mother on the triangular platform. Worried sick, the girl refused to leave Winona's side. When Winona wanted anything, all she had to do was say so and Evelyn would yell for the men to stop and tend her.

Zach rode behind the travois in a deep funk. He wanted to wipe the Pawnees out for what they had done. Were it not that his folks needed him, he might have gone off to wage war on the entire nation, single-handed.

Nate King's spirits were no higher. All too well, he knew how deadly even the smallest of wounds could be in the wilderness. Infection was a constant menace. Any cut or scrape could fester and taint a person's blood to where death was inevitable. He fretted about Winona every minute.

Blade shared the mountain man's anxiety. He could not stop blaming himself. His guilt mounted when, late in the afternoon, Evelyn cried out that her mother was burning up.

Nate was first to the travois. A hand to his wife's brow confirmed the worst. She had a raging fever and was caked with sweat. His mouth going dry, he stroked her cheek. She opened her eyes, those lovely eyes he adored, and smiled.

"One of these days you will worry yourself to death, husband. It is not healthy."

"We're making camp so I can get water boiling. We need to get some of that root into you for quelling fevers."

Winona wanted to tell him not to bother, that they could go for miles yet before the sun set, but she could not bring herself to make the effort. She was weak all over, so weak she could not lift a hand and wipe her perspiring brow. She contented herself with saying softly, "I'm sorry." Sorry that she had let herself be stabbed. Sorry that she was being so much of a burden.

"What do you have to be sorry about?" Nate wanted to know, but her eyes closed. Rising, he scanned the plain. It was as flat as a board for as far as the eye could see. "I don't like making camp in the open," he said to himself. At night a fire cold be seen from miles off, and after midnight the wind turned chill.

Blade overheard. "I'll look for a spot close by," he volunteered, applying his reins. His mount broke into a lope. He was actually grateful to have something to do. It took his mind off his mistake, and his predicament.

For the more Blade had thought about the dilemma of being thrust back in time, the more convinced he became that the prospect of seeing his own family again was extremely slim.

It was Thanatos who had rigged the portal or whatever it was as a last ditch resort. The Dark Lord had set whatever controls were involved, then leaped onto the grid just as Blade and his friends burst into the high chamber. Now all of them were trapped in the mid-nineteenth century.

The controls were the key. Unless Blade and the others could gain access to them, the portal could not be recalibrated to send them back to their own time period. Yet they could not gain access unless they *were* sent back. That was the catch. That was the reason Blade was tempted to give up hope.

Tempted. But the Warrior still clung to the dream of being returned to where he belonged. So long as life remained, he would never give up. He owed it to Jenny. He owed it to himself.

Blade spotted several buffalo to the east. To the

south the prairie went on forever, unbroken by a single tree or knoll. He figured that he would have to ride halfway to Bent's Fort before he found a sheltered nook in which to camp, but the terrain had a surprise in store. Suddenly the ground in front of him was bisected by a gully. It wasn't steep and it wasn't deep. It was perfect.

Nate was surprised to see the giant wheel and come back after going only a few hundred yards. On hearing the news, he was quick to head for the gully, make camp, and get Winona bundled in blankets next to a small fire. Tearing a strip of buckskin from a spare shirt, he soaked it with water from their water skin and applied it to her hot brow. She mumbled but did not wake up.

Zach rummaged in a parfleche for some pemmican. "I guess this will have to do for supper, Pa," he said, handing a piece to his sister.

Nate wished they had fresh meat for soup and commented as much. "We have to get something into your mother, and soup would go down easier than anything else."

"I saw some buffalo a while ago," Blade mentioned, pointing. "They're not that far."

"Let's take a gander." Nate climbed to the top of the gully. The sun had set, but it was still light enough for them to see that the buffalo had wandered off. "Too bad," he said. It would not be difficult to track them, but Nate was not about to stray from his wife's side.

"How about if Blade and I go look for game?" Zach proposed. "There are plenty of rabbits and other critters in this high grass."

Nate had been about to make the same suggestion. "Just don't stay out much after night sets in or you'll have a hard time finding this gully again."

"We'll be fine, Pa," Zach said.

Blade hoped the boy was right. Comparatively speaking, the gully was just a tiny crack in the midst of the limitless plain. Locating it in the dark would be like finding the proverbial needle in a haystack.

The Warrior and Zach rode to the southwest. Miles to the west were the foothills. Beyond, the stark silhouette of the mountains formed a jagged crown. Blade memorized the outline of the peaks to orient himself.

Neither spoke, since doing so might scare off their quarry. Half an hour went by. The only creatures they saw were sparrows and a snake.

"Maybe we'll have better luck if we split up," Zach proposed, veering to the left.

Blade did not like the idea of being separated, but he did not feel he had the right to object. He kept tabs on the boy, growing concerned when Zach was almost out of sight. It had grown much too dark to suit him. He turned.

The night swallowed Zach up. Blade marked the spot, or thought he did, but when he got there the boy was nowhere to be found. He hesitated to call out for fear of scaring off any animals that might be in the area.

A godsend in the form of a rifle shot steered Blade to where Zach should be. Drawing rein, he rose in the stirrups and strained to hear whatever sounds the stiff breeze bore his way. The rustling of grass and the distant yip of a coyote were all.

Blade waited. The boy was bound to come back soon. Minutes elapsed, however, and Zach failed to appear. It was now so dark that Blade could barely see grass a few yards away.

"Zach?" the Warrior called. "Did you get something?"

The wind intensified. There was no answer.

"Zach? Where are you?" Blade hollered. Jabbing his heels into his horse, he rode in a wide circle, shouting the boy's name every few yards. Zach never replied, leaving Blade in a quandary. Either he had misjudged where the shot came from, or Zach had already headed back.

Blade decided that the latter must be the case. The boy was probably so worried about his mother that he had raced off to the gully rather than linger until Blade showed. Accordingly, the Warrior turned to the north. He held the horse to a walk to reduce the risk from prairie dog burrows and ruts.

It seemed to take hours. Blade had not fully appreciated how far afield they had drifted. He was beginning to dread that he had overshot his companions when the pale gleam of flickering firelight guided him right to them. The moment he came to the rim, he knew that something was dreadfully wrong.

Nate King glanced up. He had just wet the buckskin for the tenth time and was gently laying it on Winona's forehead. Evelyn lay curled nearby, napping. "What did you coons bag?" he asked.

Blade wanted to crawl into one of those prairie dog dens and pull the dirt in after him. "Isn't your son here?"

Shooting to his feet, Nate ran to the crest. "No. Don't tell me that you drifted apart!"

"It was his idea," Blade said lamely. He told about the shot he had heard, and his search for Zach, concluding with, "I'll go back and look for him."

The mountain man pondered, tugging at his beard. His son was more competent than most in the wild, thanks to a lifetime of living in the mountains and the tutelage of their Shoshone kin. If Zach was all right, he would show up sooner or later. It was wiser to sit tight and wait for him than to blunder around in the dark. "No, you'd best stay with us," he said, and shared his insight.

"I hope you're right," was Blade's response. Sliding from the saddle, he led the sorrel into the gully and tethered it with the other animals.

A while earlier Nate had broken out the coffeepot and had coffee simmering. Now, taking the cook pot from a pack, he filled it halfway with water, broke pemmican and jerky into small bits and dropped them in, then set the pot beside the flames. Squatting next to his wife, he felt her cheeks and neck. The fever was higher than ever.

Blade did not know what to say. First the mother, now the son. If anything happened to Zach, he would help Nate get Winona to the post and go his own way. They had suffered enough on his account.

Nate noticed the giant's expression. It did not take a gypsy fortune teller to know what Blade was thinking. Clearing his throat, he said, "Life on the frontier is never easy. From one day to the next, we never know if we'll be around to greet the next dawn."

"Why don't you take your family back East?

They would be a lot safer there."

"Think so?" Nate added fuel to the fire. "Do you have any idea how many whites hate Indians just because of the color of their skin? No matter where we went, my wife and the children would be treated like dirt. I couldn't abide that."

Blade had not thought of that. Bigotry, apparently, was a timeless evil.

"Besides, what would we do for a living? I used to be an accountant. But I couldn't stand to sit behind a desk all day scribbling in a ledger. I don't know how I did it back then." Nate stirred the broth a few times. "We'd be outcasts in the States. Zach and Evelyn would be branded as breeds. It might break their spirits in time, and I'd hate to see that happen."

"So would I," Blade acknowledged.

Nate encompassed the prairie and the Rockies with a sweep of his brawny arm. "Out here it's different. We're free to do as we please. We're beholden to no one. Zach can grow up to be a trapper or a trader or a Shoshone warrior if he wants, and no one will hold it against him. Evelyn can do as she pleases. They can be happy."

"Every father wants the best for his kids," Blade said when the mountain man paused.

"Sure, it's mighty dangerous. But it comes with the territory. If a person wants to live wild and free, they have to live where the wild, free things do. Bears and hostiles and accidents are just Nature's way of keeping us on our toes."

Blade perceived that Nate was talking to take his mind off his missing son. He did his part by saying, "Where I come from, it's not much different. Our Home is surrounded by a stockade, and every time we step outside the walls we have to watch out for scavengers and mutants and worse. There are even chemical clouds that eat a person alive."

Nate looked at him. "I don't mind telling you, friend. Where you come from sounds like no place on God's green earth."

How could Blade possibly explain? He was mulling it over when hoofbeats brought both of them to their feet. Together they rushed to the top of the gully. It was a lone rider, coming on fast. "It's your boy," he declared happily.

"Thank God," Nate breathed. He had been debating whether to leave his wife and daughter in the giant's care so he could go hunt for his son. Now they were reunited. All was well.

In a few seconds the horse materialized, slowing as it neared them.

"It's Zach's animal, sure enough," Nate said, his elation gone. "But where is he?"

The animal stopped. Sweat caked its heaving sides, proving it had run long and hard. Nate gripped the reins and pulled the horse down into the light. They both saw the dark stain on the saddle at the same time.

It was blood.

The Dark Lord was pleased. His fledgling scheme was unfolding according to schedule. In a year he would be the undisputed master of every acre of land west of the Mississippi. In two years he would conquer the rest of the United States and set himself up as dictator for life.

It was ironic, Thanatos reflected, that he had to travel back in time to achieve the dream de-

nied him in his own time period. The Freedom
Federation had thwarted his ambition in the future. Here, there was no organized resistance to
speak of. The U.S. government hardly counted.
Their pathetic primitive weapons would be no
match for the invincible horde of red zombies he
would unleash on the unsuspecting world.

At the moment, Thanatos was strolling north
through the city. He was hungry again. He had
to find a nice secluded area so there would be no
witnesses. The street he was on was deserted. To
his right were spacious homes, to his left a thick
tangle of briars and trees. Tilting his head, he
sniffed to catch the scent of any prospective supper. Instead, he caught the scent of something
else. For the first time in many years, he was subject to surprise.

Whirling, Thanatos faced the wall of vegetation. "Show yourselves or face my wrath."

A thicket rustled. Bel Aram slithered into the
open, bowing his serpentine head. "Oh, great
one!" he intoned, "it is a joy for your humble ser-
vant to behold you again."

Again the thicket shook, limbs rending loudly.
The massive bulk of Ghanata reared onto two
legs. "Lord and master," the minotaur rasped.
"We have found you."

The Dark Lord crossed the street, his cloak
flapping in the wind. He had not given instructions for any of his minions to follow him into
the time stream. By rights he should snuff out
their worthless lives for their effrontery. "What
are you doing here?" he bluntly demanded.

Bel Aram promptly answered. He did not trust
the bumbling minotaur to present the facts ac-

curately and lucidly, and it would not do to make their feared sovereign mad at them. When he was done, he tensed for flight. Loyal he was, but he refused to die at his creator's hands as so many of his brethren had done.

Thanatos did not give their devotion a second thought. They were supposed to give their lives in his defense. It was designed into their genetic codes. He would spare them in part because it secretly pleased him to have the companionship of his children, in part because they would be of great use in the days ahead. His human lieutenants, the flotsam of St. Louis, the dregs of mortal society, were weak vessels who would stick by him only as long as it was in their best interests. The mutants would never betray him.

Another reason had to do with the Indian tribes Thanatos intended to subjugate. Having the mutants at his side would inspire such fear that most of the Indians were bound to give up without a fight.

"I am glad you have joined me," Thanatos said. "Now that you are here, you, Bel Aram, will be my right hand, and you, Ghanata, my left."

"We have news, sire," Bel Aram said, and reported on the two Warriors.

"So Blade is here, as well as that insufferably cocky gunfighter?" Thanatos said. "Their friend, Geronimo, must have also made it through. Slaying them will be our top priority. They are the only ones who stand a chance of thwarting me."

"You have only to say the word, master," Ghanata rumbled.

Bel Aram was hard pressed not to smirk. Minotaurs were forever sucking up to the Dark Lord, bending over backwards to lick his boots, as it were. "Sire, permit me a question?" he requested.

Thanatos double-checked the street. "You have it," he replied.

"There is a mystery that puzzles me—one only you can shed light on," Bel Aram said. "All of us entered the portal at about the same time, yet each of was deposited at a different point. You here in this city, Ghanata out on the grasslands, myself in the mountains. How can that be?"

Thanatos loved to discourse on his genius. Sadly, too few were able to comprehend its full extent. But he was more than pleased to make an attempt. "We were not deposited so much as we were washed ashore."

"Sire?"

"Think of time as a stream. To us, in our daily lives, it seems to move slowly, but in reality it flows as swiftly as a raging river. And what happens when you jump into one?"

Ghanata thought he knew the answer. "We get wet!" he said proudly.

"What else?" Thanatos asked. He could afford to be patient with minotaurs. They were, after all, only as smart as he had bred them to be.

"The current carries us downriver," Bel Aram offered.

The Dark Lord nodded. "Exactly." He heard a dog bark up the street and looked but no one was approaching. "Now imagine this. You take three sticks, and you throw them one after the other into the swift current. Will they all end up at the same spot?"

"No," Bel Aram said. "They will be washed ashore wherever the current carries them."

"So it is with time travel. Unless we were physically linked in some manner, we would not be cast out of the time stream at the exact same point."

"I understand now, sire. Thank you."

Ghanata scratched his broad head. "I have a question, too, master. Will we be going back to the Tower soon? I miss my feed trough."

During the six months of intense training the minotaurs underwent after emerging from the vats that spawned them, they were housed in communal dorms deep in the bowels of the Dark Tower. They wore identical insignia, slept in identical cots, trained in identical combat arenas. It was only fitting, since they were also identical in appearance.

In one respect, and in one respect only, were the mighty brutes permitted a trace of individuality. Each minotaur was assigned a personal feed trough, and the bull-men were free to embellish it in any manner they wanted.

The feed troughs were carried to the mess hall at feeding time. One by one, the horned mutants would file past a gigantic dispensing machine that squirted a set amount of slop into every trough at the press of a button. The minotaurs then filed to their assigned places, got down on all fours, and tore into the chemical concoction with gusto.

Snake hybrids such as Bel Aram found the display of hoggish behavior revolting. Which was why none of his kind were ever found in the mess hall during the feeding hour for their bullish kindred.

After each minotaur graduated from the basic

combat course, it was housed in a dorm higher in the Tower. The only item it was allowed to take was its feed trough. Frequently, the great brutes became so attached to their troughs that if another minotaur were to touch theirs, they would battle the offender to the death.

"Will we, master?" Ghanata repeated when Thanatos did not respond.

"Time will tell," the Dark Lord said dryly. "As for your trough, don't worry. So long as the Tower endures, so will it." To the south the wheels of a carriage rattled. Thanatos spoke briskly, "There is little time. We dare not risk your being discovered. The local inhabitants would accuse us of sorcery and burn us at the stake."

"How stupid!" Ghanata declared.

"I want both of you to wait for me west of the city, where the main trail west passes a stand of willows. You will be safe there."

Bel Aram bowed. "Might this humble one ask how long you want us to wait?"

"Until I arrive." Thanatos dismissed them with an imperious wave. "Now off with you. My supper is almost here."

Obedient as ever, the pair of mutants melted into the undergrowth. Thanatos did the same, but only a few steps. Standing stock still, he waited as the carriage came around a bend. Open at the front, it contained a driver on top and a young man and woman out for a starlit ride. It was to be their last.

Thanatos sniffed, inhaling their meaty odor. His mouth watered, his lips quivered. He was so hungry that his stomach growled as he sprang.

Chapter Sixteen

Hickok's reflexes were second to none. As with the other Warriors, over the years he had honed them to a superb degree. So the very instant that he set eyes on the oncoming steamboat, he dived, stroking furiously, seeking to reach the bottom of the Mississippi before the immense craft plowed over him.

The dull splash of its paddles filled his ears as water tried to fill his nose and mouth. He had sucked all the air he could into his lungs, but would it be enough?

The gunfighter knifed cleanly into the murky depths. He worried that the Colts would fall out, but he could not slow down to hold onto them. A wave buffeted him, a wave created by the water the steamboat displaced. He surged against it, fighting for every inch he gained.

The gloom darkened. The immense bulk of the vessel blotted out what little light there was just as the moon blots out the sun during an eclipse. Hickok was left in total blackness. He could not tell which way was up or which way was down. Kicking and pumping, he felt smaller shock waves roll over him. The steamboat had to be close. So very, very close.

Something tugged at his arms, at his shoulders, something sinuous and clammy. Hickok realized it was underwater growth of some kind and slowed to avoid becoming hopelessly entangled. Twisting, he saw the dim shape of the steamboat passing directly over him. It seemed to fill the river. He shuddered to think what would occur if it unexpectedly stopped. It would be impossible for him to reach the surface.

But the gargantuan craft paddled onward, the swish of its paddles like the sound a scythe makes when it slashes into grain, only magnified many times. The darkness lessened, though not by much.

Hickok had done it. He pushed off, rising swiftly. Or trying to until he was brought up short by a tug on his right ankle. He yanked without effect.

One of the plants had wrapped around his leg.

Bending, Hickok groped his ankle. It felt as if a thick, slimy cord had him in its grasp. He pried and tugged, but the plant clung to him as if it wanted to drown him for invading its watery domain. His chest hurt, his lungs burned. He had to break free.

Gripping the plant with both hands, Hickok heaved upward. It gave a little. He heaved again and it gave a little more. But plainly the roots were firm and deep. He'd die before he pulled the thing out.

The water was darkening again. Hickok did not know if it was from another passing craft or because his eyesight was dimming. His chest was on the verge of exploding.

The gloom prevented the gunfighter from determining if the plant was wrapped clockwise or counterclockwise. Straightening, he held his arms close to his sides and spun like a child's top, clockwise. The clinging growth grew tighter. Immediately, he spun in the opposite direction. Gradually, the cord loosened, but not enough for him to slip loose.

Exhausted, his senses reeling, Hickok tried one final time. He would not have the strength to attempt it again if it did not work. He spun but weakly. On the second spin the growth released him.

Raising his arms aloft, Hickok lanced toward the surface, kicking in a frenzy of rising desperation. The world around him blinked to black, returned to normal, and blinked out again. He kept on kicking, refusing to give up, as tenacious at the point of dying as he had always been in life.

Suddenly the heavy pressure and clammy sensation on his head and shoulders was gone. He sucked in sweet, invigorating air, the sweetest ever. No matter that it was humid and dank and smelled of fish and less savory odors. He breathed in deep, filling his lungs with the rich oxygen they craved.

Hickok's vision cleared. The steamboat was dozens of yards away, fading into a fog bank. It hit him that another might come along at any moment. He should get to shore while he still could.

The gunman began to swim, then remembered his Pythons and slapped his hands on his holsters. Miraculously, they were both still there. He was so happy, he laughed as he stroked for the shoreline, angling to the left of the docks in case the man who had knocked him into the river was still there.

Wisps of fog floated over him, thickening as he neared the riverbank. Hickok's feet struck the bottom and he stood. His legs were wobbly from his ordeal. Stumbling onto dry land, he knelt and bowed his head, grateful to be alive.

The fog was growing heavier by the moment. Hickok was glad. It was unlikely any nosy bystanders had noticed his plight. The last thing he wanted was to draw attention to himself with three groups of vigilantes who were prowling the city, out for his blood.

Recovering enough to stand, the Warrior walked up a grassy incline. Ahead grew the belt of vegetation he had been trying to reach all along. Smiling at the fickle whims of fate, he hiked his gunbelt, aligned the Marlin's sling so it did not pinch him under his arm, and started to cross a strip of grass.

A rush of footsteps warned Hickok that he was not out of the frying pan yet. He pivoted. Charging him was a burly man holding a long metal bar. It had to be the same one who had attacked him on the dock. Blackjack, the woman had said. Her pimp.

As a general rule Hickok did not relish resorting to his hands and feet in a fight. Although he was a skilled fighter, he would much rather rely on the Colts. They were swift and efficient. They settled disputes with a minimum of fuss.

But in this instance, in light of what the man had done and what it had almost cost him, Hickok was more than willing to make an exception. Dodging Blackjack's swing, he drove his left fist into the man's gut. Blackjack grunted and slowed, but he was tough. He swung again. Hickok skipped out of range.

The man paused. His clothes were the best money could buy. A fancy hat perched on his head, and a gold watch chain hung from a vest pocket. His cape was embroidered with fur at the collar. His looks belied his livelihood, making him appear more like a prosperous businessman than what he really was. "You're a tough bastard, I'll give you that," he said.

Hickok did not answer. Crouching, he glided to the left, seeking an opening. His fists would do his talking for him.

"I figured you were a goner for sure when that steamboat went over you," Blackjack said. "Now I have to do this the hard way." His chunky features distorted, he closed in.

A whisper of air fanned Hickok as he ducked. He shot upward as if flung from a catapult, his knuckles catching the pimp full on the jaw and rocking the man backward. Darting beyond reach of the metal bar, he tensed.

Blackjack spat blood. "Damn your bones!" he growled. "You're more bother than you're worth." When Hickok ventured no reply, he grew angrier. "Stinking cheat! You shouldn't have tried to stiff my girl."

"I didn't."

"That isn't what she claims. And I'd believe her over you any day."

"No wonder. She's a born liar and you're scum. That makes you a perfect match."

The pimp, infuriated, bounded in, aiming a blow at Hickok's head. Hickok ducked again, but not low enough. He forgot about the Marlin. The rifle's barrel extended a full foot above his right shoulder, and the bar clipped it just hard enough to unbalance him. He fell onto one knee.

"Now you get yours!"

Blackjack reared to finish him. But no Warrior would fall so easily. Hickok tucked into a roll, barreling into the pimp's legs. Blackjack was upended and squawked as he toppled. He landed beside Hickok, and the gunfighter grabbed the bar.

"Son of a bitch!" Blackjack raged, striving to wrench his makeshift weapon from Hickok's grasp. Hickok held on, shifted, and flicked a knee into the man's gut. It weakened Blackjack, though not enough for Hickok to claim sole possession of the bar.

Suddenly letting go, the Warrior rolled to safety and rose. He found himself at the brink of the incline. Eight feet below the Mississippi licked the shore. Fog swirled around him, momentarily obscuring his adversary.

The pimp capitalized on the situation by springing forward. His figure was just a spectral blur, but Hickok managed to evade the bar by jumping backward. Blackjack came after him, the bar whizzing loudly. It missed twice. By then they were near the water's edge. Just as Hickok had planned.

Blackjack was growing more incensed with each miss. Swearing lividly, he thrust instead of swung, spearing at Hickok's sternum, playing right into Hickok's hands. The gunfighter seized the bar and spun, using it as a lever, pumping down and around. Before the startled pimp quite knew what was happening, Hickok had flung him into the river.

It was only knee deep. Blackjack rose, sputtering and cursing.

Hickok leaped and tackled the man about the chest. They both went down, Hickok on top, the bar between them. The Warrior pressed, gouging the bar into the pimp's throat, pinning Blackjack, pushing him under the surface. Blackjack fought frantically and struggled to keep his face above water. Wheezing and coughing, he glowered at the gunman.

"I'll kill you yet, damn you!"

"You have it backwards," Hickok calmly said, and shoved the pimp under again. This time he applied his full weight, sliding forward on Blackjack's chest so the man could not heave him off. Blackjack tried, though. He bucked. He kicked. He thrashed. The muddy water roiled around them. Bubbles rose, turning to froth. They increased, then subsided. Finally the water was still, as still as the lifeless form that bobbed to the surface when Hickok rose and stepped back onto land.

Somewhere, a boat whistle blew.

Hickok watched the body float off, borne by the current. It was soon out of sight in the fog. Tired enough to sleep for a week, he plodded to the grass. Laying where they had scuffled was the pimp's cape. Hickok helped himself to it. Not only could he tear off a few strips to dry and clean his hardware, but it would make a dandy blanket to keep him warm until morning.

The Warrior entered the trees, looking for a spot to bed down. He saw a pine tree to his right that seemed promising. It had low branches and was ringed by high weeds. As he bent for a better look, he sensed that he was not alone. Pivoting, he saw a shadowy figure so close that he could have reached out and touched it. His right hand stabbed to his Colt. The pistol flashed clear.

The figure made no threatening moves. Whoever it was just stood there, undisturbed by the gun pointed at him.

"Step closer so I can see you, polecat," Hickok directed. "If you're a pard of Blackjack's, you're welcome to join him in hell."

The man obeyed, saying, "Do not shoot me, white-eye. I am not worth the lead."

Hickok could not hide his surprise. It was an old Indian, wrinkled and skinny and gnarled, and dressed in buckskins that had seen better days. Much better days. "What are you doing skulkin' around in the middle of the night? Fixin' to scalp folks?"

The old Indian chuckled. "What use would I have for scalps, Lightning Hands? My people never take them. They stink up the lodge and always have lice and sometimes fleas." He gave a little shudder. "I hate fleas. They make me itch and scratch. Then I must take a bath whether I want one or not."

There was no weapon on the man that Hickok could see. Slowly lowering the Colt, he asked, "Who are you?"

"In your language, it is He Who Eats Dog. My real name is—" and here the aged warrior said a long word in his native tongue that Hickok could not begin to pronounce. It had more syllables than a centipede had legs.

"What tribe are you from?"

Again the man answered in his own tongue, switching to English to say, "But your kind sometimes call us Caws, and at other times they call us the Kanzas Indians. They cannot seem to make up their minds."

Hickok caught a whiff of alcohol and wondered if the old Indian was drunk. "You still haven't answered my question about what you're doing here, old-timer."

He Who Eats Dog gestured at the vegetation. "I live here. Come. I will show you."

The Warrior allowed himself to be led a score of yards into the woodland. In a small clearing sat a rickety lean-to. Spread out under it was a threadbare blanket. Charred embers marked where a fire had been.

"My home, Lightning Hands," He Who Eats Dog said.

"Why do you keep callin' me that?"

The Indian stepped to a stack of dead branches and began breaking some in half to place on top of the embers. "I did not see your hand move when you drew your gun. So you must have hands like lightning. It is a good name, don't you think? I like it better than the one the whites gave me."

Hickok had no idea what to think. The old man was friendly enough, but he might have an ulterior motive. "Did you see what happened back there?"

"I saw nothing. Besides, the man you killed will not be missed. He was bad. He sold women as if they were pigs or chickens. That is not right."

Sitting across from the Caw, Hickok unslung his rifle and wiped it with the hem of the cape. He Who Eats Dog took a worn leather bag from the lean-to. Among other things, it contained a flint and steel. The Caw struck the two together. Before long the kindling caught and flames flared. In the glare, Hickok noticed that the man was even older than he had thought. He Who Eats Dog had to be eighty if he was a day.

"We never sell our women to the whites, as some tribes do to the north," the warrior had continued. "We are content to be left alone to grow our corn, pumpkins, and beans. But of course we are not left alone. The Pawnees are always raiding us, trying to wipe us out. The Arikaras, too, a few times. Now, *they* like to take scalps. And fingers and toes and ears. As for your kind, they treat us as if we are less than the dirt under their feet. Why should that be?"

Before Hickok could answer, the Caw went on. "I have often thought that the Great Mystery must have had too much redeye to drink when this world was made. It is the only thing that makes sense."

"Hold on there," Hickok interjected to get a word in edgewise. "Back up a bit. Why aren't you off livin' with your own people? And where did you learn to speak English so well?"

He Who Eats Dog reached into the big bag again. This time he produced a bottle. A whiskey bottle. Taking a swig, he sighed in contentment. "I like how it warms me inside. If I drink enough, it makes me feel silly. I forget all my problems and can laugh again. Of all the gifts the white man brought my people, this is the best." He patted the bottle.

"Is that why you stay in St. Louis? So you can get your hands on liquor when you have a hankerin'?"

The Caw smacked his lips. "I came many winters ago to visit my friend. Maybe you have heard of him. He is quite famous. His name was Clark."

"Can't say as I have."

He Who Eats Dog's bushy brows rose. "No? He went with another famous man, Lewis, to the Great Water where the sun sets. I thought every white man knew about them. The Great Father in Washington gave them medals. For a long while it was all the whites talked about."

It dawned on Hickok who he was referring to. "Do you mean Lewis and Clark? The first white men to reach the Pacific Ocean overland? The two who went with Sacagawea?"

The old man's expression brightened. "She was a fine woman, that one. Always kind. Always ready to help you if you were sick. I never saw why she took Charbonneau as her man. He was a scoundrel, that one. A lazy scoundrel. He worked her to death."

The implications of the innocent comments jolted Hickok. He had read about Lewis and Clark during his Schooling days, naturally, but never in his wildest dreams would he have imagined meeting someone who actually knew one of them personally.

The talkative Caw continued. "William Clark was a great friend, a great man. He cared for my people, cared for all Indians."

Hickok vaguely recollected that after the famed expedition, Clark became superintendent of Indian Affairs and later governor of the Missouri Territory.

"He took me to a man who teaches your tongue, Lightning Hands. I have worked long and hard to learn it. It is hard, because your tongue is so strange, so like the chirping of birds."

The Warrior had never heard anyone describe English quite that way before. "So what do you do with your life, besides sit around drinkin' yourself silly?"

"You do not approve. When you have seen as many winters as I have, you will think that being silly is a fine state to be in. It is better than being dead."

Hickok had no argument there. "Don't you get homesick to see your people?"

"Sometimes. I do not miss our lodges, though. They are small, shaped like eggs, made of willow branches covered with buffalo hides. They are always dirty. When it rains, you get wet. When it is cold, you are cold even if you have a fire." The ancient Indian frowned. "When I was young, I thought my lodge was the best lodge ever. I could not believe anyone would have a better one."

Hickok leaned back.

"Then I came here and saw the wooden lodges of your kind. My friend, Clark, invited me to his. It was as big as our whole village, always clean and warm. I learned an important lesson that day." He looked at the gunfighter. "Wooden floors are better than dirt floors."

The Warrior's stomach picked that moment to growl. Without being asked, He Who Eats Dog rummaged in his leather bag and handed him a small piece of jerky. "I'm obliged, old-timer," Hickok said.

"What do you do, Lightning Hands, when you are not drowning bad men and eating other people's food?"

"I'm huntin' a demon," Hickok remarked.

He Who Eats Dog perked up. "Really? That is interesting. One of your priests told me about them, but in my heart I did not believe him. I would like to see this one with my own eyes."

"It would be the last sight you ever saw. That varmint is plumb loco. He'd as soon make wolf meat of you as look at you."

"Is he like us, this demon? The priest said that some demons have horns and scales and wings. There is a story among my people of a man who had wings. It was long ago, before you whites were made. Maybe this demon is the Wind Walker."

"Hardly," Hickok said. "I've never gotten a gander at him when he wasn't wearin' his big cloak, but from what I hear he's only partly human."

The rumor was that Thanatos had performed hazardous genetic experiments on himself after he had been refused permission by the Civilized Zone government. Something had gone horribly wrong, transforming his body and snapping his mind.

"Where is his wooden lodge? I want to go see this marvel for myself."

Hickok swallowed. "Aren't I gettin' my point across? You have to treat Thanatos as you would a mean bear. Go anywhere near him and he'll rip you to pieces."

"Not me. I will stare at him and he will not touch me."

"How's that?"

The Caw poked in his bag again. A long pipe and a small pouch were taken out. "When I was young, I learned that an enemy will not hurt me if I stare at him and think in my head that he must not. It works on animals, too."

The Warrior laughed. He'd heard some mighty tall tales in his time, but this one took the cake. "Sound's like a neat trick to have up my sleeve. Maybe you can teach me."

"You poke fun at me, as you whites say," He Who Eats Dog said, "but it is true. I have tried it twice, once when the Pawnees attacked our village and once when a rattlesnake was going to bite me."

The old Caw's gaze turned inward. "I had seen just twenty snows when the Pawnees came. It was dawn. They were stealing the few horses we had and someone saw them and gave a cry. Soon all the men were fighting. I ran to the spot and saw a Pawnee smash my best friend over the head with a war club."

Hickok finished the jerky. It was barely enough to whet his appetite, but the Indian was so poor that he was not about to impose and ask for more.

"I was mad, madder than I had ever been," He Who Eats Dog said. "That Pawnee turned on me, and I looked at him and thought in my head that I wanted him to go away. And do you know what? He did. He turned and ran off without bashing my head in as he had Spotted Elk's."

"He might have done it for any number of reasons," the Warrior said.

He Who Eats Dog did not seem to hear. "Then there was the snake. I was out hunting when I came to some rocks. The rattlesnake was sunning itself and it reared up to bite me. I could not move. So I looked at it and thought to myself that it should go away and leave me alone. When I did, it crawled off," he concluded proudly.

"You were lucky, old-timer. Nothing more. Your trick wouldn't work on the Dark Lord."

He Who Eats Dog was tamping dry leaves into the bowl of his pipe. "We will see. I want you to take me to see this demon."

"How can I? I don't know where he is myself. I have to hunt him down."

"Then we will find him together. I will ask him to show me his horns or wings or whatever he has. It will prove the priest did not speak with two tongues."

A stiff gust of wind caused Hickok to shiver. "Forget it, old-timer," he said. "In the mornin' I'm going off by my lonesome to settle accounts with that buzzard. And that's final."

He Who Eats Dog would not take no for an answer. "We shall see, Lightning Hands," he said, his mouth curling in a strange little smile. "We shall see."

Chapter Seventeen

Geronimo girded every sinew in his partially paralyzed body as the enraged Blackfoot warrior bore down on him. His legs were too sluggish from having his circulation cut off for so long for him to stand. His arms were in too much torment for him to raise them to defend himself. All he could do to avoid being impaled by the eyedagg that Mad Bull streaked at his head was to roll out of harm's way—and that was exactly what he did.

Throwing himself to the left, Geronimo rolled and rolled. The eyedagg thudded into the soil twice, missing him by inches. He would have gone on rolling for as long as it took to recover from being bound, but the clearing ended before that happened. He smacked into a pine, snapping his teeth together, provoking more pain. Just what he needed.

Mad Bull had slowed. He raised his unusual weapon and barked at the Warrior.

"The heathen says not to worry, sonny," Old Hugh called. "He's not fixin' to kill you right off. He wants you to suffer first. So he'll chip at you a piece at a time."

"Tell him he does not deserve to be a Blackfoot," Geronimo answered. "Tell him that he has proven me right. Only a coward attacks a man who cannot defend himself."

Old Hugh was agape. "What are you tryin' to do? Goad him into finishin' you off that much sooner?"

"Just do it!" Geronimo commanded.

Mad Bull glanced at the trapper, growing red in the cheeks as he listened. The visage he turned to the Warrior was one of pure malice.

The delay had proven of benefit. Geronimo could flex his legs, and his fingers moved when he willed them to. He sat up, his back to the tree, his hands clawing into the brown carpet of dead needles under the pine.

Mad Bull gripped the eyedagg with both hands. Agleam with bloodlust, he lunged.

Geronimo was ready. He flung the pine needles into the Blackfoot's face even as he dodged to the right. Mad Bull bellowed and scooted back, swiping a hand at his eyes. It bought Geronimo the precious seconds he needed to push to his feet and dart past the warrior to the other eyedagg. Scooping it up, he confronted his foe.

The Blackfoot leader was incensed. His left eye watered, and dirt smeared his cheek.

The rest of the war party was caught up in the excitement of the clash. They were bantering back and forth, and gesturing, several goading Mad Bull on with shouts of encouragement.

Geronimo warily circled. The eyedagg was lighter than he anticipated, the heft nearly ideal. The shiny six-inch spike looked nasty enough to do in a grizzly. He braced as Mad Bull came at him, bringing the eyedagg up to block a blow lanced at his head. His arms responded as they should. He did not feel fully fit yet, but with each swing more of his strength returned, so that in no time he was his old self. He countered, he attacked. The Blackfoot did the same. They were evenly matched, so much so that for several minutes they waged heated battle with neither drawing blood.

Mad Bull stopped and stepped back. Sweat caked him. He appeared to be puzzled that it was taking him so long to dispatch his enemy.

The war party had largely quieted, the majority sensing that their favorite was not doing as well as they had expected.

Geronimo, without taking his eyes off Mad Bull, called out to Old Hugh. "Tell him that it is not too late to end this madness. Tell him that I have no wish to slay him, that if he lets us go in peace there will be no hard feelings."

The trapper did not reply.

"Hugh?" Geronimo said. "Did you hear me? Do as I say or we will not get out of this alive."

"Oh, I wouldn't worry there, sonny. I have everything well in hand."

There was a new note in the trapper's tone, a strange, biting arrogance out of place for someone who was a bound prisoner. It was so odd that Geronimo glanced around.

Old Hugh was no longer tied. The cut rope at his feet, he stood with a dagger in one hand and a derringer in the other. He aimed the latter at Mad Bull and said something in the Blackfoot tongue that caused all the warriors to freeze. To Geronimo, he said, "I told him that if any of his bucks move, I'll put a ball in his brain." Hugh snickered and wagged the derringer. "It never fails, sonny. Heathens are dumber than dirt. They never think to look under my moccasins for hidden weapons. I always tuck Martha and my pigsticker just under the tops. They've come in mighty handy at times."

Geronimo backed toward the trapper so that if the Blackfeet swarmed them, they could fight side by side.

Old Hugh was enjoying himself. Again he addressed Mad Bull. The leader hesitated, then angrily flung the eyedagg to the ground. After a few moments Mad Bull snapped at his warriors, who were just as reluctant to drop their own weapons but who did so to spare their leader's life.

"Now gather up our effects," Old Hugh said.

It was comforting to hold the FNC again. Geronimo reclaimed the Arminius and his tomahawk next.

Once Old Hugh had his Hawken, he wedged the dagger under his belt and stepped to the middle of the circle. Chuckling, he jabbed the rifle's muzzle into Mad Bull's gut a few times. He said something that made the Blackfoot practically quiver with rage.

Nodding at Geronimo, Hugh said, "Fetch two horses, and be quick about it, friend. One of these simpletons might get the notion to jump us. Then the rest would be on us like a bunch of riled wasps."

Geronimo picked a chestnut for himself, a gray for the trapper. Once mounted, he covered the Blackfeet while Old Hugh climbed on. If looks could kill, both of them would have dropped dead then and there.

The trapper ordered the Blackfeet to move to the middle of the clearing. They did not like doing so, but they complied. Old Hugh winked at Geronimo. "Get set to fan the breeze, sonny. I'm about to make 'em so blamed mad, they'll likely foam at the mouths."

Geronimo was denied the opportunity to ask what the trapper meant. For the very next moment Old Hugh pointed the derringer at Mad Bull and fired. As the warrior crumbled, Old Hugh bawled a lusty war whoop and spurred the gray straight into the Blackfeet, scattering them right and left. Geronimo had no choice but to follow. Several warriors started to cut him off, but they changed their minds when he swung the FNC toward them.

Old Hugh, cackling merrily, sped to where the other horses were. Yipping and hollering, he scattered them while Geronimo covered his back. When the last one had run off, Hugh trotted around the spring and through the trees in a wide loop that brought them out of the stand to the south. Behind them, the furious Blackfeet were venting their anger.

Hugh laughed and slapped his good thigh. "We taught those savages a thing or two, didn't we? Did you see the looks on their faces? They were fit to be tied!"

Geronimo did not share the trapper's sentiments. "There was no need for you to shoot Mad Bull."

Old Hugh arched a brow. "You sure are a puzzlement, neighbor. Here I done you a favor and saved your hide, and all you can do is gripe because I kilt a man who was bound and determined to do the same to you? That's plumb ungrateful, that is."

"I might have been able to reason with him, given time."

The frontiersman snorted. "Hell, sonny. You could talk to ole Mad Bull until Armageddon comes and it wouldn't do you a lick of good. Blackfeet don't cotton to whites or breeds nohow. They want every last one of us dead."

"They can't all be that way. Some must want to live in peace."

"How can you be part Blackfoot and be so danged ignorant of their ways?" Old Hugh rejoined. "There are friendly Injuns, yes. The Shoshones are our friends, and the Flatheads have never laid a finger on a white man. The Crows are nice when it suits 'em. And I've heard there are Injuns in Californy who are as tame as kittens. But they're the exceptions to the rule."

"You're wrong," Geronimo said bluntly.

"Hogwash. You just had a taste of how the Blackfeet feel about us. The Bloods and the Piegans are just as bad. Then there's the Sioux who love to count coup on whites. Down south a ways, there are the Comanches and the Apaches. Try talkin' peace to either of 'em and they'll laugh in your face while they're slittin' your throat."

It perturbed Geronimo greatly, this talk about Native Americans, as they later came to be known, being all too eager to slay anyone who did not share their skin pigment.

He reminded himself that he had to put it in a historical perspective. At one time, many tribes had indeed extolled warfare. Warriors had earned a high standing by earning coup in battle. The more coup, the more prominent they became. Other tribes, notable among them the Apaches, had not counted coup. But warfare had been just as important. Since earliest times, they had lived to raid and steal. Could they be faulted for doing that which their people had done for generation after generation?

Old Hugh had no more to say until over five miles had been covered at a gallop. Checking over a shoulder, he slowed his horse to a walk. "I reckon we can relax a spell, hoss. Those red coons will take awhile to collect their animals."

"Do you think they will come after us?"

"I *know* they will. The Blackfeet ain't about to let us get the better of 'em. They won't let us be so long as we're in their territory. Once we cross the Missouri, we should be safe."

"Should be?"

"Blackfeet are unpredictable, son. If they get a hair up their hind ends, they'd think nothin' of trackin' us all the way to Mexico."

Geronimo had better things to do than spending his days and nights trying to shake a war party of his own ancestors. He had to search for Blade and Hickok. He had to find out if Thanatos was also around somewhere. "Do you have a plan?"

"Sure do. I vote we head for Bent's Fort. It'll take us two weeks or better, but once there we'll be safe. It's the biggest post around. The Blackfeet wouldn't think of pesterin' us there."

"Two weeks? Can't we reach it any faster?"

"Not unless you can flap your arms and fly."

Geronimo regretted there was no mechanized travel in that day and age. Two weeks seemed an eternity. But if Bent's Fort was the hub of frontier activity, it stood to reason that his friends would find their way there eventually. "Bent's Fort it is, then," he said.

"Good." Old Hugh's eye jiggled. "I won't mind the company none. Fact is, a man can get powerful lonesome out here at times. There's so much space it makes you feel right puny." He paused. "You don't snore, do you?"

"Not to my knowledge."

"Good. The last coon I partnered up with was a snorin' fiend. Got so it about drove me out of my mind. But I got lucky. A bear solved the problem for me by bitin' his nose off. It also took half his arm and seven toes, but he lived. And he never snored again." Hugh beamed. "Life's grand, ain't it?"

They rode on, two tiny specks amid a sea of waving grass.

Nate King was well into the foothills when he heard the crack of a hoof on stone. Reining up, he peered through the trees in the direction the sound had come from. By his reckoning, he was no more than an hour behind the Pawnees. He had to be extra careful from then on. His son's life was at stake.

It had torn at Nate's heartstrings to leave his wife and daughter, what with Winona in a help-less fevered state and Evelyn in misery. They were in good hands, though. He had grown to trust the giant enough to know that Blade would never harm them.

Nate's black stallion raised its head, its ears pricked. Below them, riders appeared in a dry wash. Four, in all. Four Pawnees, a dead buck draped over the horse of the last warrior.

The mountain man patted the stallion to calm it so it would not nicker. He let the Pawnees get out of sight, then descended to the wash and trailed them. Overhead, the midday sun blazed. It surprised him that he had found the war party so soon. Evidently, they had made camp nearby. He fretted that they had done so for one reason: to amuse themselves by torturing his son at their leisure.

Many tribes tortured captives. It was not done out of a perverse streak of meanness. Rather, they tested the courage of their enemies by sub-jecting them to the worst torments they could devise.

Nate was careful to avoid flat rocks. The clatter of hooves from above told him that the Pawnees had not left the wash. They were smart, staying below the rim so no one could spot them from a long way off.

The wash climbed to the crest of a ridge, where it ended. From there the four warriors meandered through pines to the opposite slope. It brought them to a narrow valley.

From the top of the ridge, Nate watched them enter a tract of firs. Tendrils of smoke marked the campsite. Taking the stallion in among some saplings, he dismounted, tied the reins to one, then stalked lower on cat's feet, the Hawken primed and cocked.

Nate assumed the Pawnees had posted lookouts and acted accordingly. Deadfalls and thickets afforded ample cover. Reaching the valley floor, he slanted to the left to approach the camp from the south rather than the east. He heard voices long before he saw the small fire and the Pawnees. Most were idling the time away. Two of the hunters were skinning the buck. Lying near the fire was a wounded warrior. They had propped him on a low log and folded a buckskin shirt under his head. He was being tended by a man administering a poultice.

Now Nate comprehended. By rights they should have headed off across the prairie to their village, but they had sought a spot to lie low and aid their stricken fellow. Say what one would about the Pawnees, they did not desert their own.

Zach had been tied to a tree. He bore a big welt on his temple and his shirt was torn, but otherwise he appeared to be fine. His shoulders squared, he glared at the warriors. They took no notice.

Overjoyed at finding his son safe, Nate wormed his way around the camp to within twenty feet of his pride and joy. As yet he had not spotted a sentry. Perhaps the Pawnees believed they had given any pursuers the slip.

Frontier Strike

Just then the wounded man commenced to toss and moan. A slug had cored his chest dangerously close to his heart. It was a wonder he had lasted as long as he had.

The Pawnee with the poultice called out. Two others hurried to the log to hold the wounded man down while the healer finished. It was a lost cause. The wounded Pawnee was growing steadily worse. His breathing became ragged, his chest heaving like a bellows.

From under the low branches of a small pine, Nate monitored their doings. He had half a mind to sneak in, cut Zach loose, and run like hell. It would be futile, though, unless the Pawnees were somehow distracted. Or asleep.

Waiting until nightfall did not appeal to Nate. For one thing, the Pawnees were bound to post a guard then. For another, it meant taking that much longer to return to Winona. He'd rather get Zach out of there as soon as he could.

The healer set the poultice aside, picked up a parfleche, and moved off into the trees to the southwest. The wounded man had quieted, but he trembled from time to time, his lips moving soundlessly.

It was noteworthy that the Pawnees had tied their mounts in a string on the north side of the camp. One end of the rope was tied to a spruce, the other to an oak. Nate silently moved toward the former, lifting his arms and legs as carefully as if he were crawling over eggshells and did not want to break any.

One of the warriors was butchering the buck, slicing a haunch into thick portions. Another cut off thin strips and draped them over a crude frame constructed from thin branches. The meat would be cooked and dried for the war party's long journey home.

Behind the spruce, Nate rose high enough to untie the knot. It was on the left side of the trunk, so he had to expose his hand. He held his fingers close to the bole and pried at the rope with only two fingers. It took longer, but he eventually had the knot almost undone. A tug was all it would take.

Easing onto his stomach once more, Nate went to the oak. A few of the horses spotted him. One sniffed loudly. None whinnied, maybe because the wind was not blowing his scent to them.

This time the knot was on the side of the tree facing the Pawnees. The trunk was wider, though, so Nate could stand and lean against it as he slowly brought his hand around to the knot. Whoever had tied this end of the rope had done a thorough job. There were two knots, he learned, not one, both as tight as could be. He picked and pried, but the first one would not give a fraction.

Drawing his Green River knife, Nate sliced into the rope, partially severing it. Confident he was ready, he began to back into the undergrowth. He peeked past the trunk and saw a warrior rise and walk toward the string. Had the man seen him? Ducking into the undergrowth, he replaced the knife, training his Hawken on the Pawnee.

The warrior stopped beside a dun. He patted it, stroked its neck, spoke softly into its ear. The horse nuzzled him, as affectionate as any dog.

Nate had seen firsthand how attached warriors became to their mounts. Some Shoshones were so fond of their war horses that when there were reports of enemies near their village, they would hustle their war horses into the family's lodges at night to prevent the animals from being stolen.

This was a younger Pawnee, so young that it was probably the first raid he had ever been on. He petted his horse for nigh on fifteen minutes, then gave it a light smack on the rump and rejoined his companions.

Nate had chafed at the delay. Glad he could get on with rescuing his son, he crawled to the pine nearest Zach, picking up a pebble he passed along the way. The boy was no longer glaring at his captors. Either fatigued or depressed, he sat slumped over, his chin resting on his chest.

Cocking an arm, Nate concentrated. He threw the pebble accurately. It hit his son in the shoulder.

Zachary King was so happy to see his father that he nearly cried out in joy. He had begun to despair, to think that he would never see his pa or ma again. All because of a stupid rabbit.

The previous evening, Zach had gone much farther than he intended to after separating from Blade. Realizing how much fresh meat would mean to his mother, he had stubbornly pushed on, refusing to give up until he bagged something for their supper. It had been almost dark when he spied a rabbit that instantly bounded to the southeast. He gave chase. The rabbit soon stopped, but when he attempted to get close enough for a clear shot, it ran off again.

Several times the sequence repeated itself. The rabbit would let Zach get only so close, then off it would race. He was so intent on catching it that he did not pay much attention to anything around him. That had been his undoing.

One last time the rabbit stopped. Zach had slowly stalked it, able to see its ears and nothing else. Just when the entire rabbit was in view and he was taking a steady bead, the grass around him erupted with swarthy forms. The Pawnees had been on him so fast that he could not defend himself. In the brief scuffle his rifle had gone off. That was when one of the warriors hit him in the temple with a war club. Blood had spurted, the world had faded, and the next Zach knew, he was tied to a tree somewhere in the foothills, his head pounding so hard he could barely think straight.

The Pawnees had ignored him. They brought him neither food nor water. He tried to get the attention of several to let them know that he was parched with thirst, but they hardly glanced at him when he called out.

Zach had hoped against hope that his pa or the giant would find him. It couldn't be both, not with the shape his ma was in. His biggest worry was that the Pawnees had concealed their tracks so cleverly, no one would come.

Now, tingling with relief, Zach waited for his pa to give him a clue what to do. He grew alarmed when his father crawled out from under the pine. To reach him, his pa had to cross seven feet of open ground. The Pawnees were bound to notice.

Suddenly a warrior rose and came toward him. Zach had suspected that the raiders would get around to torturing him sooner or later. Just his luck that they chose the moment of his deliverance.

The warrior veered to the left, to where a number of dead branches lay. Gathering an armful, he carried them to the fire.

Zach exhaled. The close call had shaved a year off his life, at least. He glanced back and was stunned to see his father right behind him, sawing at the rope. It parted, and his pa raised a finger to caution him not to move. Nodding, Zach saw his father's gaze go past him, saw his father stiffen.

Two warriors had risen this time. They were heading right for the tree.

Chapter Eighteen

"All this trompin' around has given me a hankerin' for something to drink," Hickok announced. It was frustrating. Over half the day had gone by and there had been no trace of the Dark Lord. He made for a nearby tavern, sidestepping a pile left by a passing horse. "Since you've dogged my steps since sunup, you might as well come on in with me."

"I cannot," He Who Eats Dog said.

Hickok turned. The Caw had been up before he had, waiting for him to set out in search of the "demon." Over and over Hickok had explained that it was none of the Indian's affair, that he did not want the Caw along. Every word had gone in one ear and out the other. When he set off, so did He Who Eats Dog.

The gunfighter had figured that in time the old warrior would grow tired and leave him be, but the Caw seemed to have more energy than he did.

Unless Hickok wanted to shoot the old man, he was stuck with him.

To be fair, He Who Eats Dog had proven useful. He had been the one who rustled up a shabby coat and a moth-eaten cap for the Warrior to wear. The cap made Hickok's hair itch, and the coat stank of sweat and less appealing odors, but they disguised him well enough that he could move about freely.

The deaths of the constable and the zombie were the talk of the city. Hickok had lost count of the number of folks he overheard discussing it. The common consensus was that a prisoner—namely him—had escaped from jail and slain the two men in doing so.

Hickok had not been about to march up to a law officer to try and set things straight. Who in that day and age would believe that a human being could be transformed by arcane science into a murderous automaton? They'd either string him up or lock him away in an asylum somewhere.

So here it was past noon, and Thanatos was proving as elusive as ever.

"Why can't you tag along?" Hickok asked his wizened shadow. "Aren't you thirsty?"

"I am," He Who Eats Dog admitted. "But there are places Indians cannot go. This is one of them."

"Bullpuckey," Hickok grumbled, and grabbed the old man's wrist. "If I want to treat you to a drink, I darn well will." He hauled the Caw through the door and over to a scuffed bar where a skinny man with an Adam's apple the size of a melon and a dirty apron glanced up from a newspaper he was reading.

"You want something, Mister?"

"Two milks. And make it pronto."

The bartender did a double take. He glanced at the Caw, then back at the gunman. "Is this some kind of joke, stranger?"

"Do you see me laughin'?"

Straightening, the bartender leaned on the counter and fixed his dark eyes on Hickok with ill-concealed disdain. "In the first place, you jack-ass, we don't serve milk. Milk is for babies." He pointed at He Who Eats Dog. "In the second place, don't you know better than to waltz in here with a stinking Injun? We don't serve Injuns. Never have, never will."

"See? I told you," the Caw said.

Hickok did not say anything for a few moments. He stood with his head half bowed, his fingers drumming the bar. Then he exploded. His right hand seized the bartender by the front of the shirt even as his left clamped on the back of the man's head. In a swift, precise motion he smashed the bartender's face onto the counter, not once but twice. When he let go, the skinny man staggered back a step, blood pouring from his broken nose and his mashed lips.

"You son of a bitch!" he sputtered.

The right Colt leaped from its holster. As casually as if he were swatting a fly, Hickok used it to club the bartender over the head. The man went down without another word.

Pivoting, Hickok regarded the half-dozen or so patrons. None acted disposed to rise to the bartender's defense. Most wore city clothes and were speechless. A bearded man in buckskins was grinning.

"There's no excuse for poor manners," Hickok said by way of justification. "My mother always said that if you don't have something nice to say, you should keep your mouth shut. Tell that to him when he comes around."

Stepping behind the counter to where a pitcher of water sat, Hickok poured a mug for himself and the Caw and brought them back. "Here. You're a human being just like us whites. That entitles you to drink where you please."

"I thank you, Lightning Hands," He Who Eats Dog said, accepting the mug. His eyes twinkling, he took a swallow. "Your spirit is pure."

"Don't go gettin' mystical on me, Gramps," Hickok said, scanning the shelves. "I'm no more pure than you are." He peered under the counter. "This yo-yo will probably go squawk to the law when he revives. We'd best light a shuck as soon as we're done." Walking to a cabinet, he opened it. "Too bad there isn't any food here. I'm starved. That venison you treated me to last night wasn't enough to feed a mouse."

"It was not venison."

"Buffalo meat?" Hickok asked absently while still searching for something to eat.

"No."

"What then? Did you snare yourself a rabbit?"

"It was dog meat."

About to open another cabinet, Hickok glanced at the old Indian. "You didn't."

He Who Eats Dog shrugged. "A man must eat. There are many dogs that roam this city, dogs no whites want. So I help myself."

Hickok's stomach did flip-flops. "Wonderful," he said, rejoining the Caw. In a few rapid gulps he drained his mug and smacked it on the counter. "Let's skedaddle. The rate we're going, it will take us a month of Sundays to find Thanatos or Lord Seth or whatever he's callin' himself nowadays."

They turned to go. The customer in buckskins, a rough character who sat at a table between them and the door, cleared his throat. "Hold on there, you two."

Hickok drew up short, his hands lowering to his Colts. "We don't want any trouble with you, Mister," he said. "That barkeep only got what was comin' to him."

"No argument there, hoss," the customer said. "Harry always was an uppity bastard. Served him right, it did."

"Then what do you want?"

"My handle's Three-Fingered Tom." He held up his left hand to show that three fingers were gone. A better name would have been Two-Fingered Tom. "I'm partners with a man named Bucktooth Bob. He got himself involved with that Lord Seth. Went off to some secret meetin' all excited, claimin' he was goin' to be filthy rich before long." Three-fingered Tom scowled. "No one seen Bob since. But I've heard rumors. I'd like to talk to this highfalutin lord and get some questions answered."

"You'd be smart to leave it be," Hickok advised. "You have no idea how dangerous the Dark Lord can be."

Three-Fingered Tom held up his hand again. "Dangerous? Mister, I lost these fingers to a Kiowa who jumped me when I was unarmed. He whacked them off, then tried to stab me. Know what I did?" Three-Fingered Tom smiled a cold smile. "I pinned that coyote to the ground and tore out his throat with my bare teeth."

"I would have liked to see that," He Who Eats Dog said. "Neck wounds are always interesting."

Hickok was more interested in something else. "Do you know where Seth is?"

"He's left St. Louis."

"What? Already?"

Three-Fingered Tom stood, retrieving a Hawken that leaned against his table. Three pistols and two knives adorned his belt, as well as a tomahawk. "That's what I've heard. Him and a bunch of others left early this mornin', headin' west. I was of a mind to go after him, but there's a lot of them and only one of me. I might be a hellion in a pinch, but I ain't no fool."

"We're obliged for the information," Hickok said, and began to leave.

"Not so fast," Three-Fingered Tom said. "If you're set on going after him, I want to tag along. Three guns are better than two."

Hickok pondered. Actually, He Who Eats Dog did not count since the only weapon he owned was an old knife. If Thanatos had a pack of killers at his beck and call, Three-Fingered Tom could be of help. "All right, Mister. But just to make it clear. I aim to kill Lord Seth, and anyone who stands in my way."

"Fine by me. Hell, I'll even tear his throat out for you while you hold him down."

He Who Eats Dog smiled. "I would be grateful if you would let me watch. It would be something to tell my grandchildren about."

Three-Fingered Tom jerked the remaining finger on his left hand at the Caw. "Who is this loco old coot, anyhow?"

Hickok made the introductions. The next order of business was to get out of there and as far away from the tavern as they could in the shortest possible time. Half an hour later they approached a stable.

"My horse and pack animal are kept here," Three-Fingered Tom said. "You go fetch your mounts and we'll be off."

"Neither of us owns one," Hickok disclosed. Strangely, it embarrassed him to have to say it.

"You don't own a *horse?*" Three-Fingered Tom was exasperated. "I can understand the Injun. But you're a grown white man!" He blew air between his lips. "I guess that don't leave me much choice. I can lend you my pack horse. We won't be able to take much in the way of fixin's, but it won't matter if we catch up with Lord Seth quickly."

Hickok looked at He Who Eats Dog. "I reckon that leaves you out, old-timer. Sorry."

"I do not need a horse," the Caw said.

"You'd never keep up," Three-Fingered Tom responded. "We'll have to travel hard and fast."

"I will keep up," He Who Eats Dog answered. To Hickok, he said, "You go, friend. Do not worry about me. I will find you." With that, he spun on a heel and was gone, blending into the stream of pedestrians.

"That Injun is a loon," Three-Fingered Tom commented. "How in the hell does he expect to tag along when he's on foot? It can't be done." He headed for the livery. "Come on, Hickok. Seth already has more than half a day's start on us. We'll be lucky if we overtake him by tomorrow night."

The pack horse turned out to be a sturdy bay. Since Three-Fingered Tom did not have a spare saddle, Hickok had to make do without one. He did throw on an old saddle blanket the liveryman let him have for free.

They left St. Louis by back roads, arriving at the major trail west by the middle of the afternoon. Three-Fingered Tom fell in with a group of trappers, seven mountain men heading for the high country in preparation for the next trapping season. Two were friends of his.

That night, Hickok sat around the fire with the sons of the wilderness, listening to them yarn about their many and varied escapades. Some of their tall tales were outrageous, but he found himself laughing along with everyone else.

The gunfighter learned that the trappers were upset by the changes taking places in their beloved wild domain. Each year, there were fewer and fewer beaver to be had. Each year, more and more pilgrims flocked west to the Oregon Country. Some had settled along the route and more were bound to do the same as time went by. The wilderness was changing, and in the opinion of the mountain men it was not a change for the better.

Hickok sympathized. He felt a strong kinship to these hardy men who met life on its own terms and managed to wrest a living from the ever-present yawning jaws of death. They were just as he had always imagined they would be—a lusty breed who lived as they pleased, beholden to no man.

They were a dying breed, as well. Hickok knew his history. He knew that soon the prairie and the mountains would be overrun by settlers. Towns and cities would spring up where before only wild creatures had roamed. In a few short decades the mountain men would be gone, their way of life a memory. The so-called civilized types who came after them would claim that it was a change for the better. But was it?

Hickok had read about life in the pre-holocaust years. He had visited the Free State of California and the Civilized Zone. He had seen cities firsthand, and it seemed to him that they were vastly overrated.

Cities brought out the worst in people. Penned together like so many cattle, hemmed in by walls of concrete and stone, they acted more like rats in a maze than human beings. They were always in a hurry, rushing to and fro, as if there were not enough hours in the day to do all they had to get done. When they got off from work, they would slink home and collapse, spending their free time cooped up in a house or apartment no bigger than a chicken coop.

Cities bred viciousness. Many folks in big cities were notoriously rude. They were mean to strangers. They had little regard for anyone other than themselves. Maybe the pace of their lives was to blame. Maybe it was being confined like rodents to a gilded cage that was not all it seemed.

Hickok had a hunch it was all of that and more. The plain truth was that it had to be unnatural to have asphalt and concrete under foot all the time, that it was an abomination against nature for people to be cooped up like prisoners. The Good Lord had created grass and trees and the sky for a reason. The wide open spaces were man's legacy, not skyscrapers and subways.

It was midnight when the mountain men spread out to sleep. Hickok did not have a blanket, but he did have the moldy old coat the Caw had dug up for him. He spread it on the ground, curled up on top, and dozed off with no trouble.

At first light the mountain men were up and ready to depart. Since they had a string of pack animals, they could not travel fast. Three-Fingered Tom bid his friends so long and led the Warrior westward.

About ten in the morning a dark dot appeared in the distance.

"Might be a buffalo," Three-Fingered Tom declared. "We'll stuff ourselves tonight if it is."

"It's a wagon," Hickok said. He had always enjoyed exceptional eyesight. His was not quite as keen as Geronimo's at long distances, but his depth perception was superior. His ability to "distinguish spatial relationships," as a Family Elder once put it, was without peer.

Blade and Geronimo were of the opinion that the trait accounted for his extraordinary marksmanship, and Hickok was inclined to agree. He never missed when he had time to aim. Even his reflex shooting was remarkable. Once, at a shooting match in Denver, he had won the trophy by hitting the bull's-eye five hundred times out of five hundred times, a feat no one had ever performed.

"Are you sure?" Three-Fingered Tom asked.

"Positive."

The wagon sat off to one side of the trail, its tongue poking into the grass. It had wooden sides, a tailgate, and a canvas top. Or what was left of them. For as the two men drew nearer, Hickok saw that the sides had been splintered, the canvas was torn and tattered. Fist-sized holes dotted the sections of wagon that had not been broken asunder. Two of the wheels were busted, one hanging on the axle by a thread.

Personal effects lay everywhere. Clothes, silverware, cooking utensils, tools and more had been scattered about. Much of it had been trampled. Dry pools of blood marked where the occupants had fallen.

"Lord God Almighty!" Three-Fingered Tom exclaimed. "What could've done this?" He rode up to the tailgate and peered in. "Oh, Jesus!" he said, turning as pale as paper. He backed away, looking as if he were about to be sick.

Hickok took a peek. The interior was in as bad a shambles as outside, only there was more blood. That was not all. On the floor near the tailgate lay a severed human hand. The flesh showed evidence of having been chewed. Worst of all, the slender fingers and long nails were those of a little girl.

"I've done my share of killin'," Three-Fingered Tom said, "but I've never rubbed out kids, and I never will. I ain't no butcher." He dismounted and roved around the wagon, his head bent low to the ground. "There's plenty of sign. I'm not no Injun, but I can get by." Abruptly halting, he hunkered. "What in the hell made this?"

Hickok climbed down. Imbedded in soft soil was a fresh track. It resembled the hoofprint of a buffalo, but no buffalo had made it. Hickok had seen identical prints before, hundreds of years in the future. He glanced at the holes in the wagon and wanted to kick himself for not finishing the minotaur off when he had the chance.

"If I didn't know better, I'd swear a herd of buffalo attacked these poor pilgrims," Three-Fingered Tom said. "But this weren't done by no buffs. What could've done it?" he asked again.

Hickok held his peace. He circled the wagon, seeking more minotaur tracks and came on a different kind, a set made by another creature that had no business being alive in that century. This print was birdlike, with three toes and a cleft heel.

"A snake-man," the gunman said to himself. The implications upset him. Thanatos must have hooked up with the two mutants he had seen barge into the chamber in the Dark Tower right before he was whisked through time. Were there more he did not know about? Did the Dark Lord intend to gather an army of hybrids, to bring them from the future in order to conquer the past?

Among the scattered possessions were several blankets. Hickok helped himself to one that had not been ripped and was not stained with blood. He was tired of the smelly coat. Taking it off, he cast it in the grass. The same with the cap. A disguise was no longer needed.

Three-Fingered Tom was scratching his scraggly beard. "I wonder if that Lord Seth had anything to do with this. His bunch likely passed by here just yesterday afternoon."

"It was them," Hickok confirmed.

"What makes you so all-fired sure?"

"Trust me."

Hickok, folding the blanket, went to the bay. As he passed the busted rear wheel, he glanced under the wagon. Nearly hidden by the sagging tail end was a saddle. It was old and scuffed and one of the stirrups was cracked, but it would suffice. He lost no time in lugging it out from under the bed and throwing it on the bay. As he cinched up, the frontiersman came over.

"I ain't never seen the like, Hickok. I got up the nerve to take another look at that hand. It appears to me that little girl was *eaten*. But that can't be, can it?"

The gunfighter forked leather. "The gent I'm after is as vicious as they come. It might be best if you were to head back to St. Louis and leave this to me."

"I'm not no quitter," Three-Fingered Tom huffed. "I'll see this through, if you don't mind."

"You could end up like that girl."

Three-Fingered Tom blanched. "Maybe so, but I owe it to my partner to see that Seth pays for what I heard he done." He patted his rifle. "I've dropped silver-tips with this. I expect I can do the same to Lord Seth and his outfit."

Hickok regretted having let the man come. Three-Fingered Tom had no inkling of what they were up against. That Hawken, as powerful as it was, would be no match for a minotaur or the serpent-human hybrid. "I really wish you'd reconsider. No one will hold it against you."

"I would—" Three-Fingered Tom began, and broke off, gaping past the Warrior along the trail to the east. "Kick me, would you? I must've died and not known it. I can't be seein' what I think I'm seein'.'"

Hickok felt the same way when he turned. Hurrying toward them was an apparition the likes of which most people only saw in dreams. "After I kick you, you can kick me," he said.

He Who Eats Dog was mounted on an animal that had no business carrying a man. It was a dog, undeniably the largest dog in all of St. Louis, a shaggy specimen that reminded Hickok of pictures he had seen of St. Bernards. This one had great floppy ears, a dark blaze on the forehead, and paws the size of hams. It loped toward them like a hairy horse, its big tongue lolling.

The Caw sat astride the dog's back, hunched over for better balance. He beamed merrily at the gunman, his bony fingers entwined in the dog's hair, his long legs wrapped tight around its side. "Greetings, Lightning Hands! I told you that I would find you." Pulling on the hair, he brought his unique mount to a stop. "Are you pleased to see me?"

At a loss to know where to begin, Hickok blurted in amazement, "Where did you get that mutt?"

"This is Heavy Paws. He roams the streets, like

I do. Often I feed him scraps. One day I climbed on his back to see what he would do and he did nothing. So I ride him from time to time."

"It's not possible," Three-Fingered Tom said.

"You can see for yourself that it is." He Who Eats Dog patted Heavy Paws. "This will be a fine adventure for both of us."

"I thought you *eat* dogs," Hickok reminded him.

"Small dogs usually. They are plumper and taste better. Big dogs have stringy meat. They are also harder to kill." The Caw winked at the Warrior. "Besides, if we cannot find game, you will be glad I brought him."

"Has the whole world gone nuts?" Three-Fingered Tom asked no one in particular.

He Who Eats Dog jabbed his heels into his unorthodox mount and the dog hastened on down the trail. The Caw showed no interest whatsoever in the wagon or its contents. "Let us go!" he urged. "I cannot wait to see the demon with my own eyes."

Three-Fingered Tom looked at Hickok. "The demon?"

The gunfighter sighed and spurred the bay on without responding. He watched the old Indian bouncing on top of the St. Bernard or whatever it was, then shook his head in disbelief. It was just like he always said. At times life was too ridiculous for words.

Chapter Nineteen

"Those stinkin' Blackfeet are after us."

Geronimo twisted but saw nothing other than a small herd of antelope traveling to the northeast. "I don't see any sign of them," he noted.

"Neither do I, sonny," Old Hugh said, "but I can feel 'em in my bones. They're back there, all right. Probably bidin' their time until they can jump us unexpected-like. They want us to pay for what we did to Mad Bull."

"What *you* did," Geronimo emphasized. "I was all for letting him live."

The Warrior did not know whether to take the trapper's premonition seriously. They had ridden hard ever since fleeing the stand, stopping only for four hours at night and getting started well before dawn. What with the lead they had, he doubted the war party would try to catch them.

"No need to fret yet," Old Hugh said. "Unless one of our horses goes lame, we should reach Bent's Fort well ahead of those wolves."

Geronimo could hardly wait for them to get there. He yearned to locate his friends, to compare notes and figure out the next step to take.

The three of them had faced all sorts of adversaries over the years and had always won out. There had been mutants and giant insects. There had been reptiles of prehistoric proportions and creatures that defied description. There had been flesh devouring chemical clouds. Trolls, mutates, Watchers, Technics, the Assassins Guild, the Breed, and many other threats to the security of the Freedom Federation had all been dealt with.

None, though, could hold a candle to Thanatos. In terms of pure wickedness, no one rivaled his diabolical genius. He was the vile cream of the perverted crop, utterly evil through and through.

Geronimo knew that eliminating the Dark Lord would not bring an end to human suffering. It wouldn't be long before someone arose to replace him. For each menace that fell, a new one always cropped up. Sometimes it seemed as if it were an endless cycle, as if the Warriors could never get ahead, never conquer evil for good, no matter how hard they . . .

"Are you payin' attention there, sonny? I said we have company."

Looking up, Geronimo found that a pair of

bears had reared up out of the grass a hundred yards away. One was much larger than the other. Both bore the telltale humps of grizzlies.

"A sow and her youngun," Old Hugh said. "We'd best fight shy of 'em or she's liable to get temperamental on us." Suiting action to words, he angled to the east.

The bears watched them closely. The she-bear advanced ten yards, her huge head swinging ponderously from side to side, her nostrils raised to catch their scent.

"If she charges, ride like hell," Hugh suggested. "You'd be surprised how damn fast those monsters are. For short distances they can hold their own with any horse."

As if to confirm what the frontiersman claimed, the mother bear launched herself at them, flashing across the plain with astounding speed for an animal so immense.

Geronimo raked his horse with his heels, following Hugh to the southeast. As loath as he was to use precious ammo, he'd not hesitate if the bear got too close. One swipe of her paw could disembowel his mount, and that he would not allow.

But the bear merely wanted to drive them away from her offspring. She charged for a few hundred feet, then halted, rising onto her hind legs to stare after them. As added incentive to hasten their flight, she vented a grating growl that was almost a roar.

Old Hugh slowed once the sow did. "See? I told you," he said, his eye jiggling. "Feisty as cornered sidewinders, them bears. Makes you wonder why the Good Lord ever made 'em." He faced front and clucked to his mount. "Or sidewinders, for that matter."

It dawned on Geronimo that he knew very little about this odd character he had thrown in with. A number of the trapper's comments had disturbed him, so much so that he was compelled to say, "I don't mean to pry, but I need to know something."

"Ask away, sonny. We've a long way to go and I wouldn't want to discourage you from flappin' your gums. Me, I like to jaw. Helps pass the time."

"Do you hate all Indians?"

Old Hugh's good eye narrowed. "Where in tarnation did you ever get a fool notion like that?" He thought a moment, then laughed. "Oh. Probably from all those flatterin' words I had to say about the Blackfeet."

"Do you?" Geronimo persisted. It troubled him that he might be in the company of a bigot.

"Hell, no," Old Hugh said. "Just cause I'd like to see the Blackfeet turned into worm food don't mean I hate the whole red race. Matter of fact, some Indians I'm right fond of. The Shoshones and the Flatheads, for instance." He grew wistful. "Had myself a Flathead wife once. Prettiest female you ever did see."

"Where is she now?"

Old Hugh did not answer right away. It was a full minute before he went on, saying, "This was back when I was a young stallion in my prime. The cock of the woods I was, and how I loved to crow!" His weathered features cracked in a sad smile. "When I married her, I was the happiest man alive. We lived with her people for nigh on seven years. Tried like minks to have pups, but we never could."

The deep emotion in the trapper's voice proved that he was not lying. Geronimo did not pry further. If Hugh wanted to tell him the whole story, he would. If not, it was none of his business.

Old Hugh had to cough before he could go on. "Long about the spring, our village was raided. The war party run off over fifty horses. They also kilt over twenty Flatheads when we rallied to drive 'em off. A few of those rubbed out were women. One was my wife. She took an arrow meant for me." Inner torment contorted his countenance. "It was a Blackfoot war party, sonny."

"Oh." Geronimo was sorry he had brought the subject up. When would he learn not to judge a book by its cover, as the old saying had it?

"It was a long time ago. I'm pretty much over it by now," Old Hugh lied, and coughed again. "All these years I've been hopin' and prayin' that I'd get a chance to pay back the son of a bitch who kilt her, and finally I have."

A stick of dynamite went off in Geronimo's head. "Let me guess. Mad Bull?"

They rode in silence for the longest while.

Winona's groan brought Blade to her side. Kneeling, he checked her forehead. It was hotter than it had ever been. Her fever was raging out of control. Without a thermometer he could not be accurate, but he guessed it had to be one hundred and four, if not higher.

As Blade had been doing regularly ever since Nate King left, he soaked the compress and applied it to her forehead. It was an exercise in futility; it wouldn't alleviate much of her suffering. She needed proper medicine such as the Family's Healers administered.

Before he departed, the mountain man had concocted an herbal remedy from roots Winona carried in a parfleche and forced her to swallow it. So far the brew had not had much effect.

Blade suspected that infection had set in. They should get her to Bent's Fort right away, but that was out of the question until Nate returned with the boy. If they returned.

Little Evelyn was a study in despair. She sat at her mother's shoulder, her arms draped over her knees, watching Winona with sorrowful eyes. "Will my ma die, Mr. Blade?"

The question caught the Warrior off guard. She had hardly spoken two words to him since her father left. Now she wanted a reply to a question that by rights her father should be the one to answer.

"Will she?" the child asked when he hesitated.

"Not if we can help it," Blade assured her.

Evelyn laid a hand on Winona's shoulder. "I love her so much."

At that juncture one of the horses nickered. Another did so seconds later. Blade turned. Their mounts, the pack horse, and several animals that had belonged to slain Pawnees were hobbled close by. All were alert, staring westward.

Blade hoped that it was Nate King returning. Rising, he climbed partway up the slope, high enough to see over the gully rim. His hopes were dashed. Thirty yards out were wolves, nine of them, some pacing back and forth, others sitting and panting. They saw him but they made no move to attack. Yet.

"What is it?" Evelyn inquired. She wanted it to be her father. She wanted him to come back and make her mother well so that everything could be as it had been.

The Warrior was honest with her. "Wolves, but I doubt they'll bother us." Unless they were starving or rabid, wolves normally avoided humans. The pack gave no sign of being either, so they were bound to drift off sooner or later.

Just to be safe, Blade unslung the Commando. He noticed that one of the wolves was larger than the rest, a muscular male with a white band on its throat. The dominant wolf, he concluded, after another male came near and was driven off by a ferocious snarl. It would be the one to watch. The pack would follow its cue.

For a while nothing happened. The wolves did not show any inclination to go away. Then Winona, in her delirious pain-racked state, groaned loudly. The dominant male perked its ears and padded closer, its steady gaze on the Warrior. When it advanced so did four others.

Blade climbed higher, exposing more of himself on the theory they would run off once they realized what they were up against. They proved him wrong. Other than a small female that backed off a few dozen feet, the rest held their ground. They were not intimidated by him or his size. They did not appear to have any fear of man at all.

"Get out of here!" Blade shouted. Sometimes the sound of a human voice was enough to drive wild beasts away. Not this time. The leader and a few others growled. One yipped like a coyote. In fact, well beyond the pack, a pair of coyotes had appeared, as if they sensed that the wolves were closing in for a kill and wanted to be on hand to snatch whatever scraps were to be had.

Blade elevated the Commando, then lowered it again. The ammo was too valuable to waste on wolves unless they left him no choice. He glanced at Evelyn.

The girl had slid her mother's knife out and held it ready to slash, her innocent features set in lines of sober resolve. "Are they gone?"

"Not yet."

"Why don't you shoot them?"

"I will when the time is right."

The dominant male, meanwhile, had crept even nearer. It tested the air and began to circle around toward the horses.

Blade wondered if Winona's groans were to blame. Wolves were Nature's gleaners. They culled the weak and the sick from the herds of their prey. Winona's tortured cries must have triggered that instinct in the passing pack. That meant the wolves were not going anywhere any time soon.

Evelyn heard one of the predator's growl. She pressed back against her mother, prepared to sell her life dearly to preserve Winona's.

The child's fear galvanized Blade into doing what he could to spare her further anxiety. Tucking the Commando to his shoulder, he flicked the selector lever to the semi-automatic setting and tapped off a three-round burst. Miniature geysers spewed a yard from where most of the wolves were clustered. They instantly scattered, though not very far.

A second burst should suffice. The Warrior swiveled and took aim. A hint of movement and the patter of calloused pads let him know that it had been a grave mistake to take his eyes off the dominant male. Evelyn screamed as the wolf hurtled at his chest.

By a sheer fluke, the wolf snapped at Blade's neck but bit down on the Commando instead. Blade was bowled over, his shoulders absorbing the impact. In a spray of dust he slid to the bottom and twisted to regain his feet.

The wolf was not about to let him. Snarling and biting, it lunged at his abdomen, at his arm, at his face. Blade held it at bay, wielding the Commando as if it were a staff. He landed a resounding blow to the wolf's head that dazed it long enough for him to get to his knees.

Blade swung the SMG again, but this time the beast ducked and was on him before he could set himself. Fangs glittering, saliva flecking its jaws, it sprang at his throat. He had to let go of the Commando to save himself, clamping both hands on the animal's neck. Grappling fiercely, they went down, the wolf's teeth inches from his skin.

The Warrior had to end it quickly. For all he knew, the other wolves were closing in and would rush the woman and the child before he could lift a finger to protect them.

Suddenly, holding the straining wolf at arm's length with his left hand alone, he lowered his right to his Bowie. The wolf was practically berserk, snapping in a frenzy, always missing by a hair.

Blade's groping fingers found the hilt. Relying on his greater size for leverage, he rolled to the left even as he drew. The blade sank into the wolf's belly like a hot knife into butter. The stroke was perfect. It sheared through the heart. In a twinkling the wolf was dead and Blade was standing to see what the other wolves were up to.

Two of them materialized above the gully, barely slowing in their rush as they started down the slope. One made for him, the other for Evelyn and Winona.

The Warrior gave no regard to his own safety. Taking a step, he cocked his arm and threw the Bowie just as he had countless times in daily practice ever since he had been old enough to lift the big knives. The throw was as flawless as his thrust had been. The blade thudded into the wolf's side just as it coiled to spring. In a swirl of fur and tail, it tumbled to the bottom and was still.

Blade had saved the child and her mother at his own expense. The second wolf was on him before he could employ his other Bowie. He brought his left arm up as it leaped. Teeth seared into his flesh. Hot breath fanned his face. He staggered backward but did not go down.

Shifting, Blade slammed the wolf against the slope. It clung on, its teeth biting deeper, its claws digging into his legs. Since it had his left wrist in a vise, the only way he could draw his left Bowie was with his right hand. But he could not get at it, because the wolf was in the way. He punched the thrashing form twice, unable to land solid blows.

Then Blade received the shock of his life. From out of nowhere Evelyn appeared. So frail and dainty she barely came to his knees, she betrayed no fear as she stabbed her mother's knife into the wolf's neck.

The knife only went halfway in. It was enough to cause the wolf to release Blade and turn on her. The Warrior was quicker. With the speed of a striking bullwhip, he looped an arm around the beast's throat, jerked it off its feet, and squeezed. The wolf erupted like a hairy volcano. Blade held on, applying more and more pressure as he braced his right palm against the base of the wolf's head and forced it forward, inexorable inch by inexorable inch.

It was a toss-up which would happen first, strangulation or a broken neck. The crisp snap of the spinal column resolved the issue.

Blade flung the limp body down. His wrist was badly torn but not bleeding as badly as he feared. It would heal, adding yet another scar to the score he already bore.

Evelyn was standing there, tears streaking her cheeks. "Is the bad wolf dead?" she asked.

"Yes," Blade said, and remembered the rest. Scooping up the Commando, he dashed up the slope. The other wolves were almost upon them. He showed no mercy this time. Switching to full auto, he stitched those nearest with a hailstorm of heavy slugs. Three fell in as many seconds. The rest finally had enough and bolted, disappearing into the high grass. So did the coyotes.

Blade lingered, wary the pack would circle

around and try again. At last he spied them in the distance, loping off in search of easier prey.

Evelyn huddled beside Winona, her small figure shivering. She had been scared that the big man would be killed, that she would be left to save her ma by herself, which she knew she could not do. More than ever she wished that her pa would get there and make everything right.

"You're safe now," Blade said.

The horses were agitated. Frightened by the racket, panicked by the scent of fresh blood, terrified by the smell of their age-old enemies, most were trying to flee despite their hobbles.

Blade would rather have comforted the child, but he had to deal with the animals first. It took much longer than he liked to catch each one and calm it. Evelyn had stretched out beside Winona, her eyes closed, her tiny fingers clutching the top of Winona's dress. He thought that she was asleep until she looked at him.

"Is my ma safe now?"

"She's safe." Blade filled a tin cup with water from the water skin. "Care for a sip?"

"Thank you." Evelyn held the cup in both hands. The excitement had made her very thirsty. She was puzzled how the big man knew.

That was when Blade saw Winona staring at them from under hooded lids. The poor woman was barely conscious. Her lips moved but no words came out. Taking the cup from the child, he carefully tilted it so Winona could drink. She swallowed a few times, enough to moisten her throat.

"Where is my man?"

Blade hated to be the bearer of more bad tidings. He spared her the detail about blood on her son's saddle. She took the news stoically, nodding when he finished.

"Grizzly Killer will find Stalking Coyote. They will be back soon."

Blade admired her unbounded confidence in Nate King. In so many ways Winona reminded him of his own better half. "Can I get you anything? There is broth left over from last night. Or I can give you other herbs if you'll tell me which ones."

Winona had taken her daughter's hand in hers. Evelyn snuggled against her, ecstatic that she had revived. "Add chopped roots to the broth to make it stronger. They should be in my bag."

"The same ones your husband used?" Blade located them with no problem. They were on top of everything else, tied together with a short strip of buckskin. A whang, as Nate called them.

What was left of the broth was in a small pot. He diced two roots, dropped the pieces in. Then he rekindled the fire. "It will take awhile," he said.

"I am not going anywhere."

Blade grinned. That she could joke about her condition was a positive sign. Her fever, though, had not gone down any, and her skin was flushed. He would have given anything to be able to get her to a Family Healer.

Winona was touched by the worry in the giant's eyes. She had seen how gently he treated her daughter. Her misgivings about him were entirely gone. He was a decent man, if strange. She tried to sit up, but her body refused to cooperate. Her limbs were as weak as a newborn foal's. "I am sorry to be a burden," she said.

"Don't be silly."

Winona remembered that she had been awakened by loud growls and snarls. Marshaling her energy, she twisted her head and counted three dead wolves. "The blood," she warned.

"What?"

Winona had to concentrate to talk. "The scent of blood will bring any grizzly that smells it."

The last thing Blade wanted to do was tangle with one of the gigantic bears. Wasting no time, he dragged the bodies off by their tails, all three at once, and dumped them in a pile hundreds of yards from the gully. Every moment he was away made him nervous. The mother and child would be helpless should a carnivore find them.

Hastening back, the Warrior saw that both had dozed off. In repose they were angelic. Somehow it made his responsibility weigh that much heavier on his shoulders. He gazed westward, thinking out loud, "Nate King, where are you?"

Chapter Twenty

The only man who could answer that question was frozen behind a tree high in the foothills.

Nate had seen the two Pawnees coming toward his son. They were jawing, not paying much attention to what was going on around them. Reaching out, he grasped Zach's arm and hauled the boy to his feet. "Stay close to me!" he whispered, running toward the string.

About that time a Pawnee spotted them. A harsh cry rang out over the valley, bringing every last warrior to his feet.

Nate commenced hollering and bellowing and waving his arms. It did what he wanted, provoking the horses into flight. The mounts scattered every which way. He plunged into the vegetation in their wake, bearing to the right just as an arrow buzzed past his ear. His plan was to draw most of the Pawnees off, then lose the rest and circle around to his stallion.

Zach had to exert himself to keep up with his pa. War whoops and gruff shouts attended their flight. The skin between his shoulder blades prickled in expectation of taking an arrow. He glanced back and saw a warrior sight down a shaft. Throwing himself to the left at the exact instant the arrow flashed from the string, he flew by a fir and heard the arrow thunk into it.

Nate had counted on most of the warriors going after the horses, which they did. The Pawnees could ill afford to be stranded in territory claimed by the Arapaho and the Cheyenne, their bitter foes. Three-fourths bounded into the undergrowth to catch their mounts. Leaving more than enough to chase Nate and Zach.

The mountain man chose the most rugged terrain, the densest vegetation. It slowed him down, but it also slowed down the Pawnees. The only problem was Zach, who had to struggle to keep up. Nate propelled him along at critical junctures. Twice arrows rained down wide to either side.

Nate had to do something to discourage pursuit. On bursting out of the pines into a clearing, he pushed Zach toward dry brush on the left and dropped behind it moments before several Pawnees arrived.

At the crack of the Hawken, the fleetest warrior dropped stone dead. The rest retreated for cover, one sending an arrow into the brush. It came nowhere near Nate and Zach. Nate tapped his son on the shoulder and jogged to the north.

From all points of the compass came the crackle and crash of horses and Pawnees. Some of the animals had been caught, but others were unwilling to give up their new-found freedom.

Nate swung to the east. He stayed on the lookout for warriors, avoiding vague shapes wherever he spotted them. In the back of a his mind, a tiny voice told him to reload the Hawken while he could, but he elected to hold off until they reached his stallion. He still had the twin flintlocks.

Zach was in awe of his father's stealth. It seemed as if his pa were more specter than flesh and blood. Hardly a leaf rustled when his father went by. Twigs never broke under his feet. Zach tried to do the same, but he was not as skilled. He fretted that the noises he made might give them away, that he would cost them their lives.

Nate slowed when they approached the hill. All that was left was the climb to the stallion. He congratulated himself on a job well done, then learned he was getting ahead of himself when two Pawnees filled a break in the growth ahead. One led a horse. The other was scouring the vicinity. They saw Nate at the same moment he saw them.

The Pawnee on foot held a lance. Raising it, he charged, his war whoop reminiscent of the screech of a bobcat.

The other warrior vaulted onto his mount and spurred it forward. His weapon of choice was a war club which he flourished in savage exultation.

"Follow me!" Nate directed, breaking to the left to go up the hill. The slope would work in their favor, giving them the twin advantages of elevation and footing. Simply put, it was harder for a man to attack running uphill than it was going downhill.

Weaving among trees, Nate drew a pistol. The thunder of hooves heralded the mounted Pawnee, who was all-fired eager to catch him. Looking around, he saw the warrior closing the gap rapidly. He also saw, to his horror, that Zach had not done as he wanted. His son had fled in the other direction, and the warrior with the lance was after him.

Zach had not meant to disobey his pa. He had already started to retrace his steps when his father told him to go up the hill. He tried to comply, but the Pawnee with the lance was too close. Cut off, he took the only course left him.

Of all the things Zach did well, he prided himself most on being fast on his feet. Every summer, when his family would live with their Shoshone kin, he would indulge in a favorite Shoshone pastime—foot races. Boys and girls alike took part, and the whole tribe would turn out to cheer on their favorites. Most of the time he won.

The only one who could challenge him was a girl, Morning Star. She would wrap her long dress up around her thighs and skim the ground like an antelope. It was hard to say which bothered him more, her speed or her long legs. For some reason he could not take his eyes off them.

Now Zach poured all he had into running as he had never run before. Since he was smaller than the Pawnee, he darted between trees that were close together, dove into openings barely big enough for a cat, wound along rabbit trails barely wide enough for rabbits.

It helped. It slowed the Pawnee. But the warrior was no slouch. He held his own, but he could never quite get within throwing range.

A yell to the right reminded Zach that other Pawnees were abroad. He turned left, jumping a log. Large boulders offered a haven and he dashed in among them, dodging behind one the size of a bull buffalo. Crouching, he clasped a hand over his mouth to muffle his breathing. His temples were pounding, his heart hammering. Willing himself to be calm, he listened for the Pawnee.

Moccasins scraped the ground, then were still. Zach knew that the warrior had guessed what he was up to. Now it was cat and mouse. The only problem was that Zach could not stay there all day. Other warriors were bound to show up. His pa might need him. He had to sneak off.

Zach crept around the base of the boulder. A short clear space brought him to smaller ones bordering the forest. He was all set to make a break for it when a shadow fell across him.

Up on the hill, Nate King turned the moment he realized his son was missing. The mounted warrior was climbing swiftly and would soon be on him. Darting behind a tree, Nate reversed his grip on the Hawken. He disliked using it as a club since it might be damaged, but there was no time to search for a suitable dead limb.

David Thompson

The horse trotted up abreast of the tree. The warrior was preoccupied, scanning the slope above.

Acting on an impulse, Nate leaned his rifle against the bole, leaped out, and tore the war club from the Pawnee's hand. The shocked warrior attempted to rein around and get out of there, but he was too slow by half. Nate landed a blow on the man's ear that brought the warrior crashing to earth. The animal stopped.

Snatching the Hawken, Nate flung himself on and turned downhill. Somewhere down there was his son. He raced down the slope with a silent prayer that he was not too late.

Zachary King glanced up into the sneering visage of the Pawnee with the lance. The man had outwitted him. He recoiled as the warrior raised the weapon to thrust, backing against the boulder. He could not go any further. He was trapped.

Desperation prompted Zach to lash out with both legs. His feet connected with the Pawnee's left shin hard enough to jolt the man and spoil his aim. The lance tip imbedded itself in the dirt at Zach's elbow instead of in him.

Scrambling to one side, Zach heaved upright and ran. He thought that if he could gain the trees he might still escape with his life. Then his legs were swept out from under him. Smacking onto his chest and face, he inhaled enough dust to spark a coughing fit. Zach went to rise.

The Pawnee was just out of reach, smirking. He flicked the butt of the lance at Zach's head. Zach dodged, scrabbling to the rear like an oversized crawdad. The warrior came after him, jabbing again and again, laughing each time. Zach realized the man was toying with him. The blows were not delivered at full force. Those that landed, though, stung terribly.

Pausing, the Pawnee addressed him. Zach could not respond, since he did not know a lick of the tongue. Nor did he really care what the man had to say. Scouring the ground near him, he spotted a large rock and lunged.

The warrior was there before him. A foot tromped onto Zach's outstretched fingers, grinding them into the earth. Involuntarily, Zach cried out. He bit his lower lip to keep from doing it again and tugged furiously.

The Pawnee found his efforts humorous. Chuckling, the man lifted his leg, then circled, poking the butt at Zach's side, at his hip, at his shoulder. Zach was so mad that he wanted to tear into his tormentor with his nails and teeth, but he remembered his pa's advice and reined in his temper.

It had been two summers previous at the annual rendezvous. It had been evening, and a group of trappers had been seated around a crackling fire. Zach had been there, too, as fascinated by their colorful stories as always.

The topic that particular evening had been a fellow trapper by the name of Edwards, who hailed from Maine. Edwards had been with a party ambushed by Bloods several days earlier. His horse was shot out from under him in the opening volley. He still could have gotten away if he had accepted two offers to ride double with friends.

But the loss of the horse, a sorrel to which he had been quite attached, made Edwards see red.

Roaring like a bear, he had charged the Bloods, emptying his rifle and his pistols. Then, just as suddenly, he had fled back toward his party. Only to take an arrow in the back.

"That's what happens when you let your temper get the better of you," Zach's pa had commented, and most every mountain man there had nodded knowingly. "In a scrape a man has to stay calm, has to keep his wits about him. Lose your head and you lose your life."

So now Zach willed himself not to lose his. Turning as the Pawnee circled, he swatted at the lance, bruising his forearm but keeping it from landing again. His tormentor was having a grand old time, laughing and chortling.

Another boulder barred Zach's way. He broke to the right, managing two steps before the butt rammed into his gut and doubled him over in agony. The mocking laughter piled humiliation on top of the hurt.

The Pawnee suddenly grew somber. He said a few words, pointed at Zach, then at the sky. Hoisting his lance, he prepared to spear it into Zach's vitals.

Zach raised his head in defiance. If he had to meet his Maker, he would do it with dignity, as his pa had always said to. He would not give his slayer the satisfaction of seeing him cringe.

Back arched for the fatal swing, the Pawnee paused.

It was then that the underbrush crashed and a horse and rider plowed into the open. Zach looked, expecting to see another Pawnee. "Pa!"

Nate King did not stop or slow. At a gallop he bore down on the startled warrior, who spun and threw back his right arm. The horse plowed into him before he could throw. It flattened the man with the force of a falling tree. A flying hoof caught him in the forehead.

"Get on!" Nate ordered, bending so his son could grab his arm. He did not waste another look on their foe, but Zach did.

The warrior's skull was split down the middle, his brains oozing out. The lance had snapped in half and the lower part had been driven into his leg.

"Are you all right?" Nate asked, making for the hill. Judging by the racket in the woods, most of the Pawnees were still busy catching their mounts. He hoped they would go on being busy for a while yet.

"Fine, Pa," Zach answered, holding tight. "Thanks for rescuing me."

"What else are fathers for?"

The black stallion was right where it should be. Nate switched and led his son up over the crest. Harsh shouts in the valley indicated that at least one of the bodies had been found.

Anxious over Winona, Nate did not slacken the pace until they were well out on the prairie. There had been no sign of pursuit, but he would not put it past the Pawnees to come after them once the war party attended to the dead.

Zach was uncommonly quiet. His capture and subsequent narrow escape had dampened his spirits. Thanks to his carelessness, he had nearly died. So had his pa. In the future, he had to stay more alert.

It must have been half an hour later that Zach gazed at the eastern sky and felt his pulse quicken. "Pa! Are they what I think they are?"

Nate did not have to ask what his son was referring to. Half a dozen black dots could only be
one thing. "Buzzards!" he exclaimed. Very close
to where he gauged the gully to be. Bringing the
stallion to a lope, he surveyed the plain for bodies. A dozen possibilities flashed through his
mind, all of them horrible. Some of the Pawnees
had already been there, a war party from another
tribe was to blame, a grizzly had caught Blade
off guard and slain Winona and Evelyn.

They galloped madly on. Nate saw more buzzards on the ground, dozens of them covering
three prone figures. Indignation brought the
Hawken to his shoulder. He would not stand for
having his wife and daughter mutilated! His finger was curling around the trigger when he observed that one of the prone figures had a bushy
tail.

"What the—" Nate blurted. He rode closer,
spooking half the vultures into flight. Their ugly
heads bobbing, their large wings flapping noisily,
they waddled a few feet and launched themselves
into the air. Soon the sky overhead was choked
with them.

"Why, they're eating wolves, Pa!" Zach said.

To the north rose an odd sound. At first Nate
thought it was a Shoshone death chant, but on
riding closer it became apparent the language
was English. He smiled when the words sank in.

"Row, row, row your boat, gently down the
stream. Merrily, merrily, merrily, merrily, life is
but a dream."

Blade had Evelyn balanced on his knee. She
had woke up earlier crying her little heart out

and nothing he had done had stifled the tears until he hit on the brainstorm of singing. The clop-clop of horses brought them both to their feet. Blade was so glad to see who it was that he called out without thinking, "It's your father and brother!"

Winona stirred. Her eyelids cracked. She was so drowsy that she could barely keep her eyes open, but keep them open she did when she saw her man and their boy. "Husband!" she greeted Nate as he slid down the slope to her side.

Nate clasped her hand, alarmed by how hot it was. Her fever was no better than when he had left, yet the herbs should have dampened it. He wanted to examine her, but Evelyn insisted on a hug. "We saw the wolves," he remarked.

Blade gave an account of the attack, stressing the part the girl had played.

"Sissy stabbed one?" Zach asked, incredulous. His little sister had always been scared of big animals like painters and wolves. So had he, at her age. He doubted that he could have done the same.

"Why don't you take your sister for a walk?" Nate suggested. "Blade will go along to watch over you."

Zach took hold of Evelyn. "We don't need no one to protect us, Pa."

Blade guessed that the mountain man wanted to be alone with Winona to check her wound. Twice since King left, he had offered to but Winona refused, telling him flat out that the only man who could see her unclothed body was her husband. Out of respect for her wishes, he had not pressed it. Yet if Nate had not shown up when he did, Blade was going to check it whether Winona agreed or not. Her life was at stake.

Nate could tell that the giant understood. "Go with him anyway," he said. The boy looked upset; the reason was transparent. "It's not that I don't trust you, son," he elaborated, nodding at Winona.

Zach understood. "Oh. We're on our way."

"I'll teach you the song I taught your sister," Blade proposed, and gave voice to another chorus as they cleared the rim.

Nate did not delay another second. Winona had passed out again. Hunkering, he peeled the slit dress aside. A foul odor nearly made him gag. He had to avert his face and take a breath before he could go on. The dressing was red with dried blood. When he lifted it, pus clung to the bottom. The wound had festered, all right, and was rank with decay. The flesh around it was discolored, a few black streaks the darkest.

"Damn," Nate said.

He cleaned the wound as best he could. Opening her parfleche, he took out a glass canister he had obtained from a trader. Inside was a fine powder. He did not know if there was an English name for the plant it came from, which was found only at high elevations in the Rockies. Dipping his fingers in, he spent the next five minutes liberally sprinkling the wound, covering every square inch, heaviest where the pus was thickest.

The powder was supposed to be blended in a tea or made into a salve. Applying it at full strength might do more harm than good, but that was a risk Nate was willing to take. Unless the spread of infection were stopped soon, his wife's chances were slim.

Nate fitted Winona with a new bandage and covered her. He was rigging the travois when Blade and the children came back.

"It's that bad?" the giant asked.

"We're leaving for Bent's Fort as soon as we're packed up," Nate said. "If we really push, maybe we can be there by tomorrow morning. Every minute counts."

Zach gulped. His father's severe tone told him that his mother was much worse off than he had imagined. Bending, he said tenderly, "Don't you worry, Ma. We'll take good care of you. You'll be up and around before you know it."

Blade saddled his horse while Nate and the boy collected their belongings. The trapper's expression left little doubt as to how bad off Winona was. If she perished, he would never forgive himself.

As she had last time, Evelyn rode on the travois with Winona. Nate had Zach take the point and asked the Warrior to bring up the rear. "Those pesky Pawnees might show, so keep your eyes skinned."

The buzzards took wing again as they went by. The skull of each wolf had been laid bare, their bellies had been ripped open. Internal organs, some partially eaten, dotted the grass.

The swish of heavy wings reminded Blade of the time he had gone up against mutants possessing batlike wings. They had been the bane of the Dakota Territory until the Freedom Federation sent a special strike team in.

Blade envied Nate King. The mountain man

did not have to live in daily dread of clashing with vicious mutations or genetic deviates. True, the wild beasts were problem enough, but grizzlies and wolves were tame compared to the savage mutations so rampant in Blade's own time period. Often the mutants grew to immense size and had the voracious appetites of great white sharks. Blade would gladly swap places with the mountain man any day.

The travois forced them to hold to a brisk walk. Any faster and Winona would be bounced around unmercifully.

Nate tried not to think of what might occur if they could not get the help she needed at the post. They had been together for so long that the notion of life without her was unbearable. She was the reason he smiled when he woke up, the spark that kindled his zest for life. She was his heart made whole.

It was strange how love worked.

A person never knew when the mate they were destined to meet might enter their lives. Certainly he had never entertained the idea of marrying an Indian woman. Yet that first day, when he had helped save her from a band of Blackfeet, he had gazed into her eyes and known deep down that she was the one for him.

He'd fought it, of course. He'd tried to convince himself that it was a passing fancy. He'd told himself that the attraction was physical, nothing more. Yet the truth would not be denied.

Nate had no regrets. If he had it to do all over again, he would do exactly as he had done. It had taken a strange combination of circumstances to lure him to the frontier. At the time he had wondered if he were doing the right thing. Venturing hundreds of miles into unmapped territory, leaving everything he knew for the vast unknown, giving up family and friends and social standing, and all for what?

For Winona, as it had turned out. For happiness such as he had never thought existed. For the joy of having someone love him more than life itself.

Shifting in the saddle, Nate regarded his wife with affection. "You have to pull through, dearest," he whispered. "For both our sakes."

Chapter Twenty-one

"We will not catch them this day," He Who Eats Dog announced. The old Caw had climbed off his "mount" to study the trail, leaning so low that his nose almost brushed the ground.

"How can you be so sure, Injun?" Three-Fingered Tom asked. "We're not more than two hours behind them and the sun won't set for three or so."

The pair looked at Hickok as if they expected him to settle their dispute. Ignoring both, he shielded his eyes and stared westward. Thanatos and company had been holding to a steady pace. If overtaking them before dark was out of the question, then he would rather wait until daylight. It would be suicide to tangle with the mutants at night. Snake-men, especially, were famed for their ability to see in the dark.

"The demons are at the rear," He Who Eats Dog reported. "They hold back, maybe because they know we are after them."

Three-Fingered Tom slapped his leg in irritation and faced the gunfighter. "What are these demons he keeps babblin' about?"

He Who Eats Dog stood. "Go to the wooden lodges of the men who wear dresses and they will tell you."

"Shows how much you know, heathen. Men don't wear dresses. Women do."

"The men who kiss metal do. I have seen them with my own eyes."

The frontiersman shook his head. "Lord, you're hopeless. But then, you ride dogs."

The Caw grew thoughtful. "I would not need a dog if I had a bird."

"A bird? Haven't you ever heard of *horses?*"

"Long ago, when my people were the only ones in the world, they rode birds the size of buffalo. Those birds are all dead now, but I would like one. I could fly over the demons and makes faces at them."

Muttering, Three-Fingered Tom climbed on his animal. "Let's keep goin'. Listenin' to this idiot is liable to scramble my brains."

Hickok spent the next hour mulling over what the Dark Lord was up to. Why had Thanatos struck off across the prairie? What did the madman hope to accomplish with just ten men and two mutants? More than ever, Hickok wished that he could find his pards. With them at his side, he'd gladly tackle whatever Thanatos threw at him.

True to the Caw's prediction, twilight descended before they caught sight of their quarry. Three-Fingered Tom was unhappy. "It's all that damn dog's fault," he groused. "It keeps strayin' off into the grass to take a leak and we have to wait up."

"Heavy Paws can not help it," He Who Eats Dog said. "We must all be true to our natures."

Three-Fingered Tom focused his displeasure on Hickok. "When I agreed to tag along, I didn't count on travelin' clear across the plains. Why are you takin' your sweet time all of a sudden? Shed this demented Injun and this cur that thinks it's a cayuse and we could make a lot better time."

The truth was, Hickok was in no hurry. He would rather shadow the Dark Lord awhile and possibly learn what Thanatos had cooked up. It might just be that a zombie army or an entire mutant platoon had been sent through the portal ahead of everyone else and were waiting for their leader to assume command.

"Didn't you hear me?" Three-Fingered Tom snapped. "At the rate we're going, Lord Seth will be clear to California before we ever set eyes on him." He nodded at the Marlin. "I thought you wanted him dead as much as I do."

"I do. But we have to play our cards just right," Hickok said. "Otherwise. . . ."

"The demons would get us," He Who Eats Dog chimed in. He was petting Heavy Paws, who gave no sign of being tired even after carrying the warrior for so long.

Three-Fingered Tom scowled. "Will you cut it out with the demons, Injun? I don't know who told you what, but get this straight. Demons are make-believe. They don't exist in real life."

"They can if they want to."

"What do they do? Make a wish?"

The Caw was unfazed by the sarcasm. "No. They just *want* to do something and they can do it. That is how they pass from their world to ours."

Three-Fingered Tom set to work starting a small fire. "I don't know about you, Hickok, but I can only take so much of this old coot. If we don't commence drawin' blood pretty soon, I'm headin' back to St. Louis. The two of you will have to deal with Seth by your lonesome."

The Warrior offered no comment. He did not want to influence the frontiersman one way or the other. Whether Tom stayed or left was entirely up to him. Which was as it should be, considering that their lives hung in the balance.

He Who Eats Dog squatted in front of Heavy Paws. The shaggy brute was dusty and bedraggled but listened with its ears perked. "Heed me, my four-legged brother. We are hungry. You are hungry. Find us something to eat and we will share."

The frontiersman laughed. "Do you honestly think that mangy critter will do what you want? Hell, it doesn't look bright enough to know which end the food goes in and which end it comes out."

No sooner were the words out of Three-

Fingered Tom's mouth than the dog trotted off into the high grass.

"You will see," He Who Eats Dog said. "He has brought me food before. It is his way of thanking me for the food I have brought him."

"Marry him, why don't you."

Hickok was tired of their bickering. It made him think of his own constant squabbling with Geronimo, and how much he missed his friend. He saw to bedding down the horses, tethering each securely.

The sun had long since gone down. A black emptiness held sway. Stars blossomed like fireflies, but they were unable to pierce the gloom.

Hickok looked long and hard. The only light in the whole unending void was the light of their campfire. It was as if they were alone in the middle of an unseen sea, adrift on a tiny island of light, floating God knew where.

Rustling brought the Warrior and the frontiersman to their feet, guns in hand. He Who Eats Dog merely smiled, a smile that broadened when Heavy Paws came into the circle of light, a large rabbit limp in those powerful jaws.

"I'll be damned!" Three-Fingered Tom said. "I'd never have believed it if I hadn't of seen it with my own eyes."

The dog walked up to the Caw and deposited its catch. He Who Eats Dog rubbed its chin and chuckled. "I told you. We are brothers."

"Does your brother know that you aim to eat him if we run out of game?" Hickok asked.

The warrior rubbed his forehead against the dog's. "I would eat him with love in my heart. That is more than any others would do."

Three-Fingered Tom prepared supper, carving the rabbit into equal portions and roasting them by impaling each on the tip of his long knife and holding the blade over the flames. The aroma of the roast meat was tantalizing. Hickok had not realized how hungry he was until he dug into his.

"Maybe that mongrel of yours is worth his keep after all, Injun," Three-Fingered Tom begrudgingly admitted. "How is he at fightin'?"

He Who Eats Dog paused in the act of taking a bite. "I have seen him fight many dogs. He always won."

"You yack. I meant people. Will he help us if we get into a racket with Lord Seth's bunch?"

The Caw pursed his lips. "That I do not know. Maybe he will if I ask him."

Three-Fingered Tom glanced at Hickok. "We could use the cur's help. Your Injun friend here sure won't be of much use. His people are as timid as mice. They're so worthless that the only tribes who will make war on them are the Pawnees and the Arikaras, who are pretty worthless themselves."

"The Caws were great fighters once," He Who Eats Dog countered.

"When? Back when they were sproutin' from clay and ridin' birds and such?" Three-Fingered Tom smirked. "Your people are practically good for nothing'."

"We grow fine crops."

"Must come in real handy in a battle. What do you do, chuck squash and pumpkins at your enemies?"

Hickok did not like for the frontiersman to ride the old Indian like he was doing. "That's—" he began, and promptly clammed up when He Who Eats Dog motioned to do so.

"Something comes," the Caw whispered. Shooting to his feet, he disappeared into the grass, Heavy Paws at his side.

"What the hell?" Tom declared.

Hickok grabbed the Marlin. "We'd best do the same," he cautioned. He ran to the horses, swiftly freed them, and started to lead both animals into hiding. Looking back, he saw that Tom had not moved. The frontiersman sat there munching on rabbit. "Come on."

"You go ahead if you want. I'm not runnin' off like a coyote with its tail between its legs just 'cause that worthless Caw heard a sound. It's either wolves or a bear or some such, and I know how to deal with them." He patted the rifle at his side.

Hickok could think of something else it might be. "We're safer layin' low until we know for sure. It could be . . ." He hesitated, knowing the man would never believe him.

"What? Demons?" Three-Fingered Tom snickered. "I'm surprised at you, Mister, buyin' that nonsense. Don't you know that Injuns are simpletons? Why, some even think there are spirits in rocks and trees!"

"Please," Hickok said. "Come with us." Short of dragging the man off by force, it was all he could do.

Tom shook his head. "I'm not budgin'."

The Warrior entered the grass, bearing to the southeast until he was fifty yards downwind from the fire. There he hobbled the horses. Marlin in hand, he hurried back. He was halfway there when the night was rent by a piercing scream. Tom's Hawken boomed. The wind carried the sound off across the prairie as Hickok came close enough to see what was going on. His blood changed to ice.

Three-Fingered Tom should not have been so stubborn. It had cost him dearly. He sagged limp in the grasp of a mutant, the serpentine hybrid whose footprint Hickok had seen by the wagon. The creature had broken Tom's neck with the same ease a grown man might break a twig. It was sniffing the body.

Suddenly the mutant shifted, raised its hideous face, and sniffed even louder. It glanced at the bloody rabbit skin and entrails, then moved to the other side of the fire. Its long red tongue flicked out twice. It hissed as if frustrated.

Hickok had seen enough. The Marlin molded to his shoulder, and he curved his thumb around the hammer. Snake-men were not as hard to kill as minotaurs. This one wore body armor, but its head was unprotected. A single shot to the eye should suffice.

Then the grass near the camp parted and out reared the minotaur. It stomped to the fire, snorting and turning every which way.

"It isn't fair, Bel Aram. You got to kill one and I didn't." The minotaur looked hopefully at his otherworldly companion. "Are there others around? Are there any for me to smash and break?"

"Quiet, oaf!" Bel Aram snapped. He stepped to the south a few yards and sniffed some more. "There were horses but they ran off."

"Horses? Good! I like to mash their bodies and

grind their bones!" The minotaur swelled its massive chest. "Which way did they go? I will catch them."

Bel Aram glared. "You could not catch your own tail in the dark, fool. You will go nowhere. We have our orders, remember?"

The minotaur sulked just like a child. "Why do you always get to have all the fun?"

Hickok relaxed his trigger finger. It would be the same as signing his own death warrant if he opened fire now. One or the other was bound to reach cover, and once in the grass their bestial senses would give them the edge. He preferred to wait until conditions were in his favor.

Bel Aram had not stopped testing the breeze.

"What is it?" the minotaur asked.

"I cannot be sure. The blood from that rabbit hangs heavy in the air, masking all other odors," the snake-man answered. "There might have been someone else."

"Should we look?"

"No. I could be wrong." Bel Aram held Three-Fingered Tom toward the minotaur. "Carry this dung. Do not drop him, oaf. Our master will be most displeased if you bruise the meat."

The snake-man gave a last look around, gestured, and streaked westward. It was gone in the blink of an eye. The minotaur draped the frontiersman over its broad shoulder, gave a final snort, and plunged into the darkness, moving at a turtle's pace by contrast.

Hickok did not move for the longest while. It might be a ruse on their part, he mused, to lure him and the old Indian into the open. The wind picked up. The flames danced lower. Half an hour after the loathesome horrors left, Hickok walked the horses back to the campsite. Three-Fingered Tom's Hawken lay where it had fallen. He stooped to claim it.

A whisper of moving grass brought Hickok around in a blur. He Who Eats Dog rode into the light on Heavy Paws. The Caw wore a stupefied expression.

"Did you see, Lightning Hands? Did you see the demons?"

"I saw."

The aged warrior slid off the dog and raised both arms to the heavens in exultation. "I have looked on wonders with my own eyes! The men who wear dresses were right!" His wrinkled features sprouted more wrinkles. "This means that they spoke with straight tongues. This means the god of the whites is indeed a strange and powerful god."

It meant no such thing, but Hickok was in no frame of mind to set the warrior straight. "Now that you know what we're up against, maybe you'd like to light a shuck for St. Louis or your village."

"Are you going on?"

"I have to. I can't let the Dark Lord and his monsters get away. No matter how long it takes, I aim to put a stop to whatever they're schemin' to do."

He Who Eats Dog smiled. "Good. I will go with you."

Inwardly Hickok was glad. The Caw was an outstanding tracker. They could stay a full day behind Thanatos's party and still not lose them. But there was the warrior's life to think of. "You

315

could end up like Three-Fingered Tom."

"So? We get up each morning never knowing if we will go to bed at night." He Who Eats Dog gazed westward and spoke in muted awe. "I have seen marvels, Lightning Hands. I would see them again. I must know whether to give up the ways of my people and live as the men in dresses say I should."

"Don't get carried away with this demon stuff," Hickok said. He began to smother the fire, adding, "We'd best find somewhere else to sleep tonight. Those critters might come back."

"I hope they do."

The gunman noticed Three-Fingered Tom's long knife. "Here. This is yours if you want it."

He Who Eats Dog accepted the gift gratefully. "This one is finer than my own. I am glad I came on this journey. When it is over, I will be wiser and richer."

Provided you're still alive, Hickok thought. Out loud he said, "I'll take Tom's horse and you're welcome to mine."

"Why would I do that when I have a dog to ride?"

It was a week after Thanatos had gorged on the frontiersman brought back by his faithful mutant retainers that he was able to put the next stage of his master plan into effect.

Thanatos was riding westward at the head of the column when the serpentine hybrid slithered up alongside his mount, causing it to nicker and plunge. Bel Aram immediately backed off, and Thanatos brought the chestnut under control.

"Dolt. You are getting worse than Ghanata.

How many times must I tell you not to do that? Horses do not like snakes."

"My apologies, Dark Lord," Bel Aram said, bowing. "In my excitement, I erred. Please forgive me."

"What has you excited?"

Bel Aram looked up. It was always better to be the bearer of good tidings than bad tidings. A few unfortunates who had delivered the latter had been summarily snuffed out by their grim master in a fit of blind rage. "Indians, sire."

Thanatos vibrated with excitement of his own. At long last he could begin gathering his army. Within a year he would have ten thousand undead warriors at his command. Raising an arm, he brought the cutthroats to a halt. "How many and where?"

"Thirty, lord. Camped beside a stream two hours north of here."

"Find Ghanata. He's searching the sector to the northwest. Bring him to the stream. Should the two of you arrive before us, conceal yourselves. Impress on that moron that he must not do anything to scare the primitives away. They are mine."

"Your will be done." Bel Aram glided off and was soon lost in the distance.

The Dark Lord did not waste a minute. Barking commands, he galloped northward. He had to reach that stream before the Indians ventured elsewhere.

His human minions strung out behind him. After the episode with Bucktooth Bob in St. Louis, the ruffians had not given him any trouble. But Thanatos was not fooled. Their loyalty stemmed from greed, their obedience from fear. They were not devoted to him or his ideal, as were his mutants. He could trust them no further than he would a pack of piranhas. It was regrettable that he needed underlings who could carry out complicated orders which zombies lacked the mental capacity to perform, or he would have turned the whole lot of them into automatons.

The horses were lathered with sweat when Thanatos brought his band of killers to another stop. Trees framed the horizon. He called the men around him and tersely explained that they were to stay where they were. Under no circumstances must they go near those trees until he gave the word.

No one questioned him. Ever since Bel Aram and Ghanata had joined the party, the cutthroats had been unusually subdued, almost timid. They did not like the mutants. Their terror when the pair were around was so obvious, it was comical.

Thanatos was about to ride off when his test-tube creations showed. "Attend me," he ordered.

The Indians were still there. They had camped on the south bank of the shallow waterway. The remains of a dead buck told why. Most were lounging, a few sharpening knives or arrow points.

The Dark Lord left his horse at the edge of the cottonwoods. With Ghanata and Bel Aram at his heels, he stalked to the west so the wind would be in his favor. "Wait here," he directed. Inside a secret pocket on the underside of his cloak he found the item he needed. Pulling his hood low, he boldly marched into the open.

The warriors leaped to their feet in a jumble of

yells and general confusion. Some notched arrows, others brought lances or war clubs to bear. In their bewilderment, they clustered together instead of fanning out.

Thanatos smiled. Humans, whether white, black, or red, were pathetically predictable. He held the vial loosely in his right hand, selected an appropriate spot between him and the savages, and brought up his arm to hurl the container.

One of the Indians shouted, then unleased a glittering shaft. The arrow flashed toward the Dark Lord's chest, moving almost too fast for the human eye to follow. But Thanatos's eyes were not human. Nor were his reflexes. He sidestepped and snatched the shaft out of the air with his free hand. It sparked a storm of amazed outcries.

"I am the Dark Lord," Thanatos intoned, knowing full well they could not comprehend. "You are now mine to do with as I please." He hurled the vial, his aim precise. It shattered on impact, spewing green mucous identical to the slime that had transformed Scar into a zombie. Billowing clouds of bright green vapor rose twenty feet into the air and were wafted toward the startled Indians, swallowing them before they could even think to run.

Thanatos threw the arrow away, folded his arms, and waited. It had taken him years to perfect the compounds capable of sapping mortal will. The biggest stumbling block had been refining the substance so that the automatons would respond to his directions and his alone. Almost by accident he had learned that they fixated on the first person to command them once the change was complete, much as baby birds and some animals were known to become attached to the first creatures they saw after they hatched or were born.

The clouds took their sweet time dispersing. In their wake stood uneven ranks of blank-eyed Indians, their arms at their sides, their bronzed hues changed to pasty ivory.

"Come to me, my children," Thanatos instructed verbally and in sign language, which one of the men he had hired in St. Louis had taught him. The zombies did, halting when he told them to. "You are the first of many," he crowed.

Bel Aram and the minotaur had not moved. The snake-man scanned the file of walking dead and remarked, "It goes well, does it not, sire?"

The Dark Lord's eyes lit with sadistic glee. "It goes very well. Very well indeed."

Chapter Twenty-two

A mud castle. That was how Blade thought of Bent's Fort. Located on the Arkansas River in what later would become the state of Colorado, the post was the brainchild of three men. Brothers William and Charles Bent and their friend Ceran St. Vrain had foreseen a fortune to be made in the fur trade, and had built themselves the biggest and best outpost west of the Mississippi.

The front extended one hundred and thirty-seven feet, its sides were one hundred and seventy-eight from end to end. The walls were fourteen feet high, over three feet thick. They were sturdy enough to repel cannon balls, to say nothing of arrows and lead balls.

At the northwest and southeast corners stood circular towers eighteen feet in diameter. Field pieces and plenty of rifles were kept there to repel attackers.

None of the tribes had ever been foolhardy enough to actually launch an assault. Most knew that the garrison numbered upwards of two hundred men and that they were well armed.

A flag flew from a central building day in and day out. The post was always buzzing with activity. Daily, friendly Indians arrived to trade. Since the Bents and St. Vrain did not deem it wise to allow intoxicated warriors on the premises, liquor was sold through a small square porthole within rifle range of the southeast tower.

An inside corral could hold three hundred animals. There was a blacksmith shop, a storehouse, and a room for trading. Individual quarters for the three principals and lodgings for those employed by them flanked the open area of the compound.

From the first day, Blade was an object of intense curiosity. His size alone made him stand out. His unique weapons were added cause for tongues to wag. He made it a point to keep to himself—most of the time—and that in itself added to the mystery surrounding him.

Only William Bent was at the fort during the three long weeks Blade stayed there. Bent's brother and St. Vrain had gone to St. Louis and would not be back until the end of the summer. William knew Nate King well. He provided a private room for Winona and saw that all their needs were met.

At least twice a day Blade strolled around the compound, seeking newcomers. One and all he would question. Had they seen any trace of a blond man in buckskins? Of a short man with black hair in green clothes who answered to the name Geronimo? Had they heard of anyone as tall as he was who went around in a cloak? Had any unusual creatures been reported anywhere?

To all his queries Blade received the same answer: No. It was discouraging. He'd had high hopes of learning where the others were, of finding Thanatos and putting a stop to the madman once and for all.

After three weeks of fruitless waiting, Blade had reached the end of his patience. On an afternoon when dark clouds flitted overhead and the promise of a thunderstorm hung pregnant in the moisture-laden air, he crossed the compound to the room shared by the Kings and politely rapped on their door.

"Come on in," Nate called out.

All the Kings were there except Zach, who spent a lot of his time of late hanging around a girl his age. Also present was Edwin Morris, a portly man who had tended Winona during her long illness. Morris was just rising from a chair beside her bed.

"I'd say that in another week you'll be back on your feet, Mrs. King. But you must not overtax yourself or you'll be in bed again before you know it."

Winona smiled to show her appreciation for all the man had done for her, but secretly she was sick and tired of lying around doing nothing. Another week and she would be ready to yank her hair out by the roots.

Nate escorted Morris to the door. "I can't thank you enough, Edwin, for all you've done. If not for you, she wouldn't have pulled through."

"Nonsense," Morris said. "I've done little except make sure you changed her bandages regularly. It was the herb you sprinkled over the wound that stemmed the infection. I wish you had some left. I'd like to know what it was."

"The next time we come here, I'll bring you a pouch of it," Nate pledged. He shook hands, closed the door, and turned to their other visitor. "Any luck yet?"

"I wish," Blade said. Taking a seat by the window, he draped his huge arms across the back. "If you hadn't seen that mutant the day you found me, I'd be convinced that I'm wasting my time." He ran a hand through his hair. "As it is, I'm thinking of leaving soon."

Nate was not surprised. It had been clear that their giant friend was growing more and more restless. The wonder was that he had stayed as long as he had. "Where will you go? What will you do?"

"What I've been doing all along. I'll try to find my friends. There's a caravan to St. Louis heading out in five days and I plan to go along."

"We will miss you," Winona said, and meant it. Over the past few weeks she'd had a number of long talks with the strange white and had grown to like him very much. There wasn't a mean streak in the man, a compliment she could pay few besides her husband. "I will never forget how you saved Blue Flower and myself."

"Anyone would have done the same," Blade said, feeling awkward that she had brought it up. Winona had already thanked him six or seven times.

Nate did not know what to say. Like the rest of his family, he had become quite fond of their new friend. He could not understand, however, why Blade was always so sad. Nate figured that the giant had recently suffered a terrible loss, but he was not about to pry.

"If I don't pick up word of my friends there," Blade was saying, "I'll keep roaming until I do."

A knock sounded. Nate, joking, said, "I've heard of being popular but this is ridiculous."

William Bent was outside. A nattily dressed man with a receding hairline, he had a no-nonsense approach to business and operated the enterprise with an iron hand. He had to. Roughnecks of every stripe paid the fort frequent visits. Unless they were held in check, there would be brawls and bloodshed all the time. Bent removed his hat and gazed past Nate at Winona. "I do so hope I'm not bothering you, Mrs. King, but I was told that your big friend is here."

"He is," Nate confirmed.

Blade moved to the entrance. William Bent plucked at his wrist, saying, "Come with me. Hurry. I have something to show you." He hustled off before Blade could find out more, beckoning urgently.

The Fort's answer to a tavern came equipped with a rare treat on the frontier—billiards. It was the social hub of the fort, busy from the middle of the morning until it closed late at night. Blade heard the crack of the balls as they approached. Inside every table was filled. Customers lined a long plank bar and stood around slinging the bull.

Mystified, Blade watched William Bent rise on his toes to scour the room. The trader tapped him. "Is that one of the men you've been asking about? He showed up just a few minutes ago."

Blade looked and wanted to shout for joy. He barreled through the trappers and Indians, not caring one whit that many did not like being shouldered aside and gave him dirty looks. He was so elated that when he came up behind the man in the corner, he threw his arms around the stocky figure and lifted the man clear off the floor.

Geronimo thought that he was being attacked. Instinctively, he tried to get at his tomahawk.

"Lone Elk!" Blade bellowed happily. In his excited state, he used the name he had known Geronimo by during their childhood. Not until Lone Elk turned sixteen, at his Naming ceremony, had he officially chosen the name he was to bear the rest of his life.

Now it was Geronimo's turn to overflow with joy. After three nerve-wracking weeks of worrying that he might never see his friends again, three weeks of thinking that maybe, just maybe, the Warriors had met their match in Thanatos, three long weeks with no one for company but Old Hugh whose constant chatter at times made him want to scream, to hear that familiar voice and the name that only two people on the planet knew, he was so delirious with joy that he turned, threw his own arms around Blade, and kissed him on the cheek.

"Praise the Spirit! I've found you!"

The two lifelong friends stared at one another a moment. Then both became aware that every head in the place had turned in their direction.

Blade glanced around. Arched eyebrows and indignant expressions prompted him to say, "We're really good friends." Straightening, he clapped Geronimo on the shoulder. "Just when I was giving up hope, here you are!"

"I would have been here sooner," Geronimo said, and was interrupted before he could elaborate.

"Don't start your gripin' again, sonny," Old Hugh declared. "It ain't my fault it took a little longer than I figured. You didn't want my horse to come up lame, did you?"

"No," Geronimo said. It had been about a week after their clash with Mad Bull. The trapper's mount had begun to limp. They'd had to rest two whole days, then held their animals to a walk for a week afterward so the horse could heal.

Old Hugh's eye jiggled as he scrutinized Blade. "Ain't you goin' to introduce your friend here, hoss? It ain't every day that I get to shake the paw of a walkin' redwood."

Geronimo did, then steered Blade to the bar so they could talk in peace. A burning question was uppermost on his mind, one he had to ask before another moment went by. "Have you heard anything of Nathan?"

"Not a word."

They both frowned. Since the three of them had worn diapers they had been inseparable.

They had grown up together, gotten into mischief together, learned about life together. They had all decided to become Warriors and trained together to qualify. They had been assigned to the same Warrior Triad, and ever since they had worked as a well-oiled unit, waging war on the forces of darkness and destruction.

Life without the master gunfighter was unthinkable.

"Where could that idiot be?" Geronimo wondered.

"How many this time, old-timer?"

He Who Eats Dog knelt to examine the ground. Horse hoofs had made a mess of it, but not such a mess that he could not read the many tracks of horses and men as readily as whites read the strange birdlike tracks in books. "Twelve. They were Blackfeet. They tried to fight, but the demons used their magic. Now they are like the rest."

Hickok totaled the numbers out loud. "First it was thirty Arikaras, then twenty-one Pawnees, and now this bunch. That gives Thanatos sixty-three zombies, plus the riffraff he picked up in St. Louis, and the two mutants. Not bad, considering that he hasn't struck a village yet. Once he does, he'll have hundreds."

The Warrior sighed. It had been a long three weeks. The chance he had waited for had slipped through his fingers. Tackling the Dark Lord now would only get him killed. Yet he refused to give up. Where there was a will, there was a way.

Thanatos had not returned to the main trail after his encounter with the Arikaras. The madman had paralleled it instead, perhaps for secrecy's sake. Each day the two mutants had roved far afield, seeking more Indians.

Hickok and the Caw had stayed half a day behind to avoid being discovered. According to the old warrior, the closest villages were all a hundred miles or more to the north. That troubled Hickok. Thanatos was not the kind to waste time. By rights, the Dark Lord should have headed for the nearest one to recruit more zombies. Instead, his party continued westward. Thanatos had to have a reason, but for the life of him, Hickok could not imagine what it might be.

Then He Who Eats Dog stood, his voice quivering as he blurted, "Bent's Fort!"

"What?"

"You have been telling me that the demons want a lot of people for their army, and we have been thinking that they would attack a village. But we were wrong, Lightning Hands. The one you call the Dark Lord came this way to attack Bent's Fort."

"Let me guess. It's west of here?"

He Who Eats Dog nodded. "Two days away. It is a trading post. I have visited it several times. Over a hundred whites live and work there. They have many guns and much supplies."

The Caw did not have to go on. Hickok saw it all, now. Thanatos had been making for the fort all along. Hemmed in by four walls, the traders would be easy pickings. In one fell swoop the butcher would swell the ranks of his undead legion, plus have all the provisions and weapons he'd need.

Or maybe, Hickok reflected, Thanatos was

even more devious than he gave the bastard credit for. Bent's Fort was a trading post, right? That meant Indians from all over came there to barter. Thanatos would not have to go looking for recruits; they would come to him. Or maybe the Dark Lord intended to send invitations to the surrounding tribes and have them visit the post on one pretext or another so that he could transform hundreds at a time. Thanatos might even make the fort his permanent base of operations.

"Damn that varmint," Hickok grumbled. He did some fast calculations. "We have to warn the people at the fort. If we were to light a shuck and swing on around the Dark Lord's bunch, we could reach the fort a day or so ahead of him."

"This is true," He Who Eats Dog said.

"Then what are we waitin' for?"

Hickok stepped into the stirrups, and the Caw climbed onto Heavy Paws. The dog had held up well during the long journey. It had amused Hickok to see how attached He Who Eats Dog became to the animal, though the Caw tried hard not to show it.

Just the evening before Hickok had caught the old man rubbing heads with it and whispering sweet nothings in its ear.

"I am telling it to behave and stop licking me," He Who Eats Dog had responded when teased.

"Sure you are, partner," Hickok had said, smirking. "But from where I sit, it looks as if another dog-eater has bitten the dust."

Now, trailing the shaggy mongrel to the southwest, Hickok stayed on the lookout for sign of the mutants. Most of the time the pair roved to the north, but there had been exceptions.

Storm clouds moved in from the west. They blotted out the sun, creating a premature twilight. The wind intensified, buffeting the Warrior, the whangs on his buckskins flapping briskly.

Small drops fell at first. They rapidly grew bigger and colder, so that in no time Hickok felt perfectly miserable. Visibility was limited to a few dozen feet. He had to stay close to the dog in order not to lose it.

The worst was yet to come. A vivid streak of jagged light and the near deafening din that followed let Hickok know this was no simple downpour. It was a thunderstorm and no ordinary one at that. Thunderstorms on the plains were incredibly violent, so much so that only those who had experienced them could fully appreciate how severe they were.

Another flashing bolt lit up the landscape. Then another. Soon lightning crackled virtually nonstop. Thunder roared without letup. The wind howled like a crazed banshee, driving the rain into Hickok with such force the drops felt like pellets. He hunched over and protected his face with an arm.

Several times his mount shied. The extra horse tried to pull loose by tugging on the lead rope, but Hickok held on tight.

Suddenly Hickok's mount stopped cold. He was about to spur it on when he saw Heavy Paws cowering in the grass, He Who Eats Dog beside it. Dismounting, holding onto the reins, he stepped nearer and leaned down to be heard above the uproar. "We have to keep going."

The Caw had an arm around the dog's neck

and was soothing it as best he could. "Heavy Paws is too scared. He would not carry me. We must wait for the storm to end."

The prospect did not appeal to Hickok. Many a soul caught in the open in a thunderstorm had been blasted by lightning, and he did not care to be one of them. Yet what choice did he have? He could not leave the Caw behind. Hunkering, he wrapped the reins around his left arm, the lead rope around his right. The horses pressed in close, apparently comforted by his presence.

It seemed as if the elements raged for hours. The grass whipped and swayed the whole time, surrounding them with shadowy movement that in itself kept Hickok's nerves on edge. He was vastly relieved when the lightning tapered and the rain slackened. He was also soaked to the skin and covered with goosebumps.

The Warrior straightened. He had to bend backward to relieve a cramp at the base of his spine. As he did, he gazed to the north, and froze. "Don't move!" he whispered. "Don't make a peep!"

At the limits of his vision, a huge shape had appeared. It came slowly toward them, but in an odd, haphazard fashion. The creature was moving back and forth over a wide area as if it were searching for something. Or hunting prey.

Hickok rested a hand on a Python. The rain abated some more, enough for him to recognize the shape for what it was. The minotaur.

The genetic deviate acted confused. It would stomp to the east a few dozen feet, then do the same to the west. Finally, the dumb brute halted and scratched its head. Hickok realized that the thing was lost. In the confusion of the storm, its sense of direction had been scrambled. It had no idea where it was. In a few moments the monstrosity came nearer.

The gunfighter tensed. A single nicker or a yip from the mutt was all it took to make the beast charge, and he was not confident about the outcome. The Marlin had failed to do the job once already.

A break in the clouds was a lucky break for the Warrior. Gleaming shafts of sunlight streamed through, bathing part of the prairie. The minotaur squinted skyward. Now that it knew where the sun was, it knew which direction to go. Turning northward, it stomped off at a lumbering trot.

"Did you see it?" He Who Eats Dog said. "Aren't these demons wonderful?"

Hickok had another word for them. He lost no time swinging into the saddle. "Hurry up," he coaxed. "That moron might get lost again and wind up back here."

But they did not run into the minotaur again. By late evening the Caw was certain they had passed Thanatos. Hickok took nothing for granted. He stayed south of the main trail, where they were safer.

On through the night they traveled. Hickok switched horses when his flagged. Toward morning He Who Eats Dog had to coax Heavy Paws when the weary dog balked.

Dawn broke crisp and clear. In the distance to the northwest loomed what Hickok mistook for a hill.

"Bent's Fort," He Who Eats Dog declared.

It was early yet, and the front gate was not open. Hickok dismounted and pounded on it to attract attention. Presently, a bearded face appeared on the rampart above.

"What's all the racket, Mister?"

"What do you think?" Hickok retorted. "Let us in before I huff and puff and blow this thing down."

"Is that some kind of joke?" The man yawned, then noticed the Caw. His yawn widened into a gawk of astonishment. "Are my eyes playin' tricks on me, or is that Injun ridin' a dog?"

"Are you loco? That's no dog. It's a hippopotamus."

"A what?"

Hickok smacked the gate. "Just get this open, will you? I have important news for whoever runs this outfit."

"Why didn't you say so in the first place?"

The gunfighter tapped his foot with impatience, waiting for the portal to open. He nodded at the two frontiersmen who performed the chore, then stalked across an open compound toward a cluster of buildings.

Many of those who dwelled there were up and around. A blacksmith was heating his forge. Two men were toting crates. Another was giving a horse a rubdown. Six women were about to go to the river for water.

Hickok was halfway across when it occurred to him that everyone was staring at the Caw. "Will you get off that blamed mutt?" he said. "You're makin' a spectacle of yourself."

The man grooming the horse started to laugh and soon others joined in. Mirth rippled from one side of the post to the other. He Who Eats Dog sat up straighter, beaming proudly. "They like me," he said.

"They think you're a fruitcake," Hickok corrected him. Shaking his head in disgust, he walked to a hitching post and tied his two animals.

The Caw rode up alongside the gunman, then gave a little bow to their audience. "I had no idea whites could be so friendly."

Hickok rolled his eyes. "It's downright mortifyin'," he complained, walking around the horses toward a cluster of men, who should be able to direct him to the head honcho. Another burst of laughter made him look back. He Who Eats Dog had climbed down and was tying the dog to the post just as if it were a horse. Facing front, Hickok abruptly stopped.

A giant in a black leather vest and a short man in green fatigues were showing him more teeth than the snake-hybrid had. The latter chuckled.

"We should have known it would be you, Nathan."

Chapter Twenty-three

Nate King did not like it. He did not like it one bit. Standing just outside the walls of Bent's Fort, he offered his hand to the giant and said, "I still think you're making a mistake. The three of you shouldn't do it alone."

Blade shook warmly. "We've been all through this. For reasons I can't begin to explain, we have to."

Geronimo, who was mounted, nodded. "Just remember what we told you, Mr. King. If Thanatos gets past us, it will be up to you and everyone here to stop him."

Hickok, also on horseback, hefted his reins.

"Enough palaver, already. We've got us a job to do. Let's get to it, or that mangy Thanatos is liable to attack before we get two feet." Reining his animal around, he headed to the northeast. In that direction lay the Dark Lord's camp.

"Take care," Blade said to Nate, and straddled his mount. "It's been nice knowing you." With a friendly wave, he rode off in the wake of his friends and soon overtook them.

"Just the three of us again," Hickok commented. "The way it's supposed to be." He glanced at each of them. "Lordy, I can't believe how much I missed your ugly pusses. Makes me think I should have my head examined."

Never one to miss an opportunity, Geronimo responded, "Why bother? There's nothing between your ears for them to find."

"Hardy-har-har."

Blade laughed. The gunfighter was right. It was marvelous being back together again. He even enjoyed listening to them bicker like a pair of overaged kids. But it was a luxury they should indulge in later. After. If they lived that long. "Do either of you have a plan for dealing with Thanatos?"

"We waltz into his camp blazing away and hope we nail him before his hired help nails us," Hickok said.

Geronimo cocked his head at the gunman. "You call *that* a plan? As outnumbered as we're going to be, we need to come up with something better."

Blade had to agree. The element of surprise would be on their side, but that was hardly enough to compensate for the tremendous disadvantage they would be at otherwise. An important factor was their limited supply of ammo. He had the most out of the three of them, and it was not enough to tide him through a sustained battle.

"The mutants will give us the most trouble," Hickok said. "I shot that blasted minotaur in the head at close range, and it didn't do no more than dent his noggin."

Soon they were out of sight of the fort. Mile after mile they covered. Around them the waving grass shimmered golden in the glow of a newborn day.

"It can't be that much further," Hickok mentioned. He rose in the stirrups to scan the plain, and as he did, something rose up out of the grass in front of him, something that filled his horse with such terror, the animal whinnied and bucked wildly. It happened so quickly that Hickok was thrown head over heels. He landed on his back, jarring every bone, and looked up into the malice-filled eyes of the creature responsible.

"What have we here?" Bel Aram declared in a sibilant hiss. "Warriorsssssss three! What a pleasssssant sssurprissse."

Blade tried to aim the Commando, but his own horse was acting up. Rather than back off to bring it under control, he vaulted to the earth and darted to the gunfighter's side.

Only Geronimo's horse remained calm. Leveling the FNC, he said, "Three against one. Surrender, mutant, while you can."

Bel Aram would have laughed if his vocal chords were capable of producing the sound.

"Please, human slug. Do not insult my intelligence. It is you who should surrender." The tip of his forked tongue did a dance in the air. "Besides, the odds are more even than you think. Ghanata, if you please."

Blade's skin crawled as a minotaur surged to its feet to his left. Deep wounds scarred the massive head. Snorting like a maddened bull, the beast stomped its heavy hooves a few times.

"Say the word, Bel Aram, and I will crush these puny fleas!"

"Consider it given," the snake-man said.

The minotaur reached them in a blinding rush, its broad head lowered, its curved horns hooked to rend and tear. It made straight for Blade, the biggest target. He squeezed off a single shot, and then the monster was on him like a runaway express train.

Blade released the Commando to grab those wicked horns at the instant they sliced toward him. He caught one in each hand and held on, seeking to blunt the minotaur's rush. But it was like trying to blunt an avalanche. He was swept off his feet and hoisted into the air, the deviate's momentum driving him rearward. His boots touched the ground, and he attempted to brace himself, but with a mighty heave the minotaur upended him.

Hickok scrambled onto his knees, unlimbering both Pythons as Bel Aram leaped. Geronimo's FNC chattered a fraction ahead of the Colts, the slugs catching the hybrid in the chest but doing no real damage thanks to the armor it wore. Slammed backward, the mutant glided to the right, moving like molten mercury.

The minotaur closed on Blade before he could rise. He had lost the Commando when he spilled, and the next thing he knew, the minotaur had its huge arms wrapped around his waist and was lifting him off the ground.

"Ha! Ghanata has you now, Warrior! I will break you in half! My master will be pleased!"

Blade nearly cried out as indescribable pressure was applied to his midsection. He was literally being squeezed in two. It felt as if his insides might rupture out his throat at any moment. Locking an arm under the minotaur's jaw, he shoved, but he might as well have been shoving a mountain. The pressure worsened. Ghanata bellowed in glee.

Hickok and Geronimo knew that their friend was in trouble, but they had their own hands full. As the snake-man streaked toward them, the gunfighter fired four times, working the trigger so rapidly that the fours shots were like one. Yet none struck the hybrid, it was so unbelievably fast. It homed in on him, lunging at his neck.

That was when Geronimo opened up, a short burst that spanged off Bel Aram's pliable body armor and forced the serpentine creature to angle to one side.

Blade, meanwhile, was on the verge of blacking out. He slammed a fist into the minotaur's jaw, but the beast did not feel the blow. He punched its cheek, its forehead.

Ghanata laughed. "You are weak, human! Yet everyone says you are so mighty! Bah! They are all wrong."

Inside Blade, his stomach churned. He could have sworn his navel was brushing his spine.

Dizziness assailed him. Every vein on his arms and temples bulged. At any second he might explode. He strained against the minotaur's iron arms, but they were like constricting boas, immovable. His right hand slipped. His fingertips brushed the hilt of his right Bowie.

Realizing his knives were not covered by the brute's arm, Blade grabbed both.

"Ready to die, flea?" Ghanata mocked him, and stiffened for one last exertion.

Blade swept the Bowies up and around. The minotaur saw them, but it was too slow to prevent the twin blades from stabbing deep into its eyes. Blade buried them, then sagged, the last of his strength expended.

A tremendous roar tore from Ghanata's throat. Staggering, the minotaur grabbed at the hilts. Blood gushed from its nose, from its mouth, from its ears.

Flat on his back, Blade was too weak to do anything except stare as the bovine hybrid gurgled and gasped and wrenched the Bowies out. More blood spouted, covering Ghanata, peppering Blade, splattering the soil.

The minotaur swiveled to the right and the left. "Bel Aram!" it wailed, and buckled in on itself, the knobby knees folding and the enormous head collapsing on its suddenly motionless chest. Like a tree felled in a forest, the behemoth crashed to the ground, one arm outflung.

For all of five seconds no one moved. Bel Aram broke the spell, raking them with his malevolent gaze and hissing, "We will meet again, Warriorsssss! Count on it!"

Hickok raised his Colts, but the snake-man

erupted into headlong flight to the northwest, moving at a speed no animal in the world could match. In impotent anger he shook a pistol at it. "Come back here, you yellow-belly!"

Geronimo jumped down and ran to Blade, hooking an arm under the giant's shoulder as Blade rose unsteadily. "Maybe you should rest awhile," he recommended.

"No," Blade responded, his voice like sandpaper grating on sandpaper. "That thing will tell Thanatos. We have to hurry, to jump them before they can get set for us."

"Wishful thinkin', pard," Hickok said. "Bel Aram is probably halfway to their camp already."

"We have to try," Blade insisted. Once he was erect, the queasy sensation went away. He walked in a circle, tapping his reserve of stamina, feeling more like he should with every step.

Geronimo claimed the Bowies and Commando for him. "I've never heard of anyone beating a minotaur one-on-one before. Wait until the Family hears."

An awkward silence gripped them. The innocent remark was a poignant reminder that they were outcasts, adrift in the stream of time, that they might never see those who mattered most in their lives ever again.

It also reminded Blade that their only hope of returning to their own century rested in the hands of their bitterest enemy. As much as they wanted to do to the Dark Lord as he had done to so many thousands, they could not. "Remember, you two. We have to take Thanatos alive," he said softly.

"I doubt he'll let us," Hickok voiced their innermost fear.

"If we don't, we're stuck here forever," Geronimo said. The likelihood did not appeal to him. Which was strange. In their own day and age, the planet was still recovering from the worst calamity in its history. It was overrun by abominations of every stripe. It had been polluted to the point of near mass extinction.

Here, in 1840, the world was a pristine wonderland. It had clean air and pure water. The forests and valleys were lush and green. Its people lived simple lives. They were like people in any other age, and yet they were somehow different. More basic. More decent.

Yet it was Geronimo's own world that he craved, the one he had grown up in, the one where genetic deviates lurked in every shadow and chemical clouds drifted over the countryside devouring all flesh. It was his home. He wanted to go back to it more than anything. They all did.

The Warriors were somber as they rode on. In half a mile they came to a spot where the grass had been flattened in the shape of a large arrow. It pointed to the northeast.

"I'll bet that blasted snake-man did this," Hickok guessed. "It must be his notion of extendin' an invite."

"Or a challenge," Geronimo said.

Blade offered no comment. Clucking his horse into a lope, he was not surprised when half a mile further on they found another arrow. Next to it a large question mark had been made.

"That pesky reptile is beginnin' to annoy me,"

Hickok said. "He's pokin' fun at us, darin' us to keep going."

The next arrow was a mile deeper into the prairie. It was smaller and it pointed more eastward than north.

Another mile, and Hickok suddenly stiffened. "Smoke up yonder, pards," he announced. "A campfire, most likely. We've hit paydirt."

"Check your weapons," Blade directed, and did just that, insuring a fresh magazine was in the Commando. To conserve ammo, he flipped the selector lever to SEMI-AUTO.

"How do you want to play this?" Geronimo asked.

"They know we're coming, so we might as well do as Nathan proposed and ride right in on them," Blade said. "Stick close together so we can cover each other's backs."

A wide gray plume beckoned. There was much more smoke than a typical campfire would produce. Blade suspected Thanatos had ordered the fire made bigger just for their benefit. The Dark Lord wanted a showdown as much as they did.

Staying no more than five feet apart, the Warriors cautiously advanced. They saw no sign of moving figures, or men or horses or anything else.

Hickok twisted to survey the entire plain. "What gives? Where the dickens are they? We're almost on top of that smoke, yet there's no camp anywhere."

The explanation became apparent when they reined up on the rim of a wide basin, a natural bowl over one hundred yards from end to end. The fire was in the very middle; a mountain of grass had been piled up so the smoke would be thick. Scattered near it were personal effects, mainly blankets and pots and buckskin bags. At the east end of the bowl, over two dozen horses were tethered in a string. Not a living or undead soul was anywhere to be seen.

"Where are they?" Geronimo wondered.

"They ran off," Hickok said. "They suckered us in with the smoke, and the whole time they were sneakin' away. Thanatos must not want to tangle with us yet."

Geronimo was skeptical. "I can't see him passing up the chance."

Neither could Blade. He figured that they should circle the basin and look for tracks. Then the gunman pointed toward the center.

"Look there!"

Beside the fire an arrow was imbedded in the dirt. Attached to it, fluttering in the breeze, was a white sheet of paper.

"That varmint left us a note," Hickok said. Smacking his legs against his horse, he trotted down the slope to learn what it said.

"Nathan, wait!" Blade called out, but it was too late. The impetuous firebrand was at the bottom and speeding off.

Geronimo sighed. "I don't suppose we can just sit here and let that ding-a-ling be massacred?"

In response Blade spurred his mount down the incline.

"I didn't think so," Geronimo said wistfully, following. "Too bad. It might teach him a lesson."

Hickok slowed as he neared the arrow, wary of a booby-trap. He saw no tripwires, no evidence that the soil had been tampered with. Dismounting, he ground-hitched the bay and unslung the Marlin. A lingering scent hung around the fire, the aroma of roasted meat. It made his mouth water until he saw a partially charred foot laying half in the flames.

Blade and Geronimo got there just as the gunfighter bent and pulled the shaft out. They watched the rim closely, but no one appeared.

"What does it say?" Geronimo inquired.

"It's poetry, of all things," Hickok said, holding the paper still so he could read the meticulous handwriting. "Roses are red, violets are blue, minotaurs are stupid and so are you." Chuckling, he crumpled the sheet. "How come everyone claims Thanatos is a genius? My youngest sprout could do better than that."

"It got us right where he wanted us, didn't it?" Blade said, nodding.

Hickok lifted his gaze to the top of the basin. Figures had sprouted to the north, east, south, and west. On each rim two spectral ranks of undead Indians stood awaiting commands from a human cutthroat. Six mounted men appeared beside those to the north. So did the snake-man, Bel Aram. Last of all, shrouded in his billowing cloak, his hood pulled over his head, came the Dark Lord. The hood did not hide his sinister smile.

"Welcome, Warriors!" Thanatos shouted. "How gracious of you to accept our invitation!" His delight knew no bounds. Blade and the other two had been thorns in his side ever since he launched his campaign to conquer North America. To dispose of them was a pleasure too long denied.

"Mosey on down here, you pompous windbag!" Hickok replied. "I'm just itchin' for some target practice!"

Thanatos stepped to the edge of the basin. "Always the wit, eh, gunman?" he countered dryly. "What about you, Blade? Have you nothing to say?" Of all his adversaries, the giant Warrior was the only one Thanatos held in any esteem. It had been Blade's leadership of the Federation forces that resulted in his humiliating defeat and forced him to flee to his Tower. He yearned to make the giant suffer before finishing him off.

Blade had only one comment. "It ends here, evil one. One way or the other."

"On that we heartily agree!" Thanatos said. "With you and your inept associates gone, there will be no stopping me. First America, then the world!" He smugly regarded his minions. The zombies had been told to obey their human captains and would fight until they dropped. No doubt the Warriors would kill a lot of them, but so be it. Zombies were cannon fodder, nothing more, and easily replaced.

Thanatos raised his right arm. As always before a battle, emotional electricity pulsed through him. "On my order," he roared, "*attack!*"

The zombies started into the basin, marching in syncopated rhythm, their gait ungainly, their limbs twitching, their features impassive. The human captains of each section were on the right flank, ready to goad on stragglers.

The Dark Lord turned to the mounted killers. "When the zombies engage them, ride down and try to pick them off."

"What about me, sir?" Bel Aram asked.

"You are my wild card, free to do as you see fit. When an opening presents itself, take advantage of it." Thanatos became stern. "Just don't get yourself killed like that idiot Ghanata. Your services are too invaluable. It will be months before I have the portal adjusted to where it can bring dozens of your kind through at a time."

"As you will, master." Bel Aram raced to join the brewing melee.

Thanatos folded his hands behind his back and strolled lower to observe the outcome. Not that there was any doubt. The sixty-three zombies alone were enough to overwhelm the Warriors. The cutthroats and the hybrid were just so much icing on the cake, as it were. All he had to do was watch and enjoy.

Over in the center of the basin, Blade worked the cocking bolt on the Commando. "Go for their heads," he reminded his friends. He saw that the Dark Lord was staying well behind the attacking automatons, and frowned. Above all else, they had to get to him.

Hickok elevated the Marlin. It wasn't the walking dead that worried him so much as the backshooters from St. Louis. He compensated for windage and distance, fixed a bead on the foremost rider, and squeezed off a shot when the man was sixty yards out.

The cutthroat threw his arms over his head and toppled. His fellow ruffians veered to the west to keep out of range.

"Piece of cake," Hickok quipped.

"Don't get cocky," Geronimo said.

"Me? Never."

Blade noticed that the zombies to the south

348

were moving faster than the rest and pointed it out. "We take them first. If they go down, we'll only have to fight on three fronts."

"Only three?" Hickok snickered. "Good. For a minute there I thought we were in trouble."

Thanatos also noticed the breach of his battle plan. He had given specific instructions that the zombies were to engage the Warriors from all four sides simultaneously. It would render them unstoppable. Fuming at the lapse, he bellowed at the human in charge of the southern ranks.

"Slow them down! Space yourselves! Slower, damn it!"

To the Dark Lord's dismay, his command was carried out to the letter by all *four* cutthroats in charge of the undead. Each knew sign language, a smattering of Indian tongues. Each ran to the front of their squads and relayed the command. Immediately, all four prongs of the automaton army slowed to a tottering crawl just as they came within range of the Warriors.

"No!" Thanatos raged. Couldn't those dolts do anything right!

Blade, Hickok, and Geronimo were back to back.

At the moment the zombies slowed, Blade took aim at those to the south. "Now!" he barked, taking advantage of the mistake before it could be rectified. The Commando bucked against his shoulder with each tap of the trigger. He fired one round at a time, never rushing a shot, doing just as he would do on the target range only this time he was coring pale faces and not clay pigeons.

Geronimo had trained the FNC on the undead

to the east. He dropped two, three, four. Still the zombies came on, moving faster now that their overseers had realized their blunder.

Hickok had three rounds left in the .45–70. He sighted on the cutthroat heading the zombies to the north and blew the man's brains out. Swiveling, he saw that his companions were shooting the automatons, not the men in charge. So he did it for them. His next shot nailed a lanky frontiersmen leading the western ranks, his third dropped the scruffy specimen in charge of the Indians to the east.

Quickly, the gunfighter reloaded the rifle. Turning his back to the zombies on the north, he looked for the man leading those to the south. The cutthroat was shouting and gesturing sharply, trying to get his mindless charges to do something. Hickok could not hear a word above the din of the blasting SMG. He gave the fellow's throat a break by putting a hole through it. The fourth captain dropped like a rock.

Pleased with himself, Hickok looked for the three men still on horseback. They were to the southwest, circling like the vultures they were, seeking an opening so they could close in without any danger to themselves. "Fat chance," Hickok said. Hefting the Marlin, he sighted on one, taking his time in order to be sure. Out of the corner of an eye, he saw Blade reload. Then he fired.

The man on the sorrel was punched off it as if slammed by a grizzly's paw. He landed in an crumpled pile, his legs convulsing, his chest imitating Old Faithful.

"Two to go," Hickok said, grinning. He gripped

the lever and was gripped himself, from behind, by a pair of hands so cold the fingers were like ice. Too late, he remembered the zombies to the north. While his back had been turned, they had closed in.

Hickok nearly cried out. Their inhuman touch was almost enough to fill him with fear. Almost, but not quite. Spinning, he smashed the Marlin against the zombie's hands, knocking the creature back. Beside and behind it were others, reaching for him and his friends, reaching, reaching, reaching.

Hickok dropped the Marlin and drew the Colts. In that instant he lived up to the name the old Caw had given him. The Pythons were out and leveled in a fraction of an instant. He shot the zombie who had grabbed him, shot one next to it, shot another that tried to walk over them to get at him. Pivoting, he shot an automaton reaching for Geronimo's neck, shot another that tried the same. He had decimated the first row, but the next row still came on, their vacant eyes fixed unnaturally on his.

Geronimo emptied the FNC for a second time. Five of the zombies on his side still had not gone down. They were almost upon him. He filled his right hand with the Arminius, his left with his tomahawk, and took the fight to them. A war club arced at his head. Blocking it, he was startled to see that the Indian holding the club was Mad Bull! The Blackfoot leader had survived being shot by Old Hugh only to be snared by Thanatos. He sent a slug through the undead warrior's skull and pivoted to ward off another.

Blade had the most ammo of the three of them.

He was on his third magazine when the last of the automatons to the south sprawled lifeless onto the grass. Spinning to the west, he moved to confront the two rows of undead as yet unscathed.

Forty yards out a Hawken cracked. A lead ball kicked up dirt at Blade's feet. He tracked the rider and gave the man a taste of his own medicine, only the Commando shot truer. As the man fell, Blade turned the SMG on the zombies and squeezed the trigger.

The Commando jammed.

Blade had to act. The zombies were nearly there. Discarding the SMG, he resorted to his Bowies, streaking both blades clear and wading into the automatons like a human whirlwind. He struck at their necks, severing jugular after jugular, decapitating many, always in motion, never allowing them to seize hold of him, because if they did it would be all over.

A tall Indian came at him with a lance. Blade parried the tip, stepped in close, and slashed his right Bowie across the warrior's neck. The zombie halted. Its head tilted back and kept on tilting until it slid from the stump that was left and plopped at its own feet.

Blade did not break stride. It was the moment of truth. Either he shattered the zombie advance or they trod over him to attack Geronimo and Hickok. A tomahawk nearly sheared his cheek off. A knife missed his chest by a hair. He blocked, thrust, cut, and chopped, leaving severed hands and arms and heads in his wake.

The next moment Blade was in the open, the zombies dead or expiring. His knives were caked with gore, his arms smeared clear up to his elbows. He turned to see how his friends were faring. Suddenly a hooded form rose up before him. Fingers composed of living steel closed on his right wrist, others on his left.

"If you want something done right," Thanatos snarled, "do it yourself."

Ten feet away Hickok emptied his Colts and back-pedaled. Somehow he had gotten turned around so that he backed to the north, dodging outstretched arms and weapon after weapon. A lance nicked his shoulder. Another gouged his thigh.

Hickok reloaded on the fly, replacing the spent cartridges with a skill born of countless hours of practice. He flipped the loading gate on the right Python closed and fired just as a zombie rained a war club at his forehead. Another fell to a blast through the eye. Still back-pedaling, he downed two more.

It took a moment for Hickok to realize that was the last of those who were after him. He saw Geronimo battling others and went to help, taking a single step when a serpentine figure barred his path.

"We meet again, Warrior," Bel Aram said, talons poised. "Now let us discover which is truly the faster."

Geronimo, meanwhile, had two zombies left to kill. He ducked a knife and drove his tomahawk into the creature's temple. A lance speared at his heart, and he skipped to the right to avoid it.

Only one shot remained in the Arminius. Geronimo expended it on the automation with the lance. The last undead Indian, blood oozing from its split cranium, attempted to stab him. Two blows from the tomahawk ended its threat.

Panting from his exertion, Geronimo scanned the littered bodies. He was cut and bruised and sore, but he was still alive. Pivoting, he saw Hickok being attacked by Bel Aram and Blade grappling with Thanatos. He had to go to their aid, but which one should he help first?

Hickok was closer.

None of this was observed by the Dark Lord. He had eyes only for the human who had caused him so much grief. Wrenching on the giant Warrior's arms, Thanatos forced Blade to drop the Bowies. "Just because we are the same size, impudent fool, do not presume to think that you possess my raw power. You do not."

Blade was not about to dispute the fact. Try as he might, he was unable to tear his arms free. Thanatos was the strongest foe he had ever faced, bar none. It was like being an infant in the grip of a gorilla.

"First I will break your arms, then your legs," Thanatos gloated. "The rest of your bones will be broken one by one. My knowledge of the human anatomy is without peer. It will be days before you die, in the most unendurable agony."

Blade knew something about anatomy, too. He lashed out, planting his foot in the Dark Lord's groin. Thanatos roared and let go, automatically lowering a hand to cover his privates. Bending, Blade grabbed his big knives. He glimpsed Thanatos reaching under his cloak, but he struck quickest, one Bowie ripping Thanatos across the chest, the other sinking to the hilt under the Dark Lord's left arm.

Thanatos swayed. His hood fell off, revealing his contorted features. "This can't be!" he exclaimed. "It can't end like this!"

Blade yanked his Bowie out and drew it back. He stopped, seeing a metal chestplate through the tear in the cloak. It was spitting sparks and humming loudly. Dials and buttons covered the polished surface. In the center was a pulsing red button.

Suddenly Thanatos reached under his cloak and pressed that button. A twisted smile lit his face as a green glow lit his body. "So long, Warrior!"

Blade glanced around.

Bel Aram was prone, a tomahawk buried in his head, a bullet hole in his eye.

"Hickok! Geronimo!" Blade bellowed. "Grab hold of Thanatos!" He lunged, grasping the Dark Lord's shoulder. Instantly, the green glow spread up his arm, sheathing his whole body in light. His friends were retrieving their weapons. "Hurry, damn it! Do it now or else!"

Geronimo and Hickok leaped toward Blade just as the same awful, sickening sensation he had experienced during his first trip through the time portal brought him to his knees. His senses reeled. He had no idea which way was up, which was down. He could not even tell if he still had a grip on Thanatos.

The discomfort lasted longer than before. Blade's head was swimming when the green glow faded. He had to blink a few times to clear his vision, then blinked again to be sure he was not dreaming.

Hickok and Geronimo were doing the same.

The gunfighter rose first, wobbly but determined, gaping at the banks of equipment and the metal grid under their feet. "It's the same chamber! We're back! But how the dickens did we do it?"

Blade shook Thanatos. "Here's your answer." The Dark Lord lay limp, blood pouring from under his arm, a vicious sneer etched on his lips. In death he was as true to his nature as he had been in life. The chestplate had stopped sparking, and the red light had gone out. "All that counts is we're home."

"Almost, anyway," Geronimo said. "Let's get out of here. We'll come back with all the Warriors and level this place."

The three of them moved to the elevator. They took it down in somber silence. No mutants greeted them at the bottom. No zombies or other unearthly creatures tried to stop them from leaving the Tower.

Hickok breathed in the gritty air and grinned. "I can't wait to see my missus. She's probably missed me so much, she'll lock us in the bedroom for a week of wild passion."

"Either that," Geronimo remarked, "or she'll make you catch up on all the dishes you missed doing."

"I'll have you know that I wear the britches in my family, you mangy Injun. I only do the dishes every other day."

"That's right. I forgot. The other days you do laundry."

Blade smiled. After all they had been through, after all their trials and tribulations, one truth stood out above the rest. No matter what day and age it was, some things, it seemed, never changed.

T.V. OLSEN

Don't miss these double shots of classic Western action!
$7.98 values for only $4.99!
"Plenty of crunching fights and shootings!
Don't pass T.V. Olsen up!"
—*The Roundup*

McGivern. Out to avenge his woman's death, McGivern has to take on the deadliest gunrunners ever to strap on six-shooters, and whoever survives the bloody showdown will be the law of the West.
And in the same action-packed volume...
The Hard Men. Loftus Buckmaster owns half the valley and aims to own the rest. But Krag Soderstrom has other ideas, and he puts together a violent crew to stop Buckmaster. Soon the valley will ring with bullets in a battle as deadly and bitter as the hate that spawned it.
__3612-6 McGIVERN/THE HARD MEN (2 books in one) for only $4.99

A Man Called Brazos. When a murdering sidewinder steals Brazos Kane's once-in-a-lifetime stake, Kane vows that nothing will stop him from evening the score.
And in the same exciting volume...
Brand Of The Star. Although half the territory wants to cut Sam Ashby down or string him up, he can't figure out who hates him enough to kill his wife. Until Ashby catches the killer, the brave and the cowardly will fall victim to a rage no man can stop.
__3688-6 A MAN CALLED BRAZOS/BRAND OF THE STAR (2 books in one) for only $4.99

Dorchester Publishing Co., Inc.
65 Commerce Road
Stamford, CT 06902

Please add $1.75 for shipping and handling for the first book and $.50 for each book thereafter. NY, NYC, PA and CT residents, please add appropriate sales tax. No cash, stamps, or C.O.D.s. All orders shipped within 6 weeks via postal service book rate. Canadian orders require $2.00 extra postage and must be paid in U.S. dollars through a U.S. banking facility.

Name _____

Address _____

City _____ State _____ Zip _____

I have enclosed $_____ in payment for the checked book(s).

Payment <u>must</u> accompany all orders. ☐ Please send a free catalog.

DON'T MISS THESE ACTION-PACKED NOVELS BY THE WORLD'S MOST CELEBRATED WESTERN WRITER!

The Mustang Herder. Gregg isn't a big man physically, but he is as tenacious as a terrier after a rat. Raised on the tough streets of Old New York, he can outfight any brawler, outcuss any sailor, and outdraw any shootist. Armed with those talents, he heads west to make his fortune, never realizing that herding mustangs is what he'll end up doing. He doesn't know a lot about horses, but he knows anyone who stands in his way is as good as buzzard bait.

__3908-7 $4.50 US/$5.50 CAN

Gun Gentlemen. Renowned throughout the Old West, Lucky Bill has the reputation of a natural battler. Yet he is no remorseless killer. He only outdraws any gunslinger crazy enough to pull a six-shooter first. Then Bill finds himself on the wrong side of the law, and plenty of greenhorns and gringos set their sights on collecting the price on his head. But Bill refuses to turn tail and run. He swears he'll clear his name and live a free man before he'll be hunted down and trapped like an animal.

__3937-0 $4.50 US/$5.50 CAN

Dorchester Publishing Co., Inc.
65 Commerce Road
Stamford, CT 06902

Please add $1.75 for shipping and handling for the first book and $.50 for each book thereafter. NY, NYC, PA and CT residents, please add appropriate sales tax. No cash, stamps, or C.O.D.s. All orders shipped within 6 weeks via postal service book rate. Canadian orders require $2.00 extra postage and must be paid in U.S. dollars through a U.S. banking facility.

Name _____
Address _____
City _____ State _____ Zip _____
I have enclosed $_____ in payment for the checked book(s).
Payment must accompany all orders.☐ Please send a free catalog.

CHEYENNE

JUDD COLE

#15: Renegade Nation. Born the son of a great chieftain, raised by frontier settlers, Touch the Sky returns to protect his tribe. But he will never forsake his pioneer family and friends in their times of need. Then Touch the Sky's enemies join forces, striking against all his people—both Indian and white—and test his warrior and shaman skills to the limit. If the fearless brave's magic is not strong enough, he will be powerless to stop the utter annihilation of the two worlds he loves.

___3891-9 $3.99 US/$4.99 CAN

#16: Orphan Train. Raised by frontiersmen, Touch the Sky returns to the Cheyenne determined to learn their ways. Yet even while the young brave lives among his people, he never forgets his debt to the settlers. Then his enemies kidnap a train full of orphans heading west, and Touch the Sky finds himself torn between the white men and the Indians. To save the children, the mighty warrior will have to risk his life, his home, and his dreams of leading his tribe to glory.

___3909-5 $3.99 US/$4.99 CAN

GLORIETA PASS

GORDON D. SHIRREFFS

Quint Kershaw—legendary mountain man, fighter, and lover—is called from the comforts of the land he loves to battle for the Union under Kit Carson. His mission is to help preserve New Mexico from the Confederate onslaught in a tempestuous time that will test the passions of both men and women.

His sons, David and Fransisco, turn deadly rivals for the love of a shrewd and beautiful woman. His daughter, Guadelupe, yearns deeply for the one man she can never have. And Quint himself once again comes face-to-face with golden-haired Jean Calhoun, the woman he has never gotten out of his mind, now suddenly available and as ravishing as ever.

_3777-7 $4.50 US/$5.50 CAN

Dorchester Publishing Co., Inc.
65 Commerce Road
Stamford, CT 06902

Please add $1.75 for shipping and handling for the first book and $.50 for each book thereafter. NY, NYC, PA and CT residents, please add appropriate sales tax. No cash, stamps, or C.O.D.s. All orders shipped within 6 weeks via postal service book rate. Canadian orders require $2.00 extra postage and must be paid in U.S. dollars through a U.S. banking facility.

Name _____

Address _____

City _____ State _____ Zip _____

I have enclosed $_____ in payment for the checked book(s).
Payment <u>must</u> accompany all orders. ☐ Please send a free catalog.

CHEYENNE

JUDD COLE

Follow the adventures of Touch the Sky as he searches for a world he can call his own!

#3: Renegade Justice. When his adopted white parents fall victim to a gang of ruthless outlaws, Touch the Sky swears to save them—even if it means losing the trust he has risked his life to win from the Cheyenne.
_3385-2 $3.50 US/$4.50 CAN

#4: Vision Quest. While seeking a mystical sign from the Great Spirit, Touch the Sky is relentlessly pursued by his enemies. But the young brave will battle any peril that stands between him and the vision of his destiny.
_3411-5 $3.50 US/$4.50 CAN